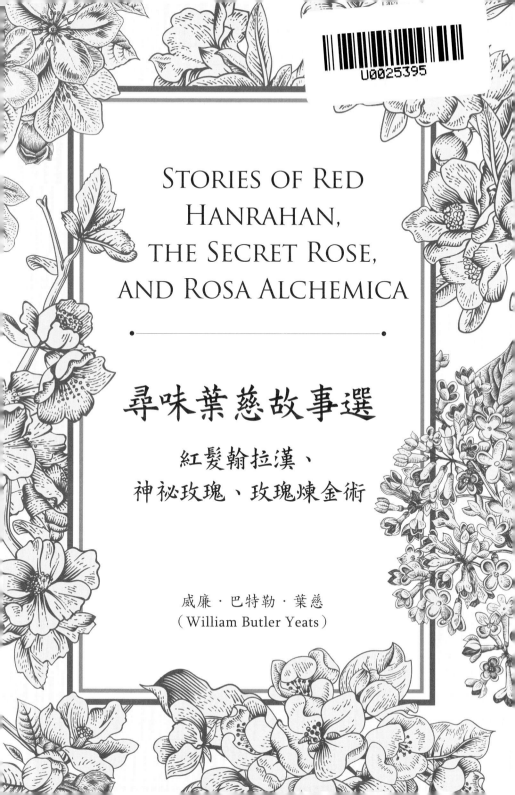

Stories of Red Hanrahan, the Secret Rose, and Rosa Alchemica

尋味葉慈故事選

紅髮翰拉漢、
神祕玫瑰、玫瑰煉金術

威廉・巴特勒・葉慈
（William Butler Yeats）

CONTENTS

前言

威廉‧巴特勒‧葉慈（William Butler Yeats, 1865–1939），愛爾蘭詩人和劇作家，曾擔任愛爾蘭國會參議員一職，並於 1923 年獲頒諾貝爾文學獎。

葉慈的早期創作，深受濫觴於十九世紀中葉的前拉斐爾派（Pre-Raphaelite Brotherhood）的影響，為華麗風格的浪漫主義，活躍於愛爾蘭文藝復興運動。葉慈在中後期，接觸了法國象徵主義（Symbolism），創作逐漸轉變為凝鍊的現代主義（Modernism）風格。

William Butler Yeats
(1865–1939)

本書收錄了三個系列故事：

《紅髮翰拉漢故事集》（*Stories of Red Hanrahan*, 1897）
《神祕玫瑰》（*The Secret Rose*, 1897）
《玫瑰煉金術》（*Rosa Alchemica*, 1896）

《紅髮翰拉漢故事集》的主角翰拉漢（Hanrahan），是依據十八世紀兩位詩人 Owen Roe O'Sullivan（1748–1782）與 Timothy O'Sullivan（1840–1882）流傳於鄉間的生平故事，再加以葉慈的創作而寫成，書寫中保留了口傳文學特色與吟遊詩人傳統。

　　《神祕玫瑰》為九篇各自獨立的民間傳說，時間自中世紀橫跨至十九世紀，內容探究自然與靈性間的對立與辯證，富含濃厚的象徵與神祕色彩。

　　《紅髮翰拉漢故事集》和《神祕玫瑰》是葉慈在奧古斯塔・桂格瑞女士（Lady Augusta Gregory, 1852–1932）協助之下完成。桂格瑞女士為愛爾蘭民俗學者與劇作家，她在愛爾蘭文藝復興（Irish Literary Revival）扮演了舉足輕重的角色。1899 年，她與葉慈、艾華・馬丁（Edward Martyn, 1859–1923）共同創立了愛爾蘭國家文學劇院（Irish Literary Theatre）。

　　桂格瑞女士以流傳於基爾泰坦（Kiltartan）一帶，帶有蓋爾語（Gaelic）語法的英語方言，和葉

Lady Augusta Gregory
(1852–1932

5

慈一同改寫愛爾蘭的民間故事。對葉慈而言，基爾泰坦語因其「未受浪漫主義的陳規和現代的抽象修辭所影響」，因而能充分表達出愛爾蘭的古老智慧，而口傳文學也能夠體現古老傳統，並展現未受英國與基督教影響的愛爾蘭獨特性。葉慈與桂格瑞女士合作之下的成果，包括《愛爾蘭鄉村的神話和民間故事集》（*Fairy and Folk Tales of the Irish Peasantry*, 1888）和多部劇作，其中最為知名的為《胡拉洪之女凱瑟琳》（*Cathleen Ni Houlihan*, 1902）。

葉慈畢生對神祕學有濃厚的興趣，他深入研究布雷克（William Blake, 1757–1827）的詩作，也廣泛涉獵新柏拉圖主義（Neo-Platonism）、印度教、佛教、神智學（Theosophy）、靈學和占星學等思想。十九世紀末時，許多神祕學團體蓬勃發展，挑戰並質疑維多利亞時代的理性主義思維與物質主義。本書所收錄的《玫瑰煉金術》，內

William Blake
(1757–1827)

容以葉慈 1890 年代所參加的黃金黎明會社（Hermetic Order of the Golden Dawn）的入會儀式為基本架構，

故事裡頭傳授靈性煉金術的麥可‧羅巴特（Michael Robartes）這一角色，也是以黃金黎明會社的創建者之一麥克葛瑞格‧馬特（MacGregor Mathers, 1854–1918）為原型，深入探究煉金術的精神面向。

本書展現葉慈早期的藝術美學，也傳達其對愛爾蘭文藝復興的信念，儘管他的民族主義熱情在日後逐漸消退，他仍十分熱衷於探索靈性與物質間的對抗與辯證，而他對神祕主義的愛好，仍是文學生涯中不斷探討的主題。

PART 1

Stories of Red Hanrahan

the Secret Rose

Rosa Alchemica

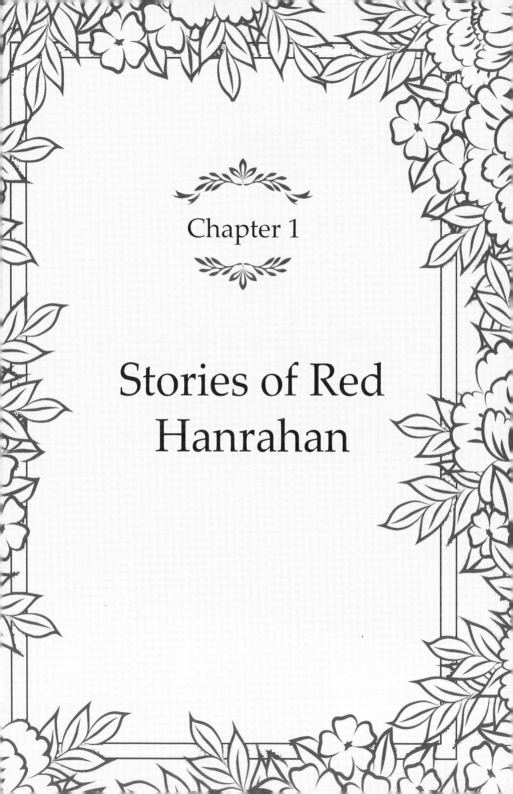

Chapter 1

Stories of Red Hanrahan

I owe thanks to Lady Gregory, who helped me to rewrite
The Stories of Red Hanrahan
in the beautiful country speech of Kiltartan,
and nearer to the tradition of the people among whom he,
of some likeness of him, drifted and is remembered.

1. Red Hanrahan

Hanrahan, the hedge schoolmaster[1], a tall, strong, red-haired young man, came into the barn where some of the men of the village were sitting on Samhain Eve[2]. It had been a dwelling-house, and when the man that owned it had built a better one, he had put the two rooms together, and kept it for a place to store one thing or another.

There was a fire on the old hearth, and there were dip candles stuck in bottles, and there was a black quart bottle upon some boards that had been put across two barrels to make a table. Most of the men were sitting beside the fire, and one of them was singing a long wandering song, about a Munster man and a Connaught man that were quarrelling about their two provinces[3].

Hanrahan went to the man of the house and said, 'I got your message'; but when he had said that, he stopped, for

---

1 hedge schoolmaster：指圍籬學校（hedge school）的老師。圍籬學校是私人辦理的學校，始於十七世紀，常借用窯屋、農舍、泥炭屋等來授課。
2 Samhain Eve：薩溫節夜，意味著收穫時節的結束與冬天的開始，通常是 10 月 31 日夜晚開始慶祝。
3 指詩人 Raftery 和兩個死對頭 Peatsy、Marcas Callinain 之間的爭執。

an old mountainy man that had a shirt and trousers of unbleached flannel, and that was sitting by himself near the door, was looking at him, and moving an old pack of cards about in his hands and muttering.

'Don't mind him,' said the man of the house; 'he is only some stranger came in awhile ago, and we bade him welcome, it being Samhain night, but I think he is not in his right wits. Listen to him now and you will hear what he is saying.'

They listened then, and they could hear the old man muttering to himself as he turned the cards, 'Spades and Diamonds, Courage and Power; Clubs and Hearts, Knowledge and Pleasure.'

'That is the kind of talk he has been going on with for the last hour,' said the man of the house, and Hanrahan turned his eyes from the old man as if he did not like to be looking at him.

'I got your message,' Hanrahan said then; '"he is in the barn with his three first cousins from Kilchriest," the messenger said, "and there are some of the neighbours with them."'

'It is my cousin over there is wanting to see you,' said the man of the house, and he called over a young frieze-coated man, who was listening to the song, and said, 'This is Red Hanrahan you have the message for.'

'It is a kind message, indeed,' said the young man, 'for it comes from your sweetheart, Mary Lavelle.'

'How would you get a message from her, and what do you know of her?'

'I don't know her, indeed, but I was in Loughrea yesterday, and a neighbour of hers that had some dealings with me was saying that she bade him send you word, if he met any one from this side in the market, that her mother has died from her, and if you have a mind yet to join with herself, she is willing to keep her word to you.'

'I will go to her indeed,' said Hanrahan.

'And she bade you make no delay, for if she has not a man in the house before the month is out, it is likely the little bit of land will be given to another.'

When Hanrahan heard that, he rose up from the bench he had sat down on.

'I will make no delay indeed,' he said, 'there is a full moon, and if I get as far as Gilchreist to-night, I will reach to her before the setting of the sun to-morrow.'

When the others heard that, they began to laugh at him for being in such haste to go to his sweetheart, and one asked him if he would leave his school in the old lime-kiln, where he was giving the children such good learning.

But he said the children would be glad enough in the morning to find the place empty, and no one to keep them at their task; and as for his school he could set it up again in any place, having as he had his little inkpot hanging from his neck by a chain, and his big Virgil and his primer in the skirt of his coat.

Some of them asked him to drink a glass before he went, and a young man caught hold of his coat, and said he must not leave them without singing the song he had made in praise of Venus and of Mary Lavelle. He drank a glass of whiskey, but he said he would not stop but would set out on his journey.

'There's time enough, Red Hanrahan,' said the man of the house. 'It will be time enough for you to give up sport when you are after your marriage, and it might be a long time before we will see you again.'

'I will not stop,' said Hanrahan; 'my mind would be on the roads all the time, bringing me to the woman that sent for me, and she lonesome and watching till I come.'

Some of the others came about him, pressing him that had been such a pleasant comrade, so full of songs and every kind of trick and fun, not to leave them till the night would be over, but he refused them all, and shook them off, and went to the door.

But as he put his foot over the threshold, the strange old man stood up and put his hand that was thin and withered like a bird's claw on Hanrahan's hand, and said: 'It is not Hanrahan, the learned man and the great songmaker, that should go out from a gathering like this, on a Samhain night. And stop here, now,' he said, 'and play a hand with me; and here is an old pack of cards has done its work many a night before this, and old as it is, there has been much of the riches of the world lost and won over it.'

One of the young men said, 'It isn't much of the riches of the world has stopped with yourself, old man,' and he looked at the old man's bare feet, and they all laughed. But Hanrahan did not laugh, but he sat down very quietly, without a word.

Then one of them said, 'So you will stop with us after all, Hanrahan'; and the old man said: 'He will stop indeed, did you not hear me asking him?'

They all looked at the old man then as if wondering where he came from.

'It is far I am come,' he said, 'through France I have come, and through Spain, and by Lough Greine of the hidden mouth, and none has refused me anything.'

And then he was silent and nobody liked to question him, and they began to play.

There were six men at the boards playing, and the others were looking on behind. They played two or three games for nothing, and then the old 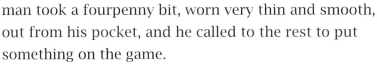 man took a fourpenny bit, worn very thin and smooth, out from his pocket, and he called to the rest to put something on the game.

Then they all put down something on the boards,

and little as it was it looked much, from the way it was shoved from one to another, first one man winning it and then his neighbour. And sometimes the luck would go against a man and he would have nothing left, and then one or another would lend him something, and he would pay it again out of his winnings, for neither good nor bad luck stopped long with anyone.

And once Hanrahan said as a man would say in a dream, 'It is time for me to be going the road'; but just then a good card came to him, and he played it out, and all the money began to come to him. And once he thought of Mary Lavelle, and he sighed; and that time his luck went from him, and he forgot her again.

But at last the luck went to the old man and it stayed with him, and all they had flowed into him, and he began to laugh little laughs to himself, and to sing over and over to himself, 'Spades and Diamonds, Courage and Power,' and so on, as if it was a verse of a song.

And after a while anyone looking at the men, and seeing the way their bodies were rocking to and fro, and the way they kept their eyes on the old man's hands, would think they had drink taken, or that the whole store they had in the world was put on the cards; but that was not so, for the quart bottle had not been disturbed since the game began, and was nearly full yet, and all that was on the game was a few sixpenny bits and shillings, and maybe a handful of coppers.

'You are good men to win and good men to lose,' said the old man, 'you have play in your hearts.'

He began then to shuffle the cards and to mix them, very quick and fast, till at last they could not see them to be cards at all, but you would think him to be making rings of fire in the air, as little lads would make them with whirling a lighted stick; and after that it seemed to them that all the room was dark, and they could see nothing but his hands and the cards.

And all in a minute a hare[4] made a leap out from between his hands, and whether it was one of the cards that took that shape, or whether it was made out of nothing in the palms of his hands, nobody knew, but there it was running on the floor of the barn, as quick as any hare that ever lived.

Some looked at the hare, but more kept their eyes on the old man, and while they were looking at him a hound made a leap out between his hands, the same way as the hare did, and after that another hound and another, till there was a whole pack of them following the hare round and round the barn.

---

4 據說女巫會化身為野兔。

The players were all standing up now, with their backs to the boards, shrinking from the hounds, and nearly deafened with the noise of their yelping, but as quick as the hounds were they could not overtake the hare, but it went round, till at the last it seemed as if a blast of wind burst open the barn door, and the hare doubled and made a leap over the boards where the men had been playing, and went out of the door and away through the night, and the hounds over the boards and through the door after it.

Then the old man called out, 'Follow the hounds, follow the hounds, and it is a great hunt you will see to-night,' and he went out after them.

But used as the men were to go hunting after hares, and ready as they were for any sport, they were in dread to go out into the night, and it was only Hanrahan that rose up and that said, 'I will follow, I will follow on.'

'You had best stop here, Hanrahan,' the young man that was nearest him said, 'for you might be going into some great danger.'

But Hanrahan said, 'I will see fair play, I will see fair play,' and he went stumbling out of the door like a man in a dream, and the door shut after him as he went.

He thought he saw the old man in front of him, but it was only his own shadow that the full moon cast on the road before him, but he could hear the hounds crying after the hare over the wide green fields of Granagh, and he followed them very fast for there was nothing to stop him; and after a while he came to smaller fields that had little walls of loose stones around them, and he threw the stones down as he crossed them, and did not wait to put them up again; and he passed by the place where the river goes under ground at Ballylee, and he could hear the hounds going before him up towards the head of the river.

Soon he found it harder to run, for it was uphill he was going, and clouds came over the moon, and it was hard for him to see his way, and once he left the path to take a short cut, but his foot slipped into a boghole and he had to come back to it.

And how long he was going he did not know, or what way he went, but at last he was up on the bare mountain, with nothing but the rough heather about him, and he could neither hear the hounds nor any other thing.

But their cry began to come to him again, at first far off and then very near, and when it came quite close to him, it went up all of a sudden into the air, and there was the sound of hunting over his head; then it went away northward till he could hear nothing more at all.

'That's not fair,' he said, 'that's not fair.'

And he could walk no longer, but sat down on the heather where he was, in the heart of Slieve Echtge, for all the strength had gone from him, with the dint of the long journey he had made.

And after a while he took notice that there was a door close to him, and a light coming from it, and he wondered that being so close to him he had not seen it before. And he rose up, and tired as he was he went in at the door, of and although it was night time outside, it was daylight he found within. And presently he met with an old man that had been gathering summer thyme and yellow flag-flowers, and it seemed as if all the sweet smells of the summer were with them.

And the old man said: 'It is a long time you have been coming to us, Hanrahan the learned man and the great songmaker.'

And with that he brought him into a very big shining house, and every grand thing Hanrahan had ever heard of, and every colour he had ever seen, were in it. There was a high place at the end of the house, and on it there was sitting in a high chair a woman, the most beautiful the world ever saw, having a long pale face and flowers about it, but she had the tired look of one that had been long waiting.

And there was sitting on the step below her chair four grey old women, and the one of them was holding a great cauldron in her lap; and another a great stone on her knees, and heavy as it was it seemed light to her; and another of them had a very long spear that was made of pointed wood; and the last of them had a sword that was without a scabbard.[5]

Hanrahan stood looking at them for a longtime, but none of them spoke any word to him or looked at him at all. And he had it in his mind to ask who that woman in the chair was, that was like a queen, and what she was waiting for; but ready as he was with his tongue and afraid of no person, he was in dread now to speak to so beautiful a woman, and in so grand a place. And then he thought to ask what were the four things the four grey old women were holding like great treasures, but he could not think of the right words to bring out.

Then the first of the old women rose up, holding the cauldron between her two hands, and she said 'Pleasure,' and Hanrahan said no word. Then the second old woman rose up with the stone in her hands, and she said 'Power'; and the third old woman rose up with the spear in her hand, and she said 'Courage'; and the last of the old women rose up having the sword in her hands, and she said 'Knowledge.'

And everyone, after she had spoken, waited as if for Hanrahan to question her, but he said nothing at all.

And then the four old women went out of the door, bringing their tour treasures with them, and as they went out one of them said, 'He has no wish for us'; and another said, 'He is weak, he is weak'; and another said, 'He is afraid'; and the last said, 'His wits are gone from him.'

5　愛爾蘭傳說中的神族的四個護身法寶，為大鍋、巨石、長矛和寶劍。故事中對四位老婦的描述，與塔羅牌中四個牌組的皇后圖示相同，分別為聖杯皇后、錢幣皇后、權杖皇后、寶劍皇后。

And then they all said 'Echtge, daughter of the Silver Hand[6], must stay in her sleep. It is a pity, it is a great pity.'

And then the woman that was like a queen gave a very sad sigh, and it seemed to Hanrahan as if the sigh had the sound in it of hidden streams; and if the place he was in had been ten times grander and more shining than it was, he could not have hindered sleep from coming on him; and he staggered like a drunken man and lay down there and then.

When Hanrahan awoke, the sun was shining on his face, but there was white frost on the grass around him, and there was ice on the edge of the stream he was lying by, and that goes running on through Daire-caol and Druim-da-rod. He knew by the shape of the hills and by the shining of Lough Greine in the distance that he was upon one of the hills of Slieve Echtge, but he was not sure how he came there; for all that had happened in the barn had gone from him, and all of his journey but the soreness of his feet and the stiffness in his bones.

It was a year after that, there were men of the village of Cappaghtagle sitting by the fire in a house on the roadside, and Red Hanrahan that was now very thin and worn and his hair very long and wild, came to the half-door[7] and asked leave to come in and rest himself; and they bid him welcome because it was Samhain night.

He sat down with them, and they gave him a glass of

whiskey out of a quart bottle; and they saw the little inkpot hanging about his neck, and knew he was a scholar, and asked for stories about the Greeks.

He took the Virgil out of the big pocket of his coat, but the cover was very black and swollen with the wet, and the page when he opened it was very yellow, but that was no great matter, for he looked at it like a man that had never learned to read. Some young man that was there began to laugh at him then, and to ask why did he carry so heavy a book with him when he was not able to read it.

It vexed Hanrahan to hear that, and he put the Virgil back in his pocket and asked if they had a pack of cards among them, for cards were better than books.

When they brought out the cards he took them and began to shuffle them, and while he was shuffling them something seemed to come into his mind, and he put his hand to his face like one that is trying to remember, and he said: 'Was I ever here before, or where was I on a night like this?' and then of a sudden he stood up and let the cards fall to the floor, and he said, 'Who was it brought me a message from Mary Lavelle?'

---

6 Silver Hand：國王 Nuada 在戰役中失去了一隻手，因此被稱為銀手 Nuada（Nuada of the Silver Hand）。
7 half-door：門做成上下兩扇，兩扇可以獨立開闔的活動門。

'We never saw you before now, and we never heard of Mary Lavelle,' said the man of the house. 'And who is she,' he said, 'and what is it you are talking about?'

'It was this night a year ago, I was in a barn, and there were men playing cards, and there was money on the table, they were pushing it from one to another here and there—and I got a message, and I was going out of the door to look for my sweetheart that wanted me, Mary Lavelle.' And then Hanrahan called out very loud: 'Where have I been since then? Where was I for the whole year?'[8]

'It is hard to say where you might have been in that time,' said the oldest of the men, 'or what part of the world you may have travelled; and it is like enough you have the dust of many roads on your feet; for there are many go wandering and forgetting like that,' he said, 'when once they have been given the touch[9].'

'That is true,' said another of the men. 'I knew a woman went wandering like that through the length of seven years; she came back after, and she told her friends she had often been glad enough to eat the food that was put in the pig's trough. And it is best for you to go to the priest now,' he said, 'and let him take off you whatever may have been put upon you.'

'It is to my sweetheart I will go, to Mary Lavelle,' said

Hanrahan; 'it is too long I have delayed, how do I know what might have happened her in the length of a year?'

He was going out of the door then, but they all told him it was best for him to stop the night, and to get strength for the journey; and indeed he wanted that, for he was very weak, and when they gave him food he eat it like a man that had never seen food before, and one of them said, 'He is eating as if he had trodden on the hungry grass[10].'

It was in the white light of the morning he set out, and the time seemed long to him till he could get to Mary Lavelle's house.

But when he came to it, he found the door broken, and the thatch dropping from the roof, and no living person to be seen. And when he asked the neighbours what had happened her, all they could say was that she had been put out of the house, and had married some labouring man, and they had gone looking for work to London or Liverpool or some big place. And whether she found a worse place or a better he never knew, but anyway he never met with her or with news of her again.

---

8 去到仙境所度過的時光，通常等於人間的一年。

9 精靈的觸摸會導致傷口、癱瘓甚至死亡。

10 hungry grass：在愛爾蘭傳說中，享用露天餐點時，如果沒有將碎屑丟給精靈，那裡就會長出一種稱為「飢餓之草」的植物。任何人只要踩到飢餓之草，就會陷入虛弱的狀態；如果沒有及時得到照護，便會死去。

2. The Twisting of the Rope

Hanrahan was walking the roads one time near Kinvara at the fall of day, and he heard the sound of a fiddle from a house a little way off the roadside. He turned up the path to it, for he never had the habit of passing by any place where there was music or dancing or good company, without going in.

The man of the house was standing at the door, and when Hanrahan came near he knew him and he said: 'A welcome before you, Hanrahan, you have been lost to us this long time.'

But the woman of the house came to the door and she said to her husband: 'I would be as well pleased for Hanrahan not to come in tonight, for he has no good name now among the priests, or with women that mind themselves, and I wouldn't wonder from his walk if he has a drop of drink taken.'

But the man said, 'I will never turn away Hanrahan of the poets from my door,' and with that he bade him enter.

There were a good many neighbours gathered in the house, and some of them remembered Hanrahan; but some of the little lads that were in the corners had only heard of him, and they stood up to have a view of him, and one of them said: 'Is not that Hanrahan that had the school, and that was brought away by Them[1]?'

But his mother put her hand over his mouth and bade him be quiet, and not be saying things like that. 'For Hanrahan is apt to grow wicked,' she said, 'if he hears talk of that story, or if anyone goes questioning him.'

One or another called out then, asking him for a song, but the man of the house said it was no time to ask him for a song, before he had rested himself; and he gave him whiskey in a glass, and Hanrahan thanked him and wished him good health and drank it off.

The fiddler was tuning his fiddle for another dance, and the man of the house said to the young men, they would all know what dancing was like when they saw Hanrahan dance, for the like of it had never been seen since he was there before.

Hanrahan said he would not dance, he had better use for his feet now, travelling as he was through the five provinces of Ireland.

---

1 在這裡，「Them」是精靈的委婉說法。

Just as he said that, there came in at the half-door Oona, the daughter of the house, having a few bits of bog deal from Connemara in her arms for the fire. She threw them on the hearth and the flame rose up, and showed her to be very comely and smiling, and two or three of the young men rose up and asked for a dance. But Hanrahan crossed the floor and brushed the others away, and said it was with him she must dance, after the long road he had travelled before he came to her.

And it is likely he said some soft word in her ear, for she said nothing against it, and stood out with him, and there were little blushes in her cheeks.

Then other couples stood up, but when the dance was going to begin, Hanrahan chanced to look down, and he took notice of his boots that were worn and broken, and the ragged grey socks showing through them; and he said angrily it was a bad floor, and the music no great things, and he sat down in the dark place beside the hearth. But if he did, the girl sat down there with him.

The dancing went on, and when that dance was over another was called for, and no one took much notice of Oona and Red Hanrahan for a while, in the corner where they were. But the mother grew to be uneasy, and she called to Oona to come and help her to set the table in the inner room. But Oona that had never refused her before, said she would come soon, but not yet, for she was listening to whatever he was saying in her ear.

The mother grew yet more uneasy then, and she would come nearer them, and let on to be stirring the fire or sweeping the hearth, and she would listen for a minute to hear what the poet was saying to her child. And one time she heard him telling about white-handed Deirdre, and how she brought the sons of Usnach to their death; and how the blush in her cheeks was not so red as the blood of kings' sons that was shed for her, and her sorrows had never gone out of mind; and he said it was maybe the memory of her that made the cry of the plover on the bog as sorrowful in the ear of the poets as the keening of young men for a comrade. And there would never have been that memory of her, he said, if it was not for the poets that had put her beauty in their songs.

And the next time she did not well understand what he was saying, but as far as she could hear, it had the sound of poetry though it was not rhymed, and this is what she heard him say:

'The sun and the moon are the man and the girl, they are my life and your life, they are travelling and ever travelling through the skies as if under the one hood. It was God made them for one another. He made your life and my life before the beginning of the world, he made

them that they might go through the world, up and down, like the two best dancers that go on with the dance up and down the long floor of the barn, fresh and laughing, when all the rest are tired out and leaning against the wall.'

The old woman went then to where her husband was playing cards, but he would take no notice of her, and then she went to a woman of the neighbours and said: 'Is there no way we can get them from one another?' and without waiting for an answer she said to some young men that were talking together: 'What good are you when you cannot make the best girl in the house come out and dance with you? And go now the whole of you,' she said, 'and see can you bring her away from the poet's talk.'

But Oona would not listen to any of them, but only moved her hand as if to send them away.

Then they called to Hanrahan and said he had best dance with the girl himself, or let her dance with one of them.

When Hanrahan heard what they were saying he said: 'That is so, I will dance with her; there is no man in the house must dance with her but myself.'

He stood up with her then, and led her out by the hand, and some of the young men were vexed, and some began mocking at his ragged coat and his broken boots. But he took no notice, and Oona took no notice, but they looked at one another as if all the world belonged to themselves alone. But another couple that had been sitting together like lovers stood out on the floor at the same time, holding one another's hands and moving their feet to keep time with the music.

But Hanrahan turned his back on them as if angry, and in place of dancing he began to sing, and as he sang he held her hand, and his voice grew louder, and the mocking of the young men stopped, and the fiddle stopped, and there was nothing heard but his voice that had in it the sound of the wind. And what he sang was a song he had heard or had made one time in his wanderings on Slieve[2] Echtge, and the words of it as they can be put into English were like this:

O Death's old bony finger
Will never find us there
In the high hollow townland
Where love's to give and to spare;
Where boughs have fruit and blossom
At all times of the year;
Where rivers are running over
With red beer and brown beer.
An old man plays the bagpipes
In a gold and silver wood;
Queens, their eyes blue like the ice,
Are dancing in a crowd.

bagpipes

And while he was singing it Oona moved nearer to him, and the colour had gone from her cheek, and her eyes were not blue now, but grey with the tears that were in them, and anyone that saw her would have thought she was ready to follow him there and then from the west to the east of the world.

But one of the young men called out: 'Where is that country he is singing about? Mind yourself, Oona, it is a long way off, you might be a long time on the road before you would reach to it.'

And another said: 'It is not to the Country of the Young you will be going if you go with him, but to Mayo of the bogs.'

Oona looked at him then as if she would question him, but he raised her hand in his hand, and called out between singing and shouting: 'It is very near us that country is, it is on every side; it may be on the bare hill behind it is, or it may be in the heart of the wood.' And he said out very loud and clear: 'In the heart of the wood; oh, death will never find us in the heart of the wood. And will you come with me there, Oona?' he said.

But while he was saying this the two old women had gone outside the door, and Oona's mother was crying, and she said: 'He has put an enchantment on Oona. Can we not get the men to put him out of the house?'

'That is a thing you cannot do', said the other woman, 'for he is a poet of the Gael, and you know well if you would put a poet of the Gael out of the house, he would put a curse on you that would wither the corn in the fields and dry up the milk of the cows, if it had to hang in the air seven years.'

'God help us,' said the mother, 'and why did I ever let him into the house at all, and the wild name he has!'

'It would have been no harm at all to have kept him outside, but there would great harm come upon you if you put him out by force. But listen to the plan I have to get him out of the house by his own doing, without anyone putting him from it at all.'

It was not long after that the two women came in again, each of them having a bundle of hay in her apron. Hanrahan was not singing now, but he was talking to Oona very fast and soft, and he was saying: 'The house is narrow but the world is wide, and there is no true lover that need be afraid of night or morning or sun or stars or shadows of evening, or any earthly thing.'

'Hanrahan,' said the mother then, striking him on the shoulder, 'will you give me a hand here for a minute?'

'Do that, Hanrahan,' said the woman of the neighbours, 'and help us to make this hay into a rope[3], for you are ready with your hands, and a blast of wind has loosened the thatch on the haystack.'

---

3 在愛爾蘭鄉間，稻草製的繩子是日常必需品，可用來製作栓繩、覆蓋屋頂和製成椅子。

'I will do that for you,' said he, and he took the little stick in his hands, and the mother began giving out the hay, and he twisting it, but he was hurrying to have done with it, and to be free again.

The women went on talking and giving out the hay, and encouraging him, and saying what a good twister of a rope he was, better than their own neighbours or than anyone they had ever seen.

And Hanrahan saw that Oona was watching him, and he began to twist very quick and with his head high, and to boast of the readiness of his hands, and the learning he had in his head, and the strength in his arms. And as he was boasting, he went backward, twisting the rope always till he came to the door that was open behind him, and without thinking he passed the threshold and was out on the road. And no sooner was he there than the mother made a sudden rush, and threw out the rope after him, and she shut the door and the half-door and put a bolt upon them.

She was well pleased when she had done that, and laughed out loud, and the neighbours laughed and praised her. But they heard him beating at the door, and saying words of cursing outside it, and the mother had but time to stop Oona that had her hand upon the bolt to open it. She made a sign to the fiddler then, and he began a reel, and one of the young men asked no leave but caught hold of Oona and brought her into the thick of the dance. And when it was over and the fiddle had stopped, there was no sound at all of anything outside, but the road was as quiet as before.

As to Hanrahan, when he knew he was shut out and that there was neither shelter nor drink nor a girl's ear for him that night, the anger and the courage went out of him, and he went on to where the waves were beating on the strand.

He sat down on a big stone, and he began swinging his right arm and singing slowly to himself, the way he did always to hearten himself when every other thing failed him. And whether it was that time or another time he made the song that is called to this day 'The Twisting of the Rope,' and that begins, 'What was the dead cat that put me in this place,' is not known.

But after he had been singing awhile, mist and shadows seemed to gather about him, sometimes coming out of the sea, and sometimes moving upon it. It seemed to him that one of the shadows was the queen-woman he had seen in her sleep at Slieve Echtge; not in her sleep now, but mocking, and calling out to them that were behind her: 'He was weak, he was weak, he had no courage.'

And he felt the strands of the rope in his hand yet, and went on twisting it, but it seemed to him as he twisted, that it had all the sorrows of the world in it.

And then it seemed to him as if the rope had changed

in his dream into a great water-worm that came out of the sea, and that twisted itself about him, and held him closer and closer, and grew from big to bigger till the whole of the earth and skies were wound up in it, and the stars themselves were but the shining of the ridges of its skin.

And then he got free of it, and went on, shaking and unsteady, along the edge of the strand, and the grey shapes were flying here and there around him. And this is what they were saying, 'It is a pity for him that refuses the call of the daughters of the Sidhe, for he will find no comfort in the love of the women of the earth to the end of life and time, and the cold of the grave is in his heart forever. It is death he has chosen; let him die, let him die, let him die.'

3. Hanrahan and Cathleen the Daughter of Hoolihan

It was travelling northward Hanrahan was one time, giving a hand to a farmer now and again in the hurried time of the year, and telling his stories and making his share of songs at wakes and at weddings.

He chanced one day to overtake on the road to Collooney one Margaret Rooney, a woman he used to know in Munster when he was a young man. She had no good name at that time, and it was the priest routed her out of the place at last.

He knew her by her walk and by the colour of her eyes, and by a way she had of putting back the hair off her face with her left hand. She had been wandering about, she said, selling herrings and the like, and now she was going back to Sligo, to the place in the Burrough where she was living with another woman, Mary Gillis, who had much the same story as herself.

She would be well pleased, she said, if he would come and stop in the house with them, and be singing his songs to the bacachs and blind men and fiddlers of the Burrough. She remembered him well, she said, and had a wish for him; and as to Mary Gillis, she had some of his songs off by heart, so he need not be afraid of not getting good treatment, and all the bacachs and poor men that heard him would give him a share of their own earnings for his stories and his songs while he was with them, and would carry his name into all the parishes of Ireland.

He was glad enough to go with her, and to find a woman to be listening to the story of his troubles and to be comforting him.

It was at the moment of the fall of day when every man may pass as handsome and every woman as comely. She put her arm about him when he told her of the misfortune of the Twisting of the Rope, and in the half light she looked as well as another.

They kept in talk all the way to the Burrough, and as for Mary Gillis, when she saw him and heard who he was, she went near crying to think of having a man with so great a name in the house.

Hanrahan was well pleased to settle down with them for a while, for he was tired with wandering; and since the day he found the little cabin fallen in, and Mary Lavelle gone from it, and the thatch scattered, he had never asked to have any place of his own; and he had never stopped long enough in any place to see the green leaves come where he had seen the old leaves wither, or to see the wheat harvested where he had seen it sown. It was a good change to him to have shelter from the wet, and a fire in the evening time, and his share of food put on the table without the asking.

He made a good many of his songs while he was living

there, so well cared for and so quiet. The most of them were love songs, but some were songs of repentance, and some were songs about Ireland and her griefs, under one name or another.

Every evening the bacachs and beggars and blind men and fiddlers would gather into the house and listen to his songs and his poems, and his stories about the old time of the Fianna, and they kept them in their memories that were never spoiled with books; and so they brought his name to every wake and wedding and pattern in the whole of Connaught. He was never so well off or made so much of as he was at that time.

One evening of December he was singing a little song that he said he had heard from the green plover of the mountain, about the fair-haired boys that had left Limerick, and that were wandering and going astray in all parts of the world.

There were a good many people in the room that night, and two or three little lads that had crept in, and sat on the floor near the fire, and were too busy with the roasting of a potato in the ashes or some such thing to take much notice of him; but they remembered long afterwards when his name had gone up, the sound of his voice, and what way he had moved his hand, and the look of him as he sat on the edge of the bed, with his shadow falling on the whitewashed wall behind him, and as he moved going up as high as the thatch.

And they knew then that they had looked upon a king of the poets of the Gael, and a maker of the dreams of men.

Of a sudden his singing stopped, and his eyes grew misty as if he was looking at some far thing.

Mary Gillis was pouring whiskey into a mug that stood on a table beside him, and she left off pouring and said,' Is it of leaving us you are thinking?'

Margaret Rooney heard what she said, and did not know why she said it, and she took the words too much in earnest and came over to him, and there was dread in her heart that she was going to lose so wonderful a poet and so good a comrade, and a man that was thought so much of, and that brought so many to her house.

'You would not go away from us, my heart?' she said, catching him by the hand.

'It is not of that I am thinking,' he said, 'but of Ireland and the weight of grief that is on her.'

And he leaned his head against his hand, and began to sing these words, and the sound of his voice was like the wind in a lonely place.

The old brown thorn trees break in two
high over Cummen Strand
Under a bitter black wind that blows
from the left hand;
Our courage breaks like an old tree
in a black wind and dies,

But we have hidden in our hearts the flame out of the eyes
Of Cathleen the daughter of Hoolihan.

The winds has bundled up the clouds high over Knocknarea
And thrown the thunder on the stones for all that Maeve[1] can
  say.
Angers that are like noisy clouds have set our hearts abeat,
But we have all bent low and low and kissed the quiet feet
Of Cathleen the daughter of Hoolihan.

The yellow pool has overflowed high up on Clooth-na-Bare,
For the wet winds are blowing out of the clinging air;
Like heavy flooded waters our bodies and our blood,
But purer than a tall candle before the Holy Rood
Is Cathleen the daughter of Hoolihan.

While he was singing, his voice began to break, and tears came rolling down his cheeks, and Margaret Rooney put down her face into her hands and began to cry along with him. Then a blind beggar by the fire shook his rags with a sob, and after that there was no one of them all but cried tears down.

---

1 Maeve：愛爾蘭傳說中的女神。

4. Red Hanrahan's Curse

One fine May morning a long time after Hanrahan had left Margaret Rooney's house, he was walking the road near Collooney[1], and the sound of the birds singing in the bushes that were white with blossom set him singing as he went. It was to his own little place he was going, that was no more than a cabin, but that pleased him well.

For he was tired of so many years of wandering from shelter to shelter at all times of the year, and although he was seldom refused a welcome and a share of what was in the house, it seemed to him sometimes that his mind was getting stiff like his joints, and it was not so easy to him as it used to be to make fun and sport through the night, and to set all the boys laughing with his pleasant talk, and to coax the women with his songs.

And a while ago, he had turned into a cabin that some poor man had left to go harvesting and had never come to again. And when he had mended the thatch and made a bed in the corner with a few sacks and bushes,

and had swept out the floor, he was well content to have a little place for himself, where he could go in and out as he liked, and put his head in his hands through the length of an evening if the fret was on him, and loneliness after the old times.

One by one the neighbours began to send their children in to get some learning from him, and with what they brought, a few eggs, or an oaten cake or a couple of sods of turf, he made out a way of living[2]. And if he went for a wild day and night now and again to the Burrough[3], no one would say a word, knowing him to be a poet, with wandering in his heart.

It was from the Burrough he was coming that May morning, light-hearted enough, and singing some new song that had come to him. But it was not long till a hare ran across his path, and made away into the fields, through the loose stones of the wall. And he knew it was no good sign a hare to have crossed his path, and he remembered the hare that had led him away to Slieve Echtge the time Mary Lavelle was waiting for him, and how he had never known content for any length of time since then.

---

1 Collooney：斯萊戈（Sligo）南方八英里處的小村莊。
2 圍籬學校的私塾教師，通常以日用品維生。
3 Burrough：斯萊戈（Sligo）城內最舊的地區。

'And it is likely enough they are putting some bad thing before me now,' he said.

And after he said that he heard the sound of crying in the field beside him, and he looked over the wall. And there he saw a young girl sitting under a bush of white hawthorn, and crying as if her heart would break. Her face was hidden in her hands, but her soft hair and her white neck and the young look of her, put him in mind of Bridget Purcell and Margaret Gillane and Maeve Connelan and Oona Curry and Celia Driscoll[4], and the rest of the girls he had made songs for and had coaxed the heart from with his flattering tongue.

She looked up, and he saw her to be a girl of the neighbours, a farmer's daughter.

'What is on you, Nora?' he said.

'Nothing you could take from me, Red Hanrahan.'

'If there is any sorrow on you it is I myself should be well able to serve you,' he said then, 'for it is I know the history of the Greeks, and I know well what sorrow is and parting, and the hardship of the world. And if I am not able to save you from trouble,' he said, 'there is many a one I have saved from it with the power that is in my songs, as it was in the songs of the poets that were before me from the beginning of the world. And it

---

4　這些都是作者改編這本民間傳說時，所虛構出來的角色。

is with the rest of the poets I myself will be sitting and talking in some far place beyond the world, to the end of life and time,' he said.

The girl stopped her crying, and she said, 'Owen Hanrahan, I often heard you have had sorrow and persecution, and that you know all the troubles of the world since the time you refused your love to the queen-woman in Slieve Echtge; and that she never left you in quiet since. But when it is people of this earth that have harmed you, it is yourself knows well the way to put harm on them again. And will you do now what I ask you, Owen Hanrahan?' she said.

'I will do that indeed,' said he.

'It is my father and my mother and my brothers,' she said, 'that are marrying me to old Paddy Doe, because he has a farm of a hundred acres under the mountain. And it is what you can do, Hanrahan,' she said, 'put him into a rhyme the same way you put old Peter Kilmartin in one the time you were young, that sorrow may be over him rising up and lying down, that will put him thinking of Collooney churchyard and not of marriage. And let you make no delay about it, for it is for to-morrow they have the marriage settled, and I would sooner see the sun rise on the day of my death than on that day.'

'I will put him into a song that will bring shame and sorrow over him; but tell me how many years has he, for I would put them in the song?'

'O, he has years upon years. He is as old as you yourself. Red Hanrahan.'

'As old as myself,' said Hanrahan, and his voice was as if broken; 'as old as myself; there are twenty years and more between us! It is a bad day indeed for Owen Hanrahan when a young girl with the blossom of May in her cheeks thinks him to be an old man. And my grief!' he said, 'you have put a thorn in my heart.'

He turned from her then and went down the road till he came to a stone, and he sat down on it, for it seemed as if all the weight of the years had come on him in the minute. And he remembered it was not many days ago that a woman in some house had said: 'It is not Red Hanrahan you are now but yellow Hanrahan, for your hair is turned to the colour of a wisp of tow.'

And another woman he had asked for a drink had not given him new milk but sour; and sometimes the girls would be whispering and laughing with young ignorant men while he himself was in the middle of giving out his poems or his talk.

And he thought of the stiffness of his joints when he first rose of a morning, and the pain of his knees after making a journey, and it seemed to him as if he was come to be a very old man, with cold in the shoulders and speckled shins and his wind breaking and he himself withering away. And with those thoughts there came on him a great anger against old age and all it brought with it.

And just then he looked up and saw a great spotted eagle sailing slowly towards Ballygawley, and he cried out: 'You, too, eagle of Ballygawley, are old, and your wings are full of gaps, and I will put you and your ancient comrades, the Pike of Dargan Lake and the Yew[5] of the Steep Place of

great spotted eagle

the Strangers[6] into my rhyme, that there may be a curse on you forever[7].'

There was a bush beside him to the left, flowering like the rest, and a little gust of wind blew the white blossoms over his coat.

'May blossoms,' he said, gathering them up in the hollow of his hand, 'you never know age because you die away in your beauty, and I will put you into my rhyme and give you my blessing.'

He rose up then and plucked a little branch from the bush, and carried it in his hand. But it is old and broken he looked going home that day with the stoop in his shoulders and the darkness in his face.

---

5 老鷹、梭魚和紫杉，皆代表長壽和年老。
6 Steep Place of the Strangers：指 Cope's Mountain 北方的峭壁。
7 據說愛爾蘭吟遊詩人能夠透過寫詩，來讓敵人生病或死亡。

When he got to his cabin there was no one there, and he went and lay down on the bed for a while as he was used to do when he wanted to make a poem or a praise or a curse. And it was not long he was in making it this time, for the power of the curse-making bards was upon him. And when he had made it he searched his mind how he could send it out over the whole countryside.

Some of the scholars began coming in then, to see if there would be any school that day, and Hanrahan rose up and sat on the bench by the hearth, and they all stood around him.

They thought he would bring out the Virgil or the Mass book[8] or the primer, but instead of that he held up the little branch of hawthorn he had in his hand yet. 'Children,' he said, this is a new lesson I have for you to-day.

'You yourselves and the beautiful people of the world are like this blossom, and old age is the wind that comes and blows the blossom away. And I have made a curse upon old age and upon the old men, and listen now while I give it out to you.' And this is what he said,—

The poet, Owen Hanrahan, under a bush of may
Calls down a curse on his own head because it withers grey;

---

8 Mass book：世俗人在參加天主教彌撒時所閱讀的手冊，
內容有聖經文、祈禱文和聖歌等

Then on the speckled eagle cock of Ballygawley Hill,
Because it is the oldest thing that knows of cark and ill;
And on the yew that has been green from the times out of mind
By the Steep Place of the Strangers and the Gap of the Wind;
And on the great grey pike that broods in Castle Dargan Lake
Having in his long body a many a hook and ache;
Then curses he old Paddy Bruen of the Well of Bride
Because no hair is on his head and drowsiness inside.
Then Paddy's neighbour, Peter Hart, and Michael Gill, his
    friend,
Because their wandering histories are never at an end.

And then old Shemus Cullinan, shepherd of the Green Lands
Because he holds two crutches between his crooked hands;
Then calls a curse from the dark North upon old Paddy Doe,
Who plans to lay his withering head upon a breast of snow,
Who plans to wreck a singing voice and break a merry heart.
He bids a curse hang over him till breath and body part;
But he calls down a blessing on the blossom of the may,
Because it comes in beauty, and in beauty blows away.

He said it over to the children verse by verse till all of
them could say a part of it, and some that were the quickest
could say the whole of it.

'That will do for to-day,' he said then. 'And what you have
to do now is to go out and sing that song for a while, to the

tune of the Green Bunch of Rushes, to everyone you meet, and to the old men themselves.'

'I will do that,' said one of the little lads; 'I know old Paddy Doe well. Last Saint John's Eve[9] we dropped a mouse down his chimney, but this is better than a mouse.'

'I will go into the town of Sligo and sing it in the street,' said another of the boys.

'Do that,' said Hanrahan, 'and go into the Burrough and tell it to Margaret Rooney and Mary Gillis, and bid them sing it, and to make the beggars and the bacachs sing it wherever they go.'

The children ran out then, full of pride and of mischief, calling out the song as they ran, and Hanrahan knew there was no danger it would not be heard[10].

He was sitting outside the door the next morning, looking at his scholars as they came by in twos and threes. They were nearly all come, and he was considering the place of the sun in the heavens to know whether it was time to begin, when he heard a sound

---

9　Saint John's Eve（聖約翰之夜）：在夏至舉辦的節慶，人們會在山頂升起營火。

10　人們會透過這種方式來表達對老男人與年輕女孩結婚的反對，小男孩尤其熱衷這種活動。

that was like the buzzing of a swarm of bees in the air, or the rushing of a hidden river in time of flood.

Then he saw a crowd coming up to the cabin from the road, and he took notice that all the crowd was made up of old men, and that the leaders of it were Paddy Bruen, Michael Gill and Paddy Doe, and there was not one in the crowd but had in his hand an ash stick or a blackthorn. As soon as they caught sight of him, the sticks began to wave hither and thither like branches in a storm, and the old feet to run.

He waited no longer, but made off up the hill behind the cabin till he was out of their sight.

After a while he came back round the hill, where he was hidden by the furze growing along a ditch. And when he came in sight of his cabin he saw that all the old men had gathered around it, and one of them was just at that time thrusting a rake with a wisp of lighted straw on it into the thatch.

'My grief,' he said, 'I have set Old Age and Time and Weariness and Sickness against me, and I must go wandering again. And, O Blessed Queen of Heaven,' he said, 'protect me from the Eagle of Ballygawley, the Yew Tree of the Steep Place of the Strangers, the Pike of Castle Dargan Lake, and from the lighted wisps of their kindred, the Old Men!'

5. Hanrahan's Vision

It was in the month of June Hanrahan was on the road near Sligo, but he did not go into the town, but turned towards Ben Bulben; for there were thoughts of the old times coming upon him, and he had no mind to meet with common men. And as he walked he was singing to himself a song that had come to him one time in his dreams:

O Death's old bony finger
Will never find us there
In the high hollow townland
Where love's to give and to spare;
Where boughs have fruit and blossom
At all times of the year;
Where rivers are running over
With red beer and brown beer.
An old man plays the bagpipes
In a gold and silver wood;
Queens, their eyes blue like the ice,
Are dancing in a crowd.

The little fox he murmured,
'O what of the world's bane?'
The sun was laughing sweetly,
The moon plucked at my rein;
But the little red fox murmured,
'O do not pluck at his rein,
He is riding to the townland
That is the world's bane.'

When their hearts are so high
That they would come to blows.
They unhook their heavy swords
From golden and silver boughs;
But all that are killed in battle
Awaken to life again;
It is lucky that their story
Is not known among men.
For O, the strong farmers
That would let the spade lie,
Their hearts would be like a cup
That somebody had drunk dry.

Michael will unhook his trumpet
From a bough overhead.
And blow a little noise
When the supper has been spread.

Gabriel will come from the water
With a fish tail, and talk
Of wonders that have happened
On wet roads where men walk,
And lift up an old horn
Of hammered silver, and drink
Till he has fallen asleep
Upon the starry brink.

Hanrahan had begun to climb the mountain then, and he gave over singing, for it was a long climb for him, and every now and again he had to sit down and to rest for a while.

And one time he was resting he took notice of a wild briar bush, with blossoms on it, that was growing beside a rath, and it brought to mind the wild roses he used to bring to Mary Lavelle, and to no woman after her. And he tore off a little branch of the bush, that had buds on it and open blossoms, and he went on with his song:

The little fox he murmured,
'O what of the world's bane?'
The sun was laughing sweetly,
The moon plucked at my rein;
But the little red fox murmured,

'O do not pluck at his rein,
He is riding to the townland
That is the world's bane.'

And he went on climbing the hill, and left the rath, and there came to his mind some of the old poems that told of lovers, good and bad, and of some that were awakened from the sleep of the grave itself by the strength of one another's love, and brought away to a life in some shadowy place, where they are waiting for the judgment and banished from the face of God.

And at last, at the fall of day, he came to the Steep Place of the Strangers, and there he laid himself down along a ridge of rock, and looked into the valley, that was full of grey mist spreading from mountain to mountain.

And it seemed to him as he looked that the mist changed to shapes of shadowy men and women, and his heart began to beat with the fear and the joy of the sight. And his hands, that were always restless, began to pluck off the leaves of the roses on the little branch, and he watched them as they went floating down into the valley in a little fluttering troop.

Suddenly he heard a faint music, a music that had more laughter in it and more crying than all the music of this world. And his heart rose when he heard that, and he began to laugh out loud, for he knew that music was made by some who had a beauty and a greatness beyond the people of this world.

And it seemed to him that the little soft rose leaves[1] as they went fluttering down into the valley began to change their shape till they looked like a troop of men and women far off in the mist, with the colour of the roses on them. And then that colour changed to many colours, and what he saw was a long line of tall beautiful young men, and of queen-women, that were not going from him but coming towards him and past him, and their faces were full of tenderness for all their proud looks, and were very pale and worn, as if they were seeking and ever seeking for high sorrowful things.

And shadowy arms were stretched out of the mist as if to take hold of them, but could not touch them, for the quiet that was about them could not be broken.

And before them and beyond them, but at a distance as if in reverence, there were other shapes, sinking and rising and coming and going, and Hanrahan knew them by their whirling flight to be the Sidhe, the ancient defeated gods; and the shadowy arms did not rise to take hold of them, for they were of those that can neither sin nor obey. And they all lessened then in the distance, and they seemed to be going towards the white door that is in the side of the mountain.

---

1 在本書第三篇故事〈玫瑰煉金術〉裡，玫瑰花瓣也幻化為生命。

The mist spread out before him now like a deserted sea washing the mountains with long grey waves, but while he was looking at it, it began to fill again with a flowing broken witless life that was a part of itself, and arms and pale heads covered with tossing hair appeared in the greyness.

It rose higher and higher till it was level with the edge of the steep rock, and then the shapes grew to be solid, and a new procession half lost in mist passed very slowly with uneven steps, and in the midst of each shadow there was something shining in the starlight. They came nearer and nearer, and Hanrahan saw that they also were lovers, and that they had heart-shaped mirrors instead of hearts, and they were looking and ever looking on their own faces in one another's mirrors.

They passed on, sinking downward as they passed, and other shapes rose in their place, and these did not keep side by side, but followed after one another, holding out wild beckoning arms, and he saw that those who were followed were women, and as to their heads they were beyond all beauty, but as to their bodies they were but shadows without life, and their long hair was moving and trembling about them, as if it lived with some terrible life of its own.

And then the mist rose of a sudden and hid them, and then a light gust of wind blew them away towards the north-east, and covered Hanrahan at the same time with a white wing of cloud.

He stood up trembling and was going to turn away from the valley, when he saw two dark and half-hidden forms standing as if in the air just beyond the rock, and one of them that had the sorrowful eyes of a beggar said to him in a woman's voice, 'Speak to me, for no one in this world or any other world has spoken to me for seven hundred years.'

'Tell me who are those that have passed by,' said Hanrahan.

'Those that passed first,' the woman said 'are the lovers that had the greatest name in the old times, Blanad and Deirdre and Grania and their dear comrades, and a great many that are not so well known but are as well loved. And because it was not only the blossom of youth they were looking for in one another, but the beauty that is as lasting as the night and the stars, the night and the stars hold them forever from the warring and the perishing, in spite of the wars and the bitterness their love brought into the world. And those that came next,' she said, 'and that still breathe the sweet air and have the mirrors in their hearts, are not put in songs by the poets, because they sought only to triumph one over the other, and so to prove their strength and beauty, and out of this they made a kind of love. And as to the women with shadow-bodies, they desired neither to triumph nor to love but only to be loved, and there is no blood in their hearts or in their bodies until it flows through them from a kiss, and their life is but for a moment. All these are unhappy, but I am the unhappiest of all, for I am Dervadilla, and this is Dermot, and it was our sin brought the Norman into Ireland. And the curses of all the generations are upon us, and none are punished as we are punished. It was but the blossom of the man and of the woman we loved in one another, the dying beauty of the dust and not the everlasting beauty. When we died there was no lasting unbreakable quiet about us, and the bitterness of the battles we brought into Ireland turned to our own punishment. We go wandering together forever, but Dermot that was my lover sees me always as a body that has been a long time in the ground, and I know that is the way he sees me. Ask me more, ask me more, for all the years have left their wisdom in my heart, and no one has listened to me for seven hundred years.'

A great terror had fallen upon Hanrahan, and lifting his arms above his head he screamed out loud three times, and the cattle in the valley lifted their heads and lowed, and the birds in the wood at the edge of the mountain awaked out of their sleep and fluttered through the trembling leaves. But a little below the edge of the rock, the troop of rose leaves still fluttered in the air, for the gateway of Eternity had opened and shut again in one beat of the heart.

6. The Death of Hanrahan

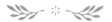

Hanrahan, that was never long in one place, was back again among the villages that are at the foot of Slieve Echtge, Illeton and Scalp and Ballylee, stopping sometimes in one house and sometimes in another, and finding a welcome in every place for the sake of the old times and of his poetry and his learning.

There was some silver and some copper money in the little leather bag under his coat, but it was seldom he needed to take anything from it, for it was little he used, and there was not one of the people that would have taken payment from him. His hand had grown heavy on the blackthorn he leaned on, and his cheeks were hollow and worn, but so far as food went, potatoes and milk and a bit of oaten cake, he had what he wanted of it; and it is

not on the edge of so wild and boggy a place as Echtge a mug of spirits would be wanting, with the taste of the turf smoke on it.

He would wander about the big wood at Kinadife, or he would sit through many hours of the day among the rushes about Lake Belshragh, listening to the streams from the hills, or watching the shadows in the brown bog pools; sitting so quiet as not to startle the deer that came down from the heather to the grass and the tilled fields at the fall of night.

As the days went by it seemed as if he was beginning to belong to some world out of sight and misty, that has for its mearing the colours that are beyond all other colours and the silences that are beyond all silences of this world.

And sometimes he would hear coming and going in the wood music that when it stopped went from his memory like a dream; and once in the stillness of midday he heard a sound like the clashing of many swords, that went on for long time without any break. And at the fall of night and at moonrise the lake would grow to be like a gateway of silver and shining stones, and there would come from its silence the faint sound of keening and of frightened laughter broken by the wind, and many pale beckoning hands.

He was sitting looking into the water one evening in harvest time, thinking of all the secrets that were shut

into the lakes and the mountains, when he heard a cry
coming from the south, very faint at first, but getting
louder and clearer as the shadow of the rushes grew
longer, till he could hear the words, 'I am beautiful, I am
beautiful; the birds in the air, the moths under the leaves,
the flies over the water look at me, for they never saw any
one so beautiful as myself. I am young; I am young: look
upon me, mountains; look upon me, perishing woods,
for my body will shine like the white waters when you
have been hurried away. You and the whole race of men,
and the race of the beasts and the race of the fish and
the winged race are dropping like a candle that is nearly
burned out, but I laugh out because I am in my youth.'

The voice would break off from time to time, as if
tired, and then it would begin again, calling out always
the same words, 'I am beautiful, I am beautiful.'

Presently the bushes at the edge of the little lake
trembled for a moment, and a very old woman forced her
way among them, and passed by Hanrahan, walking with
very slow steps. Her face was of the colour of earth, and
more wrinkled than the face of any old hag that was ever
seen, and her grey hair was hanging in wisps, and the
rags she was wearing did not hide her dark skin that was
roughened by all weathers. She passed by him with her
eyes wide open, and her head high, and her arms hanging
straight beside her, and she went into the shadow of the
hills towards the west.

A sort of dread came over Hanrahan when he saw her, for he knew her to be one Winny Byrne, that went begging from place to place crying always the same cry, and he had often heard that she had once such wisdom that all the women of the neighbours used to go looking for advice from her, and that she had a voice so beautiful that men and women would come from every part to hear her sing at a wake or a wedding; and that the Others, the great Sidhe, had stolen her wits one Samhain night many years ago, when she had fallen asleep on the edge of a rath, and had seen in her dreams the servants of Echtge of the hills.

And as she vanished away up the hillside, it seemed as if her cry, 'I am beautiful, I am beautiful,' was coming from among the stars in the heavens.

There was a cold wind creeping among the rushes, and Hanrahan began to shiver, and he rose up to go to some house where there would be a fire on the hearth. But instead of turning down the hill as he was used, he went on up the hill, along the little track that was maybe a road and maybe the dry bed of a stream. It was the same way Winny had gone, and it led to the little cabin where she stopped

when she stopped in any place at all.

He walked very slowly up the hill as if he had a great load on his back, and at last he saw a light a little to the left, and he thought it likely it was from Winny's house it was shining, and he turned from the path to go to it. But clouds had come over the sky, and he could not well see his way, and after he had gone a few steps his foot slipped and he fell into a bog drain, and though he dragged himself out of it, holding on to the roots of the heather, the fall had given him a great shake, and he felt better fit to lie down than to go travelling. But he had always great courage, and he made his way on, step by step, till at last he came to Winny's cabin, that had no window, but the light was shining from the door. He thought to go into it and to rest for a while, but when he came to the door he did not see Winny inside it, but what he saw was four old grey-haired women playing cards, but Winny herself was not among them. Hanrahan sat down on a heap of turf beside the door, for he was tired out and out, and had no wish for talking or for card-playing, and his bones and his joints aching the way they were.

He could hear the four women talking as they played, and calling out their hands. And it seemed to him that they were saying, like the strange man in the barn long ago: 'Spades and Diamonds, Courage and Power. Clubs and Hearts, Knowledge and Pleasure.'

And he went on saying those words over and over to

himself; and whether or not he was in his dreams, the pain that was in his shoulder never left him.

And after a while the four women in the cabin began to quarrel, and each one to say the other had not played fair, and their voices grew from loud to louder, and their screams and their curses, till at last the whole air was filled with the noise of them around and above the house, and Hanrahan, hearing it between sleep and waking, said: 'That is the sound of the fighting between the friends and the ill-wishers of a man that is near his death. And I wonder,' he said, 'who is the man in this lonely place that is near his death.'

It seemed as if he had been asleep a long time, and he opened his eyes, and the face he saw over him was the old wrinkled face of Winny of the Cross Road. She was looking hard at him, as if to make sure he was not dead, and she wiped away the blood that had grown dry on his face with a wet cloth, and after a while she partly helped him and partly lifted him into the cabin, and laid him down on what served her for a bed. She gave him a couple of potatoes from a pot on the fire, and, what served him better, a mug of spring water.

He slept a little now and

again, and sometimes he heard her singing to herself as she moved about the house, and so the night wore away.

When the sky began to brighten with the dawn he felt for the bag where his little store of money was, and held it out to her, and she took out a bit of copper and a bit of silver money, but she let it drop again as if it was nothing to her, maybe because it was not money she was used to beg for, but food and rags; or maybe because the rising of the dawn was filling her with pride and a new belief in her own great beauty.

She went out and cut a few armfuls of heather, and brought it in and heaped it over Hanrahan, saying something about the cold of the morning, and while she did that he took notice of the wrinkles in her face, and the greyness of her hair, and the broken teeth that were black and full of gaps.

And when he was well covered with the heather she went out of the door and away down the side of the mountain, and he could hear her cry, ' I am beautiful, I am beautiful,' getting less and less as she went, till at last it died away altogether.

Hanrahan lay there through the length of the day, in his pains and his weakness, and when the shadows of the evening were falling he heard her voice again coming up the hillside, and she came in and boiled the potatoes and shared them with him the same way as before.

And one day after another passed like that, and the

weight of his flesh was heavy about him. But little by little as he grew weaker he knew there were some greater than himself in the room with him, and that the house began to be filled with them; and it seemed to him they had all power in their hands, and that they might with one touch of the hand break down the wall the hardness of pain had built about him, and take him into their own world.

And sometimes he could hear voices, very faint and joyful, crying from the rafters or out of the flame on the hearth, and other times the whole house was filled with music that went through it like a wind. And after a while his weakness left no place for pain, and there grew up about him a great silence like the silence in the heart of a lake, and there came through it like the flame of a rushlight the faint joyful voices ever and always.

One morning he heard music somewhere outside the door, and as the day passed it grew louder and louder until it drowned the faint joyful voices, and even Winny's cry upon the hillside at the fall of evening.

About midnight and in a moment, the walls seemed to melt away and to leave his bed floating on a pale misty light that shone on every side as far as the eye could see; and after the first blinding of his eyes he saw that it was full of great shadowy figures rushing here and there.

At the same time the music came very clearly to him, and he knew that it was but the continual clashing of swords.

'I am after my death,' he said, 'and in the very heart of the music of Heaven. Cherubim and Seraphim, receive my soul!'

At his cry the light where it was nearest to him filled with sparks of yet brighter light, and he saw that these were the points of swords turned towards his heart; and then a sudden flame, bright and burning like God's love or God's hate, swept over the light and went out and he was in darkness.

At first he could see nothing, for all was as dark as if there was black bog earth about him, but all of a sudden the fire blazed up as if a wisp of straw had been thrown upon it. And as he looked at it, the fight was shining on the big pot that was hanging from a hook, and on the flat stone where Winny used to bake a cake now and again, and on the long rusty knife she used to be cutting the roots of the heather with, and on the long blackthorn stick he had brought into the house himself.

And when he saw those four things, some memory came into Hanrahan's mind, and strength came back to him, and he rose sitting up in the bed, and he said very loud and clear: 'The Cauldron, the Stone, the Sword, the Spear. What are they? Who do they belong to? And I have asked the question this time,' he said.

And then he fell back again, weak, and the breath going from him.

Winny Byrne, that had been tending the fire, came

over then, having her eyes fixed on the bed; and the faint laughing voices began crying out again, and a pale light, grey like a wave, came creeping over the room, and he did not know from what secret world it came. He saw Winny's withered face and her withered arms that were grey like crumbled earth, and weak as he was he shrank back farther towards the wall.

And then there came out of the mud-stiffened rags arms as white and as shadowy as the foam on a river, and they were put about his body, and a voice that he could hear well but that seemed to come from a long way off said to him in a whisper: 'You will go looking for me no more upon the breasts of women.'

'Who are you?' he said then.

'I am one of the lasting people, of the lasting unwearied Voices, that make my dwelling in the broken and the dying, and those that have lost their wits; and I came looking for you, and you are mine until the whole world is burned out like a candle that is spent. And look up now,' she said, 'for the wisps that are for our wedding are lighted.'

He saw then that the house was crowded with pale shadowy hands, and that every hand was holding what was sometimes like a wisp lighted for a marriage, and sometimes like a tall white candle for the dead.

When the sun rose on the morning of the morrow Winny of the Cross Roads rose up from where she was sitting beside the body, and began her begging from townland to townland, singing the same song as she walked, 'I am beautiful, I am beautiful. The birds in the air, the moths under the leaves, the flies over the water look at me. Look at me, perishing woods, for my body will be shining like the lake water after you have been hurried away. You and the old race of men, and the race of the beasts, and the race of the fish, and the winged race, are wearing away like a candle that has been burned out. But I laugh out loud, because I am in my youth.'

She did not come back that night or any night to the cabin, and it was not till the end of two days that the turf cutters going to the bog found the body of Red Owen Hanrahan, and gathered men to wake him and women to keen him, and gave him a burying worthy of so great a poet.

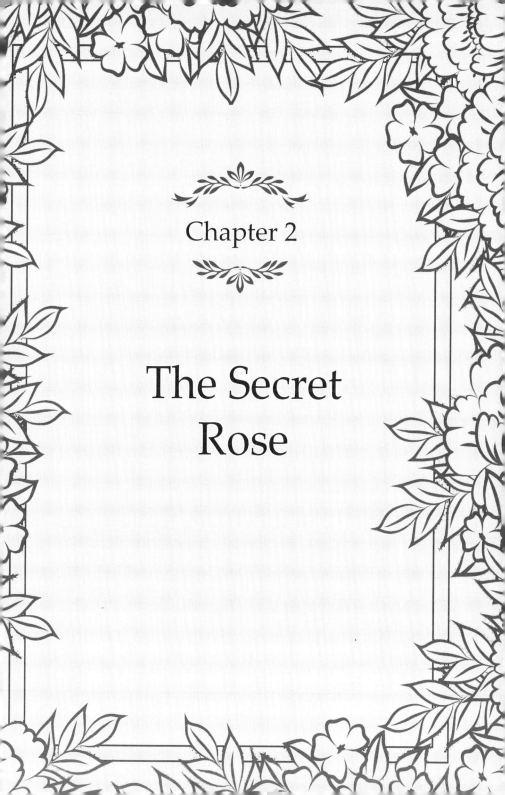

Chapter 2

The Secret Rose

My dear A. E.[1]—I dedicate this book to you because, whether you think it well or ill written, you will sympathize with the sorrows and the ecstasies of its personages, perhaps even more than I do myself. Although I wrote these stories at different times and in different manners, and without any definite plan, they have but one subject, the war of spiritual with natural order; and how can I dedicate such a book to anyone but to you, the one poet of modern Ireland who has moulded a spiritual ecstasy into verse?

My friends in Ireland sometimes ask me when I am going to write a really national poem or romance, and by a national poem or romance I understand them to mean a poem or romance founded upon some famous moment of Irish history, and built up out of the thoughts and feelings which move the greater number of patriotic Irishmen.

I on the other hand believe that poetry and romance cannot be made by the most conscientious study of famous moments and of the thoughts and feelings of others, but only by looking into that little, infinite, faltering, eternal flame that we call ourselves. If a writer wishes to interest a certain people among whom he has grown up, or fancies he has a duty towards them, he may choose for the symbols of his art their legends, their history, their beliefs, their opinions, because he has a right to choose among things less than himself, but he cannot choose among the substances of art.

So far, however, as this book is visionary it is Irish, for Ireland which is still predominantly Celtic has preserved with some less excellent things a gift of vision, which has died out among more hurried and more successful nations: no shining candelabra have prevented us from looking into the darkness, and when one looks into the darkness there is always something there.

W. B. YEATS.
London, 1896.

74

As for living, our servants will do that for us.
—Villiers de L'Isle Adam[2]

*Helen, when she looked in her mirror, seeing the withered
wrinkles made in her face by old age, wept, and wondered why
she had twice been carried away.*
—From Leonardo da Vinci's note books

1　A.E. 為愛爾蘭作家 George William Russell（1867–1935）的筆名。
2　Villiers de L'Isle Adam（1838–1889），法國象徵主義作家、詩人、
　　劇作家。

1. To the Secret Rose

Far off, most secret, and inviolate Rose,
Enfold me in my hour of hours; where those
Who sought thee at the Holy Sepulchre,
Or in the wine-vat, dwell beyond the stir
And tumult of defeated dreams; and deep
Among pale eyelids heavy with the sleep
Men have named beauty. Your great leaves enfold
The ancient beards, the helms of ruby and gold
Of the crowned Magi[1]; and the king whose eyes
Saw the Pierced Hands and Rood of Elder rise
In druid vapour and make the torches dim;
Till vain frenzy awoke and he died; and him
Who met Fand[2] walking among flaming dew,
By a grey shore where the wind never blew,
And lost the world and Emir[3] for a kiss;
And him who drove the gods out of their liss
And till a hundred morns had flowered red
Feasted, and wept the barrows of his dead;

And the proud dreaming king who flung the crown
And sorrow away, and calling bard and clown
Dwelt among wine-stained wanderers in deep woods;
And him who sold tillage and house and goods,
And sought through lands and islands numberless years
Until he found with laughter and with tears
A woman of so shining loveliness
That men threshed corn at midnight by a tress,
A little stolen tress. I too await
The hour of thy great wind of love and hate.
When shall the stars be blown about the sky,
Like the sparks blown out of a smithy, and die?
Surely thine hour has come, thy great wind blows,
Far off, most secret, and inviolate Rose?

---

1 Magi：在基督教傳統中，指三賢人（Three
  Wise Men），他們帶著金子、乳香和沒藥，
  在耶穌出生時來拜訪。
2 Fand：愛爾蘭神話中，一位超凡脫俗的女子。
3 Emir：愛爾蘭神話中，英雄庫胡林
  （Cúchulainn）的妻子。

2. The Crucifixion of the Outcast

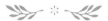

A man, with thin brown hair and a pale face, half ran, half walked, along the road that wound from the south to the town of Sligo. Many called him Cumhal, the son of Cormac, and many called him the Swift, Wild Horse; and he was a gleeman, and he wore a short parti-coloured doublet, and had pointed shoes, and a bulging wallet. Also he was of the blood of the Ernaans, and his birth-place was the Field of Gold; but his eating and sleeping places were the four provinces of Eri[1], and his abiding place was not upon the ridge of the earth.

His eyes strayed from the Abbey tower of the White Friars and the town battlements to a row of crosses which stood out against the sky upon a hill a little to the eastward of the town, and he clenched his fist, and shook it at the crosses.

He knew they were not empty, for the birds were fluttering about them; and he thought how, as like as not, just such another vagabond as himself was hanged on one of them; and he muttered: 'If it were hanging or bowstringing, or stoning or beheading, it would be bad enough. But to have the birds pecking your eyes and the wolves eating your feet! I would that the red wind[2] of the Druids had withered in his cradle the soldier of Dathi[3], who brought the tree of death out of barbarous lands, or that the lightning, when it smote Dathi at the foot of the mountain, had smitten him also, or that his grave had been dug by the green-haired and green-toothed merrows[4] deep at the roots of the deep sea.'

While he spoke, he shivered from head to foot, and the sweat came out upon his face, and he knew not why, for he had looked upon many crosses. He passed over two hills and under the battlemented gate, and then round by a left-hand way to the door of the Abbey. It was studded with great nails, and when he knocked at it, he roused the lay brother who was the porter, and of him he asked a place in the guest-house.

Then the lay brother took a glowing turf on a shovel, and led the way to a big and naked outhouse strewn with very dirty rushes; and lighted a rush-candle fixed between two of the stones of the wall, and set the glowing turf upon the hearth and gave him two unlighted

---

1 Eri：葉利，古愛爾蘭的主要氏族，這裡用來代表愛爾蘭人。
2 古愛爾蘭人認為有十二種不同顏色的風。
3 Dathi：大提王，愛爾蘭國王，最後在阿爾卑斯山上被雷電擊斃。
4 merrow：愛爾蘭傳說中的美人魚。

sods and a wisp of straw, and showed him a blanket
hanging from a nail, and a shelf with a loaf of bread and
a jug of water, and a tub in a far corner. Then the lay
brother left him and went back to his place by the door.

And Cumhal the son of Cormac began to blow upon
the glowing turf that he might light the two sods and the
wisp of straw; but the sods and the straw would not light,
for they were damp. So he took off his pointed shoes,
and drew the tub out of the corner with the thought of
washing the dust of the highway from his feet; but the
water was so dirty that he could not see the bottom.

He was very hungry, for he had not eaten all that day;
so he did not waste much anger upon
the tub, but took up the black loaf,
and bit into it, and then spat out
the bite, for the bread was hard and
mouldy. Still he did not give way to his anger, for he had
not drunken these many hours; having a hope of heath
beer or wine at his day's end, he had left the brooks
untasted, to make his supper the more delightful.

Now he put the jug to his lips, but he flung it from
him straightway, for the water was bitter and ill-smelling.
Then he gave the jug a kick, so that it broke against the
opposite wall, and he took down the blanket to wrap it
about him for the night. But no sooner did he touch it
than it was alive with skipping fleas.

At this, beside himself with anger, he rushed to the

door of the guest-house, but the lay brother, being well accustomed to such outcries, had locked it on the outside; so he emptied the tub and began to beat the door with it, till the lay brother came to the door and asked what ailed him, and why he woke him out of sleep.

'What ails me!' shouted Cumhal, 'are not the sods as wet as the sands of the Three Rosses[5]? and are not the fleas in the blanket as many as the waves of the sea and as lively? and is not the bread as hard as the heart of a lay brother who has forgotten God? and is not the water in the jug as bitter and as ill-smelling as his soul? and is not the foot-water the colour that shall be upon him when he has been charred in the Undying Fires?'

The lay brother saw that the lock was fast, and went back to his niche, for he was too sleepy to talk with comfort.

And Cumhal went on beating at the door, and presently he heard the lay brother's foot once more, and cried out at him, 'O cowardly and tyrannous race of friars, persecutors of the bard and the gleeman, haters of life and joy! O race that does not draw the sword and tell the truth![6] O race that melts the bones of the people with

---

5　Three Rosses：三諾斯，位於羅席斯半島（Rosses Point peninsula）的三個路岬。

6　這裡提到愛爾蘭分離主義者 John O'Leary（1830–1907）的話：「我的信仰，就是拉弓戰鬥和傳頌真理。」（I have but one religion, to bend the bow and tell the truth.）

cowardice and with deceit!'

'Gleeman,' said the lay brother, 'I also make rhymes; I make many while I sit in my niche by the door, and I sorrow to hear the bards railing upon the friars. Brother, I would sleep, and therefore I make known to you that it is the head of the monastery, our gracious abbot, who orders all things concerning the lodging of travellers.'

'You may sleep,' said Cumhal, 'I will sing a bard's curse on the abbot.'[7]

And he set the tub upside down under the window, and stood upon it, and began to sing in a very loud voice. The singing awoke the abbot, so that he sat up in bed and blew a silver whistle until the lay brother came to him.

'I cannot get a wink of sleep with that noise,' said the abbot. 'What is happening?'

'It is a gleeman,' said the lay brother, 'who complains of the sods, of the bread, of the water in the jug, of the foot-water, and of the blanket. And now he is singing a bard's curse upon you, O brother abbot, and upon your father and your mother, and your grandfather and your grandmother, and upon all your relations.'

'Is he cursing in rhyme?'

'He is cursing in rhyme, and with two assonances in every line of his curse.'

The abbot pulled his night-cap off and crumpled it in his hands, and the circular brown patch of hair in the middle of his bald head looked like an island in the midst of a pond, for in Connaught they had not yet abandoned the ancient tonsure[8] for the style then coming into use.

tonsure

'If we do not somewhat,' he said, 'he will teach his curses to the children in the street, and the girls spinning at the doors, and to the robbers upon Ben Bulben[9].'

'Shall I go, then,' said the other, 'and give him dry sods, a fresh loaf, clean water in a jug, clean foot-water, and a new blanket, and make him swear by the blessed Saint Benignus, and by the sun and moon, that no bond be lacking, not to tell his rhymes to the children in the street, and the girls spinning at the doors, and the robbers upon Ben Bulben?'

'Neither our Blessed Patron nor the sun and moon would avail at all,' said the abbot; 'for tomorrow or the next day the mood to curse would come upon him, or a pride in those rhymes would move him, and he would teach his lines to the children, and the girls, and the robbers. Or else he would tell another of his craft how he

---

7 據說愛爾蘭的吟遊詩人，能夠藉由作詩，來讓敵人生病或死亡。

8 Tonsure：頭頂剃光的樣式於八世紀廢除。

9 the robbers upon Ben Bulben：布本山的強盜也出現在另一個故事〈玫瑰信念〉之中。

fared in the guest-house, and he in his turn would begin to curse, and my name would wither. For learn there is no steadfastness of purpose upon the roads, but only under roofs and between four walls. Therefore I bid you go and awaken Brother Kevin, Brother Dove, Brother Little Wolf, Brother Bald Patrick, Brother Bald Brandon, Brother James and Brother Peter. And they shall take the man, and bind him with ropes, and dip him in the river that he shall cease to sing. And in the morning, lest this but make him curse the louder, we will crucify him.'

'The crosses are all full,' said the lay brother.

'Then we must make another cross. If we do not make an end of him another will, for who can eat and sleep in peace while men like him are going about the world? Ill should we stand before blessed Saint Benignus, and sour would be his face when he comes to judge us at the Last Day, were we to spare an enemy of his when we had him under our thumb! Brother, the bards and the gleemen are an evil race, ever cursing and ever stirring up the people, and immoral and immoderate in all things, and heathen in their hearts, always longing after the Son of Lir, and Aengus, and Bridget, and the Dagda, and Danna the mother[10], and all the false gods of the old days; always making poems in praise of those kings and queens of the demons, Finvaragh, whose home is under Cruachmaa, and Red Aodh of Cnocna-Sidhe, and Cleena of the Wave, and Aoibhell of the Grey Rock, and him they call Donn[11] of the

Vats of the Sea; and railing against God and Christ and the blessed Saints.'

While he was speaking he crossed himself, and when he had finished he drew the night-cap over his ears, to shut out the noise, and closed his eyes, and composed himself to sleep.

The lay brother found Brother Kevin, Brother Dove, Brother Little Wolf, Brother Bald Patrick, Brother Bald Brandon, Brother James and Brother Peter sitting up in bed, and he made them get up. Then they bound Cumhal, and they dragged him to the river, and they dipped him in it at the place which was afterwards called Buckley's Ford[12].

'Gleeman,' said the lay brother, as they led him back to the guest-house, 'why do you ever use the wit which God has given you to make blasphemous and immoral tales and verses? For such is the way of your craft. I have, indeed, many such tales and verses well nigh by rote, and so I know that I speak true! And why do you praise with rhyme those demons, Finvaragh, Red Aodh,

---

10 the Son of Lir，曾被後母施以法術。Aengus，愛情與欺騙之神。Bridget，詩人和預言家。Dagda，豐饒之神。Danna the mother：愛爾蘭傳說中的諸神之母。

11 Finvaragh，愛爾蘭精靈之王。Red Aodh，死亡之神。Cleena，芒斯特的仙子。Aoibhell，克琳娜的姊妹。Donn，死亡之神。

12 位於斯萊戈郡（Sligo）。

Cleena, Aoibhell and Donn? I, too, am a man of great wit and learning, but I ever glorify our gracious abbot, and Benignus our Patron, and the princes of the province. My soul is decent and orderly, but yours is like the wind among the salley gardens. I said what I could for you, being also a man of many thoughts, but who could help such a one as you?'

'Friend,' answered the gleeman, 'my soul is indeed like the wind, and it blows me to and fro, and up and down, and puts many things into my mind and out of my mind, and therefore am I called the Swift, Wild Horse.'

And he spoke no more that night, for his teeth were chattering with the cold.

The abbot and the friars came to him in the morning, and bade him get ready to be crucified, and led him out of the guest-house. And while he still stood upon the step a flock of great grass-barnacles[13]

great grass-barnacles

passed high above him with clanking cries. He lifted his arms to them and said, 'O great grass-barnacles, tarry a little, and mayhap my soul will travel with you to the waste places of the shore and to the ungovernable sea!

'At the gate a crowd of beggars gathered about them, being come there to beg from any traveller or pilgrim who might have spent the night in the guest-house. The abbot and the friars led the gleeman to a place in the woods at some distance, where many straight young trees were growing, and they made him cut one down and fashion it to the right length, while the beggars stood round them in a ring, talking and gesticulating. The abbot then bade him cut off another and shorter piece of wood and nail it upon the first.

So there was his cross for him; and they put it upon his shoulder, for his crucifixion was to be on the top of the hill where the others were.

A half-mile on the way he asked them to stop and see him juggle for them; for he knew, he said, all the tricks of Aengus the Subtle-hearted. The old friars were for pressing on, but the young friars would see him: so he did many wonders for them, even to the drawing of live frogs out of his ears.

But after a while they turned on him, and said his tricks were dull and a shade unholy, and set the cross on his shoulders again.

Another half-mile on the way, and he asked them to stop and hear him jest for them, for he knew, he said, all the jests of Conan the Bald, upon whose back a sheep's wool grew[14]. And the young friars, when they had heard

---

13 great grass-barnacles：白額黑燕，在愛爾蘭北部和西部過冬。

14 在鄉間流傳的故事中，加南（Conan）在失去背部的皮膚之後，他的夥伴跑向一群綿羊，剝下羊皮綁在 Conan 的背上。

his merry tales, again bade him take up his cross, for it ill became them to listen to such follies.

Another half-mile on the way, he asked them to stop and hear him sing the story of White-breasted Deirdre, and how she endured many sorrows, and how the sons of Usna died to serve her. And the young friars were mad to hear him, but when he had ended they grew angry, and beat him for waking forgotten longings in their hearts. So they set the cross upon his back and hurried him to the hill.

When he was come to the top, they took the cross from him, and began to dig a hole to stand it in, while the beggars gathered round, and talked among themselves.

'I ask a favour before I die,' says Cumhal.

'We will grant you no more delays,' says the abbot.

'I ask no more delays, for I have drawn the sword, and told the truth, and lived my vision, and am content.'

'Would you, then, confess?'

'By sun and moon, not I; I ask but to be let eat the food I carry in my wallet. I carry food in my wallet whenever I go upon a journey, but I do not taste of it unless I am well-nigh starved. I have not eaten now these two days.'

'You may eat, then,' says the abbot, and he turned to help the friars dig the hole.

The gleeman took a loaf and some strips of cold fried bacon out of his wallet and laid them upon the ground.

'I will give a tithe to the poor,' says he, and he cut a tenth part from the loaf and the bacon. 'Who among you is the poorest?'

And thereupon was a great clamour, for the beggars began the history of their sorrows and their poverty, and their yellow faces swayed like Gara Lough[15] when the floods have filled it with water from the bogs.

He listened for a little, and, says he, 'I am myself the poorest, for I have travelled the bare road, and by the edges of the sea; and the tattered doublet of particoloured cloth upon my back and the torn pointed shoes upon my feet have ever irked me, because of the towered city full of noble raiment which was in my heart. And I have been the more alone upon the roads and by the sea because I heard in my heart the rustling of the rose-bordered dress of her who is more subtle than Aengus, the Subtle-hearted, and more full of the beauty of laughter than Conan the Bald, and more full of the wisdom of tears than White-breasted Deirdre, and more lovely than a bursting dawn to them that are lost in the darkness. Therefore, I award the tithe to myself; but yet, because I am done with all things, I give it unto you.'

So he flung the bread and the strips of bacon among the beggars, and they fought with many cries until the

---

15 Gara Lough：位於斯萊戈郡（Sligo）西南方。

last scrap was eaten. But meanwhile the friars nailed the gleeman to his cross, and set it upright in the hole, and shovelled the earth in at the foot, and trampled it level and hard.

So then they went away, but the beggars stayed on, sitting round the cross. But when the sun was sinking, they also got up to go, for the air was getting chilly. And as soon as they had gone a little way, the wolves, who had been showing themselves on the edge of a neighbouring coppice, came nearer, and the birds wheeled closer and closer.

'Stay, outcasts, yet a little while,' the crucified one called in a weak voice to the beggars, 'and keep the beasts and the birds from me.'

But the beggars were angry because he had called them outcasts, so they threw stones and mud at him, and went their way.

Then the wolves gathered at the foot of the cross, and the birds flew lower and lower. And presently the birds lighted all at once upon his head and arms and shoulders, and began to peck at him, and the wolves began to eat his feet.

'Outcasts,' he moaned, 'have you also turned against the outcast?'

3. Out of the Rose

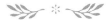

One winter evening an old knight in rusted chain-armour rode slowly along the woody southern slope of Ben Bulben, watching the sun go down in crimson clouds over the sea. His horse was tired, as after a long journey, and he had upon his helmet the crest of no neighbouring lord or king, but a small rose made of rubies that glimmered every moment to a deeper crimson. His white hair fell in thin curls upon his shoulders, and its disorder added to the melancholy of his face, which was the face of one of those who have come but seldom into the world, and always for its trouble, the dreamers who must do what they dream, the doers who must dream what they do.

After gazing a while towards the sun, he let the reins fall upon the neck of his horse, and, stretching out

both arms towards the west, he said, 'Divine Rose of Intellectual Flame, let the gates of thy peace be opened to me at last!'

And suddenly a loud squealing began in the woods some hundreds of yards further up the mountain side. He stopped his horse to listen, and heard behind him a sound of feet and of voices. 'They are beating them to make them go into the narrow path by the gorge,' said someone, and in another moment a dozen peasants armed with short spears had come up with the knight, and stood a little apart from him, their blue caps in their hands.

'Where do you go with the spears?' he asked; and one who seemed the leader answered: 'A troop of wood-thieves came down from the hills a while ago and carried off the pigs belonging to an old man who lives by Glen Car Lough, and we turned out to go after them. Now that we know they are four times more than we are, we follow to find the way they have taken; and will presently tell our story to De Courcey, and if he will not help us, to Fitzgerald; for De Courcey and Fitzgerald have lately made a peace, and we do not know to whom we belong.'

'But by that time,' said the knight, 'the pigs will have been eaten.'

'A dozen men cannot do more, and it was not reasonable that the whole valley should turn out and risk their lives for two, or for two dozen pigs.'

'Can you tell me,' said the knight, 'if the old man to whom the pigs belong is pious and true of heart?'

'He is as true as another and more pious than any, for he says a prayer to a saint every morning before his breakfast.'

'Then it were well to fight in his cause,' said the knight, 'and if you will fight against the wood-thieves I will take the main brunt of the battle, and you know well that a man in armour is worth many like these wood-thieves, clad in wool and leather.'

And the leader turned to his fellows and asked if they would take the chance; but they seemed anxious to get back to their cabins.

'Are the wood-thieves treacherous and impious?'

'They are treacherous in all their dealings,' said a peasant, 'and no man has known them to pray.'

'Then,' said the knight, 'I will give five crowns for the head of every wood-thief killed by us in the fighting'; and he bid the leader show the way, and they all went on together.

After a time they came to where a beaten track wound into the woods, and, taking this, they doubled back upon their previous course, and began to ascend the wooded slope of the mountains. In a little while the path grew very straight and steep, and the knight was forced to dismount and leave his horse tied to a tree-stem. They knew they were on the right track: for they could see the marks of pointed shoes in the soft clay and mingled with them the cloven footprints of the pigs.

Presently the path became still more abrupt, and they knew by the ending of the cloven footprints that the thieves were carrying the pigs. Now and then a long mark in the clay showed that a pig had slipped down, and been dragged along for a little way.

They had journeyed thus for about twenty minutes, when a confused sound of voices told them that they were coming up with the thieves. And then the voices ceased, and they understood that they had been overheard in their turn. They pressed on rapidly and cautiously, and in about five minutes one of them caught sight of a leather jerkin half hidden by a hazel-bush. An arrow struck the knight's chain-armour, but glanced off harmlessly, and then a flight of arrows swept by them with the buzzing sound of great bees.

They ran and climbed, and climbed and ran towards the thieves, who were now all visible standing up among the bushes with their still quivering bows in their hands: for they had only their spears and they must at once come hand to hand.

The knight was in the front and struck down first one and then another of the wood-thieves. The peasants shouted, and, pressing on, drove the wood-thieves before them until they came out on the flat top of the mountain, and there they saw the two pigs quietly grubbing in the short grass, so they ran about them in a circle, and began to move back again towards the narrow path: the old knight coming now the last of all, and striking down thief after thief.

The peasants had got no very serious hurts among them, for he had drawn the brunt of the battle upon himself, as could well be seen from the bloody rents in his armour; and when they came to the entrance of the narrow path he bade them drive the pigs down into the valley, while he stood there to guard the way behind them.

So in a moment he was alone, and, being weak with loss of blood, might have been ended there and then by the wood-thieves he had beaten off, had fear not made them begone out of sight in a great hurry.

An hour passed, and they did not return; and now the knight could stand on guard no longer, but had to lie down upon the grass. A half-hour more went by, and then a young lad with what appeared to be a number of cock's feathers stuck round his hat, came out of the path behind him, and began to move about among the dead thieves, cutting their heads off.

Then he laid the heads in a heap before the knight, and said: 'great knight, I have been bid come and ask you for the crowns you promised for the heads: five crowns a head. They bid me to tell you that they have prayed to God and His Mother to give you a long life, but that they are poor peasants, and that they would have the money before you die. They told me this over and over for fear I might forget it, and promised to beat me if I did.'

The knight raised himself upon his elbow, and opening a bag that hung to his belt, counted out the five crowns for each head. There were thirty heads in all.

'O great knight,' said the lad, 'they have also bid me take all care of you, and light a fire, and put this ointment upon your wounds.'

And he gathered sticks and leaves together, and, flashing his flint and steel under a mass of dry leaves, had made a very good blaze. Then, drawing off the coat of mail, he began to anoint the wounds: but he did it clumsily, like one who does by rote what he had been told.

The knight motioned him to stop, and said: 'You seem a good lad.'

'I would ask something of you for myself.'

'There are still a few crowns,' said the knight; ' shall I give them to you?'

'O no,' said the lad. 'They would be no good to me.

There is only one thing that I care about doing, and I have no need of money to do it. I go from village to village and from hill to hill, and whenever I come across a good cock I steal him and take him into the woods, and I keep him there under a basket until I get another good cock, and then I set them to fight. The people say I am an innocent, and do not do me any harm, and never ask me to do any work but go a message now and then. It is because I am an innocent that they send me to get the crowns: anyone else would steal them; and they dare not come back themselves, for now that you are not with them they are afraid of the wood-thieves. Did you ever hear how, when the wood-thieves are christened, the wolves are made their god-fathers[1], and their right arms are not christened at all?'

'If you will not take these crowns, my good lad, I have nothing for you, I fear, unless you would have that old coat of mail which I shall soon need no more.'

'There was something I wanted: yes, I remember now,' said the lad. 'I want you to tell me why you fought like the champions and giants in the stories and for so little a thing. Are you indeed a man like us? Are you not rather an old wizard who lives among these hills, and will not a wind arise presently and crumble you into dust?'

---

1 據說古愛爾蘭人崇拜野狼，人們會對野狼禱告，
並且讓野狼當孩子的教父。

'I will tell you of myself,' replied the knight, 'for now that I am the last of the fellowship, I may tell all and witness for God. Look at the Rose of Rubies on my helmet, and see the symbol of my life and of my hope.'

And then he told the lad this story, but with always more frequent pauses; and, while he told it, the Rose shone a deep blood-colour in the firelight, and the lad stuck the cock's feathers in the earth in front of him, and moved them about as though he made them actors in the play.

'I live in a land far from this, and was one of the Knights of St. John,' said the old man; 'but I was one of those in the Order who always longed for more arduous labours in the service of the Most High. At last there came to us a knight of Palestine[2], to whom the truth of truths had been revealed by God Himself. He had seen a great Rose of Fire, and a Voice out of the Rose had told him how men would turn from the light of their own hearts, and bow down before outer order and outer fixity, and that then the light would cease, and none escape the curse except the foolish good man who could not, and the passionate wicked man who would not, think. Already, the Voice told him, the wayward light of the heart was shining out upon the world to keep

---

2 十九世紀時，「巴勒斯坦」一詞才用為指稱地域。十四世紀時，這則故事就流傳於鄉間，因此「巴勒斯坦」在這裡是時代上的誤用。

it alive, with a less clear lustre, and that, as it paled, a strange infection was touching the stars and the hills and the grass and the trees with corruption, and that none of those who had seen clearly the truth and the ancient way could enter into the Kingdom of God, which is in the Heart of the Rose, if they stayed on willingly in the corrupted world; and so they must prove their anger against the Powers of Corruption by dying in the service of the Rose of God. While the Knight of Palestine was telling us these things we seemed to see in a vision a crimson Rose spreading itself about him, so that he seemed to speak out of its heart, and the air was filled with fragrance. By this we knew that it was the very Voice of God which spoke to us by the knight, and we gathered about him and bade him direct us in all things, and teach us how to obey the Voice. So he bound us with an oath, and gave us signs and words whereby we might know each other even after many years, and he appointed places of meeting, and he sent us out in troops into the world to seek good causes, and die in doing battle for them. At first we thought to die more readily by fasting to death in honour of some saint; but this he told us was evil, for we did it for the sake of death, and thus took out of the hands of God the choice of the time and manner of our death, and by so doing made His power the less. We must choose our service for its excellence, and for this alone, and leave it to God to reward us at His own time and in His own manner. And after this he compelled us to eat always two at a table to watch each other lest we fasted unduly, for some among us said that if one fasted for a love of the holiness of saints and then died, the death would be acceptable. And the years passed, and one by one my fellows died in the Holy Land, or in warring upon the evil princes of the earth, or in clearing the roads of robbers; and among them died the knight of Palestine, and at last I was alone. I fought in every cause where the few contended against the many, and my hair grew white, and a terrible fear lest I had fallen under the displeasure of God came upon me. But, hearing at last how this western isle was fuller of wars and rapine than any other land, I came hither, and I have found the thing I sought, and, behold! I am filled with a great joy.'

Thereat he began to sing in Latin, and, while he sang, his voice grew fainter and fainter. Then his eyes closed, and his lips fell apart, and the lad knew he was dead.

'He has told me a good tale,' he said, 'for there was fighting in it, but I did not understand much of it, and it is hard to remember so long a story.'

And, taking the knight's sword, he began to dig a grave in the soft clay. He dug hard, and a faint light of dawn had touched his hair and he had almost done his work when a cock crowed in the valley below.

'Ah,' he said, 'I must have that bird'; and he ran down the narrow path to the valley.

4. The Wisdom of the King

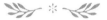

The High-Queen of Ireland had died in childbirth, and her child was put to nurse with a woman who lived in a hut of mud and wicker, within the border of the wood.

One night the woman sat rocking the cradle, and meditating upon the beauty of the child, and praying that the gods might grant him wisdom equal to his beauty. There came a knock at the door, and she got up, not a little wondering, for the nearest neighbours were in the dun of the High-King a mile away; and the night was now late.

'Who is knocking?' she cried, and a thin voice answered, 'Open! for I am a crone of the grey hawk, and I come from the darkness of the great wood.'

In terror she drew back the bolt, and a grey-clad woman, of a great age, and of a height more than human, came in and stood by the head of the cradle. The nurse shrank back against the wall, unable to take her eyes from the woman, for she saw by the gleaming of the firelight that the feathers of the

grey hawk were upon her head instead of hair.

But the child slept, and the fire danced, for the one was too ignorant and the other too full of gaiety to know what a dreadful being stood there.

'Open!' cried another voice, 'for I am a crone of the grey hawk, and I watch over his nest in the darkness of the great wood.'

The nurse opened the door again, though her fingers could scarce hold the bolts for trembling, and another grey woman, not less old than the other, and with like feathers instead of hair, came in and stood by the first.

In a little, came a third grey woman, and after her a fourth, and then another and another and another, until the hut was full of their immense bodies. They stood a long time in perfect silence and stillness, for they were of those whom the dropping of the sand has never troubled, but at last one muttered in a low thin voice: 'Sisters, I knew him far away by the redness of his heart under his silver skin'; and then another spoke: 'Sisters, I knew him because his heart fluttered like a bird under a net of silver cords'; and then another took up the word: 'Sisters, I knew him because his heart sang like a bird that is happy in a silver cage.'

And after that they sang together, those who were nearest rocking the cradle with long wrinkled fingers; and their voices were now tender and caressing, now like the wind blowing in the great wood, and this was their song:

Out of sight is out of mind:
Long have man and woman-kind,
Heavy of will and light of mood,
Taken away our wheaten food.
Taken away our Altar stone;
Hail and rain and thunder alone,
And red hearts we turn to grey,
Are true till Time gutter away.

When the song had died out, the crone who had first spoken, said: 'We have nothing more to do but to mix a drop of our blood into his blood.'

And she scratched her arm with the sharp point of a spindle, which she had made the nurse bring to her, and let a drop of blood, grey as the mist, fall upon the lips of the child; and passed out into the darkness. Then the others passed out in silence one by one; and all the while the child had not opened his pink eyelids or the fire ceased to dance, for the one was too ignorant and the other too full of gaiety to know what great beings had bent over the cradle.

When the crones were gone, the nurse came to her courage again, and hurried to the dun[1] of the High-

---

1 dun：古時或中世紀時的堡壘。

King, and cried out in the midst of the
assembly hall that the Sidhe, whether
for good or evil she knew not, had
bent over the child that night; and the
king and his poets and men of law,
and his hunstmen, and his cooks, and
his chief warriors went with her to the

hut and gathered about the cradle, and were as noisy as
magpies, and the child sat up and looked at them.

Two years passed over, and the king died fighting
against the Fer Bolg; and the poets and the men of law
ruled in the name of the child, but looked to see him
become the master himself before long, for no one had
seen so wise a child, and tales of his endless questions
about the household of the gods and the making of the
world went hither and thither among the wicker houses
of the poor.

Everything had been well but for a miracle that began
to trouble all men; and all women, who, indeed, talked
of it without ceasing. The feathers of the grey hawk had
begun to grow in the child's hair, and though his nurse
cut them continually, in but a little while they would be
more numerous than ever.

This had not been a matter of great moment, for
miracles were a little thing in those days, but for an
ancient law of Eri that none who had any blemish of
body could sit upon the throne; and as a grey hawk was

a wild thing of the air which had never sat at the board, or listened to the songs of the poets in the light of the fire, it was not possible to think of one in whose hair its feathers grew as other than marred and blasted; nor could the people separate from their admiration of the wisdom that grew in him a horror as at one of unhuman blood.

Yet all were resolved that he should reign, for they had suffered much from foolish kings and their own disorders, and moreover they desired to watch out the spectacle of his days; and no one had any other fear but that his great wisdom might bid him obey the law, and call some other, who had but a common mind, to reign in his stead.

When the child was seven years old the poets and the men of law were called together by the chief poet, and all these matters weighed and considered. The child had already seen that those about him had hair only, and, though they had told him that they woo had had feathers but had lost them because of a sin committed by their forefathers, they knew that he would learn the truth when he began to wander into the country round about.

After much consideration they made a new law commanding everyone upon pain of death to mingle artificially the feathers of the grey hawk into his hair; and they sent men with nets and slings and bows into the countries round about to gather a sufficiency of feathers. They decreed also that any who told the truth to the child should be flung from a cliff into the sea.

The years passed, and the child grew from childhood into boyhood and from boyhood into manhood, and from being curious about all things he became busy with strange and subtle thoughts which came to him in dreams, and with distinctions between things long held the same and with the resemblance of things long held different.

Multitudes came from other lands to see him and to ask his counsel, but there were guards set at the frontiers, who compelled all that came to wear the feathers of the grey hawk in their hair. While they listened to him his words seemed to make all darkness light and filled their hearts like music; but, alas, when they returned to their own lands his words seemed far

off, and what they could remember too strange and subtle to help them to live out their hasty days.

A number indeed did live differently afterwards, but their new life was less excellent than the old: some among them had long served a good cause, but when they heard him praise it, they returned to their own lands to find what they had loved less lovable and their arm lighter in the battle, for he had taught them how little a hair divides the false and true; others, again, who had served no cause, but built up in peace the welfare of their own households, when he had expounded the meaning of their purpose, found their bones softer and their will less ready for toil, for he had shown them greater purposes; and numbers of the young, when they had heard him upon all these things, remembered certain strange words that became like a fire in their hearts, and made all kindly joys and traffic between man and man as nothing, and went different ways, but all into vague regret.

When any asked him concerning the common things of life; disputes about the mear of a territory, or about the straying of cattle, or about the penalty of blood; he would turn to those nearest him for advice; but this was held to be from courtesy, for none knew that these matters were hidden from him by thoughts and dreams that filled his mind like the marching and counter-marching of armies.

Among those who came to look at him and to listen to him was the daughter of a little king who lived a great way off; and when he saw her he loved, for she was beautiful, with a strange and pale beauty unlike the women of his land; but Dana, the great mother, had decreed her a heart that was but as the heart of others, and when she thought of the mystery of the hawk feathers she was troubled with a great horror.

He called her to him when the assembly was over and told her of her beauty, and praised her simply and frankly as though she were a fable of the bards; and he asked her humbly to give him her love, for he was only subtle in his dreams.

Overwhelmed with his greatness, she half consented, and yet half refused, for she longed to marry some warrior who could carry her over a mountain in his arms. Day by day the king gave her gifts; gold enameled cups and cloths the merchants had carried from India or maybe from China itself; and still she was ever between a smile and a frown; between yielding and withholding.

He laid down his wisdom at her feet, and told how the heroes when they die return to the world and begin their labour anew; and a multitude of things that even the Sidhe have forgotten, either because they happened so long ago or because they have not time to think of them; and still she half refused, and still he hoped, because he could not believe that such a beauty so much like wisdom could hide a common heart.

There was a tall young man in the house who had yellow hair, and was skilled in wrestling and in the training of horses; and one day when the king walked in the orchard, which was between the foss and the forest, he heard his voice among the salley bushes which hid the waters of the foss.

'My dear,' it said, 'I hate them for making you weave these dingy feathers into your beautiful hair, and all that the bird of prey upon the throne may sleep easy o' nights'; and then the low, musical voice he loved answered: 'My hair is not beautiful like yours; and now that I have plucked the feathers out of your hair I will put my hands through it, thus, and thus, and thus; for it casts no shadow of terror and darkness upon my heart.'

Then the king remembered many things that he had forgotten without understanding them, doubtful words of his poets and his men of law, doubts that he had reasoned away, his own continual solitude; and he called to the lovers in a trembling voice.

They came from among the salley bushes and threw themselves at his feet and prayed for pardon, and he stooped down and plucked the feathers out of the hair of the woman and turned away towards the dun without a word.

He strode into the hall of assembly, and having gathered his poets and his men of law about him, stood upon the dais and spoke in a loud, clear voice: 'Men of law, why did you make me sin against the laws of Eri? Men of verse, why did you make me sin against the secrecy of wisdom, for law was made by man for the welfare of man, but wisdom the gods have made, and no man shall live by its light, for it and the hail and the rain and the thunder follow a way that is deadly to mortal things? Men of law and men of verse, live according to your kind, and call Eocha[2] of the Hasty Mind to reign over you, for I set out to find my kindred.'

He then came down among them, and drew out of the hair of first one and then another the feathers of the grey hawk, and, having scattered them over the rushes upon the floor, passed out, and none dared to follow him, for his eyes gleamed like the eyes of the birds of prey; and no man saw him again or heard his voice.

Some believed that he found his eternal abode among the demons, and some that he dwelt henceforth with the dark and dreadful goddesses, who sit all night about the pools in the forest watching the constellations rising and setting in those desolate mirrors.

2　Eocha：愛爾蘭傳說中的國王。

5. The Heart of the Spring [1]

A very old man, whose face was almost as fleshless as the foot of a bird, sat meditating upon the rocky shore of the flat and hazel-covered isle which fills the widest part of Lough Gill. A russet-faced boy of seventeen years sat by his side, watching the swallows dipping for flies in the still water. The old man was dressed in threadbare blue velvet and the boy wore a frieze coat and a blue cap, and had about his neck a rosary of blue beads.

Behind the two, and half hidden by trees, was a little monastery. It had been burned down a long while before by sacrilegious men of the Queen's party[2], but had been roofed anew with rushes by the boy, that the old man might find shelter in his last days.

He had not set his spade, however, into the garden

---

about it, and the lilies and the roses of the monks had spread out until their confused luxuriance met and mingled with the narrowing circle of the fern. Beyond the lilies and the roses the ferns were so deep that a child walking among them would be hidden from sight, even though he stood upon his toes; and beyond the fern rose many hazels and small oak trees.

'Master,' said the boy, 'this long fasting, and the labour of beckoning after nightfall with your rod of quicken wood to the beings who dwell in the waters and among the hazels and oak-trees, is too much for your strength. Rest from all this labour for a little, for your hand seemed more heavy upon my shoulder and your feet less steady under you to-day than I have known them. Men say that you are older than the eagles, and yet you will not seek the rest that belongs to age.'

He spoke eagerly, as though his heart were in the words; and the old man answered slowly and deliberately, as though his heart were in distant days and events.

'I will tell you why I have not been able to rest,' he said. 'It is right that you should know, for you have served me faithfully these five years, and even with affection, taking away thereby a little of the doom of loneliness which always falls upon the wise. Now, too, that the end of my labour and the triumph of my hopes is at hand, it is the more needful for you to have this knowledge.'

'Master, do not think that I would question you. It is for me to keep the fire alight, and the thatch close against the rain, and strong, lest the wind blow it among the trees; and to take down the heavy books from the shelves, possessing the while an incurious and reverent heart, for God has made out of His abundance a separate wisdom for everything which lives, and to do these things is my wisdom.'

'You are afraid,' said the old man, and his eyes shone with a momentary anger.

'Sometimes at night,' said the boy, 'when you are reading, with the rod of quicken wood in your hand, I look out of the door and see, now a great grey man driving swine among the hazels, and now many little people in red caps who come out of the lake driving little white cows before them. I do not fear these little people so much as the grey man; for, when they come near the house, they milk the cows, and they drink the frothing milk, and begin to dance; and I know there is good in the heart that loves dancing; but I fear them for all that. And I fear the tall white-armed ladies who come out of the air, and move slowly hither and thither, crowning themselves with the roses or with the lilies, and shaking about their living hair, which moves, for so I have heard them tell each other, with the motion of their thoughts, now spreading out and now gathering close to their heads. They have mild, beautiful faces, Aengus, son of

Forbis, but I am afraid of the Sidhe, and afraid of the art which draws them about us.'

'Why,' said the old man, 'do you fear the ancient gods who made the spears of your father's fathers to be stout in battle, and the little people who came at night from the depth of the lakes and sang among the crickets upon their hearths? And in our evil day they still watch over the loveliness of the earth. But I must tell you why I have fasted and laboured when others would sink into the sleep of age, for without your help once more I shall have fasted and laboured to no good end. When you have done for me this last thing, you may go and build your cottage and till your fields, and take some girl to wife, and forget the ancient gods. I have saved all the gold and silver pieces that were given to me by earls and knights and squires for keeping them from the evil eye and from the love-weaving enchantments of witches, and by earls' and knights' and squires' ladies for keeping the people of the Sidhe from making the udders of their cattle fall dry, and taking the butter from their churns. I have saved it all for the day when my work should be at an end, and now that the end is at hand you shall not lack for gold and silver pieces enough to make strong the roof-tree of your cottage and to keep cellar and larder full. I have sought through all my life to find the secret of life. I was not happy in my youth, for I knew that it would pass; and I was not happy in my manhood for I knew that age was coming; and so I gave myself, in youth and manhood and age, to the search for the Great Secret. I longed for a life whose abundance would fill centuries, I scorned the life of fourscore winters. I would be—no, I will be!—like the Ancient Gods of the land. I read in my youth, in a Hebrew manuscript I found in a Spanish monastery, that there is a moment after the Sun has entered the Ram and before he has passed the Lion, which trembles[3] with the Song of the Immortal Powers, and that whosoever finds this moment and listens to the Song shall become like the Immortal Powers themselves; I came back to Ireland and asked the fairy men, and the cow-doctors[4], if they knew when this moment was; but though all had heard of it, there was none could find the moment upon the hour-glass. So I gave myself to magic, and spent my life in fasting and in labour that I might bring the Gods and the Fairies to my side; and now at last one of the Fairies has told me that the moment is at hand. One, who wore a red cap and whose lips were white with the froth of the new milk, whispered it into my ear. Tomorrow, a little before the close of the first hour after dawn, I shall find the moment, and then I will go away to a southern land

---

3 「顫抖」的時刻，指的是夏至。

4 cow-doctor：乳牛獸醫，指能和精靈溝通，並擁有神奇治癒疾病能力的人。

and build myself a palace of white marble amid orange trees, and gather the brave and the beautiful about me, and enter into the eternal kingdom of my youth. But, that I may hear the whole Song, I was told by the little fellow with the froth of the new milk on his lips, that you must bring great masses of green boughs and pile them about the door and the window of my room; and you must put fresh green rushes upon the floor, and cover the table and the rushes with the roses and the lilies of the monks. You must do this tonight, and in the morning at the end of the first hour after dawn, you must come and find me.'

'Will you be quite young then?' said the boy.

'I will be as young then as you are, but now I am still old and tired, and you must help me to my chair and to my books.'

When the boy had left Aengus son of Forbis in his room, and had lighted the lamp which, by some contrivance of the wizard's, gave forth a sweet odour as of strange flowers, he went into the wood and began cutting green boughs from the hazels, and great bundles of rushes[5] from the western border of the isle, where the small rocks gave place to gently sloping sand and clay.'

5　愛爾蘭傳統中，村子裡的年輕人會在仲夏夜去附近的沼澤割採燈芯草，然後撒在屋子內外。

It was nightfall before he had cut enough for his purpose, and well-nigh midnight before he had carried the last bundle to its place, and gone back for the roses and the lilies. It was one of those warm, beautiful nights when everything seems carved of precious stones. Sleuth Wood away to the south looked as though cut out of green beryl, and the waters that mirrored them shone like pale opal. The roses he was gathering were like glowing rubies, and the lilies had the dull lustre of pearl.

Everything had taken upon itself the look of something imperishable, except a glow-worm, whose faint flame burnt on steadily among the shadows, moving slowly hither and thither, the only thing that seemed alive, the only thing that seemed perishable as mortal hope.

The boy gathered a great armful of roses and lilies, and thrusting the glow-worm among their pearl and ruby, carried them into the room, where the old man sat in a half-slumber. He laid armful after armful upon the floor and above the table, and then, gently closing the door, threw himself upon his bed of rushes, to dream of a peaceful manhood with his chosen wife at his side, and the laughter of children in his ears.

At dawn he rose, and went down to the edge of the lake, taking the hour-glass with him. He put some bread and a flask of wine in the boat, that his master might not lack food at the outset of his journey, and then sat down to wait until the hour from dawn had gone by.

Gradually the birds began to sing, and when the last grains of sand were falling, everything suddenly seemed to overflow with their music. It was the most beautiful and living moment of the year; one could listen to the spring's heart beating in it.

He got up and went to find his master. The green boughs filled the door, and he had to make a way through them. When he entered the room the sunlight was falling in flickering circles on floor and walls and table, and everything was full of soft green shadows.

But the old man sat clasping a mass of roses and lilies in his arms, and with his head sunk upon his breast. On the table, at his left hand, was a leathern wallet full of gold and silver pieces, as for a journey, and at his right hand was a long staff.

The boy touched him and he did not move. He lifted the hands but they were quite cold, and they fell heavily.

'It were better for him,' said the lad, 'to have told his beads and said his prayers like another, and not to have spent his days in seeking amongst the Immortal Powers what he could have found in his own deeds and days had he willed. Ah, yes, it were better to have said his prayers and kissed his beads!'

He looked at the threadbare blue velvet, and he saw it was covered with the pollen of the flowers, and while he was looking at it a thrush, who had alighted among the boughs that were piled against the window, began to sing.

6. The Curse of the Fires and of the Shadows

One summer night, when there was peace, a score of Puritan troopers under the pious Sir Frederick Hamilton, broke through the door of the Abbey of the White Friars which stood over the Gara Lough at Sligo. As the door fell with a crash they saw a little knot of friars gathered about the altar, their white habits glimmering in the steady light of the holy candles. All the monks were kneeling except the abbot, who stood upon the altar steps with a great brass crucifix in his hand.

'Shoot them!' cried Sir Frederick Hamilton, but nobody stirred, for all were new converts, and feared the crucifix and the holly candles.

The white lights from the altar threw the shadows of the troopers up on to roof and wall. As the troopers moved about, the shadows began a fantastic dance among the corbels and the memorial tablets. For a little while all was silent, and then five troopers who were the body-guard of Sir Frederick Hamilton lifted their muskets, and shot down five of the friars. The noise and the smoke drove away the mystery of the pale altar lights, and the other troopers took courage and began to strike. In a moment the friars lay about the altar steps, their white habits stained with blood.

'Set fire to the house!' cried Sir Frederick Hamilton, and at his word one went out, and came in again carrying a heap of dry straw, and piled it against the western wall, and, having done this, fell back, for the fear of the crucifix and of the holy candles was still in his heart.

Seeing this, the five troopers who were Sir Frederick Hamilton's body-guard darted forward, and taking each a holy candle set the straw in a blaze. The red tongues of fire rushed up and flickered from corbel to corbel and from tablet to tablet, and crept along the floor, setting in a blaze the seats and benches. The dance of the shadows passed away, and the dance of the fires began. The troopers fell back towards the door in the southern wall, and watched those yellow dancers springing hither and thither.

For a time the altar stood safe and apart in the midst of its white light; the eyes of the troopers turned upon it. The abbot whom they had thought dead had risen to his feet and now stood before it with the crucifix lifted in both hands high above his head.

Suddenly he cried with a loud voice, 'Woe unto all who smite those who dwell within the Light of the Lord, for they shall wander among the ungovernable shadows, and follow the ungovernable fires!'

And having so cried he fell on his face dead, and the brass crucifix rolled down the steps of the altar.

The smoke had now grown very thick, so that it drove the troopers out into the open air. Before them were burning houses. Behind them shone the painted windows of the Abbey filled with saints and martyrs, awakened, as from a sacred trance, into an angry and animated life.

The eyes of the troopers were dazzled, and for a while could see nothing but the flaming faces of saints and martyrs. Presently, however, they saw a man covered with dust who came running towards them.

'Two messengers,' he cried, 'have been sent by the defeated Irish to raise against you the whole country about Manor Hamilton, and if you do not stop them you will be overpowered in the woods before you reach home again! They ride north-east between Ben Bulben and Cashel-na-Gael.'

Sir Frederick Hamilton called to him the five troopers who had first fired upon the monks and said, 'Mount quickly, and ride through the woods towards the mountain, and get before these men, and kill them.'

In a moment the troopers were gone, and before many moments they had splashed across the river at what is now called Buckley's Ford, and plunged into the woods. They followed a beaten track that wound along the northern bank of the river. The boughs of the birch and quicken trees mingled above, and hid the cloudy moonlight, leaving the pathway in almost complete darkness.

They rode at a rapid trot, now chatting together, now watching some stray weasel or rabbit scuttling away in the darkness. Gradually, as the gloom and silence of the woods oppressed them, they drew closer together, and began to talk rapidly; they were old comrades and knew each other's lives.

One was married, and told how glad his wife would be to see him return safe from this harebrained expedition against the White Friars, and to hear how fortune had made amends for rashness.

The oldest of the five, whose wife was dead, spoke of a flagon of wine which awaited him upon an upper shelf; while a third, who was the youngest, had a sweetheart watching for his return, and he rode a little way before the others, not talking at all. Suddenly the young man stopped, and they saw that his horse was trembling[1].

'I saw something,' he said, 'and yet I do not know but it may have been one of the shadows. It looked like a

---

1 愛爾蘭許多地區的人們相信，馬能夠和另一個世界的幽靈、精靈溝通。

great worm with a silver crown upon his head.'[2]

One of the five put his hand up to his forehead as if about to cross himself, but remembering that he had changed his religion he put it down, and said: 'I am certain it was but a shadow, for there are a great many about us, and of very strange kinds.'

Then they rode on in silence. It had been raining in the earlier part of the day, and the drops fell from the branches, wetting their hair and their shoulders. In a little they began to talk again. They had been in many battles against many a rebel together, and now told each other over again the story of their wounds, and so awakened in their hearts the strongest of all fellowships, the fellowship of the sword, and half forgot the terrible solitude of the woods.

Suddenly the first two horses neighed, and then stood still, and would go no further. Before them was a glint of water, and they knew by the rushing sound that it was

a river. They dismounted, and after much tugging and coaxing brought the horses to the riverside.

In the midst of the water stood a tall old woman with grey hair flowing over a grey dress. She stood up to her knees in the water, and stooped from time to time as though washing. Presently they could see that she was washing something that half floated. The moon cast a flickering light upon it, and they saw that it was the dead body of a man, and, while they were looking at it, an eddy of the river turned the face towards them, and each of the five troopers recognised at the same moment his own face.

While they stood dumb and motionless with horror, the woman began to speak, saying slowly and loudly: 'Did you see my son? He has a crown of silver on his head, and there are rubies in the crown.'

Then the oldest of the troopers, he who had been most often wounded, drew his sword and said: 'I have fought for the truth of my God, and need not fear the shadows of Satan,' and with that rushed into the water. In a moment he returned. The woman had vanished, and though he had thrust his sword into air and water he had found nothing.

The five troopers remounted, and set their horses at the ford, but all to no purpose. They tried again and again, and went plunging hither and thither, the horses foaming and rearing.

---

2 巨大水蛇常出現在愛爾蘭的傳說故事中。

'Let us,' said the old trooper, 'ride back a little into the wood, and strike the river higher up.'

They rode in under the boughs, the ground-ivy crackling under the hoofs, and the branches striking against their steel caps. After about twenty minutes' riding they came out again upon the river, and after another ten minutes found a place where it was possible to cross without sinking below the stirrups.

The wood upon the other side was very thin, and broke the moonlight into long streams. The wind had arisen, and had begun to drive the clouds rapidly across the face of the moon, so that thin streams of light seemed to be dancing a grotesque dance among the scattered bushes and small fir-trees. The tops of the trees began also to moan, and the sound of it was like the voice of the dead in the wind; and the troopers remembered the belief that tells how the dead in purgatory are spitted upon the points of the trees and upon the points of the rocks. They turned a little to the south, in the hope that they might strike the beaten path again, but they could find no trace of it.

Meanwhile, the moaning grew louder and louder, and the dance of the white moon-fires more and more rapid. Gradually they began to be aware of a sound of distant music. It was the sound of a bagpipe, and they rode towards it with great joy.

It came from the bottom of a deep, cup-like hollow. In the midst of the hollow was an old man with a red cap and withered face. He sat beside a fire of sticks, and had a burning torch thrust into the earth at his feet, and played an old bagpipe furiously. His red hair dripped over his face like the iron rust upon a rock.

'Did you see my wife?' he said, looking up a moment; 'she was washing! she was washing!'

'I am afraid of him,' said the young trooper, 'I fear he is one of the Sidhe.'

'No,' said the old trooper, 'he is a man, for I can see the sun-freckles upon his face. We will compel him to be our guide; and at that he drew his sword, and the others did the same.

They stood in a ring round the piper, and pointed their swords at him, and the old trooper then told him that they must kill two rebels, who had taken the road between Ben Bulben and the great mountain spur that is called Cashel-na-Gael, and that he must get up before one of them and be their guide, for they had lost their way.

The piper turned, and pointed to a neighbouring tree, and they saw an old white horse ready bitted, bridled, and saddled. He slung the pipe across his back, and, taking the torch in his hand, got upon the horse, and started off before them, as hard as he could go.

The wood grew thinner now, and the ground began to slope up toward the mountain. The moon had already set, and the little white flames of the stars had come out everywhere. The ground sloped more and more until at last they rode far above the woods upon the wide top of the mountain. The woods lay spread out mile after mile below, and away to the south shot up the red glare of the burning town. But before and above them were the little white flames.

The guide drew rein suddenly, and pointing upwards with the hand that did not hold the torch, shrieked out, 'Look; look at the holy candles!' and then plunged forward at a gallop, waving the torch hither and thither.

'Do you hear the hoofs of the messengers?' cried the guide. 'Quick, quick! or they will be gone out of your hands!' and he laughed as with delight of the chase.

The troopers thought they could hear far off, and as if below them, rattle of hoofs; but now the ground began to slope more and more, and the speed grew more head-long moment by moment. They tried to pull up, but in vain, for the horses seemed to have gone mad.

The guide had thrown the reins on to the neck of the old white horse, and was waving his arms and singing a wild Gaelic song. Suddenly they saw the thin gleam of a river, at an immense distance below, and knew that they were upon the brink of the abyss that is now called Lug-na-Gael, or in English the Stranger's Leap.

The six horses sprang forward, and five screams went up into the air, a moment later five men and horses fell with a dull crash upon the green slopes at the foot of the rocks.

7. The Old Men of the Twilight

At the place, close to the Dead Man's Point, at the Rosses, where the disused pilot-house looks out to sea through two round windows like eyes, a mud cottage stood in the last century. It also was a watchhouse, for a certain old Michael Bruen, who had been a smuggler in his days, and was still the father and grandfather of smugglers, lived there, and when, after nightfall, a tall schooner crept over the bay from Roughley, it was his business to hang a horn lanthorn in the southern window, that the news might travel to Dorren's Island, and from thence, by another horn lanthorn, to the village of the Rosses.

But for this glimmering of messages, he had little communion with mankind, for he was very old, and had no thought for anything but for the making of his soul, at the foot of the Spanish crucifix of carved oak that hung by his chimney, or bent double over the rosary of stone beads brought to him a cargo of silks and laces out of France.

One night he had watched hour after hour, because a gentle and favourable wind was blowing, and La Mere de Misericorde was much overdue; and he was about to lie down upon his heap of straw, seeing that the dawn was whitening the east, and that the schooner would not dare to round Roughley and come to an anchor after daybreak; when he saw a long line of herons flying slowly from Dorren's Island and towards the pools which lie, half choked with reeds, behind what is called the Second Rosses. He had never before seen herons flying over the sea, for they are shore-keeping birds, and partly because this had startled him out of his drowsiness, and more because the long delay of the schooner kept his cupboard empty, he took down his rusty shot-gun, of which the barrel was tied on with a piece of string, and followed the herons towards the pools.

In a little he came upon the herons, of whom there were a great number, standing with lifted legs in the shallow water; and crouching down behind a bank of rushes, looked to the priming of his gun, and bent for a moment over his rosary to murmur: 'Patron Patrick, let me shoot a heron; made into a pie it will support me for nearly four days, for I no longer eat as in my youth. If you keep me from missing I will say a rosary to you every night until the pie is eaten.'

Then he lay down, and, resting his gun upon a large stone, turned towards a heron which stood upon a bank of smooth grass over a little stream that flowed into the pool; for he feared to take the rheumatism by wading, as he would have to do if he shot one of those which stood in the water.

But when he looked along the barrel the heron was gone, and, to his wonder and terror, a man of infinitely great age and infirmity stood in its place. He lowered the gun, and the heron stood there with bent head and motionless feathers, as though it had slept from the beginning of the world.

He raised the gun, and no sooner did he look along the iron than that enemy of all enchantment brought the old man again before him, only to vanish when he lowered the gun for the second time.

He laid the gun down, and crossed himself three times, and said a Paternoster and an Ave Maria, and muttered half aloud: 'Some enemy of God and of my patron is standing upon the smooth place and fishing in the blessed water,' and then aimed very carefully and slowly.

He fired, and when the smoke had gone saw an old man, huddled upon the grass and a long line of herons flying with clamour towards the sea. He went round a bend of the pool, and coming to the little stream looked down on a figure wrapped in faded clothes of black and green of an ancient pattern and spotted with blood. He shook his head at the sight of so great a wickedness.

Suddenly the clothes moved and an arm was stretched upwards towards the rosary which hung about his neck, and long wasted fingers almost touched the cross. He started back, crying: 'Wizard, I will let no wicked thing touch my blessed beads'; and the sense of a great danger just escaped made him tremble.

'If you listen to me,' replied a voice so faint that it was like a sigh, 'you will know that I am not a wizard, and you will let me kiss the cross before I die.'

'I will listen to you' he answered, 'but I will not let you touch my blessed beads,' and sitting on the grass a little way from the dying man, he reloaded his gun and laid it across his knees and composed himself to listen.

'I know not how many generations ago we, who are now herons, were the men of learning of King Leaghaire; we neither hunted, nor went to battle, nor listened to the Druids preaching, and even love, if it came to us at all, was but a passing fire. The Druids and the poets told us, many and many a time, of a new Druid Patrick; and most among them were fierce against him, while a few thought his doctrine merely the doctrine of the gods set out in new symbols, and were for giving him welcome; but we yawned when they spoke of him. At last they came crying that he was coming to the king's house, and fell to their dispute, but we would listen to neither party, for we were busy with a dispute about the merits of the Great and of the Little Metre; nor were we disturbed when they passed our door with sticks of enchantment under their arms, traveling towards the forest to contend against his coming, nor when they returned after nightfall with torn coats and despairing cries; for the click of our knives writing our thoughts in Ogham[1] filled us with peace and our dispute filled us with joy; nor even when in the morning crowds passed us to hear the strange Druid preaching the commandments of his god. The crowds passed, and one, who had laid down his knife to yawn and stretch himself, heard a voice speaking far off, and knew that the Druid Patrick was preaching within the king's house; but our hearts were deaf, and we carved and disputed and read, and laughed a thin laughter together. In a little we heard many feet coming towards the house, and presently two tall figures stood in the

---

1 Ogham：歐甘文，為古愛爾蘭文。

door, the one in white, the other in a crimson coat; like a great lily and a heavy poppy; and we knew the Druid Patrick and our King Leaghaire. We laid down the slender knives and bowed before the king, but when the black and green robes had ceased to rustle, it was not the loud rough voice of King Leaghaire that spoke to us, but a strange voice in which there was a rapture as of one speaking from behind a battlement of Druid flame: "I preached the commandments of the maker of the world" it said; "within the king's house and from the centre of the earth to the windows of Heaven there was a great silence, so that the eagle floated with unmoving wings in the white air, and the fish with unmoving fins in the dim water, while the linnets and the wrens and the sparrows stilled their ever-trembling tongues in the heavy boughs, and the clouds were like white marble, and the rivers became their motionless mirrors, and the shrimps in the far-off sea-pools became still, enduring eternity in patience, although it was hard." And as he named these things, it was like a king numbering his people. "But your slender knives went click, click! upon the oaken staves, and, all else being silent, the sound shook the angels with anger. O, little roots, nipped by the winter, who do not awake although the summer pass above you with innumerable feet. O, men who have no part in love, who have no part in song, who have no part in wisdom, but dwell with the shadows of memory where the feet of angels cannot touch you as they pass over your heads, where the hair of demons cannot sweep about you as they pass under your feet, I lay upon you a curse, and change you to an example for ever and ever; you shall become grey herons and stand pondering in grey pools and flit over the world in that hour when it is most full of sighs; having forgotten the flame of the stars and not yet found the flame of the sun; and you shall preach to the other herons until they also are like you, and are an example for ever and ever; and your deaths shall come to you by chance and unforeseen, for you shall not be certain about anything for ever and ever."'

The voice of the old man of learning became still, but the voteen[2] bent over his gun with his eyes upon the ground, too stupid to understand what he had heard; and he had remained so, it may be for a long time, had not a tug at his rosary made him start out of his dream. The old man of learning had crawled along the grass, and was now trying to draw the cross down low enough for his lips to reach it.

'You must not touch my blessed beads,' cried the voteen, and struck the long withered fingers with the barrel of his gun.

He need not have trembled, for the old man fell back

2　voteen：在鄉村口語的用法中，是 devotee（虔誠的信者）的意思。

upon the grass with a sigh and was still.

He bent down and began to consider the black and green clothes, for his fear had begun to pass away when he came to understand that he had something the man of learning wanted and pleaded for, and now that the blessed beads were safe, his fear had nearly all gone; and surely, he thought, if that big cloak, and that little tight-fitting shirt under it, were warm and without holes, Saint Patrick would take the enchantment out of them and leave them fit for human use.

But the black and green clothes fell away wherever his fingers touched them, and while this was a new wonder, a slight wind blew over the pool and crumbled the old man of learning and all his ancient gear into a little heap of dust, and then made the little heap less and less until there was nothing but the smooth green grass.

8. Where There Is Nothing, There Is God

Abbot Malathgeneus, Brother Dove, Brother Bald Fox, Brother Peter, Brother Patrick, Brother Bittern, Brother Fair-Brows sat about the fire, one mending lines to lay in the river for eels, one fashioning a snare for birds, one mending the broken handle of a spade, one writing in a large book, and one hammering at the corner of a gold box that was to hold the book; and among the rushes at their feet lay the scholars, who would one day be Brothers.

One of these, a child of eight or nine years, called Olioll, lay upon his back looking up through the hole in the roof, through which the smoke went, and watching the stars appearing and disappearing in the smoke.

He turned presently to the Brother who wrote in the big book, and whose duty was to teach the children, and said, 'Brother Dove, to what are the stars fastened?'

The Brother, pleased to find so much curiosity in the stupidest of his scholars, laid down the pen and said,

'There are nine crystalline spheres, and on the first the Moon is fastened, on the second the planet Mercury, on the third the planet Venus, on the fourth the Sun, on the fifth the planet Mars, on the sixth the planet Jupiter, on the seventh the planet Saturn; these are the wandering stars; and on the eighth are fastened the fixed stars; but the ninth sphere is a sphere made out of the First Substance.'[1]

'What is beyond that?' said the child.

'There is nothing beyond that; there is God.'

And then the child's eyes strayed to the gold box, and he said, 'Why has Brother Peter put a great ruby on the side of his box?'

'The ruby is a symbol of the love of God.'

'Why is the ruby a symbol of the love of God?'

'Because it is red, like fire, and fire burns up everything, and where there is nothing, there is God.'

The child sank into silence, but presently sat up and said, 'There is somebody outside.'

'No,' replied the Brother. 'It is only the wolves; I have heard them moving about in the snow for some time. They are growing very wild, now that the winter drives them from the mountains. They broke into a fold last night and carried off many sheep, and if we are not

---

1 在托勒密的天動學說中，地球固定在世界中心，為九顆行星所環繞，而天堂包覆著全世界。

careful they will devour everything.'

'No, it is the footstep of a man, for it is heavy; but I can hear the footsteps of the wolves also.'

He had no sooner done speaking than somebody rapped three times, but with no great loudness.

'I will go and open, for he must be very cold.'

'Do not open, for it may be a man-wolf, and he may devour us all.'

But the boy had already drawn back the heavy wooden bolt, and all the faces, most of them a little pale, turned towards the slowly-opening door.

'He has beads and a cross, he cannot be a man-wolf,' said the child, as a man with the snow heavy on his long, ragged beard, and on his matted hair, that fell over his shoulders and nearly to his waist, and dropping from the tattered cloak that but half-covered his withered brown body, came in and looked from face to face with mild, ecstatic eyes.

Standing some way from the fire, and with eyes that had rested at last upon the Abbot Malathgeneus, he cried out, 'O blessed abbot, let me come to the fire and warm myself and dry the snow from my beard an my hair and my cloak; that I may not die of the cold of the mountains, and anger the Lord with a willful martyrdom.'

'Come to the fire,' said the abbot, 'and warm yourself,

and eat the food the boy Olioll will bring you. It is sad indeed that any for whom Christ has died should be as poor as you.'

The man sat over the fire, and Olioll took away his now dripping cloak and laid meat and bread and wine before him; but he would eat only of the bread, and he put away the wine, asking for water.

When his beard and hair had begun to dry a little and his limbs had ceased to shiver, he spoke again. 'Set me to some labour, the hardest there is, for I am the poorest of God's poor.'

Then the Brothers discussed together what work they could put him to, and at first to little purpose, for there was no labour that had not found its labourer; but at last one remembered that Brother Bald Fox, whose business it was to turn the great quern in the quern-house, for he was too stupid for anything else, was getting old; and so he could go to the quern-house in the morning.

The cold passed away, and the spring grew to summer, and the quern was never idle, nor was it turned with grudging labour, for when any passed the beggar was heard singing as he drove the handle round.

The last gloom, too, had passed from that happy community, for Olioll, who had always been stupid and unteachable, grew clever, and this was the more miraculous because it had come of a sudden.

One day he had been even duller than usual, and was

beaten and told to know his lesson better on the morrow
or be sent into a lower class among little boys who would
make a joke of him.

He had gone out in tears, and when he came the next
day, although his stupidity, born of a mind that would
listen to every wandering sound and brood upon every
wandering light, had so long been the byword of the
school, he knew his lesson so well that he passed to
the head of the class, and from that day was the best of
scholars.

At first Brother Dove thought this was an answer to
his own prayers and grew proud; but when many far
more fervid prayers for more important things had
failed, he convinced himself
that the child was trafficking
with bards, or druids[2], or
witches, and resolved to follow
and watch.

He had told his thought to
the abbot, who bid him come
to him the moment he hit the
truth; and the next day, which
was a Sunday, he stood in the
path when the abbot and the

druid

---

2 Druid（德魯伊人）：在古愛爾蘭，德魯伊人是由教士組成
   的社會階級，被認為擁有魔法般的力量。

Brothers were coming from vespers, and took the abbot by the sleeve and said, 'The beggar is of the greatest of saints and of the workers of miracle. I followed Olioll but now, and when he came to the little wood by the quern-house I knew by the path broken in the under-wood and by the foot-marks in the muddy places that he had gone that way many times. I hid behind a bush where the path doubled upon itself at a sloping place, and understood by the tears in his eyes that his stupidity was too old and his wisdom too new to save him from terror of the rod. When he was in the quern-house I went to the window and looked in, and the birds came down and perched upon my head and my shoulders, for they are not timid in that holy place; and a wolf passed by, his right side shaking my habit, his left the leaves of a bush. Olioll opened his book and turned to the page I had told him to learn, and began to cry, and the beggar sat beside him and comforted him until he fell asleep. When his sleep was of the deepest the beggar knelt down and prayed aloud, and said, "O Thou Who dwellest beyond the stars, show forth Thy power as at the beginning, and let knowledge sent from Thee awaken in his mind, wherein is nothing from the world, that the nine orders of angels may glorify Thy name"; and then a light broke out of the air and wrapped Olioll, and I smelt the breath of roses. I stirred a little in my wonder, and the beggar turned and saw me, and, bending low, said, "O Brother Dove, if I have done wrong, forgive me, and I will do penance. It was my pity moved me"; but I was afraid and I ran away, and did not stop running until I came here.'

Then all the Brothers began talking together, one saying it was such and such a saint, and one that it was not he but another; and one that it was none of these, for they were still in their brotherhoods, but that it was such and such a one; and the talk was as near to quarrelling as might be in that gentle community, for each would claim so great a saint for his native province.

At last the abbot said, 'He is none that you have named, for at Easter I had greeting from all, and each was in his brotherhood; but he is Aengus the Lover of God, and the first of those who have gone to live in the wild places and among the wild beasts. Ten years ago he felt the burden of many labours in a brotherhood under the Hill of Patrick and went into the forest that he might labour only with song to the Lord; but the fame of his holiness brought many thousands to his cell, so that a little pride clung to a soul from which all else had been driven. Nine years ago he dressed himself in rags, and from that day nobody has seen him, unless, indeed, it be true that he has been seen living among the wolves on the M mountains and eating the grass of the fields. Let us go to him and bow down before him; for at last, after long seeking, he has found the nothing that is God.'

9. Of Costello the Proud, of Una the Daughter of Macdermot, and of the Bitter Tongue

Costello[1] had come up from the fields and lay upon the ground before the door of his square tower, resting his head upon his hands and looking at the sunset, and considering the chances of the weather.

Though the customs of Elizabeth and James, now going out of fashion in England, had begun to prevail among the gentry, he still wore the great cloak of the native Irish; and the sensitive outlines of his face and the greatness of his indolent body had a commingling of pride and strength which belonged to a simpler age.

His eyes wandered from the sunset to where the long white road lost itself over the south-western horizon and to a horseman who toiled slowly up the hill. A few more minutes and the horseman was near enough for his little and shapeless body, his long Irish cloak, and the dilapidated bagpipes hanging from his shoulders, and the rough-haired garron under him, to be seen distinctly in the grey dusk.

So soon as he had come within earshot, he began crying: 'Is it

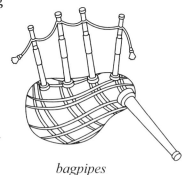

bagpipes

sleeping you are, Tumaus Costello, when better men break their hearts on the great white roads? Get up out of that, proud Tumaus, for I have news! Get up out of that, you great omadhaun! Shake yourself out of the earth, you great weed of a man!'

Costello had risen to his feet, and as the piper came up to him seized him by the neck of his jacket, and lifting him out of his saddle threw him on to the ground.

'Let me alone, let me alone,' said the other, but Costello still shook him.

'I have news from MacDermot's[2] daughter, Una.'

The great fingers were loosened, and the piper rose gasping.

'Why did you not tell me,' said Costello, 'that you came from her? You might have railed your fill.'

'I have come from her, but I will not speak until I am paid for the shaking.'

Costello fumbled at the bag in which he carried his money, and it was some time before it would open, for the hand that had overcome many men shook with fear and hope.

'Here is all the money in my bag,' he said, dropping a stream of French and Spanish money into the hand of the

---

1 在中世紀時，Costello 家族曾是瑪佑地區勢力龐大的家族。
2 MacDermot 家族因其與修道院的關係，曾是洛奇地區最有勢力的家族。

piper, who bit the coins before he would answer.

'That is right, that is a fair price, but I will not speak till I have good protection, for if the MacDermots lay their hands upon me in any boreen after sundown, or in Cool-a-vin[3] by day, I will be left to rot among the nettles of a ditch, or hung on the great sycamore, where they hung the horse-thieves last Beltaine[4] four years.'

And while he spoke he tied the reins of his garron to a bar of rusty iron that was mortared into the wall.

'I will make you my piper and my body-servant,' said Costello, 'and no man dare lay hands upon the man, or the goat, or the horse, or the dog that is Tumaus Costello's.'

'And I will only tell my message,' said the other, flinging the saddle on the ground, 'in the corner of the chimney with a noggin in my hand, and a jug of the Brew of the Little Pot beside me, for though I am ragged and empty, my old fathers were well clothed and full until their house was burnt and their cattle driven away seven centuries ago by the Dillons, whom I shall yet see on the hob of hell, and they screeching'

Costello led him into the great rush-strewn hall, where were none of the comforts which had begun to grow

---

3 Cool-a-vin：MacDermot 家族的住處。

4 Beltaine：古塞爾特族的慶祝會。

common among the gentry, but a mediaeval gauntness and bareness, and pointed to the bench in the great chimney; and when he had sat down, filled up a horn noggin and set it on the bench beside him, and set a great black jack of leather beside the noggin, and lit a torch that slanted out from a ring in the wall, his hands trembling the while; and then turned towards him and said: 'Will MacDermot's daughter come to me, Duallach, son of Daly?'

'MacDermot's daughter will not come to you, for her father has set women to watch her, but she bid me tell you that this day week will be the eve of St. John and the night of her betrothal to MacNamara of the Lake, and she would have you there that, when they bid her drink to him she loves best, as the way is, she may drink to you, Tumaus Costello, and let all know where her heart is, and how little of gladness is in her marriage; and I myself bid you to go with good men about you, for I saw the horse-thieves with my own eyes, and they dancing the "Blue Pigeon" in the air.'

And then he held the now empty noggin towards Costello, his hand closing round it like the claw of a bird, and cried: 'Fill my noggin again, for I wish the day had come when all the water in the world is to shrink into a periwinkle-shell, that I might drink nothing but Poteen.'

Finding that Costello made no reply, but sat in a dream, he burst out: 'Fill my noggin, I tell you, for no

Costello is so great in the world that he should not wait upon a Daly, even though the Daly travel the road with his pipes and the Costello have a bare hill, an empty house, a horse, and a handful of cows.'

'Praise the Dalys if you will,' said Costello as he filled the noggin, 'for you have brought me a kind word from my love.'

For the next few days Duallach went here and there trying to raise a bodyguard, and every man he met had some story of Costello, how he killed the wrestler when but a boy by so straining at the belt that went about them both that he broke the big wrestler's back; how when somewhat older he dragged fierce horses through a ford for a wager; how when he came to manhood he broke the steel horseshoe in Mayo; and of many another deed of his strength and pride; but he could find none who would trust themselves with any so passionate and poor in a quarrel with careful and wealthy persons like MacDermot of the Sheep and MacNamara of the Lake.

Then Costello went out himself, and after listening to many excuses and in many places, brought in a big half-witted fellow, who followed him like a dog, a farm-labourer who worshipped him for his strength, a fat farmer whose forefathers had served his family, and a couple of lads who looked after his goats and cows; and marshalled them before the fire in the empty hall.

They had brought with them their heavy sticks, and

Costello gave them an old pistol apiece, and kept them all night drinking Spanish ale and shooting at a white turnip which he pinned against the wall with a skewer.

Duallach of the pipes sat on the bench in the chimney playing ' The Green Bunch of Rushes' 'The Unchion Stream' and 'The Princes of Breffeny'[5] on his old pipes, and abusing now the appearance of the shooters, now their clumsy shooting, and now Costello because he had no better servants.

The labourer, the half-witted fellow, the farmer and the lads were well accustomed to Duallach's abusiveness, for it was as inseparable from wake or wedding as the squealing of his pipes, but they wondered at the forbearance of Costello, who seldom came either to wake or wedding, and if he had would not have been patient with a scolding piper.

On the next evening they set out for Cool-a-vin, Costello riding a tolerable horse and carrying a sword, the others upon rough-haired ponies, and with their cudgels under their arms. As they rode over the bogs and in the boreens among the hills they could see fire answering fire from hill to hill, from horizon to horizon, and everywhere groups who danced in the red light of the turf.

When they came to MacDermot's house they saw before the door an unusually large group of the very poor,

---

5 這些都是傳統的愛爾蘭曲調。

dancing about a fire, in the midst of which was a blazing cartwheel, that circular dance which is so ancient that the gods, long dwindled to be but fairies, dance no other. From the door and through the loopholes on either side came the light of candles and the sound of many feet dancing a dance of Elizabeth and James.

They tied their horses to bushes, for the number so tied already showed that the stables were full, and shoved their way through a crowd of peasants who stood about the door, and went into the big hall where the dance was. The labourer, the half-witted fellow, the farmer and the two lads mixed with a group of servants who were looking on from an alcove, and Duallach sat with the pipers on their bench, but Costello made his way through the dancers to where MacDermot of the Sheep stood with MacNamara of the Lake pouring Poteen out of a porcelain jug into horn noggins with silver rims.

'Tumaus Costello,' said the old man, 'you have done a good deed to forget what has been, and to fling away enmity and come to the betrothal of my daughter to MacNamara of the Lake.'

'I come,' answered Costello, 'because when in the time of Costello De Angalo my ancestors overcame your ancestors and afterwards made peace, a compact was made that a Costello might go with his body-servants and his piper to every feast given by a MacDermot for ever, and a MacDermot with his body-servants and his piper to every feast given by a Costello for ever.'

'If you come with evil thoughts and armed men,' said the son of MacDermot flushing, 'no matter how good you are with your weapons, it shall go badly with you, for some of my wife's clan have come out of Mayo, and my three brothers and their servants have come down from the Ox Mountains'; and while he spoke he kept his hand inside his coat as though upon the handle of a weapon,

'No,' answered Costello, 'I but come to dance a farewell dance with your daughter.'

MacDermot drew his hand out of his coat and went over to a tall pale girl who was now standing but a little way off with her mild eyes fixed upon the ground.

'Costello has come to dance a farewell dance, for he knows that you will never see one another again.'

The girl lifted her eyes and gazed at Costello, and in her gaze was that trust of the humble in the proud, the gentle in the violent, which has been the tragedy of woman from the beginning.

Costello led her among the dancers, and they were soon drawn into the rhythm of the Pavane, that stately dance which, with the Sara-band, the Gallead, and the Morrice dances, had driven out, among all but the most Irish of the gentry, the quicker rhythms of the verse-interwoven, pantomimic dances of earlier days; and while they danced there came over them the weariness with the world, the melancholy, the pity one for the other, the vague anger against common hopes and fears, which is the exultation of love.

And when a dance ended and the pipers laid down the pipes and lifted the noggins, they stood a little from the others waiting pensively and silently for the dance to begin again and the fire in their hearts to leap up and to wrap them anew; and so they danced and danced Pavane and Saraband and Gallead and Morrice the night long, and many stood still to watch them, and the peasants came about the door and peered in, as though they understood that they would gather their children's children about them long hence, and tell how they had seen Costello dance with MacDermot's daughter Una, and become by the telling themselves a portion of ancient romance; but through all the dancing and piping MacNamara went hither and thither talking loudly and making foolish jokes that all might seem, and old MacDermot grew redder and redder, and looked oftener and oftener at the doorway to see if the candles there grew yellow in the dawn.

At last he saw that the moment to end had come, and, in a pause after a dance, cried out that his daughter would now drink the cup of betrothal; then Una came over to where he was, and the guests stood round in a half-circle, Costello close to the wall to the right, and the piper, the labourer, the farmer, the half-witted man and the two farm lads close behind him.

The old man took out of a niche in the wall the silver cup from which her mother and her mother's mother had drunk the toasts of their betrothals, and poured Poteen out of a porcelain jug and handed the cup to his daughter with the customary words, 'Drink to him whom you love the best.'

She held the cup to her lips for a moment, and then said in a clear soft voice: 'I drink to my true love, Tumaus Costello.'

And then the cup rolled over and over on the ground, ringing like a bell, for the old man had struck her in the face and the cup had fallen, and there was a deep silence.

There were many of MacNamara's people among the servants now come out of the alcove, and one of them, a story-teller and poet, who had a plate and a chair in MacNamara's kitchen, drew a French knife out of his girdle and made as though he would strike at Costello, but in a moment a blow had been hurled to the ground, his shoulder sending the cup rolling and ringing again.

The click of steel had followed quickly, had not there come a muttering and shouting from the peasants about the door and from those crowding up behind them; for all knew that these were no children of Queen's Irish[6], but of the wild Irish about Lough Gara and Lough Cara, Kellys,

---

6 children of Queen's Irish：女皇的愛爾蘭後裔，
指接受英國統治與文化的人。

Dockerys, Drurys, O'Re-gans, Mahons, and Lavins, who had left the right arms of their children unchristened that they might give better blows, and were even said to have named the wolves godfathers to their children.

Costello's hand rested upon the handle of his sword, and his knuckles had grown white, but now he drew it away, and, followed by those who were with him, strode towards the door, the dancers giving way before him, went toward the door, the dancers giving way before him, the most angrily and slowly, and with glances at the muttering and shouting peasants, but some gladly and quickly, because the glory of his fame was over him.

He passed through the fierce and friendly peasant faces, and came where his horse and the ponies were tied to bushes; and mounted and bade his ungainly bodyguard mount also and ride into the narrow boreen.

When they had gone a little way, Duallach, who rode last, turned towards the house where a little group of MacDermots and MacNamaras stood next to a bigger group of countrymen, and cried: 'MacDermot, you deserve to be as you are this hour, for your hand was ever niggardly to piper and fiddler and to poor travelling people.'

He had not done before the three old MacDermots from the Ox Mountains had run towards their horses, and old MacDermot himself had caught the bridle of a pony belonging to the MacNamaras and was calling to the others to follow him; and many blows and many deaths had been had not the countrymen caught up still blazing sticks from the ashes of the fires and thrown them among the horses with loud cries, making all plunge and rear, and some break from those who held them, the whites of their eyes gleaming in the dawn.

For the next few weeks Costello had no lack of news of Una, for now a woman selling eggs, and now a man or a woman going to the Holy Well, would tell him how his love had fallen ill the day after St. John's Eve, and how she was a little better or a little worse; and the country people still remember how when night had fallen he would bid Duallach of the Pipes tell out, 'The Son of Apple,' 'The Beauty of the World,' 'The King of Ireland's Son,' or some like tale; and while the world of the legends was abuilding, would abandon himself to the dreams of his sorrow.

Costello cared only for the love sorrows, and no matter where the stories wandered, Una alone endured their shadowy hardships; for it was she and no king's daughter who was hidden in the steel tower under the water with the folds of the Worm of Nine Eyes round and about her prison; and it was she who won by seven years of service the right to deliver from hell all she could carry, and carried away multitudes clinging with worn fingers to the hem of her dress; and it was she who endured dumbness for a year because of the little thorn of enchantment the fairies had thrust into her tongue; and it was a lock of her hair, coiled in a little carved box, which gave so great a light that men threshed by it from sundown to sunrise, and awoke so great a wonder that kings spent years in wandering or fell before unknown armies in seeking to discover her hiding-place.

There was no beauty in the world but hers, no tragedy in the world but hers; for he was of those ascetics of passion who keep their hearts pure for love or for hatred as other men for God, for Mary and for the Saints.

One day a serving-man rode up to Costello, who was helping his two lads to reap a meadow, and gave him a letter, and rode away; and the letter contained these words in English: 'Tumaus Costello, my daughter is very ill. She will die unless you come to her. I therefore command you come to her whose peace you stole by treachery.'

Costello threw down his scythe, and sent one of the lads for Duallach, who had become woven into his mind with Una, and himself saddled his horse and Duallach's pony.

When they came to MacDermot's house it was late afternoon, and Lough Gara lay down below them, blue, and deserted; and though they had seen, when at a distance, dark figures moving about the door, the house appeared not less deserted than the Lough. The door stood half open, and Costello knocked upon it again and again, but there was no answer.

'There is no one here,' said Duallach, 'for MacDermot is too proud to welcome Proud Costello,' and he threw the door open, and they saw a ragged, dirty, very old woman, who sat upon the floor leaning against the wall.

Costello knew that it was Bridget Delaney, a deaf and dumb beggar; and she, when she saw him, stood up and made a sign to him to follow, and led him and his companion up a stair and down a long corridor to a closed door.

She pushed the door open and went a little way off and sat down as before; Duallach sat upon the ground also, but close to the door, and Costello went and gazed upon Una sleeping upon a bed.

He sat upon a chair beside her and waited, and a long time passed and still she slept, and then Duallach motioned to him through the door to wake her, but he hushed his very breath, that she might sleep on.

Presently he turned to Duallach and said: 'It is not right that I stay here where there are none of her kindred, for the common people are always ready to blame the beautiful.'

And then they went down and stood at the door of the house and waited, but the evening wore on and no one came.

'It was a foolish man that called you Proud Costello,' Duallach cried at last; 'had he seen you waiting and waiting where they left none but a beggar to welcome you, it is Humble Costello he would have called you.'

Then Costello mounted and Duallach mounted, but when they had ridden a little way Costello tightened the reins and made his horse stand still.

Many minutes passed, and then Duallach cried: 'It is no wonder that you fear to offend MacDermot of the Sheep, for he has many brothers and friends, and though he is old, he is a strong man and ready with his hands, and he is of the Queen's Irish, and the enemies of the Gael are upon his side.'

And Costello answered flushing and looking towards the house: 'I swear by the Mother of God that I will never return there again if they do not send after me before I pass the ford in the Brown River,' and he rode on, but so very slowly that the sun went down and the bats began to fly over the bogs.

When he came to the river he lingered awhile upon the edge, but presently rode out into the middle and stopped his horse in a shallow. Duallach, however, crossed over and waited on a further bank above a deeper place.

After a good while Duallach cried out again, and this time very bitterly: 'It was a fool who begot you and a fool who bore you, and they are fools who say you come of an old and noble stock, for you come of whey-faced beggars who travelled from door to door, bowing to serving-men.

With bent head, Costello rode through the river and

stood beside him, and would have spoken had not hoofs clattered on the further bank and a horseman splashed towards them. It was a serving-man of MacDermot's, and he said, speaking breathlessly like one who had ridden hard: 'Tumaus Costello, I come to bid you again to MacDermot's house. When you had gone, his daughter Una awoke and called your name, for you had been in her dreams.'

Bridget Delaney the Dummy saw her lips move and the trouble upon her, and came where we were hiding in the wood above the house and took MacDermot by the coat and brought him to his daughter. He saw the trouble upon her, and bid me ride his own horse to bring you the quicker.'

Then Costello turned towards the piper Duallach Daly, and taking him about the waist lifted him out of the saddle and threw him against a big stone that was in the river, so that he fell lifeless into a deep place, and the waters swept over the tongue which had been made bitter, it may be, that there might be a story in men's ears in after time.

Then plunging his spurs into the horse, he rode away furiously toward the north-west, along the edge of the river, and did not pause until he came to another and smoother ford, and saw the rising moon mirrored in the water. He paused for a moment irresolute, and then rode into the ford and on over the Ox Mountains, and down

towards the sea; his eyes almost continually resting upon the moon.

But now his horse, long dark with sweat and breathing hard, for he kept spurring it, fell heavily, throwing him on the roadside. He tried to make it stand up, and failing in this, went on alone towards the moonlight; and came to the sea and saw a schooner lying there at anchor.

Now that he could go no further because of the sea, he found that he was very tired and the night very cold, and went into a shebeen close to the shore and threw himself down upon a bench. The room was full of Spanish and Irish sailors who had just smuggled a cargo of wine, and were waiting a favourable wind to set out again. A Spaniard offered him a drink in bad Gaelic. He drank it greedily and began talking wildly and rapidly.

For some three weeks the wind blew inshore or with

too great violence, and the sailors stayed drinking and talking and playing cards, and Costello stayed with them, sleeping upon a bench in the shebeen, and drinking and talking and playing more than any.

He soon lost what little money he had, and then his long cloak and his spurs and even his boots. At last a gentle wind blew towards Spain, and the crew rowed out to their schooner, and in a little while the white sails had dropped under the horizon.

Then Costello turned homeward, his life gaping before him, and walked all day, coming in the early evening to the road that went from near Lough Gara to the southern edge of Lough Cay. Here he overtook a great crowd of peasants and farmers, who were walking very slowly after two priests and a group of well-dressed persons, certain of whom were carrying a coffin.

He stopped an old man and asked whose burying it was and whose people they were, and the old man answered: 'It is the burying of Una, MacDermot's daughter, and we are the MacNamaras and the MacDermots and their following, and you are Tumaus Costello who murdered her.'

Costello went on towards the head of the procession, passing men who looked angrily at him, and only vaguely understanding what he had heard, for now that he had lost the understanding that belongs to good health, it seemed impossible that so much gentleness and beauty could pass away.

Presently he stopped and asked again whose burying it was, and a man answered: 'We are carrying MacDermot's daughter Una, whom you murdered, to be buried in the island of the Holy Trinity,' and the man stooped and picked up a stone and threw it at Costello, striking him on the cheek and making the blood flow out over his face.

Costello went on scarcely feeling the blow, and coming to those about the coffin, shouldered his way into the midst of them, and laying his hand upon the coffin, asked in a loud voice: 'Who is in this coffin?'

The three Old MacDermots from the Ox Mountains caught up stones and told those about them do the same; and he was driven from the road, covered with wounds, and but for the priests would surely have been killed.

When the procession had passed on, Costello began to follow again, and saw from a distance the coffin laid upon a large boat, and those about it get into other boats, and the boats move slowly over the water to Insula Trinitatis; and after a time he saw the boats return and their passengers mingle with the crowd upon the bank, and all scatter by many roads and boreens.

It seemed to him that Una was somewhere on the island smiling gently, and when all had gone he swam in the way the boats had been rowed and found the new-made grave beside the ruined Abbey, and threw himself upon it, calling to Una to come to him.

He lay there all that night and through the day after, from time to time calling her to come to him, but when the third night came he had forgotten, worn out with hunger and sorrow, that her body lay in the earth beneath; but only knew she was somewhere near and would not come to him.

Just before dawn, the hour when the peasants hear his ghostly voice crying out, his pride awoke and he called loudly: 'If you do not come to me, Una, I will go and never return to the island of the Holy Trinity,' and before his voice had died away a cold and whirling wind had swept over the island and he saw many figures rushing past, women of the Sidhe with crowns of silver and dim floating drapery; and then Una, but no longer smiling, for she passed him swiftly and angrily, and as she passed struck him upon the face crying: 'Then go and never return.'

He would have followed, and was calling out her name, when the whole company went up into the air, and, rushing together in the shape of a great silvery rose, faded into the ashen dawn.

Costello got up from the grave, understanding nothing but that he had made his sweetheart angry and that she wished him to go, and wading out into the lake, began to swim.

He swam on and on, but his limbs were too weary to keep him afloat, and when he had gone a little way he sank without a struggle.

The next day a fisherman found him among the reeds upon the lake shore, lying upon the white sand, and carried him to his own house.

And the very poor lamented over him and sang the keen, and when the time had come, laid him in the Abbey on Insula Trinitatis with only the ruined altar between him and MacDermot's daughter, and planted above them two ash-trees that in after days wove their branches together and mingled their trembling leaves.

Chapter 3

Rosa
Alchemica

O blessed and happy he, who knowing the mysteries of the gods, sanctifies his life, and purifies his soul, celebrating orgies in the mountains with holy purifications.

—Euripides

I

It is now more than ten years since I met, for the last time, Michael Robartes, and for the first time and the last time his friends and fellow students; and witnessed his and their tragic end, and endured those strange experiences, which have changed me so that my writings have grown less popular and less intelligible, and driven me almost to the verge of taking the habit of St. Dominic[1].

St. Dominic

I had just published *Rosa Alchemica*, a little work on the Alchemists, somewhat in the manner of Sir Thomas Browne[2], and had received many letters from believers in the arcane sciences, upbraiding what they called my timidity, for they could not believe so evident sympathy but the sympathy of the artist, which is half pity, for everything which has moved men's hearts in any age.

---

1 St. Dominic（1170–1221），西班牙教士與聖道明會的建立者，堅守刻苦的生活，遊歷講道時，跣足步行。

2 Sir Thomas Browne（1605–1682），英格蘭散文家和醫師。

I had discovered, early in my researches, that their doctrine was no merely chemical phantasy, but a philosophy they applied to the world, to the elements and to man himself; and that they sought to fashion gold out of common metals  merely as part of an universal transmutation of all things into some divine and imperishable substance; and this enabled me to make my little book a fanciful reverie over the transmutation of life into art, and a cry of measureless desire for a world made wholly of essences.

I was sitting dreaming of what I had written, in my house in one of the old parts of Dublin; a house my ancestors had made almost famous through their part in the politics of the city and their friendships with the famous men of their generations; and was feeling an unwonted happiness at having at last accomplished a long-cherished design, and made my rooms an expression of this favourite doctrine.

The portraits, of more historical than artistic interest, had gone; and tapestry, full of the blue and bronze of peacocks, fell over the doors, and shut out all history and activity untouched with beauty and peace; and now when I looked at my Crevelli[3] and pondered on the rose in the hand of the Virgin, wherein the form was so delicate and precise that it seemed more like a thought than a flower, or at the grey dawn and rapturous faces of my Francesca[4], I knew all a Christian's ecstasy without his slavery to rule and custom; when I pondered over the antique bronze gods and goddesses, which I had mortgaged my house to buy, I had all a pagan's delight in various beauty and without his terror at sleepless destiny and his labour with many sacrifices; and I had only to go to my bookshelf, where every book was bound in leather, stamped with intricate ornament, and of a carefully chosen colour: Shakespeare in the orange of the glory of the world, Dante in the dull red of his anger, Milton in the blue grey of his formal calm; and I could experience what I would of human passions without their bitterness and without satiety.

I had gathered about me all gods because I believed in none, and experienced every pleasure because I gave myself to none, but held myself apart, individual, indissoluble, a mirror of polished steel[5]: I looked in the triumph of this imagination at the birds of Hera[6],

---

3 Carlo Crevelli（1430–1495），文藝復興時期的義大利藝術家。

4 Piero della Francesca（?–1492），文藝復興時期的早期義大利畫家。

5 有聚焦能力的金屬鏡，例如望遠鏡中使用的凹面鏡。

6 在希臘神話中，孔雀拉著宙斯的妻子希拉所乘坐的戰車，
孔雀也是希拉的聖鳥。

glowing in the firelight as though they were wrought of jewels; and to my mind, for which symbolism was a necessity, they seemed the doorkeepers of my world, shutting out all that was not of as affluent a beauty as their own; and for a moment I thought as I had thought in so many other moments, that it was possible to rob life of every bitterness except the bitterness of death; and then a thought which had followed this thought, time after time, filled me with a passionate sorrow.

All those forms: that Madonna with her brooding purity, those rapturous faces singing in the morning light, those bronze divinities with their passionless dignity, those wild shapes rushing from despair to despair, belonged to a divine world wherein I had no part; and every experience however profound, every perception, however exquisite, would bring me the bitter dream of a limitless energy I could never know, and even in my most perfect moment I would be two selves, the one watching with heavy eyes the other's moment of content.

I had heaped about me the gold born in the crucibles of others; but the supreme dream of the alchemist, the transmutation of the weary heart into a weariless spirit, was as far from me as, I doubted not, it had been from him also.

I turned to my last purchase, a set of alchemical apparatus which, the dealer in the Rue le Peletier had

assured me, once belonged to Raymond Lully[7], and as I
joined the alembic to the athanor and laid the lavacrum
maris at their side, I understood the alchemical doctrine,
that all beings, divided from the great deep where
spirits wander, one and yet a multitude, are weary; and
sympathized, in the pride of my connoisseurship, with
the consuming thirst for destruction which made the
alchemist veil under his symbols of lions and dragons,
of eagles and ravens, of dew and of nitre, a search for an
essence which would dissolve all mortal things.[8]

I repeated to myself the ninth key of Basilius
Valentinus[9], in which he compares the fire of the last
day to the fire of the alchemist, and the world to the
alchemist's furnace, and would have us know that all
must be dissolved before the divine substance, material
gold or immaterial ecstasy, awake.

I had dissolved indeed the mortal world and lived
amid immortal essences, but had obtained no miraculous
ecstasy.

---

7 Raymond Lulle（1235–1315），加泰羅尼亞作家、邏輯學家、神祕
主義神學家。

8 這是煉金術各個步驟與各個階段的象徵。綠獅代表綠色、硫
酸、硝石，也有侵蝕的意象；蟠龍代表煉金步驟開始與結束的
兩個階段；老鷹代表物質轉為白色；渡鴉代表物質轉為黑色；
露水據說能夠溶解黃金。

9 Basilius Valentinus：十五世紀初期的煉金術師，曾出版煉金術的
神學圖案書，並發表鹽酸的製作方法。

As I thought of these things, I drew aside the curtains and looked out into the darkness, and it seemed to my troubled fancy that all those little points of light filling the sky were the furnaces of innumerable divine alchemists, who labour continually, turning lead into gold, weariness into ecstasy, bodies into souls, the darkness into God; and at their perfect labour my mortality grew heavy, and I cried out, as so many dreamers and men of letters in our age have cried, for the birth of that elaborate spiritual beauty which could alone uplift souls weighted with so many dreams.

My reverie was broken by a loud knocking at the door, and I wondered the more at this because I had no visitors, and had bid my servants do all things silently, lest they broke the dream of my inner life. Feeling a little curious, I resolved to go to the door myself, and, taking one of the silver candlesticks from the mantlepiece, began to descend the stairs.

The servants appeared to be out, for though the sound poured through every corner and crevice of the house there was no stir in the lower rooms. I remembered that because my needs were so few, my part in life so little, they had begun to come and go as they would, often leaving me alone for hours. The emptiness and silence of a world from which I had driven everything but dreams suddenly overwhelmed me, and I shuddered as I drew the bolt.

I found before me Michael Robartes, whom I had not seen for years, and whose wild red hair, fierce eyes, sensitive, tremulous lips and rough clothes, made him look now, just as they used to do fifteen years before, something between a debauchee, a saint, and a peasant.

He had recently come to Ireland, he said, and wished to see me on a matter of importance: indeed, the only matter of importance for him and for me.

His voice brought up before me our student years in Paris, and remembering the magnetic power he had once possessed over me, a little fear mingled with much annoyance at this irrelevant intrusion, as I led the way up the wide staircase, where Swift[1] had passed joking and railing, and Curran[2] telling stories and quoting Greek, in simpler days, before men's minds, subtilized and complicated by the romantic movement in art and literature, began to tremble on the verge of some unimagined revelation.

I felt that my hand shook, and saw that the light of the candle wavered and quivered more than it need have upon the Maenads on the old French panels, making them look like the first beings slowly shaping in the formless and void darkness.

When the door had closed, and the peacock curtain, glimmering like many-coloured flame, fell between us and the world, I felt, in a way I could not understand, that some singular and unexpected thing was about to happen.

I went over to the mantlepiece, and finding that a little chainless bronze censer, set, upon the outside, with

pieces of painted china by
Orazio Fontana[3], which I had
filled with antique amulets,
had fallen upon its side and
poured out its contents, I
began to gather the amulets
into the bowl, partly to collect
my thoughts and partly with
that habitual reverence which
seemed to me the due of things so long connected with
secret hopes and fears.

'I see,' said Michael Robartes, 'that you are still fond
of incense, and I can show you an incense more precious
than any you have ever seen,' and as he spoke he took
the censer out of my hand and put the amulets in a little
heap between the athanor and the alembic.

I sat down, and he sat down at the side of the fire, and
sat there for a while looking into the fire, and holding
the censer in his hand.

'I have come to ask you something,' he said, 'and the

---

1 Dr Jonathan Swift（1667-1745），英國和愛爾蘭作家,《格列佛遊記》
  （*Gulliver's Travels*）的作者。
2 John Philpot Curran（1750-1817），愛爾蘭律師、演說家、愛爾蘭國
  會成員。
3 Orazio Fontana（1510–1571），義大利的陶藝工匠。

incense will fill the room, and our thoughts, with its sweet odour while we are talking. I got it from an old man in Syria, who said it was made from flowers, of one kind with the flowers that laid their heavy purple petals upon the hands and upon the hair and upon the feet of Christ in the Garden of Gethsemane[4], and folded Him in their heavy breath, until he cried against the cross and his destiny.'

He shook some dust into the censer out of a small silk bag, and set the censer upon the floor and lit the dust which sent up a blue stream of smoke, that spread out over the ceiling, and flowed downwards again until it was like Milton's[5] banyan tree.

It filled me, as incense often does, with a faint sleepiness, so that I started when he said, 'I have come to ask you that question which I asked you in Paris, and which you left Paris rather than answer.'

He had turned his eyes towards me, and I saw them glitter in the firelight, and through the incense, as I replied: 'You mean, will I become an initiate of your Order of the Alchemical Rose[6]? I would not consent in Paris, when I was full of unsatisfied desire, and now that I have at last fashioned my life according to my desire, am I likely to consent?'

'You have changed greatly since then,' he answered. 'I have read your books, and now I see you among all these images, and I understand you better than you do yourself, for I have been with many and many dreamers at the same cross-ways. You have shut away the world and gathered the gods about you, and if you do not throw yourself at their feet, you will be always full of lassitude, and of wavering purpose, for a man must forget he is miserable in the bustle and noise of the multitude in this world and in time; or seek a mystical union with the multitude who govern this world and time.'

And then he murmured something I could not hear, and as though to someone I could not see. For a moment the room appeared to darken, as it used to do when he was about to perform some singular experiment, and in the darkness the peacocks upon the doors seemed to glow with a more intense colour.

I cast off the illusion, which was, I believe, merely caused by memory, and by the twilight of incense, for I would not acknowledge that he could overcome my now mature intellect; and I said: 'Even if I grant that I need a

---

4 Garden of Gethsemane：這個花園位於耶路撒冷。耶穌在最後的晚餐之後，來到這個花園裡，被猶大出賣。隔日，耶穌被釘在十字架上。

5 John Milton（1608-1674）：英國詩人、思想家。

6 Alchemical Rose：「玫瑰煉金術教團」承襲許多玫瑰十字會（Rosicrucian）的傳統。在葉慈所加入的黃金黎明教團（Hermetic Order of Golden Dawn）中，玫瑰也是重要的象徵意象。

spiritual belief and some form of worship, why should I go to Eleusis[7] and not to Calvary[8]?'

He leaned forward and began speaking with a slightly rhythmical intonation, and as he spoke I had to struggle again with the shadow, as of some older night than the night of the sun, which began to dim the light of the candles and to blot out the little gleams upon the corner of picture-frames and on the bronze divinities, and to turn the blue of the incense to a heavy purple; while it left the peacocks to glimmer and glow as though each separate colour were a living spirit. I had fallen into a profound dream-like reverie in which I heard him speaking as at a distance.

'And yet there is no one who communes with only one god,' he was saying, 'and the more a man lives in imagination and in a refined understanding, the more gods does he meet with and talk with, and the more does he come under the power of Roland[9], who sounded in the Valley of Roncesvalles[10] the last trumpet of the body's will and pleasure; and of Hamlet[11], who saw them perishing away, and sighed; and of Faust[12], who looked for them up and down the world and could not find them; and under the power of all those countless divinities who have taken upon themselves spiritual bodies in the minds of the modern poets and romance writers, and under the power of the old divinities, who since the Renaissance have won everything of their ancient worship except the sacrifice of birds and fishes, the fragrance of garlands and the smoke of incense. The many think humanity made these divinities, and that it can unmake them again; but we who have seen them pass in rattling harness, and in soft robes, and heard them speak with articulate voices while we lay in deathlike trance, know that they are always making and unmaking humanity, which is indeed but the trembling of their lips.'

He had stood up and begun to walk to and fro, and had become in my waking dream a shuttle weaving an immense purple web whose folds had begun to fill the room. The room seemed to have become inexplicably silent, as though all but the web and the weaving were at an end in the world.

'They have come to us; they have come to us,' the voice began again; 'all that have ever been in your reverie, all that you have met with in books. There is Lear[13], his head still wet with the thunder-storm, and he laughs because you thought yourself an existence who are but

7 Eleusis：希臘神話中，膜拜豐收女神狄蜜特（Demeter）的地點。

8 Calvary：加爾瓦略山，耶穌被釘上十字架的地方。

9 Roland：《羅蘭之歌》（*The Song of Roland*），法國史詩。

10 Valley of Roncesvalles：位於西班牙北方的一座小村落。

11 Hamlet：莎士比亞作品《哈姆雷特》（*Hamlet*）的主角。

12 Faust：歌德作品《浮士德》（*Faust*）的主角。

13 Lear：莎士比亞所作之悲劇《李爾王》（*King Lear*）的主角。

a shadow, and him a shadow who is an eternal god; and there is Beatrice[14], with her lips half parted in a smile, as though all the stars were about to pass away in a sigh of love; and there is

the mother of the God of humility[15] who cast so great a spell over men that they have tried to unpeople their hearts that he might reign alone, but she holds in her hand the rose whose every petal is a god; and there, O swiftly she comes! is Aphrodite[16] under a twilight falling from the wings of numberless sparrows, and about her feet are the grey and white doves.'

In the midst of my dream I saw him hold out his left arm and pass his right hand over it as though he stroked the wings of doves. I made a violent effort which seemed almost to tear me in two, and said with forced determination: 'You would sweep me away into an indefinite world which fills me with terror; and yet a man is a great man just in so far as he can make his mind reflect everything with indifferent precision like a mirror.'

I seemed to be perfectly master of myself, and went on, but more rapidly: 'I command you to leave me at once, for your ideas and phantasies are but the illusions that creep like maggots into civilizations when they begin to decline, and into minds when they begin to decay.'

I had grown suddenly angry, and seizing the alembic from the table, was about to rise and strike him with it, when the peacocks on the door behind him appeared to grow immense; and then the alembic fell from my fingers and I was drowned in a tide of green and blue and bronze feathers, and as I struggled hopelessly I heard a distant voice saying: 'Our master Avicenna[17] has written that all life proceeds out of corruption.'

The glittering feathers had now covered me completely, and I knew that I had struggled for hundreds of years, and was conquered at last.

I was sinking into the depth when the green and blue and bronze that seemed to fill the world became a sea of flame and swept me away, and as I was swirled along I heard a voice over my head cry, 'The mirror is broken in two pieces,' and another voice answer, 'The mirror is broken in four pieces,' and a more distant voice cry with

---

14 Beatrice Portinari：但丁《神曲》(*Divine Comedy*) 中的人物。

15 the mother of the God of humility：指聖母瑪利亞。

16 Aphrodite：希臘神話中的愛神。

17 Avicenna (Ibn Sina, 980–1037)：中世紀的波斯哲學家、醫學家、自然科學家、文學家。

an exultant cry, 'The mirror is broken into numberless pieces'; and then a multitude of pale hands were reaching towards me, and strange gentle faces bending above me, and half wailing and half caressing voices uttering words that were forgotten the moment they were spoken.

I was being lifted out of the tide of flame, and felt my memories, my hopes, my thoughts, my will, everything I held to be myself melting away; then I seemed to rise through numberless companies of beings who were, I understood, in some way more certain than thought, each wrapped in his eternal moment, in the perfect lifting of an arm, in a little circlet of rhythmical words, in dreaming with dim eyes and half-closed eyelids.

And then I passed beyond these forms, which were so beautiful they had almost ceased to be, and, having endured strange moods, melancholy, as it seemed, with the weight of many worlds, I passed into that Death which is Beauty herself, and into that Loneliness which all the multitudes desire without ceasing.[18]

All things that had ever lived seemed to come and dwell in my heart, and I in theirs; and I had never again known mortality or tears, had I not suddenly fallen from the certainty of vision into the uncertainty of dream, and become a drop of molten gold falling with immense

---

18 對葉慈而言，心境代表主觀的經驗。

rapidity, through a night elaborate with stars, and all about me a melancholy exultant wailing.

I fell and fell and fell, and then the wailing was but the wailing of the wind in the chimney, and I awoke to find myself leaning upon the table and supporting my head with my hands. I saw the alembic swaying from side to side in the distant corner it had rolled to, and Michael Robartes watching me and waiting.

'I will go wherever you will,' I said, 'and do whatever you bid me, for I have been with eternal things.'

'I knew,' he replied, 'you must need answer as you have answered, when I heard the storm begin. You must come to a great distance, for we were commanded to build our temple between the pure multitude by the waves and the impure multitude of men.'

III

I did not speak as we drove through the deserted streets, for my mind was curiously empty of familiar thoughts and experiences; it seemed to have been plucked out of the definite world and cast naked upon a shoreless sea.

There were moments when the vision appeared on the point of returning, and I would half-remember, with an ecstasy of joy or sorrow, crimes and heroisms, fortunes and misfortunes; or begin to contemplate, with a sudden leaping of the heart, hopes and terrors, desires and ambitions, alien to my orderly and careful life; and then I would awake shuddering at the thought that some great imponderable being had swept through my mind.

It was indeed days before this feeling passed perfectly away, and even now, when I have sought refuge in the only definite faith, I feel a great tolerance for those people with incoherent personalities, who gather in the chapels and meeting-places of certain obscure sects, because I also have felt fixed habits and principles dissolving before a power, which was hysterica passion or sheer madness, if you will, but was so powerful in its melancholy exultation that I tremble lest it wake again and drive me from my new-found peace.

When we came in the grey light to the great half-empty terminus, it seemed to me I was so changed that I was no more, as man is, a moment shuddering at eternity, but eternity weeping and laughing over a moment; and when we had started and Michael Robartes had fallen asleep, as he soon did, his sleeping face, in which there was no sign of all that had so shaken me and that now kept me wakeful, was to my excited mind more like a mask than a face.

The fancy possessed me that the man behind it had dissolved away like salt in water, and that it laughed and sighed, appealed and denounced at the bidding of beings greater or less than man.

'This is not Michael Robartes at all: Michael Robartes is dead; dead for ten, for twenty years perhaps,' I kept repeating to myself.

I fell at last into a feverish sleep, waking up from time to time when we rushed past some little town, its slated roofs shining with wet, or still lake gleaming in the cold morning light. I had been too preoccupied to ask where we were going, or to notice what tickets Michael Robartes had taken, but I knew now from the direction of the sun that we were going westward; and presently I knew also, by the way in which the trees had grown

into the semblance of tattered beggars flying with bent heads towards the east, that we were approaching the western coast. Then immediately I saw the sea between the low hills upon the left, its dull grey broken into white patches and lines.

When we left the train we had still, I found, some way to go, and set out, buttoning our coats about us, for the wind was bitter and violent. Michael Robartes was silent, seeming anxious to leave me to my thoughts; and as we walked between the sea and the rocky side of a great promontory, I realized with a new perfection what a shock had been given to all my habits of thought and of feelings, if indeed some mysterious change had not taken place in the substance of my mind, for the grey waves, plumed with scudding foam, had grown part of a teeming, fantastic inner life; and when Michael Robartes pointed to a square ancient-looking house, with a much smaller and newer building under its lee, set out on the very end of a dilapidated and almost deserted pier, and said it was the Temple of the Alchemical Rose, I was possessed with the phantasy that the sea, which kept covering it with showers of white foam, was claiming it as part of some indefinite and passionate life, which had begun to war upon our orderly and careful days, and was about to plunge the world into a night as obscure as that which followed the downfall of the classical world.

One part of my mind mocked this phantastic terror, but the other, the part that still lay half plunged in vision, listened to the clash of unknown armies, and shuddered at unimaginable fanaticisms, that hung in those grey leaping waves. We had gone but a few paces along the pier when we came upon an old man, who was evidently a watchman, for he sat in an overset barrel, close to a place where masons had been lately working upon a break in the pier, and had in front of him a fire such as one sees slung under tinkers' carts.

I saw that he was also a voteen, as the peasants say, for there was a rosary hanging from a nail on the rim of the barrel, and I saw I shuddered, and I did not know why I shuddered. We had passed him a few yards when

I heard him cry in Gaelic, 'Idolaters, idolaters, go down to Hell with your witches and your devil; go down to Hell that the herrings may come again into the bay'; and for some moments I could hear him half screaming and half muttering behind us.

'Are you not afraid,' I said, 'that these wild fishing people may do some desperate thing against you?' 'I and mine,' he answered, 'are long past human hurt or help, being incorporate with immortal spirits, and when we die it shall be the consummation of the supreme work. A time will come for these people also, and they will sacrifice a mullet to Artemis[1], or some other fish to some new divinity, unless indeed their own divinities set up once more their temples of grey stone. Their reign has never ceased, but only waned in power a little, for the Sidhe still pass in every wind, and dance and play at hurley, but they cannot build their temples again till there have been martyrdoms and victories, and perhaps even that long-foretold battle in the Valley of the Black Pig[2].'

Keeping close to the wall that went about the pier on the seaward side, to escape the driving foam and the wind, which threatened every moment to lift us off our feet, we made our way in silence to the door of the square building.

Michael Robartes opened it with a key, on which I saw the rust of many salt winds, and led me along a bare passage and up an uncarpeted stair to a little room surrounded with bookshelves. A meal would be brought, but only of fruit, for I must submit to a tempered fast before the ceremony, he explained, and with it a book on the doctrine and method of the Order, over which I was to spend what remained of the winter daylight. He then left me, promising to return an hour before the ceremony.

dervish

I began searching among the bookshelves, and found one of the most exhaustive alchemical libraries I have ever seen. There were the works of Morienus[3], who hid his immortal body under a shirt of hair-cloth; of Avicenna[4], who was a drunkard and yet controlled numberless legions of spirits; of Alfarabi[5], who put so

---

1 Artemis：希臘神話中的月亮女神與狩獵的象徵。
2 葉慈在《蘆葦間的風》(*The Wind Among the Reeds*, 1899) 提到：「黑豬谷之役，是明白清楚的世界與古代黑暗事物之間的戰爭。」
3 Morienus：七世紀的一位基督教隱士。
4 Avicenna (980–1037)：波斯醫師、哲學家，對中世紀的伊斯蘭哲學影響深遠。葉慈從《煉金術哲學家》(*Lives of Alchemistical Philosophers*) 一書中，得到他的思想。
5 Alfarabi (870–950 年代)：喀喇汗王朝初期著名的醫學家、哲學家、心理學家、音樂學家。

many spirits into his lute that he could make men laugh, or weep, or fall in deadly trance as he would; of Lully[6], who transformed himself into the likeness of a red cock; of Flamel[7], who with his wife Parnella achieved the elixir many hundreds of years ago, and is fabled to live still in Arabia among the Dervishes[8]; and of many of less fame.

There were very few mystics but alchemical mystics, and because, I had little doubt, of the devotion to one god of the greater number and of the limited sense of beauty, which Robartes would hold an inevitable consequence; but I did notice a complete set of facsimiles of the prophetical writings of William Blake[9], and probably because of the multitudes that thronged his illumination and were 'like the gay fishes on the wave when the moon sucks up the dew[10].'

I noted also many poets and prose writers of every age, but only those who were a little weary of life, as indeed the greatest have been everywhere, and who cast their imagination to us, as a something they needed no longer now that they were going up in their fiery chariots.

William Blake

Presently I heard a tap at the door, and a woman came in and laid a little fruit upon the table. I judged that she had once been handsome, but her cheeks were hollowed by what I would have held, had I seen her anywhere else, an excitement of the flesh and a thirst for pleasure, instead of which it doubtless was an excitement of the imagination and a thirst for beauty.

I asked her some question concerning the ceremony, but getting no answer except a shake of the head, saw that I must await initiation in silence. When I had eaten, she came again, and having laid a curiously wrought bronze box on the table, lighted the candles, and took away the plates and the remnants. So soon as I was alone, I turned to the box, and found that the peacocks of Hera spread out their tails over the sides and lid, against a background, on which were wrought great stars, as though to affirm that the heavens were a part of their glory.

6　Ramon Lully（1235–1316）：加泰羅尼亞作家與神祕主義神學家。

7　Nicolas Flamel（約 1330–1418）：法國瓦盧瓦王朝煉金術士，研究煉金術界的傳奇物質「賢者之石」，以此聞名。

8　Dervish：指伊斯蘭教蘇非派的托缽僧。

9　William Blake（1757-1827）：威廉·布萊克，英國詩人、畫家，浪漫主義文學代表人物。對葉慈的美學有深刻影響。

10　出自威廉·布萊克的作品〈歐洲：預言〉（*Europe: A Prophecy*）中的蝕刻版畫。

In the box was a book bound in vellum, and having upon the vellum and in very delicate colours, and in gold, the alchemical rose with many spears thrusting against it, but in vain, as was shown by the shattered points of those nearest to the petals. The book was written upon vellum, and in beautiful clear letters, interspersed with symbolical pictures and illuminations, after the manner of the *Splendor Solis*[11].

The first chapter described how six students, of Celtic descent, gave themselves separately to the study of alchemy, and solved, one the mystery of the Pelican, another the mystery of the green Dragon, another the mystery of the Eagle, another that of Salt and Mercury[12].

What seemed a succession of accidents, but was, the book declared, the contrivance of preternatural powers, brought them together in the garden of an inn in the South of France, and while they talked together the thought came to them that alchemy was the gradual distillation of the contents of the soul, until they were ready to put off the mortal and put on the immortal.

An owl passed, rustling among the vine-leaves overhead, and then an old woman came, leaning upon a stick, and, sitting close to them, took up the thought where they had dropped it. Having expounded the whole principle of spiritual alchemy, and bid them found the Order of the Alchemical Rose, she passed from among them, and when they would have followed was nowhere to be seen.

They formed themselves into an Order, holding their goods and making their researches in common, and, as they became perfect in the alchemical doctrine, apparitions came and went among them, and taught them more and more marvellous mysteries.

The book then went on to expound so much of these as the neophyte was permitted to know, dealing at the outset and at considerable length with the independent reality of our thoughts, which was, it declared, the doctrine from which all true doctrines rose.

If you imagine, it said, the semblance of a living being, it is at once possessed by a wandering soul, and goes hither and thither working good or evil, until the

---

11 Splendor Solis:《太陽的光輝》(*Splendor Solis*),著名的彩色插圖煉金術手稿,於 1532–1535 間寫成。

12 Pelican:一種煉金術的容器,圓形的壺身加上細長的壺口,像是鵜鶘彎著脖子餵食幼鳥的樣子。綠龍,沒有精確指向任何煉金術的隱喻或是階段步驟,較常見的是使用綠獅,象徵第三個步驟時物質轉為綠色。綠龍一詞可能是葉慈閱讀《太陽的光輝》(*Splendor Solis*)時,對雙龍插圖印象深刻。老鷹,是第二個步驟時物質轉為白色。鹽巴和水銀,指的是煉金術中的第一元素(prima materia)。

moment of its death has come; and gave many examples, received, it said, from many gods. Eros had taught them how to fashion forms in which a divine soul could dwell, and whisper what they would into sleeping minds; and Ate[13], forms from which demonic beings could pour madness, or unquiet dreams, into sleeping blood; and Hermes[14], that if you powerfully imagined a hound at your bedside it would keep watch there until you woke, and drive away all but the mightiest demons, but that if your imagination was weakly, the hound would be weakly also, and the demons prevail, and the hound soon die; and Aphrodite, that if you made, by a strong imagining, a dove crowned with silver and had it flutter over your head, its soft cooing would make sweet dreams of immortal love gather and brood over mortal sleep; and all divinities alike had revealed with many warnings and lamentations that all minds are continually giving birth to such beings, and sending them forth to work health or disease, joy or madness.

If you would give forms to the evil powers, it went on, you were to make them ugly, thrusting out a lip, with the thirsts of life, or breaking the proportions of a body with the burdens of life; but the divine powers would only appear in beautiful shapes, which are but, as it were, shapes trembling out of existence, folding up into a timeless ecstasy, drifting with half-shut eyes, into a sleepy stillness.

The bodiless souls who descended into these forms were what men called the moods; and worked all great changes in the world; for just as the magician or the artist could call them when he would, so they could call out of the mind of the magician or the artist, or if they were demons, out of the mind of the mad or the ignoble, what shape they would, and through its voice and its gestures pour themselves out upon the world.

In this way all great events were accomplished; a mood, a divinity, or a demon, first descending like a faint sigh into men's minds and then changing their thoughts and their actions until hair that was yellow had grown black, or hair that was black had grown yellow, and empires moved their border, as though they were but drifts of leaves.

The rest of the book contained symbols of form, and sound, and colour, and their attribution to divinities and demons, so that the initiate might fashion a shape for any divinity or any demon, and be as powerful as Avicenna among those who live under the roots of tears and of laughter.

---

13 Ate：詛咒女神，宙斯的長女。
14 Hermes：希臘神話人物，十二主神之一，是眾神的使者，
　　也是商業之神、旅者之神。

IV

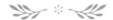

A couple of hours after sunset Michael Robartes
returned and told me that I would have to learn the
steps of an exceedingly antique dance, because before
my initiation could be perfected I had to join three times
in a magical dance, for rhythm was the wheel of Eternity,
on which alone the transient and accidental could be
broken, and the spirit set free.

I found that the steps,
which were simple enough,
resembled certain antique
Greek dances, and having been
a good dancer in my youth and
the master of many curious
Gaelic steps, I soon had them
in my memory.

He then robed me and himself in a costume[1] which
suggested by its shape both Greece and Egypt, but by
its crimson colour a more passionate life than theirs;
and having put into my hands a little chainless censer
of bronze, wrought into the likeness of a rose, by some
modern craftsman, he told me to open a small door
opposite to the door by which I had entered.

I put my hand to the handle, but the moment I did so the fumes of the incense, helped perhaps by his mysterious glamour, made me fall again into a dream, in which I seemed to be a mask[2], lying on the counter of a little Eastern shop. Many persons, with eyes so bright and still that I knew them for more than human, came in and tried me on their faces, but at last flung me into a corner with a little laughter; but all this passed in a moment, for when I awoke my hand was still upon the handle.

I opened the door, and found myself in a marvellous passage, along whose sides were many divinities wrought in a mosaic, not less beautiful than the mosaic in the Baptistery at Ravenna[3], but of a less severe beauty; the predominant colour of each divinity, which was surely a symbolic colour, being repeated in the lamps that hung from the ceiling, a curiously-scented lamp before every divinity.

I passed on, marvelling exceedingly how these enthusiasts could have created all this beauty in so remote a place, and half persuaded to believe in a

---

1 所有黃金黎明教團裡的成員，在儀式中依照他們的位階，穿上不同顏色的長袍和腰帶。
2 葉慈曾寫道：「在拜倫的詩作中，人物角色像是個面具，是用來傳達主觀意識的媒介。」
3 Ravenna：位於義大利艾米利亞—羅馬涅區的城市。

material alchemy, by the sight of so much hidden wealth; the censer filling the air, as I passed, with smoke of ever-changing colour.

I stopped before a door, on whose bronze panels were wrought great waves in whose shadow were faint suggestions of terrible faces. Those beyond it seemed to have heard our steps, for a voice cried: 'Is the work of the Incorruptible Fire at an end?' and immediately Michael Robartes answered: 'The perfect gold has come from the athanor.'

The door swung open, and we were in a great circular room, and among men and women who were dancing slowly in crimson robes. Upon the ceiling was an immense rose wrought in mosaic; and about the walls, also in mosaic, was a battle of gods and angels, the gods glimmering like rubies and sapphires, and the angels of the one greyness, because, as Michael Robartes whispered, they had renounced their divinity, and turned from the unfolding of their separate hearts, out of love for a God of humility and sorrow.

Pillars supported the roof and made a kind of circular cloister, each pillar being a column of confused shapes, divinities, it seemed, of the wind, who rose as in a whirling dance of more than human vehemence, and playing upon pipes and cymbals; and from among these shapes were thrust out hands, and in these hands were censers.

I was bid place my censer also in a hand and take my place and dance, and as I turned from the pillars towards the dancers, I saw that the floor was of a green stone, and that a pale Christ on a pale cross was wrought in the midst. I asked Robartes the meaning of this, and was told that they desired 'To trouble His unity with their multitudinous feet.'

The dance wound in and out, tracing upon the floor the shapes of petals that copied the petals in the rose overhead, and to the sound of hidden instruments which were perhaps of an antique pattern, for I have never heard the like; and every moment the dance was more passionate, until all the winds of the world seemed to have awakened under our feet.

After a little I had grown weary, and stood under a pillar watching the coming and going of those flame-like figures; until gradually I sank into a half-dream, from which I was awakened by seeing the petals of the great rose, which had no longer the look of mosaic, falling slowly through the incense-heavy air, and, as they fell, shaping into the likeness of living beings of an extraordinary beauty.[4]

4　在《The Secret Rose》裡，也有玫瑰花瓣轉化為永恆
生命的意象。

Still faint and cloudlike, they began to dance, and as they danced took a more and more definite shape, so that I was able to distinguish beautiful Grecian faces and august Egyptian faces, and now and again to name a divinity by the staff in his hand or by a bird fluttering over his head; and soon every mortal foot danced by the white foot of an immortal; and in the troubled eyes that looked into untroubled shadowy eyes, I saw the brightness of uttermost desire as though they had found at length, after unreckonable wandering, the lost love of their youth.

Sometimes, but only for a moment, I saw a faint solitary figure with a veiled face, and carrying a faint torch, flit among the dancers, but like a dream within a dream, like a shadow of a shadow, and I knew by an understanding born from a deeper fountain than thought, that it was Eros himself, and that his face was veiled because no man or woman from the beginning of the world has ever known what love is, or looked into his eyes, for Eros alone of divinities is altogether a spirit, and hides in passions not of his essence if he would commune with a mortal heart. So that if a man love nobly he knows love through infinite pity, unspeakable trust, unending sympathy; and if ignobly through vehement jealousy, sudden hatred, and unappeasable desire; but unveiled love he never knows.

While I thought these things, a voice cried to me from the crimson figures: 'Into the dance! there is none that can be spared out of the dance; into the dance! into the dance! that the gods may make them bodies out of the substance of our hearts'; and before I could answer, a mysterious wave of passion, that seemed like the soul of the dance moving within our souls, took hold of me, and I was swept, neither consenting nor refusing, into the midst.

I was dancing with an immortal august woman, who had black lilies in her hair, and her dreamy gesture seemed laden with a wisdom more profound than the darkness that is between star and star, and with a love like the love that breathed upon the waters; and as we danced on and on, the incense drifted over us and round us, covering us away as in the heart of the world, and ages seemed to pass, and tempests to awake and perish in the folds of our robes and in her heavy hair.

Suddenly I remembered that her eyelids had never quivered, and that her lilies had not dropped a black petal, or shaken from their places, and understood with a great horror that I danced with one who was more or less than human, and who was drinking up my soul as an ox drinks up a wayside pool; and I fell, and darkness passed over me.

V

I awoke suddenly as though something had awakened me, and saw that I was lying on a roughly painted floor, and that on the ceiling, which was at no great distance, was a roughly painted rose, and about me on the walls half -finished paintings. The pillars and the censers had gone; and near me a score of sleepers lay wrapped in disordered robes, their upturned faces looking to my imagination like hollow masks; and a chill dawn was shining down upon them from a long window I had not noticed before; and outside the sea roared.

I saw Michael Robartes lying at a little distance and beside him an overset bowl of wrought bronze which looked as though it had once held incense. As I sat thus, I heard a sudden tumult of angry men and women's voices mix with the roaring of the sea; and leaping to my feet, I went quickly to Michael Robartes, and tried to shake him out of his sleep.

I then seized him by the shoulder and tried to lift him, but he fell backwards, and sighed faintly; and the voices became louder and angrier; and there was a sound of heavy blows upon the door, which opened on to the pier.

Suddenly I heard a sound of rending wood, and I knew

it had begun to give, and I ran to the door of the room. I pushed it open and came out upon a passage whose bare boards clattered under my feet, and found in the passage another door which led into an empty kitchen; and as I passed through the door I heard two crashes in quick succession, and knew by the sudden noise of feet and the shouts that the door which opened on to the pier had fallen inwards.

I ran from the kitchen and out into a small yard, and from this down some steps which descended the seaward and sloping side of the pier, and from the steps clambered along the water's edge, with the angry voices ringing in my ears. This part of the pier had been but lately refaced with blocks of granite, so that it was almost clear of seaweed; but when I came to the old part, I found it so slippery with green weed that I had to climb up on to the roadway.

I looked towards the Temple of the Alchemical Rose, where the fishermen and the women were still shouting, but somewhat more faintly, and saw that there was no one about the door or upon the pier; but as I looked, a little crowd hurried out of the door and began gathering large stones from where they were heaped up in readiness for the next time a storm shattered the pier, when they would be laid under blocks of granite.

While I stood watching the crowd, an old man, who was, I think, the voteen, pointed to me, and screamed out something, and the crowd whitened, for all the faces had turned towards me. I ran, and it was well for me that pullers of the oar are poorer men with their feet than with their arms and their bodies; and yet while I ran I scarcely heard the following feet or the angry voices, for many voices of exultation and lamentation, which were forgotten as a dream is forgotten the moment they were heard, seemed to be ringing in the air over my head.

There are moments even now when I seem to hear those voices of exultation and lamentation, and when the indefinite world, which has but half lost its mastery over my heart and my intellect, seems about to claim a perfect

mastery; but I carry the rosary about my neck, and when I hear, or seem to hear them, I press it to my heart and say: 'He whose name is Legion is at our doors deceiving our intellects with subtlety and flattering our hearts with beauty, and we have no trust but in Thee[1]'; and then the war that rages within me at other times is still, and I am at peace.

1 出自《聖經》的〈馬可福音〉，故事如下：

　　耶穌在格拉森人（Gerasenes）土地上遇見一位被污靈附身的人，那人遠遠地看見耶穌，連忙跑過來，跪在耶穌面前，大聲喊道：「至高上帝的兒子耶穌，你為甚麼來打擾我呢？我指著上帝求求你，不要折磨我！」（他會這樣講，是因為耶穌已經吩咐說：「污靈，從那人身上出來！」）

　　耶穌問他：「你叫什麼名字？」

　　他回答：「我名叫『群』（Legion），因為我們數目眾多！」他再三哀求耶穌不要趕他們離開。

　　在附近山坡上，剛好有一大群豬在吃東西，污靈就央求耶穌，說：「把我們趕進豬群，讓我們附身在豬群裡面吧。」

　　耶穌准了他們，污靈就從那人身上出來，進了豬群。整群的豬（約兩千隻），衝下山崖，跌入湖裡，淹死了。

PART 2

Chapter 1

紅髮翰拉漢
故事集

感謝桂格瑞女士的協助，
讓我能夠以優美的基爾泰坦方言，
來改寫《紅髮翰拉漢故事集》，得以更貼近鄉間傳說。
翰拉漢的形象，傳流民間，
留存在人們的記憶裡。

1. 紅髮翰拉漢

　　翰拉漢是一位私塾先生[1]，他年輕、高大、強壯，一頭紅髮，薩溫節夜[2]這一晚，他走進一間坐著一些村裡男人的穀倉。這間穀倉原本是住家，屋主另外蓋了間比較好的房子，就把這裡的兩間房間打通，用來存放雜物。

　　老舊的壁爐燃著火，瓶子裡插著浸製蠟燭，兩個木桶上擱著幾塊板子，充作桌子，上頭擺了一個黑色的夸脫罐。屋內的人大多圍坐在火爐旁，當中有個人正在唱著一首長曲子，那是一首漂泊之歌，內容講一個芒斯特人和一個康諾特人，為自己的家鄉地在爭吵[3]。

　　翰拉漢走向屋主，說道：「我收到你的通知了。」話說完就打住，因為有個山裡來的老人正盯著他看，老人穿著襯衫和一條原色的法蘭絨長褲，獨自坐在門邊，兩隻手摸著一副舊紙牌，嘴裡唸唸有詞。

1　指圍籬學校（hedge school）的老師。圍籬學校是私人辦理的學校，始於十七世紀，常借用窯屋、農舍、泥炭屋等來授課。
2　薩溫節夜（Samhain Eve），意味著收穫時節的結束與冬天的開始，通常是 10 月 31 日夜晚開始慶祝。
3　指詩人 Raftery 和兩個死對頭 Peatsy、Marcas Callinain 之間的爭執。

「別理他。」屋主說：「不知道他是誰，他剛剛才來到這裡，今天是薩溫節夜，我們讓他進來。但我想他精神不太正常，你現在聽聽看，就能知道他在講什麼。」

　　他們側耳傾聽，老人一邊翻動紙牌，一邊喃喃自語說：「黑桃和方塊，勇氣與力量；梅花和紅心，知識與喜悅。」

　　「他就這樣一直唸了個把鐘頭。」屋主說完，翰拉漢便將眼神從老人的身上移開，一副不想看到他的樣子。

　　翰拉漢接著說：「我收到你的通知了。傳話的人說：『那個人在穀倉，夥同三個奇魁司來的堂兄弟，還有幾個鄰居跟他們在一起。』」

　　「那是我堂弟在那裡，他要找你。」屋主說道，然後把一個正在聽著歌曲、穿著起絨粗呢外套的年輕人叫過來，對他說道：「這就是你要帶話給他的人，紅髮翰拉漢。」

　　「我帶來的口信，可感人了，是你的情人瑪莉・拉維要我帶話給你的。」年輕人說。

　　「你怎麼會有她的口信？你怎麼認識她的？」

　　「我並不認識她。我昨天在灰湖鎮，跟她的鄰居做買賣，她交代那鄰居說，如果在市集遇到從我們這邊去的人，就請對方帶個口信給你，說是瑪莉的母親過世了，已經離她而去，要是你還有心要跟她在一起，她願意信守對你的承諾。」

　　「我一定會去找她。」翰拉漢說。

「她要你立刻去找她，因為在月底之前，如果屋子裡沒有個男人，她的那小塊地很可能會被讓給別人。」

　　翰拉漢一聽，便從剛坐下的長凳上起身。

　　「我立刻出發，今天是滿月，今晚要是能趕到奇魁司，就可以在明天日落之前趕到她那裡。」他說。

　　眾人聞言，揶揄他這麼急著去找情人。有人問他，他該不會丟下舊石灰窯私塾吧，孩子們在那裡學到了很多學問。

　　但是他說，孩子們早上去上課，要是發現那裡空蕩蕩的，沒有人會逼他們寫作業，一定會樂壞了。至於私塾，只要他的脖子上還掛著小墨水罐、外套的衣襬裡還塞著維吉爾的大部頭著作和識字讀本，他處處都可以開個私塾。

　　有人要他喝一杯再走，還有個年輕人抓住他的外套，要他唱完他寫的那首歌頌維納斯和瑪莉・拉維的歌曲，方可離開。翰拉漢喝了一杯威士忌，說他不會耽擱，要動身啟程了。

　　「時間還很充裕，紅髮翰拉漢。等你結婚了，多的是時間不去鬼混，我們恐怕要很久以後才能見到你了。」屋主說。

　　「我不拖延了，我的心已經上路了，帶我去招喚著我的女子身邊。她的寂寞芳心，正引頸期盼我的到來。」翰拉漢說。

又有一些人走到他的身邊，勸他過了今晚再離開，因為他一向是個討人喜歡的夥伴，會唱很多歌，能玩的把戲和樂子也很多。不過，翰拉漢不加理會，擺脫人了群，走向門口。

　　當他的腳正跨過門檻時，那位怪異的老人站了起來，伸出細長乾枯、鳥爪般的手，抓住翰拉漢的手，說道：「博學之士、偉大的作曲家翰拉漢啊，你不該在薩溫節夜離開這樣的聚會，留下來，跟我玩一把吧！這一副老舊的紙牌，經歷過無數的夜晚，雖然很老舊了，但是有那麼多的世間財富，因它一夕而失、一夕而得。」

　　一位年輕人說道：「世間的財富，倒是沒怎麼為你停留啊，老頭子。」他說完，打量了一下老人的一雙赤腳，眾人哄堂大笑。不過，翰拉漢並沒有笑，反而是很快地坐了下來，未發一語。

　　有人說道：「翰拉漢啊，你終究還是會留下來陪我們。」

　　老人說：「他當然會留下來，你們沒聽到我要他留下來嗎？」

　　大家都盯著老人看，似乎在納悶著他是何方神聖。

　　「我從很遠的地方來。」老人說：「我穿越法蘭西，橫跨西班牙，沿著格恩湖的隱密湖口來到這裡，這一路上還沒有人拒絕過我。」

之後，他一陣沉默，人們也不再質疑他。接著，大家就玩起牌來。

有六個男人在木板搭起的桌上玩牌，其他人在後方圍觀著。他們玩了兩、三輪，並沒有下賭注。這時，老人從口袋裡拿出一枚磨得又薄又光滑的四便士，慫恿其他人也拿一點出來下賭注。

於是每個人都在牌桌上押了賭注，雖然賭注不多，但是這樣移來推去，感覺就堆了很多。一開始，有人贏了，接著，輪到他旁邊的那個人贏。每當有人的手氣差到輸得一毛不剩時，就會有人借他一點錢，然後他就能夠贏錢來還錢。手氣不管是好是壞，都不會在誰的身上停留太久。

每當翰拉漢如夢囈般地呢喃著：「我該上路了。」就會拿到一張好牌，他一把牌打出來，所有的錢就會跑到他這裡來；然而，每當他想起瑪莉·拉維，嘆了口氣，那一刻好運就會溜走，接著他又會把她給忘了。

最後，好運來到老人這邊停住了，所有的錢都流向他，他開始自顧自地輕輕發笑，逕自地反覆唱著歌：「黑桃和方塊，勇氣與力量」，把諸如此類的話當成歌詞來唱。

一陣子之後，這群人的身子搖來晃去，眼睛死盯老人的手，任誰看了都會覺得他們喝醉了，或是他們把全部的家當都拿來玩牌了。但事實並非如此，玩牌到現在，夸脫罐都還沒有人碰過，裡頭的酒幾乎還是滿的，而全部的賭金也不過是幾個六便士硬幣和先令，銅幣抓起來大概也只有一把那麼多而已。

老人說：「是輸是贏，都好，因為牌戲就在你們的心中。」

他開始洗牌，動作飛快，最後快到看不出來是紙牌，反倒像是在空中做出一個個火環，就像小夥子拿著火棒旋轉那樣。這一刻，整個空間彷彿陷入一片漆黑，除了老人的雙手和紙牌，什麼都看不見。

忽然，有一隻野兔[4]從他的手中跳出來，沒人知道兔子到底是從紙牌變成的，還是憑空從他的手掌中出現的。野兔以最快的速度，在穀倉地板上飛快地奔跑。

有些人盯著野兔看，但有更多人盯著老人瞧。在他們目不轉睛地盯著老人之際，就像剛剛跳出來一隻野兔那樣，老人的雙手中又跳出來一隻獵犬，而且一隻接著一隻跳出來，最後只見一大群獵犬追著野兔，繞著穀倉跑。

這時，玩牌的人都站了起來，用背部抵著牌桌，閃避著獵犬。獵犬的吠叫聲震耳欲聾，牠們使勁地追趕，但是就是追不上野兔。最後，穀倉大門像是被一陣狂風給吹開，野兔猛地一跳，躍過牌桌，衝出大門，奔進了夜色之中。獵犬也跟著跳過牌桌，穿過門追了出去。

4 據說女巫會化身為野兔。

老人大叫：「快跟著獵犬出去！快跟著獵犬出去！今晚打獵就會大豐收！」便跟著追出去。

雖然他們有捕獵野兔的習慣，而且對任何娛樂隨時都躍躍欲試，可是卻不敢在黑夜裡闖出去。這時，只有翰拉漢站起身來，說道：「讓我來追！讓我來追！」

「你最好待在這裡，翰拉漢！以免遭遇危險。」離他最近的年輕人說。

但是翰拉漢說：「我會親眼看到一場公平的競賽！我會親眼看到一場公平的競賽！」然後像個夢遊的人，搖搖晃晃地走了出去，他身後的門隨之關上。

翰拉漢以為老人走在他的前方，但那只是滿月將他自己的身影投射在前方的路上罷了。他聽到遼闊的格納原野那邊，傳來獵犬追捕野兔的嗥叫聲，於是他快步跟上前去，什麼都阻擋不了他。一會兒後，他來到一片稍小的原野，那裡圍著一道由鬆散石頭堆起來的矮牆。他移開幾塊石頭，越過矮牆，也沒停下來把石頭再放回去。他越過有地下暗河流經貝里里的那邊，聽到前方的獵犬正朝著河流的源頭奔去。

很快地，他發現自己愈跑愈吃力，原來他正往山上跑去。雲朵遮住了月亮，他看不清楚前方的路。有一次，他抄了捷徑，雙腳卻滑入了沼穴，只得再返回路上。

他不知自己走了多遠，也不知走了哪些路。最後來到光禿禿的山上，周圍除了亂糟糟的石南花，什麼也沒有，也聽不到獵犬的叫聲或其他任何聲音。

就在這時，他又聽見獵犬的嗥叫聲。聲音一開始從遠處傳來，但又突然變得很近，就在聲音接近時，又突然升至他的頭頂旋繞著，然後朝北方飄去，最後再也聽不見任何聲響。

　　「這不公平，不公平！」他說。

　　他再也沒力氣行走了，走了這麼遠的路，筋疲力竭了。他就地坐在石南花叢旁，那裡是葉格山脈的中央地區一帶。

　　過了一會兒，他注意到旁邊有扇門離他很近，門後透出亮光，他納悶自己怎麼沒有注意到旁邊這扇門。他雖然很疲憊，還是站起身來，走進門裡。此時門外雖正值深夜，門裡頭卻是白晝。很快地，他看到一位老人正在摘採夏日百里香和黃色鳶尾花，夏日所有芬芳彷彿都瀰漫在花間。

　　老人說：「博學之士、偉大的作曲家翰拉漢，你花了好一陣子才來到這裡。」

　　隨後，老人帶領翰拉漢走進一間金碧輝煌的大房子。翰拉漢耳聞過的豪華擺設、眼見過的各種繽紛色彩，房子裡都有。屋子盡頭有一高處，有位女子正坐在上面的高椅子上，她有著絕世美貌，花朵環繞著她細長蒼白的臉龐，臉上卻流露出等候多時的疲倦神情。

　　她椅子下方的階梯上坐著四位白髮老婦。其中一位腿上抱著大鍋；另一位膝上擺了塊大石頭，沉甸甸的石頭對她而言，似乎很輕；還有一位老婦，手中握著一根很長的木製尖頭長矛；最後那位老婦抓著一把沒有劍鞘的寶劍 5。

翰拉漢注視她們良久，但是沒有人招呼他或是瞥上一眼。他決定要問椅子上那位貴如皇后的女子是誰，還有她是在等待什麼。他誰也不怕，也準備好要開口發問，然而，在這麼富麗堂皇之處，面對這麼美麗的女子，他退縮了。他也想問問，四位白髮老婦抱著像是稀世珍寶的那些東西是什麼，但是他想不出來要怎麼問。

　　這時，第一位老婦站了起來，兩手提著大鍋，說道：「喜悅。」翰拉漢沒有說話；接著，第二位老婦站起來，雙手抱著巨石，說道：「力量。」再來是第三位老婦，她站起身，手上握著長矛，說道：「勇氣。」最後一位老婦也站了起來，雙手抓著寶劍，說道：「知識。」

　　她說完之後，彷彿大家都在等著翰拉漢提問，但是翰拉漢靜默不語。

　　最後，四位老婦各自帶著四件寶物，走出大門。就在要走出門時，一位老婦說：「他對我們沒有任何期待。」另一位說：「他很懦弱，很懦弱。」第三位說：「他害怕了。」最後一位說：「他失去理智了。」

　　她們一齊喊道：「銀手⁶之女葉格，只能繼續在夢中沉睡了。真可惜，真是可惜！」

5　愛爾蘭傳說中的神族的四個護身法寶，為大鍋、巨石、長矛和寶劍。故事中對四位老婦的描述，與塔羅牌中四個牌組的皇后圖示相同，分別為聖杯皇后、錢幣皇后、權杖皇后、寶劍皇后。

6　銀手（Silver Hand），國王 Nuada 在戰役中失去了一隻手，因此被稱為銀手 Nuada（Nuada of the Silver Hand）。

那位貴如皇后的女子，悲傷地嘆了口氣，嘆息聲聽在翰拉漢的耳裡，就像是伏流流過的聲音。他身處的這個地方，要是再華麗、輝煌個十倍，他大概就抵擋不住睡意的來襲了。這時，他像個醉漢般，腳步踉蹌，當場倒了下來。

　　翰拉漢醒來時，太陽正照耀著臉龐，身旁的草地覆上了白霜。他躺在結了冰的河沿，這條河潺潺流過岱科和朱達羅。從小丘的輪廓，還有遠處閃閃發亮的格恩河，他認出了自己正躺在葉格山脈的一座小山上，但他不曉得自己怎麼會到這裡來。穀倉裡發生的事情，已離他遠去；這趟旅程下來，只留下痠痛的雙腳和僵硬的身子。

　　一年後，在卡帕塔村路邊的一間屋子裡，人們正圍坐在火爐旁。這時，瘦骨嶙峋的紅髮翰拉漢，頂著一頭雜亂長髮，來到雙扇活動門旁 7，請求讓他進門休息。人們讓他進了門，因為那天是薩溫節夜。

　　他跟大家坐在一起，他們從夸脫酒瓶中倒了一杯威士忌，遞給他。他們看見翰拉漢的頸子上掛著小墨水罐，知道他是個讀書人，就要他講講希臘人的故事。

　　他從外套的大口袋裡掏出維吉爾的書，封面骯髒不堪，也因為潮濕，脹得鼓鼓的，他翻開書，內頁也泛黃了，但這些倒不打緊，因為翰拉漢看書的樣子，就像個文盲一樣。那裡有幾個年輕人嘲笑起他，問他又不識字，何必帶著一本這麼厚重的書。

　　這些話惹怒了翰拉漢，他把維吉爾的書放回口袋，問

他們身上是否有紙牌，至少紙牌比書本還受人歡迎。

　　他們掏出紙牌，他拿來開始洗牌。這時突然心底浮現了什麼事，他用雙手蒙住臉，努力回想。他問道：「我以前來過這裡嗎？還是我在哪裡也度過這樣的夜晚？」他突然站了起來，紙牌掉了一地。「是誰帶給我瑪莉‧拉維的消息？」他問。

　　「我們沒見過你，也沒聽過瑪莉‧拉維這個人，她是誰？你到底在說什麼？」主人說。

　　「一年前，同樣是在薩溫節夜，我在一間穀倉裡，人們正玩著紙牌，桌上押著錢幣，錢幣從這邊推給那個人，一下子又從那邊推給另一個人──然後我得到口信，動身要去見我的情人瑪莉‧拉維，她要我去找她。」翰拉漢這時大吼道：「我在那之後去了哪裡？這整整一年間，我又在哪裡？」[8]

　　「很難說你那段時間可能去了哪裡，或是遊歷了世間的哪些地方。」年紀最大的男人說：「應該可以確定的是，你的雙腳積了許多路上的塵沙。一旦被精靈觸摸了，許多人就跟你一樣，四處漂泊，遺忘了過去。」[9]

7　門做成上下兩扇，兩扇可以獨立開闔的活動門，英文為 half-door。
8　去到仙境所度過的時光，通常等於人間的一年。
9　精靈的觸摸會導致傷口、癱瘓甚至死亡。

「的確如此。就我知道的，有位女人像那樣遊蕩了七年，後來回來了還跟友人說，她從前常常很慶幸可以吃到豬槽裡的食物。你現在最好快去神父那裡，讓他為你卸下心中的重擔。」另一個人說道。

「我要去找我的情人瑪莉・拉維。我耽擱了太久了，要怎樣才能知道她這一年來經歷了哪些事？」翰拉漢說。

他準備走出門，但大夥勸他今天最好留宿一晚，才有體力上路，而這也正是他所需要的，他已經虛弱不堪了。人們遞給他食物時，他一副好像沒見過食物的樣子，有人還說：「他吃東西的樣子，就像是踩到了飢餓之草。」[10]

在隔日的晨光中，他動身出發，因為要到瑪莉家，可能還需要不少時間。

到了瑪莉家，看到大門已經壞了，茅草屋頂傾頹倒塌，裡頭不見半個人影。他跟鄰居打聽她的事，他們只知道她被趕出了屋子，後來嫁給了一位工人。他們一起去了倫敦或利物浦之類的大城市找工作。翰拉漢不知道她去到的地方是好是壞，他再也沒見過她，她就此杳無音訊。

---

10 在愛爾蘭傳說中，享用露天餐點時，如果沒有將碎屑丟給精靈，那裡就會長出一種稱為「飢餓之草」（hungry grass）的植物。任何人只要踩入飢餓之草，就會陷入虛弱的狀態；如果沒有及時得到照護，便會死去。

2. 編繩

　　某天日暮時分，翰拉漢行走在金瓦拉附近的道路上，聽見路旁不遠處的一間屋子裡，傳出小提琴樂音。他循著聲音的方向，轉入通往屋子的小路。只要是有音樂、舞蹈或是好夥伴的地方，他都不會錯過。

　　屋子的主人正站在門口，等翰拉漢一走近，主人認出了他。他說：「翰拉漢，誠摯歡迎你的到來，好久沒有聽到你的消息了。」

　　然而，女主人卻走到門口來，對丈夫說道：「翰拉漢今晚要是不進門來，我會很高興的。他現在在神父的口中惡名昭彰，在潔身自愛的女子眼裡，也是聲名狼藉。況且，看他走路的樣子，就知道他剛喝了酒。」

　　屋主說：「我永遠都不會在家門口把詩人翰拉漢攆走。」便請他進到屋子裡。

屋子裡聚集了許多鄰居，有一些人還記得翰拉漢，但是那些坐在角落的小伙子，只對他略有耳聞。他們站起來，一睹他的風采。一個小伙子說道：「他不就是那位私塾先生翰拉漢，被『他們』¹給帶走的那個人嗎？」

　　但小伙子的母親用手摀住他的嘴，命令他安靜下來，不許他提那些事。她說：「翰拉漢要是聽到有人談到那件事，或是有誰向他問起那件事，他會變得很討人厭。」

　　有幾個人開始起鬨，要他唱首歌。但屋主說，先讓他稍事休息後，才能請他唱歌，便遞給他一杯威士忌，翰拉漢道過謝，祝他身體健康，把酒給乾了。

　　小提琴手正為下一首舞曲調音，屋主對年輕小伙子們說，等看過翰拉漢的舞藝，就會知道什麼才是真正的舞蹈。翰拉漢上次在那裡跳過舞之後，人們就無緣再見到那樣的舞蹈了。

　　但是，翰拉漢說他不準備跳舞，他的兩隻腳現在應該用在更重要的事情上，去遍遊愛爾蘭的五個省分。

　　他話才說完，屋主的女兒歐娜推開雙扇的活動門，走了進來。她抱著幾塊從康內馬拉泥煤田採來的松木，準備升火。她將木頭丟進壁爐裡，燃起的火光，映照出她迷人的模樣和笑顏。有兩、三位年輕男士站起身來，邀請歐娜跳舞，但翰拉漢穿越過地板，將他們推開。他說，他歷經了長途跋涉，才得以見到歐娜，歐娜一定要跟他跳一曲。

---

1 在這裡，「他們」是精靈的委婉說法。

歐娜沒有表示拒絕，站到了他身旁，臉頰泛起了紅暈，大概是翰拉漢在她耳邊說了什麼動聽的話。

　　有幾對舞伴站了起來，就在要跳舞之時，翰拉漢偶然一個低頭，瞥見到自己磨損綻裂的靴子，破爛的灰襪還露了出來，就氣惱地抱怨舞池差、音樂又不入流，然後一屁股在壁爐旁的暗處坐了下來。歐娜看見他坐在那裡，也跟著坐在他身旁。

　　大家繼續跳舞，一首舞曲才結束，下一首又旋即開始。有好一陣子，大家都不太留意角落裡的歐娜和翰拉漢倆，但是歐娜的母親不安了起來，就叫歐娜去裡面幫忙張羅餐桌。歐娜從不曾違抗母親的吩咐，說自己一會兒就過去，但不是現在，因為她只顧聽著翰拉漢在她耳邊的綿綿絮語。

　　母親越來越感到不安，便走到他們身旁，假裝在撥弄火堆和打掃壁爐，想聽一下這位詩人對她的孩子說了些什麼。這時，她聽到他在講狄兒瑞公主的故事，說著她如何殺死烏許納荷之子，而她臉頰上的紅暈，比不上各國王子為她所流的鮮血那樣的鮮紅，讓她始終難以走出悲傷。他還說，或許就是她的這些記憶，使得沼澤地裡的鴿鳥啼哭聲，在詩人的耳裡聽來，就像年輕人在為同袍之死慟哭一樣。翰拉漢說，詩人如果沒有將她的美麗寫入歌曲，就沒有人會記得她。

他接下來所說的，歐娜不太聽得懂，只是聽起來好像是一段沒有押韻的詩歌。她聽到他說：

「太陽和月亮，是男人和女人，是我們生命的泉源。上帝為他們創造了彼此，他們同在一穹蒼下，永不停歇地在空中穿梭運行。在世界未始之前，祂就創造了你我的生命，祂也創造日月，使其升起落下、穿越整個世界，就像兩名優異的舞者，在長長的穀倉地板上，來回地舞動著。當其他人都累得倚著牆壁休息、喘氣，他們仍然精力充沛，神情愉悅。」

老婦人去牌桌找丈夫，但是丈夫正在玩牌，無暇理會她，於是她去問鄰婦：「難道真的沒有方法可以將他們分開嗎？」不等對方回答，又對幾個正在聊天的年輕小伙子說：「要你們邀屋子裡最好的女孩共舞，連這個都做不到，你們還有什麼用？現在全部給我過去，看看能不能讓她擺脫那位詩人的一派胡言。」

但是歐娜誰的話也不肯聽，她揮揮手，作勢要趕他們走。

他們轉而向翰拉漢喊道，他要是不跟歐娜跳舞，就把機會讓給其他人。

翰拉漢聽了，回答道：「我當然會跟她跳，這屋子裡只有我可以跟她跳舞。」

他和歐娜一同站起身來。他牽著她的手，走出角落，

有些小伙子被惹惱，有些嘲笑他襤褸的外套和一雙破靴子，但他完全不放在心上，歐娜也不在意。他們彼此互望，彷彿整個世界只屬於兩人。另一對坐在那裡仿若情侶的兩人，也同時間站上舞池，緊握彼此雙手，和著音樂，緩緩起舞。

這時翰拉漢轉身背對著他們，狀似生氣了。他舞不跳了，卻唱起了歌，並握著她的雙手，歌聲越發嘹亮。小伙子不再嘲笑他，小提琴也停下了演奏，那一刻只聽得見他的歌聲，和著風聲。他唱的歌，是他在葉格山流浪時，所聽到或是所作的曲子，歌詞在英文裡的意思是這樣的：

噢，死神那瘦削的手指，
永遠無法尋獲我們的蹤跡，
在空曠的高地教區，
愛情是給予和分享；
樹稍掛著果實和花朵，
一年四季始終如此；
河水溢滿出來，
挾帶著紅色、棕色啤酒。
一位老人吹奏著風笛，
笛木閃耀著金銀光彩；
女王們的眸子藍如冰，
在人群中翩翩起舞。

翰拉漢唱著這首歌，歐娜靠得他更近了，她的臉頰失去血色，目光不復湛藍，黯然盈滿著淚水，任誰看到她這番模樣，都知道她此時此刻已準備好要跟隨翰拉漢，去到世界各處。

　　這時，一個小伙子大聲說道：「他歌曲中說的國度，是在哪裡？歐娜，你得好好照顧自己，那裡很遙遠，要一番跋涉才能到達。」

　　又有人說：「你要是跟他去，你去的地方不會是青春的國度，而是沼澤遍佈的瑪佑郡。」

　　歐娜看了看他，好像想開口問些什麼，但是翰拉漢拉起她的手，半高歌、半喊道：「那裡近在咫尺，又無所不在，可能就在寸草不生的山丘後方，也可能就在森林深處。」他大聲而清晰地說：「在森林的深處，噢，在森林的深處，死神永遠找不到我們。你願意跟我一道前往嗎，歐娜？」他問。

　　在他說話之際，兩名老婦走到門外，歐娜的母親哭著說：「他在歐娜身上施了法術，我們能叫那些男人來把他攆出屋子嗎？」

　　婦人回答：「萬萬不可，他是蓋爾族的詩人，你明白，要是把蓋爾族詩人攆出門外，他就會施咒語，讓你田裡的穀物枯萎、母牛的乳汁枯竭，咒語會持續七年之久。」

　　「上天救救我們吧，我到底為什麼會讓這麼聲名狼藉的人進到屋子裡！」母親說。

　　「要是不讓他進門，就會沒事。但是現在，你要是硬

把他趕出去，就會有災厄降臨。你聽聽我的主意，我會讓他自己離開，不需要任何人去把他趕走。」

不久，兩位婦人又走進屋子，圍裙上各自攢著一綑稻草。翰拉漢不再唱歌，而是用急切而輕柔的語調，對著歐娜說：「屋子這麼狹隘，世界這麼寬廣，真心相愛的人，用不著害怕夜晚和清晨、太陽和星辰、夜裡的幽靈，或是塵世諸事。」

母親拍了一下翰拉漢的肩膀，說道：「翰拉漢，你能幫我一下嗎？」

「翰拉漢，來。」鄰婦說：「幫我們把這些乾草捲成繩子吧，你的雙手看起來很靈巧。乾草堆的稻草頂蓋，被一陣大風給吹散了。」[2]

「我來幫你們吧！」翰拉漢說。他接過小樹枝，母親遞給他稻草，他將稻草纏繞在小樹枝上，動作急促，想趕快做完好脫手。

婦女倆繼續對他說話、遞給他稻草、鼓勵他，誇讚他真是編繩高手，技藝比這一帶的人都要好，甚至比她們所認識的誰都還要好。

翰拉漢看到歐娜正望著他，便昂起頭，飛快地扭著繩子，誇耀自己的雙手多麼靈巧、學識多麼豐富、雙臂多麼強壯有力。他一邊吹噓，一邊往後退，手中不停搓著繩子，

2　在愛爾蘭鄉間，稻草製的繩子是日常必需品，可用來製作栓繩、覆蓋屋頂和製成椅子。

退到身後敞開的屋門，也沒多想，就跨出門檻，來到路上。這時，母親急忙衝向前，將繩子往外丟，然後關起大門和內門，插上門閂。

　　終於把他掃地出門了，她開懷大笑，鄰居們也笑著稱讚她。然而，他們聽見翰拉漢在外頭拍打著門，還口出穢言。歐娜的手已經放在門栓上，準備要開門，母親連忙阻止她。母親向小提琴手打手勢，他開始拉起輕快的雙人舞曲，有個年輕人也沒有問過歐娜，就把她拉進舞池。跳完舞後，小提琴手放下琴弓，這時門外靜悄悄的，路上一如往常的寂靜。

　　當翰拉漢意識到自己被關在門外，失去了那晚的歇腳處、美酒，還有聽他訴衷情的女孩，他的怒氣和勇氣頓時消失，只好朝著海浪不停拍打的海濱處走去。

　　他坐在大石頭上，開始晃著右臂，悠悠地對自己唱起歌。每逢遇到挫折他就會這樣唱著歌鼓舞自己。這歌是他那時還是什麼時候做的，如今被稱為《編繩》歌，開頭唱道：「是哪隻死貓，帶我來到這裡。」

　　唱了一會兒，霧靄與幽靈向他聚攏而來，時而浮現海面，時而盤旋海上。當中有個幽靈彷彿是那葉格山沉睡的女王，但此刻她不再沉睡了，只嘲弄著他，對著身後幽靈說：「他太懦弱了，太懦弱了，根本沒有膽量。」

　　他感覺到繩股仍在手中，於是他繼續扭編著。他一邊編著，一邊覺得自己把世上所有的悲傷，都編進繩子裡了。

在睡夢中，他感覺繩子好像變成一隻大水怪，從海裡浮現出來，逕自纏繞著，愈來越緊地纏繞著他。水怪越來越巨大，整個天地都被捲入其中，星辰成了水怪脊背上閃耀的光芒。

後來，他從中掙脫開來，步履蹣跚地沿著海岸走著，幽靈灰色的形影在他的四周飄竄，這麼說著：「很遺憾的，他拒絕了精靈之女的召喚，他此生都無法在世間女子的愛情裡尋得慰藉。他的心底，將永駐著墓穴般的荒涼。是他自己選擇了死亡，讓他死吧，讓他死吧，讓他死吧！」

3.翰拉漢和胡勒漢之女凱瑟琳

有一回，翰拉漢朝著北方旅行。遇到農忙時節，他偶爾會幫農夫幹點活；遇到守靈夜或婚禮時也會跟人們講自己的經歷，或是獻上歌聲。

一日，在通往喀魯尼的路上，他碰巧遇見瑪格麗特・魯尼，他年輕時在芒斯特就認識她了。當時，她因為名聲不好，神父命令她離開。

翰拉漢從她走路姿態、眼睛顏色，還有她用左手將頭髮撥至耳後的樣子，認出了瑪格麗特・魯尼。她一直都在這一帶漂泊，販賣鯡魚等漁貨。這時她正要返回斯萊戈

郡，她和一位叫瑪莉‧吉爾斯的婦女，一起住在柏勒，兩人有著相似的過往。

瑪格麗特‧魯尼說，翰拉漢要是能夠去她們家住一住，並為柏勒的瘸子、盲人、遊民獻唱，她會很開心。她說，自己很清楚地記得他，並給了他祝福。瑪莉‧吉爾斯還記得他的幾首歌，所以翰拉漢不用擔心她們會款待不周。聽過翰拉漢這號人物的瘸子和窮人，當翰拉漢來陪他們，跟他們說故事、唱歌，會給他一點酬勞，而他的名聲也會傳遍愛爾蘭所有的教區。

他很高興能跟她一道走，有女子願意傾聽他的苦難經歷，為他帶來慰藉。

日暮時分，來來往往的每個男女，個個都長得很俊俏美麗。當他告訴她編繩那件倒楣事時，瑪格麗特‧魯尼環抱著他，在昏暗的天色中，她看起來和其他來往的人一樣美麗。

往柏勒的一路上，他們聊個不停。當瑪莉‧吉爾斯見到他，得知他就是翰拉漢，想到能有這麼一位聲名遠播的人來到家中作客，激動得差點哭了出來。

翰拉漢很開心能夠在她們這裡小住，因為他已厭倦了漂泊的生活。當他看到瑪莉‧拉維的小屋子早已坍塌頹倒，她人也已經不知去向，只見散落一地的屋頂茅草，這一天起，他就成了居無定所的人。他未曾在何處久留過，未曾在枯葉凋零之處又見綠葉抽芽，也不曾在初播種的土地上見到小麥收成。像現在這樣，能有個地方避雨，夜晚

能有爐火，毋需請求，桌上就擺著一份他的食物，這何嘗不好。

他待在這裡的期間，受到悉心的照顧，生活平靜閒適，寫下了很多歌謠。歌謠大都是情歌，但也有一些在講悔恨，有一些談到愛爾蘭和它所經歷的種種苦難。

每晚，瘸子、盲人、遊民聚集在屋子裡，聆聽翰拉漢的歌謠和詩句，還有他編講的古代勇士芬尼亞的故事。這些故事留存在他們的記憶裡，未曾受過書籍的汙染。就這樣，他們將翰拉漢的名字帶到康諾省裡的每個守靈夜、婚禮等儀式之中。當時的翰拉漢未曾如此富足，受到這麼多的愛戴。

十二月的一個夜晚，他唱著一首從山中的綠千鳥那裡聽來的歌，歌詞中的金髮少年們離開利默里克，在世界各處流浪，迷失了方向。

當晚，屋子裡有很多人，兩、三位小男孩也溜了進來，坐在爐火邊的地板上，忙著烤爐子裡的馬鈴薯，或是諸如此類的事，沒有注意到翰拉漢。許久之後，當翰拉漢的名字被提起，他們記起了他的聲音、他揮手的方式、他坐在床沿上的神情，那時他的身影落在身後的灰白牆上，當他移身站起來，都跟茅草屋頂一樣高了。

此刻，他們意識到這個他們所仰望的人，正是蓋爾族的詩王，是人類夢想的創造者。

他突然停止歌唱，眼神憂悒，彷彿望著遠方某處。

瑪莉‧吉爾斯站在他身邊的桌子旁，正在將威士忌酒倒進杯子裡，她停下來問道：「你正想要離開我們嗎？」

瑪格麗特‧魯尼聽到這句話，不明白她怎麼會這麼說。她太在意這句話，便走到翰拉漢身邊，她很憂心，怕會失去這麼出色的詩人，而且又是這麼好的夥伴。他受人們敬重，為她的屋子裡帶來這麼多的東西。

「親愛的，你不會離開我們吧？」她抓著他的手問道。

他回答：「我不是在想這件事，而是想到愛爾蘭及其所肩負的苦痛。」

他用手抵著頭，唱起了歌，歌聲猶如孤寂之地的風聲。

在高高的庫門海岸上，從左方
　　襲來一陣刺骨的黑風，
棕色的荊棘老樹，裂為兩半；
我們的勇氣，就像黑風中的
　　老樹，破滅死去，
但是我們的內心深處，
藏著胡勒漢之女凱瑟琳眼中
　　噴射的火光。

狂風襲捲納內瑞山高空的白雲，
擲下雷電，劈打岩石，道出美依芙女王[1]所能說的。
憤怒就像轟轟的黑雲，逼促我們的心怦怦跳動，
但我們卻低低彎下腰，
親吻胡勒漢之女凱瑟琳靜靜擺著的雙足。

黃濁的池水，淹沒克魯納貝爾高地，
凝滯的空氣中，吹來潮濕的風；
我們的身體和血液，就像氾濫的洪水，
但胡勒漢之女凱瑟琳，
卻比神聖十字架前的長蠟燭更加純潔。

　　他唱著歌，聲音嘶啞，臉上流下了淚水。瑪格麗特・魯尼將臉埋入手中，和他一起哭泣。火爐邊的一個盲眼乞丐的破爛衣服，也因為啜泣而顫抖。最後，整屋子的人都哭了，流下了眼淚。

1　美依芙女王（Maeve）為愛爾蘭傳說中的女神。

4. 紅髮翰拉漢的詛咒

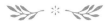

　　一個晴朗的五月早晨，翰拉漢已經離開瑪格麗特·魯尼的住處好一陣子，走在科盧尼一帶的路上，長滿白花的樹叢中，傳來鳥兒的啼唱聲，翰拉漢走著走著也不禁唱起了歌。他正要走回自己小小的住處，雖然那不過是一間簡陋的小屋，但他已心滿意足。

　　畢竟，他也厭倦了這麼多年來的漂泊，終年不停地從一處輾轉漂蕩至他處，即使人們大多會請他進門，享用食物。有時候，他覺得他的腦袋就跟關節一樣，越來越

僵硬。要通宵達旦地狂歡作樂，講有趣的話來逗男孩子們笑，用詩歌來哄女人，對他來說不是那麼容易了。

前一陣子，他住進了一位窮人出門收割莊稼不回而留下來的屋子。翰拉漢修葺了茅草屋頂，用幾個麻袋和木叢枝做了張床，擺在屋子的角落裡，還打掃了地板。能有個自己的小地方，他感到心滿意足，他可以隨意地進出。當憂愁或是年老所致的孤寂感襲來，他也可以將頭枕在手上，度過漫漫長夜。

鄰居一個個送自己的小孩來跟著翰拉漢學習，他們帶來雞蛋、燕麥蛋糕、泥炭，翰拉漢便靠這些維生。偶爾，他去柏勒狂歡個一天一夜，鄰居也不會有閒話，因為他們知道翰拉漢是個詩人，有個四處漂泊的靈魂。

五月的那天早晨，他正從柏勒返回，心情愉悅，哼著腦中浮現的曲調。沒多久，一隻野兔從他眼前橫越過去，穿過鬆落的石牆，跑進了田野裡。他知道，看到野兔從前方路上橫越而過，不是什麼好兆頭。他想起了那隻野兔，把他帶到了葉格山，那時瑪莉·拉維正在等著他。從此，他的內心不曾一刻感到滿足。

「這下子，他們大概又要讓我大禍臨頭了。」他說。

他話才一說完，就聽見一旁的田野傳來哭泣的聲音。他往牆的另一邊望去，看到白色山楂花的樹叢下，坐著一個正在哭泣的少女，傷心欲絕。她把臉埋在手裡，柔軟的秀髮、潔白的頸項、青春的模樣，讓翰拉漢想起了布姬·柏賽、瑪格麗特·吉連、瑪芙·康內藍、歐娜·柯里、瑟

莉亞‧杜斯寇，還有其他的女孩們，他為她們寫過歌，用甜言蜜語贏得過她們的芳心。

她抬起頭看了看，翰拉漢認出來她是附近農夫的女兒。

「諾拉，發生了什麼事？」他問道。

「你是幫不上忙的，紅髮翰拉漢。」

「只要你心中有一絲絲哀愁，我都會隨侍在候。」他說：「我通曉希臘人的歷史，深知悲傷和分離是何物，也很清楚世間的苦難。我自己要是無法將你從煩惱中拯救出來，那麼就讓我的詩歌來拯救你，我曾用詩歌裡的魔力，讓許多人得到解脫。自世界初始至今，詩人的詩歌就蘊含力量。我自己也會在塵世之外的某個遠方，和其他的詩人坐在一起交談，直到生命與時間的盡頭。」

女孩不再哭泣，她說：「歐文‧翰拉漢，我常聽人說，你在葉格山的時候，拒絕去愛那位貴如皇后的女子，從此以後，她就不曾讓你的內心平靜過。你經歷了傷痛和放逐，你了解世間的一切苦難。如果世間的人傷害了你，你也知道如何報復。歐文‧翰拉漢，如果我現在要你做什麼，你就會去做嗎？」

「我會去做。」翰拉漢回答。

她說：「我的父母和兄弟打算把我嫁給老皮迪‧多烏，因為他在山下擁有上百畝的農地。翰拉漢，你所能為我做的事，就是將他寫入詩歌中，就像你年輕時候將彼得‧奇馬汀寫入詩歌那樣。這麼一來，悲傷將日日夜夜籠罩著

他，他會一直想著喀魯尼墓地，就不會去想結婚的事了。請你務必儘快，因為婚禮即將在明日舉行。如果明天太陽升起來，我就得嫁給他，那我寧可選擇死去。」

「我會將他寫入詩歌，帶給他恥辱與悲傷。請告訴我他的年紀，我會在歌詞中寫上他的歲數。」

「噢，他年紀很大了，跟你一樣年邁，紅髮翰拉漢。」

「年紀跟我一樣！」翰拉漢說道，聲音彷彿岔開了，「跟我一樣大，我和你差了二十多歲！一位臉頰上綻放五月花朵光澤的少女，竟然認為翰拉漢是個老人，這對歐文翰拉漢來說，真是悲慘的一天。我太難過了！」他說：「你刺傷了我的心。」

他轉身離開她，繼續走在路上，來到一塊石頭邊坐了下來。一時之間，歲月的重量彷彿壓在了他的身上。他想起來，就在幾天前，有戶人家的婦女對他說：「你現在不是紅髮翰拉漢，而是黃髮翰拉漢了。你頭髮的顏色，就像是一綹拖繩。」

還有一次，他向婦女要東西喝，她沒給鮮奶，卻給了酸奶。有的時候，當他在朗誦詩歌或發表談話時，底下的女孩們也會和無知的男子們竊竊私語，或開心地胡鬧。

他又想到，他清晨起床時僵硬的關節，以及旅行後疼痛的膝蓋，覺得自己已經垂垂老矣。雙肩感到寒氣，腿上佈滿斑點，呼吸會喘，體衰氣弱。這些念頭一出來，他不禁對年老與年老之後的狀態心生憤怒。

就在這時候，他抬頭一看，有一隻花鷸正徐緩地朝

貝里貝飛去，他大喊道：「你也一樣呀，貝里貝的花鵰，你也老了，你的翅膀都是裂痕，我會把你和你的古老夥伴——達甘湖的梭魚，還有生長於『外來者陡坡』山崖上的紫杉樹[1]，一起寫入我的詩歌，永遠詛咒你們[2]。」

他左方的灌木叢就如其他灌木叢般盛開著花朵，一陣風將白色的花朵，吹落在他的外套上。

「五月的花朵」，他說著，一邊將花朵聚攏在掌心，「你永遠無法了解歲月是怎麼一回事，因為你在美麗綻放的時刻死去，我也會將你寫入詩歌，獻上我的祝福。」

他站了起來，從樹叢扯下一根小樹枝，拿在手中。那天回家的路途上，他肩背佝僂，神情陰鬱，顯得衰老不堪。

當他回到小屋時，屋子裡沒有人。他在床上躺了一會兒，每當他想作詩、讚頌或是詛咒時，他就會這樣。這一次，他很快就開始作起詩來，因為寫詛咒的吟遊詩人所擁有的力量灌注在他身上。作品完成後，他思索著如何讓這首詩傳遍整個鄉間。

有幾位學生走進屋子，想知道今天是否有排課。翰拉漢起身，坐在火爐旁的長椅上，學生圍繞著他站立著。

---

1 老鷹、梭魚和紫杉，皆代表長壽和年老。「外來者陡坡」（Steep Place of the Strangers）是地名，指 Cope's Mountain 北方的峭壁。
2 據說愛爾蘭吟遊詩人能夠透過寫詩，來讓敵人生病或死亡。

他們以為翰拉漢會拿出維吉爾的書、彌撒守則[3]或是識字讀本，然而，他舉起手中的山楂樹枝，說道:「孩子們，這是我今天為你們準備的新課文。」

　　「你們和世間美麗的人們，就像這朵花一樣，而歲月就是風，將花朵吹落。我作了一首詩來詛咒年邁和老人，我現在就要教你們，仔細聽好！」以下是他所說的:

詩人翰拉漢，在五月的灌木叢下，
詛咒他自己的腦袋，因為它已衰老花白;
接著，他詛咒貝里貝山上的花鵰，
因為牠最早知悉了苦惱與疾病;
他也詛咒那臨著『外來者陡坡』和埡口、
未曾吐出綠芽的紫杉樹;
他又詛咒在達甘城堡湖底沉思的大灰梭魚，
要牠的長長身軀滿是魚鉤和疼痛;
再來，為了新娘的幸福，詛咒落在老皮迪‧布恩身上，
因為他已經頂上無毛，內心渾噩。
他也詛咒皮迪的鄰居彼得‧哈特和友人麥可‧吉爾，
因為他們飄泊的故事永無結束的一刻。

接著是老西莫斯‧庫里南，綠色曠野的牧羊人，
因為他變形的雙手，抓著兩根拐杖;
之後，從黑暗的北方召喚詛咒，落在老皮迪‧多烏的身上，
他打算將他的衰老的頭，倒在雪白的胸脯上，

他打算摧毀歡唱的歌喉，傷害快樂的心。
他對他下詛咒，直到氣息離開他的身體；
但他給予五月的花朵祝福，
因為花朵生於美麗，又在美麗中消逝。

　　他逐行地唸給孩子們聽，讓他們每個人最少都能夠唸出幾句，學得快的孩子，還能唸出整首詩。

　　「今天的課就上到這裡，你們現在要做的，就是走出這裡，高唱一會兒這首歌，唱給綠色的燈芯草聽，唱給你遇見的每個人聽，也唱給老人聽。」翰拉漢說。

　　「我會照做的，我和老皮迪・多烏熟得很。去年的聖約翰之夜[4]，我們丟了一隻老鼠到他的煙囪裡，而這首詩要比丟老鼠來得更妙了。」一個小伙子說。

　　「我會去斯萊戈城的街上，高唱這首歌。」另一位男孩說。

　　翰拉漢說：「去吧！也去柏勒唱給瑪格麗特・魯尼和瑪麗・吉爾斯聽，請她們一起唱這首歌，也讓乞丐和瘸子走到哪裡就唱到哪裡。」

3　彌撒守則（Mass book）是世俗人在參加天主教彌撒時所閱讀的手冊，內容有聖經文、祈禱文和聖歌等。

4　聖約翰之夜（Saint John's Eve）是夏至舉辦的節慶，人們會在山頂升起營火。

孩子們於是信心滿滿又淘氣地跑出去了，邊跑邊大聲歌唱。翰拉漢知道，這首歌將無人不曉[5]。

　　隔天一早，他坐在門外，看著學生三三兩兩走進來，幾乎全員到齊，他端詳著太陽在天空中的位置，來判斷是否要開始上課了。這時，他聽到像是一群蜜蜂嗡嗡作響的聲音，又像是伏流氾濫的奔流聲。

　　他看見路上有一群人朝著小屋走過來，他注意到這群人都是老人，帶頭的是皮迪・布恩、麥可・吉爾，以及皮迪・多烏。這群人的手上都各自拿著樺樹木棍或是李樹手杖，一看到翰拉漢就開始上下揮舞著手中的棍棒，像是暴風雨中狂舞的樹枝，接著年邁的腳步跑了起來。

　　翰拉漢毫不遲疑地逃往小屋後方的山丘上，直到逃離他們的視線。

　　他藏身進壕溝旁的金雀花叢中，一陣子後才從山丘上返回。當他看見小屋時，發現老人都圍在小屋周圍，其中一人正打算將插著火稻草的長柄草耙，擲向茅草屋頂。

　　「太悲慘了！我讓年老、時間、困頓和疾病都與我作對，我又要去流浪了！」他說：「啊，神聖的天國女王啊，請讓我安然遠離貝里貝花鷂，遠離『外來者陡坡』上的紫杉，遠離達甘城堡湖裡的梭魚，遠離這一票老人們手中點燃的火把！」

5　人們透過這種方式來表達對老男人與年輕女孩結婚的反對，小男孩尤其熱衷這種活動。

5. 翰拉漢的靈視

　　六月的一天，翰拉漢走在斯萊戈附近的路上，他沒進城，反倒朝布本山走去，因為過去的回憶襲上心頭，他不想見到人們。走著走著，他自個兒唱起了曾經出現在他夢中的歌謠：

　　噢，死神那瘦削的手指，
　　永遠無法尋獲我們的蹤跡，
　　在空曠的高地教區，
　　愛情是給予和分享；
　　樹稍掛著果實和花朵，
　　一年四季始終如此；
　　河水溢滿出來，
　　挾帶著紅色、棕色啤酒。
　　一位老人吹奏著風笛，
　　笛木閃耀著金銀光彩；
　　女王們的眸子藍如冰，
　　在人群中翩翩起舞。

　　小狐狸低語著：
　　「啊，世間的禍根是什麼？」

太陽親切地笑著，
月亮拉著我的韁繩；
但那隻小紅狐低語著：
「噢，別拉他的韁繩，
他正要騎去教區，
那是世間的禍根。」

當他們志得意滿，
便會彼此拳腳相向。
他們從閃耀著金銀光彩的樹枝上，
取下沉重的利劍；
然而所有在戰役中死去的人，
又再度重獲生命；
幸運的是，
無人知曉他們的經歷。
啊，因為體魄強健的農夫，
將會把鐵鍬放下，
他們的心將會如同酒杯，
早已被人一飲而盡。

麥克爾將從頭頂上的樹枝，
取下他的號角。
張羅好晚餐之時，
他將輕吹一聲。

加百利將從水中走來，
帶著一條魚的尾巴，
述說奇蹟之事，
在人們行走的潮濕路上，
他會舉起一支古老的錘銀角杯，
將酒飲下，
直到他進入夢鄉，
在繁星燁燁的杯緣。

翰拉漢開始走上山，對他來說，上山的路還很長，他不時得坐下來休息一會兒，於是他停止了歌唱。

有一次，他在休息時，注意到堡壘旁有一株開花的野荊棘，他憶起他以前常摘給瑪莉·拉維的野玫瑰，之後，他就不再帶花給其他女子。他從樹叢扯下一根小樹枝，上頭長著花苞，還綻放著花朵。他又唱起了歌：

小狐狸低語著：
「啊，世間的禍根是什麼？」
太陽親切地笑著，
月亮拉著我的韁繩；
但那隻小紅狐低語著：

「噢，別拉他的韁繩，

他正要騎去教區，

那是世間的禍根。」

　　他離開堡壘，繼續走上山。幾首關於戀人的古老詩歌，浮現他的心頭，裡頭是幸與不幸的愛情故事；詩歌中也說著，有些人被戀人的愛情力量所喚醒，然後被帶到幽暗之地，等待著在上帝的面前接受審判與懲罰。

　　最後在黃昏時刻，他來到了「外來者陡坡」。他倚著陡坡的石脊，俯瞰山谷，灰色的霧靄瀰漫在連綿的山間。

　　看著看著，霧氣幻化成一群朦朧的幽靈，幽靈有男有女，這景象讓他既害怕又驚喜，心臟怦怦跳個不停。他那雙閒不下來的手，開始把小樹枝上的玫瑰葉子拔下來，他看著葉子迴旋地飄下山谷，像是一小支飄動的軍隊。

　　突然，他聽到一陣微弱的樂音，裡頭的悲喜之情，勝過世間所有的音樂。他一聽到這個樂音，心情立刻激昂起來，開始放聲大笑，因為他知道這樂音出自一位美麗而偉大的人，在世人之上。

　　柔軟的玫瑰小葉子[1]飄落山谷，在遠方霧靄中幻化為一群玫瑰色的男女，色彩變化萬千。他看見長長一列高大俊美的年輕男子，和貴如皇后的女人，他們沒有走開，反

1　在本書第三篇故事〈玫瑰煉金術〉裡，玫瑰花瓣也幻化為生命。

倒是走向他，從他身邊經過。他們傲氣的神情中帶著溫柔，面色蒼白而疲憊，彷彿始終在尋覓悲傷之事。

迷霧中出現了幽靈的手，像是要抓住他們，但是又搆不到，因為他們周遭籠罩著一種無法被打破的寂靜。

還有一些幽靈，像是出於敬意，和他們保持一段距離，在他們前方遠處，浮浮沉沉、來來去去。翰拉漢從他們迴旋飛行的模樣，看出來那是「賽德」，他們是古代戰敗的眾神。幽靈沒有伸手要去抓他們，因為他們並不邪惡，但也不會輕易服從。之後，他們都朝著山邊的一扇白色大門走去，逐漸消失在遠方。

霧靄在他面前散開，出現一片荒涼之海，長長的灰白波浪刷洗著山峰。看著看著，又開始浮現、流動著生命的破碎軀殼，灰白波浪中漂滿了手臂和披著散髮的蒼白頭顱。

霧氣不停地上湧，一直到和陡峭的石崖一樣高，幽靈逐漸變得具體，新的一列隊伍半沒入在霧靄中，踏著錯落的步伐，緩緩走過。每個幽靈體內都有某個東西在星光下閃爍著。當他們越來越靠近，翰拉漢注意到他們都是戀人，但是沒有心臟，只有一面面心型的鏡子，他們在彼此的鏡子中，不停地找尋自己的臉孔。

他們繼續向前，在經過翰拉漢的身邊時沉落下去，但其他的幽靈會現身遞補。他們不是並排行走，而是一個接著一個地前進，他們伸出手臂，揮動示意。翰拉漢注意到，那些跟隨而上的都是女人，有著絕美的頭部，但是身軀卻

是缺乏生命的幻影。她們的長髮飛揚舞動著，彷彿頭髮本身有著令人毛骨悚然的生命。

突然間，霧靄湧起，掩蓋住了她們，一陣輕風將她們吹往東北方。這時，一陣白翼般的煙霧也籠罩了翰拉漢。

他打了個冷顫，站起身來，準備離開山谷。他看到岩石後方的半空中，立著兩個半掩的黑色形體。其中一個眼神很哀傷，像乞丐一樣，用女人的聲音對他說：「和我說說話吧，七百年來，不管是這個世間還是別的世界，都沒有人跟我說過話。」

「請告訴我，剛才經過的那些幽靈是誰吧！」翰拉漢說。

女人說：「最先走過的那幾位，是古代名聲最響亮的戀人，像是布拉納德、迪爾德利、格尼爾，還有他們親愛的同伴，而另外那一群雖然較不為人所知，但也是一樣被深深愛過的人。由於他們不只是在彼此身上，找尋如花綻放的青春，也追尋著如同黑夜和繁星那樣永垂不朽的美，所以儘管他們的愛情為世間帶來戰爭與苦痛，黑夜和繁星讓他們永遠遠離戰爭與死亡。」她接著說：「再接下來的那些人，他們呼吸著甜美的空氣，內心也有一面鏡子，但是詩人卻不將他們寫入歌謠，因為他們所追尋的，只是想透過戰勝他人，以證明自己的力量和美麗，他們之間的愛情是這樣產生的。至於有著幽靈身體的女人，她們所欲求的，並非是戰勝別人或是去愛人，而是只想要被愛。除非有人親吻，不然心臟與身體都不會有一絲血色，生命也只

能存活一瞬。這些人都不快樂，但最不快樂的人是我。我是德娃蒂雅，這位是德莫特，是我們鑄下大錯，將諾曼人帶進愛爾蘭，世世代代的詛咒都落到了我們身上，從未有人像我們一樣受到這麼嚴厲的懲罰。我們愛著彼此綻放美麗時的樣子，我們愛著塵世間轉瞬即逝的美，而非那永垂不朽之美。死亡之時，沒有恆久不滅的寧靜在側。我們悲慟不已，因為我們將戰爭帶給了愛爾蘭，這苦痛就是對我們的懲罰。自此，我們永無止境地遊蕩，但我的愛人德莫特視我為長埋地下的一具軀體，我知道他是這麼看待我的。再問我吧，再問我更多問題吧，歲月讓我的內心增長不少智慧，但七百年來，沒有人聆聽我說話。」

一股巨大的恐懼籠罩了翰拉漢，他將雙臂高舉過頭頂，咆哮了三聲，山谷中的牛隻抬起頭來哞哞叫，山邊林間的鳥兒從睡夢中驚醒，在顫抖的樹葉間振翅亂飛。在岩壁邊緣的下方，玫瑰葉片隊伍仍在空中飄盪，因為通向永生的門，在一個心跳的瞬間，開啟之後，又關上了。

6. 翰拉漢之死

　　翰拉漢從不在一處久留，這次他又重返葉格山山腳下的伊爾頓、斯卡普和巴利里小村落。他時而在這間屋子歇歇腳，時而在那間屋子停留幾天，因為他過去的經歷、他的詩歌才華和廣博的學識，所到之處都受到人們的歡迎。

　　他外套裡面的小皮革袋子裡有一些銀幣和銅幣，但他很少拿出來，因為他錢花得少，而且沒有人會向他收取金錢。他握著李樹手杖的手日益沉重，臉頰深陷憔悴，但他還是能吃得到他想吃的食物，馬鈴薯、牛奶、小塊燕麥蛋糕，而且在葉格森林一帶這麼荒涼泥濘之地，是不缺大罐烈酒的，裡頭還有泥炭的煙煤味。

　　他會在齊納迪佛廣袤的森林裡漫步，或是坐在貝沙格湖畔的燈芯草叢中，消磨幾個小時的時光，聽著山上流下來的潺潺溪流，或是凝視棕色泥塘裡的幽靈。他安靜地坐著，以免驚擾到夜色中走出石南叢、來到草地和田野的小鹿。

　　日子緩緩流過，他似乎開始屬於某個來自靈視和霧靄的世界，在兩個世界的接壤之處，那裡的色彩超越世間的一切色彩，那裡的寂靜超越世間的一切寂靜。

　　有時，他會聽見森林中傳出忽隱忽現的音樂，當音樂

停止時，那些樂音又彷彿是來自他如夢的記憶。有一次，在正午的寂靜之中，他聽見像是刀劍的鏗鏘聲，聲音不間斷地持續了好一陣子。日暮時分，月升之際，湖水會變得像是一道由銀和寶石所做成的大門，寂靜的湖面會傳來微弱的慟哭聲，還有像是被風撕裂的駭人笑聲，並有許多蒼白的手在空中招著手。

收割時節的一個晚上，他坐著凝視水面，思索著所有被封藏在湖泊山岳之中的奧祕。這時，他聽見南方傳來一陣呼喊，起初十分微弱，但隨著燈芯草的影子越拉越長，聲音也逐漸變得清晰而響亮。終於，他能聽見呼喊裡頭的字句：「我真美麗動人！我真是美麗動人啊！空中的飛鳥、葉背的蠹蛾、水面的昆蟲都望著我看，因為未曾見過像我這樣美麗的女人。我真年輕貌美！我真是年輕貌美啊！山巒，看看我！枯萎的森林，看看我！當你們匆匆走過我的

身旁，我的身軀將如銀白的湖水那樣閃爍著光芒。你們和所有的人類、獸類、魚類、羽類都正在凋零，就像是即將燃燒殆盡的蠟燭，而我卻我暢聲歡笑，因為我正值青春年華。」

聲音斷斷續續，彷彿是疲倦了，但不久又再次呼喊著同樣的字句：「我真美麗動人，我真是美麗動人啊！」

這時，湖邊的灌木叢一陣搖晃，一位老嫗吃力地走出來，腳步很緩慢，經過翰拉漢身旁。她的面色如土，臉上的皺紋比任何老太婆都還要多，她的灰髮一束束地垂著，襤褸的衣衫遮不住那飽受日曬雨淋、又黑又粗糙的皮膚。她直瞪著雙眼，走過翰拉漢身旁，頭抬得高高的，兩側的雙手直挺挺地擺動著，然後走進山丘西邊的陰影之中。

看到她，翰拉漢打了一陣寒顫，因為他認出來她就是溫妮‧拜尼，她四處乞討，總是呼喊著同樣的話。他常聽人說，她以前智慧過人，附近的婦女常來請教她。她也有著美妙的嗓音，各地的人都樂於在守靈夜或是婚禮上聽到她的歌聲。但在多年前的薩溫節夜，那個世界的人，也就是偉大的「賽德」，趁她睡在城堡邊時偷走了她的智慧，而在她的夢中看到了葉格的僕從。

這時，她消失在山坡彼端，天上的星辰似乎傳來她的呼喊：「我真美麗動人，我真是美麗動人啊！」

燈芯草裡吹入一陣冷風，翰拉漢開始打起冷顫，於是他站了起來，想找個有爐火的屋子。然而，他不像往常一樣走下山坡，而是沿著山路或乾河床的小徑向上走。溫妮

離開時，也是走這條路，通往如她往常歇腳暫棲的小屋。

　　他緩慢地走在小坡上，彷彿背上揹著重擔。最後，他看見左邊有微弱的光亮，他猜想那可能是溫妮的房子，正在閃爍著火光，於是他走出小徑，朝屋子走去。但是就在這時，天空烏雲密佈，他看不清楚眼前的路，才走了幾步，便滑了一跤，跌進泥溝裡面。他抓著石南叢的根部，把自己拉出水溝，不過，這一摔卻讓他覺得躺著比向前走還要舒服。然而，他一向很有膽量的，他一步一步地往前移動，最後終於來到溫妮的小屋，屋子沒有窗戶，閃爍的火光從門裡透出來。

　　他打算進去休息一會兒，他走到門邊，沒有看見溫妮，只有四位灰髮老婦在玩著紙牌，溫妮也沒有在裡頭。翰拉漢坐在門邊的一堆草皮上，他累壞了，不想說話，也不想玩牌，他的骨頭和關節一如往常疼痛不堪。

　　他聽到四名婦人一邊玩牌，一邊交談著，叫著她們手中的牌。她們正在說的話，在他聽起來就像很久以前在穀倉裡那位怪老頭所說的話：「黑桃和方塊，勇氣與力量！梅花和紅心，知識與喜悅！」

　　他自言自語不停地重複這些字句，但無論是夢是醒，他肩上的疼痛不曾消失。

　　沒多久，屋裡的四位婦人開始爭吵了起來，互相指責對方作弊，她們不停地尖叫、咒罵，嗓門越來越大，最後整間屋子裡裡外外都充斥著她們的聲音。翰拉漢半夢半醒間，聽見她們在爭吵，便說道：「這聲音是來自朋友與瀕

死咒罵者之間的爭執，我納悶，在這個人跡罕至的地方，那個瀕死之人是誰？」

他彷彿沉睡了很長的時間，當他睜開雙眼，眼前出現的是「十字路口溫妮」那一張長滿皺紋的蒼老面容。她聚精會神盯著他看，彷彿是要確定他還一息尚存。她用濕布擦去他臉上乾掉的血漬，半攙扶著他進到屋子裡，讓他躺在她的床鋪。她從火爐上的鍋子裡，拿出幾顆馬鈴薯給他，也遞給他一杯泉水，這是他最需要的。

他躺在床上睡睡醒醒，有時會聽到溫妮唱著歌，在屋裡走動著，那一晚就這麼過了。

天光漸亮，晨曦之際，他摸到了那裝著一點錢的袋子，把袋子拿給了溫妮。她從裡頭拿出幾個銅幣和銀幣，但是又讓錢幣掉回袋子裡，一副不看在眼裡的樣子，可能是她一向不是乞討金錢，而是乞討食物和衣服，也可能是因為黎明的到來，讓她對自己的美貌充滿了驕傲與自信。

她出門砍石南花叢，抱了幾叢回屋子，堆在翰拉漢的旁邊，一邊說著清晨的天氣有多麼寒冷，這時翰拉漢注意到她臉上的皺紋、灰白的頭髮，還有滿是黑色窟窿的一口爛牙。

幫他鋪好石南叢之後，她就出門，往山邊走去，他聽見她的呼喊道：「我真美麗動人！我真是美麗動人啊！」

隨著她遠去，聲音越來越微弱，最後消失了。

　　翰拉漢的身體痠痛又虛弱，一整天都躺在那裡。當夜幕垂下，他又聽見她從山中傳來的聲音。一會兒，她走進屋子，煮了馬鈴薯，像先前一樣和他分著吃。

　　這樣的日子一天天地過去，他感到身體的沉重，他日漸虛弱，也逐漸明白屋子裡存在著某種比他還強大的東西，正逐漸佔據整個空間。他覺得他們的手擁有無限的力量，只需輕輕一碰，就能瓦解苦痛在他四周所築起的牆，然後把他帶進他們的世界裡。

　　有時候，他能聽見微弱而快活的聲音，從橡木或是爐火中傳出來。又有時候，整間屋子會充滿音樂聲，像一陣風吹入了屋內。漸漸地，虛弱讓他感覺不到苦痛了，四周越來越寧靜，就像是湖心那樣的寂靜，然後又像從燈芯的火光中那樣，傳來微弱的永恆歡樂聲。

　　一個早上，他聽見門外傳來了樂音，聲音一天比一天大聲，把那個微弱的歡樂聲都掩蓋住了，甚至連溫妮日落時分在山中的呼喊聲也聽不見了。

　　約莫午夜時分，房子的牆像是瞬間融化了，他的床漂浮在白霧的朦朧光線中，光線充斥著整個空間。他的眼睛突然什麼都看不到，接著他看到幽靈般的形體在屋內四處亂竄。

　　就在這個時候，他可以清楚聽見那音樂了，他知道那是持續不斷的刀劍撞擊聲。

　　「我即將死去，在天國的樂音中安息。基路柏和撒拉

弗，接引我的靈魂吧！」他說。

　　就在他呼喊之時，離他最近的那道光芒突然充滿著四射的火光，變得更加耀眼，他看到這些都是指向他心臟的劍鋒。突然間，一陣火焰竄起，如上帝的愛與憎那般地炙烈燃燒著，火焰捲走了所有光芒，衝向外頭，將他留在黑暗之中。

　　一時之間，他什麼都看不見，一切都黑得像是置身在沼澤泥塘中。這時，火焰突然燃燒起來，彷彿有人丟入了一綑稻草。他注視著火焰，那掛在勾子上的大鍋、溫妮用來烤蛋糕的石板、她用來採割石南的生鏽長刀，都閃著光芒，還有他帶進屋裡的李樹木杖，也映上了火光。

　　他盯著這四樣東西，腦海中浮現過往記憶，身體又重新充滿力量。他起身坐在床上，大聲而清楚地說：「大鍋、石頭、寶劍、長矛，到底是什麼？又是屬於誰的？這一次我終於問了這個問題。」

　　他又倒下身來，生命的氣息正在離他而去。

　　剛才在生火的溫妮‧拜尼走了過來，雙眼注視著床舖。這時，微弱的笑聲又出現了，蒼白的光線如海浪般悄悄佔據整間屋子，他不知道光線是來自什麼神祕世界。他看見溫妮憔悴的面容，還有她乾枯得如碎裂泥土般的雙臂，儘管他十分虛弱，他還是盡力向身後的牆壁退去。

　　這時，從乾泥僵硬的破布中，伸出來白如河水泡沫的手臂，將他的身體纏繞住，一個像是來自遠方但又能清晰聽見的聲音對他低語：「你再也不需要在其他女人的懷中，

尋找我的身影了。」

「你是誰？」他問。

「我屬於永生不老的族類，有著永不消逝的聲音，我居住在衰老、死亡之中，以及失去理智的人們之中。我是來尋找你的，在整個世界如蠟燭般燃燒殆盡之前，你都屬於我。」她說：「你抬頭看，我們婚禮的火炬已經點燃了。」

他看見屋子裡擠滿了蒼白模糊的手，每隻手都舉著點燃的火把，像是為婚禮所準備的，也像是為亡者所點燃的白色長蠟燭。

翌日清晨，太陽升起之時，「十字路口的溫妮」從屍體旁站了起來，開始在城鎮間乞討。她一邊走著，一邊唱著同樣的曲調：「我真美麗動人！我真是美麗動人啊！空中的飛鳥、葉背的蟲蛾、水面的昆蟲，牠們都望著我看，因為未曾見過像我這樣美麗的女人。我真年輕貌美！我真是年輕貌美啊！山巒，看看我！枯萎的森林，看看我！當你們匆匆走過我的身旁，我的身軀將如銀白的湖水那樣閃爍著光芒。你們和所有的人類、獸類、魚類、羽類都正在凋零，就像是即將燃燒殆盡的蠟燭，而我卻我暢聲歡笑，因為我正值青春年華。」

那晚之後，她再也沒有回到小屋。整整兩天過去，前往沼澤採割草皮的人們才發現紅髮歐文・翰拉漢的軀體。他們召集男人來為他守靈，婦女為他唱起輓歌，並為他舉行了一場與偉大詩人相稱的喪禮。

Chapter 2

神祕玫瑰

我所摯愛的 A.E.[1]——我將這本書獻給你，不管你覺得寫得如何，你都能體會到書中人物的悲傷與歡喜，或許還比我更能感同身受。雖然我在不同的時期，以不同的方式寫下這些故事，寫作過程中也沒有任何明確的計畫，但這些故事都圍繞著同一個主題，也就是靈性與自然法則之間的對抗。你是愛爾蘭現代詩人，你將靈魂中的狂喜鑄於詩句之間，我除了將本書獻給你，還能獻給誰呢？

　　愛爾蘭的朋友有時會問，我什麼時候要寫首真正的民族詩歌，或是寫篇羅曼史。就我對民族詩歌與羅曼史的了解，這意味著以愛爾蘭歷史某個重要時刻為背景的詩作或愛情故事，而且能感動大多數愛國的愛爾蘭人的思想和感受。

　　另一方面，我也認為，我們無法藉由嚴謹調查過去重大事件，或是依靠研究他人的思想和感受，來寫出詩歌與羅曼史。我們應該去探索我們自己內在那微小卻無垠、搖曳卻永恆的火焰。一位作家如果希望引起自己成長環境中那些人們的興趣，或是覺得自己對他們負有某種責任，那麼他可以在創作中加入一些來自人們的傳說、歷史事件、信仰、看法的象徵意象，因為作家有權選擇他可掌握的事物，但無法選擇創作的本質。

　　這本極富想像力的書籍具有愛爾蘭的風格，主要由凱爾特民族所組成的愛爾蘭，雖然有一些不盡完美的事物，卻保存了幻想的才能。在腳步匆促、成功的國家，這種想像力已經消失殆盡：華麗閃耀的燭台，無法阻撓我們窺視黑暗；當我們直視黑暗，那裡面總有東西等待著我們。

威廉・巴特勒・葉慈
倫敦，1896

至於生活，讓僕人為我們去操煩吧。

—— Villiers de L'Isle Adam [2]

海倫注視著鏡中的自己，看見歲月在她臉上畫下的
一道道皺紋，她哭了，她感到疑惑，
為什麼她會又一次被奪去生命。

——摘自達文西的筆記本

1　A.E. 為愛爾蘭作家 George William Russell（1867–1935）的筆名。

2　Villiers de L'Isle Adam（1838–1889），法國象徵主義作家、詩人、
劇作家。

1. 致神祕玫瑰

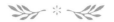

遙遠的、最祕密的、不曾被褻瀆的玫瑰啊，
請在緊要關頭包覆著我；
那些在聖墓裡或酒缸中尋找你的人們，
住在失敗夢境的騷動與混亂之外；
深居於因睡意而沉重的蒼白眼瞼之中，
人們稱之為美。你大片的葉子，
包覆了古老的鬍鬚，加冕的三聖人[1]，
他們那飾滿紅寶石和黃金的舵柄；
國王親眼見證刺穿的雙手，
以及基督受難的接骨木十字架，
在德魯伊的幻想中矗立，黯淡了火炬；
最後在徒然的瘋狂中醒來，然後死去；
他遇到芳德[2]在燃燒的露水中，
走在風永遠吹不到的灰色海岸上，
只因為一個吻，他失去了世界和葉蜜兒[3]；
他將眾神從神邸裡驅趕出來，
直到一百個黎明綻放紅霞之後，
在他的墳前痛哭；

那個做著夢的驕傲國王，丟開王冠和憂傷，
從深林裡那些酒漬斑斑的流浪者之中，
召喚來詩人和小丑；
他賣掉耕地、房屋、家當，
在陸地和島嶼中尋覓了無數個年歲，
最後，他又是哭、又是笑地，
終於找到了一位耀眼的美麗女子。
午夜裡，人們用一綹頭髮在打穀，
那是一綹偷來的頭髮。我也在等待著，
等待你那愛與恨的狂風到來的時刻。
什麼時候，繁星將在天空中被吹得四散，
就像鐵匠鋪中噴濺的火花，然後消逝？
毫無疑問，你的時刻已經到來，你的狂風吹襲著，
遙遠的、最祕密的、不曾被褻瀆的玫瑰？

---

1 在基督教傳統中，三聖人（Magi）帶著金子、乳香和沒藥，在耶穌
  出生時來拜訪。
2 愛爾蘭神話中，芳德（Fand）是一位超凡脫俗的女子。
3 愛爾蘭神話中，葉蜜兒（Emir）是英雄庫胡林（Cúchulainn）的妻子。

2. 十字架上的放逐者

　　一位男子邊跑邊走在自南方蜿蜒通往斯萊戈城的路上，他有一頭稀疏棕色頭髮和蒼白臉龐，大家叫他庫爾，寇瑪之子，也有人叫他迅疾野馬。他是吟遊詩人，穿著色彩繽紛的緊身上衣和尖頭鞋，身上背著鼓起的旅行袋。他體內流著厄爾斯的血液，出生於金色田野（Field of Gold），吃睡的地方在葉利人[1]的四個省分，住的地方不在大地的山脊上。

　　他的目光從白衣修道會的教堂移到城垛，最後停在一列十字架上，十字架矗立在小城外偏東的山丘，背景襯著一片藍天。他握緊拳頭，對著十字架揮舞。

　　他知道十字架上並非空無一物，因為十字架的周圍有鳥在振翅盤旋。他思索著，另一位和他一樣的吟遊詩人，可能如何地被釘死在眼前的十字架上。他低聲咕噥道：「被吊死、被勒死、被石頭砸死、被砍頭，這樣就夠慘了，還要被鳥啄食雙眼、被野狼啃食雙腳！大提王[2]從蠻夷之地帶回來死亡之樹，但願大提王在襁褓時，德魯伊的赤風[3]就消滅了他的士兵；或者，大提王在山腳下被雷電擊中時，就被擊敗；又或者，讓深海底下的綠髮碧齒美人魚，挖掘他的墳墓吧。」

　　十字架他可是見多了，但不知怎地，他一邊咕噥著，

從頭到腳直打著哆嗦，臉上也滲出汗水。他越過兩座小丘，來到城垛大門，再沿著左側的路，來到修道院門口，門上佈滿了碩大的裝飾用門釘。他敲門，叫醒看門的修士，向他要了間客房。

隨後，修士用鐵鍬鏟了一塊灼熱的泥炭，帶他來到一間寬敞、未加陳設的外屋，屋子裡鋪滿了髒兮兮的燈芯草。修士點燃固定在牆上兩塊石頭之間的燈芯草蠟燭，將灼熱的泥炭放進火爐，並給了庫爾兩塊尚未點燃的草皮和一束稻草，指給他看掛在釘子上的毛毯、放著麵包和水罐的架子，以及角落裡的木盆，就返回看門處。

寇瑪之子庫瑪開始對著火紅灼熱的泥炭吹氣，想點燃另外兩片草皮和那束稻草，但是煤炭跟稻草過於潮濕，無法點燃。他脫下尖頭鞋，從角落拉出木盆，想要洗去一路沾在腳上的塵土，但是水太髒了，髒到見不到底。

他一整天沒吃東西了，飢腸轆轆，不想浪費太多力氣對木盆發怒。他拿起黑麵包，用力咬下，卻立刻吐了出來，麵包很硬，還發了霉。他的脾氣仍未發作，因為他好幾個小時沒喝水了。他稍早的時候，沒喝溪水就啟程了，他期待一天結束之後，能來杯石南啤酒或葡萄酒，這樣搭配晚餐更美味。

---

1 葉利（Eri）為古愛爾蘭的主要氏族，這裡用來代表愛爾蘭人。
2 大提王（Dathi）為愛爾蘭國王，最後在阿爾卑斯山上被雷電擊斃。
3 古愛爾蘭人認為有十二種不同顏色的風。

他把水罐一拿到嘴邊，就立刻扔掉，因為水的味道又苦澀又難聞。他踢了水罐一腳，水罐撞上對面的牆壁破掉了。他取下毯子，打算裹著度過夜晚，但他才一碰毯子，裡頭滿是活蹦亂跳的跳蚤。

這下子他氣瘋了，立刻衝向房門。修士早習慣了這種激烈的抗議，所以把門從外面給鎖上了。庫爾把木桶中的水倒掉，用木桶敲打著房門，最後修士總算來到門邊，問他發生了什麼事，搞得這麼火大，擾人清夢。

「你問我發生了什麼事！」庫爾咆哮道：「難道不是因為木炭濕得像三諾斯[4]的沙子？難道不是因為毯子裡的跳蚤像海浪一樣，又多又活蹦蹦的？難道不是因為麵包跟背離上帝的修士心腸一樣硬？難道不是因為罐子裡的水，就像修士那難聞的靈魂一樣苦澀嗎？難道不是因為洗腳水的顏色，就像修士被地獄之火烤焦的顏色嗎？」

修士看到門鎖牢靠得很，就轉身回到看門處，他太睏了，講不上安慰的話。

庫爾繼續敲打房門，他又聽見修士的腳步聲響起，便對他大叫：「懦弱又專橫的化緣修士，你們是吟遊詩人的迫害者！你們憎恨生命與歡笑！你們從不拔劍，也不傳頌真理[5]！你們以怯懦和欺騙，融化人們的骨頭！」

「吟遊詩人啊，我也作詩，我在看門的時候寫下很多詩作，我很遺憾聽見吟遊詩人咒罵修士。兄弟啊！我要睡了，所以我要讓你知道，是修道院上頭的人，也就是我們仁慈的修道院院長，在安排旅人的下榻。」修士說。

「你可以睡了，我要用吟遊詩人的詩歌來咒罵修道院長。」[6] 庫爾說。

他把木桶倒放在窗戶下方，站上去大聲唱歌。歌聲把院長吵醒了，院長起來坐在床上，吹著銀色口哨，直到修士過來。

院長說：「這麼吵，根本沒辦法闔眼，是怎麼回事？」

「有個吟遊詩人在抱怨草皮、麵包、罐裡的水、洗腳水、毛毯，他正在唱著吟遊詩人的詩歌來咒罵您。噢，院長修士，他也咒罵您的父母、祖父母和所有的親戚。」修士說。

「他用詩歌來咒罵？」

「是，他用詩歌來咒罵，而且每句詩都有兩個半諧音。」

修道院院長扯下睡帽，捏在手中，他禿頭中央處的圓形棕色頭髮，看上去就像池塘中央的島嶼，康納這個地方還沒有因為要施行新樣式，而廢除剔光頭頂的樣式[7]。

修道院長說：「我們要是不採取行動，他會讓街上的

4　三諾斯（Three Rosses）位於羅席斯半島（Rosses Point peninsula）的三個路岬。

5　這裡提到愛爾蘭分離主義者 John O'Leary（1830–1907）的話：「我的信仰，就是拉弓戰鬥和傳頌真理。」（I have but one religion, to bend the bow and tell the truth.）

6　據說愛爾蘭的吟遊詩人，能夠藉由作詩，來讓敵人生病或死亡。

7　頭頂剃光的樣式（Tonsure）於八世紀廢除。

孩子、門邊紡紗的女孩、布本山的強盜，學會那些詛咒的。」

另一修士說：「那我是不是應該要給他乾草皮、新鮮麵包、一壺乾淨的水、乾淨的洗腳水和一條新毯子，然後要他對著神聖的聖貝尼涅（Saint Benignus）發誓，也對太陽和月亮發誓，決不會去教導街上的孩子、門邊紡紗的女孩、布本山的強盜，吟唱他所作的詩歌？」

修道院院長說：「不論是我們神聖的守護者或是日月，都幫不上忙，因為到了明天或後天，他又會陷入咒罵的情緒之中，或者又為自己的詩作感到自豪，使得他的態度動搖了，那他就會去教導孩子、女孩、強盜那些詩句，又或者他會把在客房的遭遇跟別的吟遊詩人講，然後換成別人來咒罵，我就會名譽掃地。在路上學到的東西，沒有一貫的道理，教學應該是要在有天花板和四面牆壁的屋子裡才對。因此，我命令你喚醒凱文弟兄、德夫弟兄、小沃爾夫弟兄、禿頂派翠弟兄、禿頂布萊登弟兄、詹姆士弟兄和彼得弟兄，叫他們把這個人抓起來，用繩子捆住，浸在河裡，這樣他就會停止唱歌。但怕這樣做會讓他唱得更大聲，明天早上我們就把他釘死在十字架上。」

「十字架已經滿了。」修士說。

「那麼我們就再做個十字架。就算我們沒有將他處死，別人也會這麼做，像他這樣的人去到世界各地，有誰能安穩地吃飯睡覺？神聖的聖貝尼涅都讓庫爾來到我們的手掌心了，要是我們放過敵人，祂在世界末日審判我們之時，一定會震怒！修士們，你們要知道，吟遊詩人和唱遊

詩人都是邪惡之徒，他們老是咒罵、煽動人群，凡事都無視道德，缺乏節制，他們的內心追隨著里爾之子、安格斯、布里吉特、達哥達、母神黛娜，還有古代所有的罪惡之神。他們總是作詩讚美邪惡的國王跟王后：居住在克拉克瑪下方的芬瓦拉、科諾加納仙國中的里德奧哈、海浪克琳娜、灰色岩石之上的阿伊亥爾、大海中的道恩[8]。他們還批評上帝、耶穌和神聖的聖徒。」

　　修道院長說完，劃了個十字，然後拉下睡帽，蓋住耳朵，擋住噪音，接著閉上眼睛，平靜下來入眠。

　　修士發現凱文弟兄、德夫弟兄、小沃爾夫弟兄、禿頂派翠弟兄、禿頂布萊登弟兄、詹姆士弟兄和彼得弟兄，早就在床上坐起來了，便叫他們下床。他們把庫爾捆起來，拖到河邊，再將他浸到河裡。人們之後稱那個地方為巴克利淺灘。

　　弟兄們領著庫爾回到客房，修士問道：「吟遊詩人，你為何要用上帝賜給你的智慧，去創作褻瀆和悖德的故事跟詩歌？這就是你的狡猾之處！我知道我說的是對的，因為事實上我記誦了許多這樣的故事跟詩歌。為什麼你要用

8　里爾之子（Son of Lir），曾被後母施以法術。安格斯（Aengus），愛情與欺騙之神。布里吉特（Bridget），詩人和預言家。達哥達（Dagda），豐饒之神。母神黛娜（Danna the mother），愛爾蘭傳說中的諸神之母。芬瓦拉（Finvaragh），愛爾蘭精靈之王。里德奧哈（Red Aodh），死亡之神。克琳娜（Cleena），芒斯特的仙子。阿伊亥爾（Aoibhell），克琳娜的姊妹。道恩（Donn），死亡之神。

詩歌讚美芬瓦拉、里德奧哈、克琳娜、阿伊亥爾和道恩這些魔鬼呢？我也是明智、學識淵博的人，但我從來就只會讚美我們仁慈的修道院院長、我們的庇護者聖貝尼涅、主教轄區的王子。我的靈魂是高貴又愛好和平的，但你的靈魂卻是像柳樹園裡的風。我也是很有想法的人，我能說的都說了，但是像你這樣的人，又有誰能夠拯救你？」

「朋友啊！」吟遊詩人回答：「我的靈魂確實是像風一般，來來回回吹拂著我，為我的內心帶來許多想法，也從我的內心帶走許多思緒，因此人們稱我為迅疾野馬。」

那天晚上，他再也沒說話，因為寒冷讓他的牙齒不住顫抖。

隔天早上，修道院院長和化緣修士去找他，要他準備好被釘上十字架，然後帶他離開客房。他站在台階上，一群白額黑燕飛越他頭頂的天空，發出尖銳的叫聲。他向牠們伸出雙臂，說：「噢！偉大的白額黑燕啊，請停留一會兒，也許我的靈魂能跟你們一起旅行到岸邊的荒蕪之地，以及那深不可測的大海！」

大門前，一群乞丐將他們團團圍住，向那些下榻客房的遊子或朝聖者乞討。修道院院長跟化緣修士領著吟遊詩人，來到一段距離外的樹林中，那裡生長著許多筆直的小樹，他們要吟遊詩人砍下其中的一棵，並鋸成適合的長度。這時候，那群乞丐站在附近圍成一圈，指指點點說著話。修道院長又命令他砍下另一棵較矮的樹，釘在第一棵上，這樣一來十字架就完成了。

和其他被釘死的人一樣，他也會被釘死在山頂上，所以他們把十字架放在他的肩上。

　　走了半英哩，他請求大家停下來看他變戲法，他說他知道「敏感之心安格斯」的所有戲法。年長的化緣修士催促大家繼續向前走，但年輕的化緣修士想看他變戲法，他便為他們表演了許多魔術，還從他的耳朵裡拉出活蹦亂跳的青蛙。

　　但沒多久，他們的臉色都變了，說他的把戲既無趣又下流，便又把十字架放到他的肩上。

　　又走了半英哩，他請大家停下來聽他說笑話，說他知道所有「禿子加南」的把戲，據說那人的背上可以長出羊毛[9]。聽完了他說的好笑故事，年輕的化緣修士們又再度要他扛起十字架，因為他們厭煩了聽他說那些蠢事。

　　又再走了半英哩，他要他們停下來聽他唱「乳白胸脯迪爾德麗」的故事，她是如何忍受那麼多的苦痛，而烏斯納之子是如何渴望服侍她。年輕化緣修士們狂熱地想要聽他的故事，但等他說完之後，卻火大地揍了他一頓，因為他撩起他們心裡沉睡已久的渴望。他們重新把十字架放到他肩上，催趕著他上山。

　　到達山頂時，他們把十字架從他身上拿下，開始挖洞，要把十字架插在裡頭。乞丐聚集過來閒言閒語。

---

[9] 在鄉間流傳的故事中，加南（Conan）在失去背部的皮膚之後，他的夥伴跑向一群綿羊，剝下羊皮綁在 Conan 的背上。

「在死之前，我有一個請求。」庫爾說。

「我們不會再讓你拖延一分一秒。」修道院院長說。

「我不再要求延後，因為我奮戰過，說出了真理，也實現了我的理想，我已經滿足了。」

「那麼，你願意懺悔嗎？」

「我對著日月宣誓，我毋須懺悔，我只求讓我享用我放在行囊裡的食物。我旅行時，行囊裡都會帶上食物，但只有在我快要餓死的時候，才會吃上一口。這兩天，我什麼都沒吃。」

「你吃吧。」修道院長說完，就轉身幫化緣修士挖洞。

吟遊詩人從旅行袋裡拿出一條麵包和幾條冷掉的炸培根，把它們擺在地上。

「我會給窮人十分之一的食物。」說完，就切下十分之一的麵包跟培根，問道：「你們當中誰最窮苦？」

人群中隨即一陣大騷動，乞丐們開始訴說自己有多苦、多窮，他們發黃的臉扭動著，像是洪水來襲時灌滿沼澤渾水的加拉湖。

他聽了一會兒，說道：「我才是最貧窮的，我走過荒涼的道路與海洋的邊界，身上穿著襤褸的衣服，腳下踩著破損的尖頭鞋，我為此苦惱不已，因為我心裡有座聳入雲霄的城市，充滿高尚的服飾。我行走在路上與海邊，是更孤單的，因為我的心中聽見大海玫瑰花邊的裙子，發出窸窸窣窣的聲響，比『敏感之心安格斯』的把戲，更難以捉摸，比『禿子加南』的笑聲，更加充滿歡樂，比『乳白胸

脯迪爾德麗』的經歷，更富有憂傷的智慧，也比消失在黑暗中的黎明，更加迷人可愛。因此我將這十分之一給自己當作獎賞，但因為我此生無憾了，我將這十分之一送給你們。」

然後他將麵包和培根條拋到乞丐之中，乞丐們邊喊叫、邊搶食，直到最後一點碎屑也被吃光。就在這同時，化緣修士將吟遊詩人釘在十字架上，然後把十字架直立插入洞裡，在他的腳邊鏟起泥土，覆蓋起來，再將泥土結實地踩平。

修士們都離開了，但乞丐仍待在那裡圍著十字架坐著，然而隨著太陽落下，天氣轉涼，他們也起身準備離開。他們才剛走不遠，出現在附近灌木林旁的野狼就靠近過來，空中徘徊的鳥也越飛越低。

「被放逐的人，請留步，就算只是一下子也好。」被釘在十字架上的庫爾，以微弱的聲音對乞丐說：「請幫我趕走那些野獸和鳥吧。」

但是乞丐們很生氣，因為庫爾稱呼他們為被放逐的人，所以向他扔石頭和泥土，然後離開了。

狼群聚集在十字架的底下，鳥兒也越飛越低，降落在他的頭頂、手臂、肩膀，開始啄食他的肉，狼群也開始啃食他的雙腳。

「被放逐的人們！難道你們也同樣敵視被放逐的人嗎？」他呻吟著。

3. 玫瑰信念

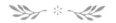

　　冬夜裡，一位老騎士穿著生鏽的鏈條盔甲，騎馬行走在布本山南面森林覆蓋的斜坡上，看著太陽落入海上緋紅的雲層裡。歷經了長途跋涉，他的馬已經疲倦了。騎士的頭盔上頭，鑲著的不是鄰近貴族或國王的紋飾，而是紅寶石雕刻成的一朵小小玫瑰花，花朵閃著微光，每閃爍一次就更加緋紅。他雜亂無章的微捲白髮披在肩上，臉龐更顯憂傷。他這種人總是擔憂著世間苦難，鮮少能夠享受當下的時刻，他是為理想付諸行動的夢想家，也是堅持理想的實踐者。

　　他凝視落日一會兒，鬆開馬的韁繩，面向西方伸出雙臂，說道：「智慧火焰的神聖玫瑰啊！請在最終的時刻向我敞開祢的和平之門吧！」

　　突然間，遠在幾百碼外山邊的森林裡，傳來一陣長長的尖叫聲，他停下馬，仔細聆聽，身後響起了腳步聲和談話聲。其中一人說道：「他們抽打那幾隻豬，把牠們趕進峽谷裡的狹窄小徑。」過了一下子，十多位帶著短矛的農人追上騎士，手上拿著藍色無邊帽，站在騎士旁。

　　「你們拿著短矛，要去哪裡？」騎士問。像是帶頭的人回答：「不久之前，一群山賊從山上下來，搶走了住在格林佳湖畔老人的豬隻，我們打算追趕那些山賊。但是他

們的人數比我們多四倍，所以我們只能跟蹤他們。我們打算立刻去上報狄柯西，他要是不願幫我們，那我們就去找費茲傑羅。狄柯西和費茲傑羅最近簽訂了停戰條約，我們不知道自己屬於哪一方。」

「等到那時候，豬都被吃掉了。」騎士說。

「我們這十幾個人力量有限，別說是為了兩頭豬，就算是二十幾頭豬，也不能因此讓整座山谷裡的人冒著生命危險。」

「你告訴我，那養豬老人是個虔誠的老實人嗎？」騎士說。

「他跟大家一樣老實，信仰上比大家都虔誠，他每天早上用早飯之前，都會向聖徒禱告。」

騎士說：「那麼我們就應該為他而戰。如果你們要打山賊，我願意擔綱主力，你們應該很清楚，一位穿盔甲的男子，比得上好幾位穿羊毛衣與皮革的山賊。」

帶頭的人轉身問大家，是否要賭上一把，但是他們一副想趕快回家的樣子。

「那些山賊是不是狡詐又不敬神？」

「他們做的每件事情都背信忘義，而且沒人見過他們禱告。」農夫說。

騎士說：「這樣好了，只要你們在戰鬥中取下一顆山賊的頭顱，我就給你們五克朗當作獎賞。」他命令帶頭的人為他指路，所有人便一道前行。

走了一會兒，他們來到一條前人踩出的小徑，蜿蜒

通往森林，他們循著這條路，回到農夫們先前走過的路線，開始攀爬樹木繁盛的山坡。很快地，道路變得筆直而陡峭，騎士只好下馬，把馬匹綁在樹幹上。他們知道走這條路是對的，因為軟泥土上有尖頭皮鞋踩過的痕跡，當中還混雜著豬的蹄印。

　　沒多久，山路更陡峭了，豬的蹄印也消失了，他們推測是因為山賊把豬扛在背上走，而泥土中不時出現的長長拖痕，顯示豬隻滑了下來，還被拖行了一小段路。

　　大概又走了二十分鐘，一陣嘈雜的聲音讓他們知道就要趕上山賊了。後來聲音停了下來，他們猜想山賊已經有所察覺了。他們小心翼翼地迅速逼近，過了五分鐘左右，一位農夫看見穿著皮製緊身上衣的人，躲藏在榛木旁。這時，一支利箭射向騎士的鎖鏈盔甲，隨即彈開，騎士毫髮無傷。一陣亂箭射向農夫們，發出蜂群般的嗡嗡聲響。

　　他們朝著山賊的方向奔跑攀爬，最後看到了藏匿在樹叢中的所有山賊，他們手中握著的弓還顫抖著。農夫的手中只有短矛，只能跟山賊打肉搏戰。

　　騎士衝鋒陷陣，打倒一個又一個山賊，農夫咆哮著向前逼近，將面前的山賊驅趕至山頂的平地，那裡有兩隻小

豬靜靜地在草地裡挖土。他們圍著豬隻，把豬趕回狹窄的小徑。老騎士走在隊伍的最後方，把山賊一個個打倒在地。

農夫們的傷勢並不嚴重，因為騎士為他們擋下了最激烈的搏鬥，鮮血從他盔甲上的破洞汩汩流出。當他們來到狹窄的小徑入口，騎士吩咐農夫們先把豬隻趕回山谷，他自己會留在原地，從後方掩護他們。

不久，四周就只剩他一人。他流了很多血，身體很虛弱，生命可能就要在這裡結束，死在被他打倒的山賊旁邊，但只有這麼做，才能確保農夫能夠趕緊離開這一帶。

一小時過去了，農夫們沒有回來。騎士無法再站著守衛下去了，他得躺在草地上。又過了半個多小時，帽上插著像是公雞羽毛的一個年輕小伙子，從後方的小徑走過來。他在山賊的屍體間穿梭，用刀砍下他們的頭顱。

小伙子把頭顱堆在騎士的面前說道：「偉大的騎士，我被派來向你索取你承諾的獎賞，一顆頭換五克朗。他們吩咐我告訴你，他們已向上帝和聖母祈禱，願你長命百歲，但他們是貧窮的農夫，所以希望在你死之前能夠拿到錢。他們一再叮嚀我，生怕我忘記，說我要是忘記了，一定會教訓我。」

騎士用手肘把自己撐起來，打開腰帶上掛著的袋子，數了數錢，一個頭值五克朗，一共有三十顆頭。

「噢！偉大的騎士！他們也吩咐我要盡力照顧你，幫你點起火堆，在你的傷口擦上藥膏。」小伙子說。

他把樹枝跟葉子堆在一起，用打火石點燃乾枯的葉

子，火堆熊熊燃燒起來。他為騎士脫去盔甲外套，開始用軟膏塗抹傷口，但是他笨手笨腳，別人怎麼教，他就怎麼做，動作笨拙。

騎士用手示意，要他停下來，接著對他說：「你看起來是個好孩子。」

「我也想替自己向你要些東西。」

「還有五克朗，要把這些給你嗎？」騎士說。

小伙子說：「噢，不，那對我沒什麼用。我只在乎一件事，那不需要用到錢。我在村莊山間穿梭時，只要看到健壯的公雞，就會把牠偷來，藏在森林中的竹筐底下，等到偷到另一隻公雞，就讓兩隻搏鬥。人們說我是個傻子，他們不會傷害我，也不會要我工作，只會偶爾要我帶個口信。也因為我是個傻子，他們才叫我來向你要錢，要是換成別人，錢會被私吞。沒有你在旁邊，他們不敢返回來，怕遇到山賊。你聽說過嗎？這些山賊受洗的時候，把野狼奉為教父[1]，而且他們的右臂根本就沒有受洗。」

「我的好孩子，你不接受這些錢，我恐怕就沒東西好給你了，除非你想要我這件老盔甲，我很快就不需要它了。」

「我是有想要的東西的，對，我現在記起來了！」小伙子說：「我想知道，你為什麼會為了這麼一件小事，就

---

1 據說古愛爾蘭人崇拜野狼，人們會對野狼禱告，並且讓野狼當孩子的教父。

像故事中的戰士和巨人那樣地去戰鬥。你和我們一樣是凡人嗎？還是你是居住在山中的老巫師？該不會現在一陣風吹起，你就會碎裂為塵土吧？」

騎士答道：「讓我親口來告訴你，因為我的同伴都已經死去，上帝作證，我將如實道來。看看我的頭盔上那朵紅寶石做成的玫瑰花，這是我的生命與希望的象徵。」

他告訴小伙子以下的事蹟，但是在述說的過程中，他越來越常停下來。在他講述著事蹟之際，玫瑰花在火光的映照下閃耀著血色光芒。小伙子把公雞羽毛插在他面前的泥土地，不停擺弄著羽毛，彷彿他們是戲裡的演員。

老人說：「我居住在遙遠的土地上，是聖約翰的座前騎士。在騎士團裡面，我是渴望承擔最艱苦任務的騎士，為的是那至高無上的真理。後來，一位巴勒斯坦[2]的騎士來到我們這裡，上帝已親自向他展現真理中的真理。他看見一朵巨大的火玫瑰，來自玫瑰的聲音讓他了解到，人們是如何不去理睬內心的光芒，只服膺於外在的指令與圭臬，這麼一來，光芒就會消失。愚蠢善良

---

2 十九世紀時，「巴勒斯坦」一詞才用為指稱地域。十四世紀時，這則故事就流傳於鄉間，因此「巴勒斯坦」在這裡是時代上的誤用。

的人無法思考，臣服於情慾的邪惡之徒不去思考，除了這兩種人，所有其他人都無法逃離這個詛咒。玫瑰的聲音又告訴巴勒斯坦騎士，那難以捉摸的心靈之光，仍在世上閃耀，照看著這個世界，但是光澤已經不如從前那般純粹了。隨著光芒逐漸黯淡，墮落就像傳染病，在星辰、山峰、草地、樹木間肆虐，而那些有能力洞悉真理、擁有古老智慧的人們，如果還願意繼續生活在這個墮落的世界，就無法進入神的國度，也就是玫瑰之心。因此，為了證明他們對於墮落力量的憤怒，他們要為玫瑰之神而殉身。在巴勒斯坦騎士為我們闡述之際，我們似乎在幻覺中看見一朵緋紅的玫瑰在他的四周展開，他似乎是從花心中對我們訴說這些事，空氣中也盈滿花香。我們明白到，這就是上帝透過騎士在對我們說話，於是我們聚集在騎士身旁，懇請他為我們指明所有事物的真理，教導我們如何遵循那道聲音的指示。他用誓言讓我們團結一致，賜予我們信號與暗語。這樣一來，在多年之後我們仍然可以認出彼此。他還為我們指定了會面地點，將我們這群人送入世間，要我們去找尋偉大崇高的目標，為之戰鬥而死。起初，我們很願意為了彰顯某位聖人的榮耀，禁食而亡，但騎士告訴我們，這麼做是敗德的，因為我們只是為了死亡本身而行動，而且還阻撓了上帝安排我們的死期和死亡的方式，如此將削弱祂的力量。我們應該為了奉獻而犧牲，而且僅僅是為了奉獻本身，然後再讓上帝以祂的方式，在祂選定的時刻，來

獎勵我們。於是，在那之後，他強制我們吃飯時要兩人同桌，看顧彼此，以免我們不當禁食，因為我們當中有人說過，如果是出自對於聖人的聖潔之愛禁食而死，那麼這種死法是可以被接受的。好幾年過去了，我的同伴一個個犧牲在神聖的土地上，與世上邪惡的王子戰鬥而死，或是因阻止強盜的惡行而死。最後，巴勒斯坦騎士也過世了，只剩下我孤零零一人。為了理想，我在每個以寡擊眾的戰場上戰鬥，如今我的頭髮逐漸花白，心中滿是恐懼，害怕上帝對我的表現不悅。但是後來，聽聞這個西方小島充斥著比任何地方都還要嚴重的戰爭與掠奪，我就來到這裡，並且找到了我所追尋的事物。啊，看哪！我全身上下充滿了無比的喜悅！」

騎士開始以拉丁語唱起了歌，他的聲音越來越微弱，眼睛也隨之闔上，嘴唇微開，小伙子知道他已經斷氣了。

「他跟我說了一個精彩的故事，因為裡頭提到了戰鬥。不過，我不是很了解故事的內容，而且故事太長了，我也記不住。」小伙子說。

他拿起騎士的寶劍，開始在軟土中挖掘墳墓。他使勁地挖著，黎明的微弱光線灑落在他的頭髮上，當山谷裡的公雞啼叫時，他差不多要挖好了。

「啊，我要去抓那隻雞！」說完，就沿著狹窄的小徑跑向山谷了。

4. 國王的智慧

　　愛爾蘭皇后死於難產，孩子被交由奶媽照顧。奶媽居住在柳條與泥漿搭起的簡陋小屋，位於森林的邊界。

　　一個夜晚，奶媽坐在搖籃旁搖著搖籃，仔細看著美麗的孩子，祈求上帝能賜予孩子和俊美的外表相稱的智慧。這時，有人敲門，她立刻站身，因為離這裡最近的住家是一哩外的國王宮殿，何況現在已是深夜了。

　　「誰在敲門？」她大聲問道。一個微弱的聲音回應：「開門！我是灰鷹老婦，來自廣袤森林的幽暗之處。」

　　奶媽驚恐地拉開門閂，一位高於常人、灰髮覆蓋的老婦走進屋子，站在搖籃前方。奶媽縮到牆角，目光緊盯著老婦，搖曳的火光中，她看到老婦頭頂上長的不是頭髮，而是灰鷹的羽毛。

　　孩子這時沉睡著，爐子裡的火光不停搖曳，孩子天真單純，爐火興高采烈，並不知道站在那裡的是多麼可怕的生物。

　　「開門！」又一個聲音大喊：「我是灰鷹老婦，我從廣袤森林的幽暗之處，照看著他的搖籃。」

　　奶媽顫抖的手指，差一點握不住門閂，但她還是又開了門。這位灰髮老婦和先前那位一般蒼老，也同樣頂著一

頭羽毛。她進門後，站在第一
位老婦的身旁。

　　很快地，第三位、第四
位灰髮老婦進來，一位接著一
位，直到整間屋子被她們碩大
的身軀塞得滿滿的。她們一動
也不動地站了許久，不發聲
響。她們是那種連沙子掉落的
聲音，都不會受驚擾的族類。
最後，一位老婦用微弱的聲音說道：「姊妹們，他銀色肌
膚下血紅心臟的色澤，讓我在遠處就注意到他了。」另一
位老婦說：「姊妹們，我會注意到他，是因為他心臟的跳
動，就像鳥兒在銀線織成的鳥巢裡拍動著翅膀。」另一老
婦又說：「姊妹們，我會知道他，是因為他的心跳聲像是
在銀色籠子裡快樂啼唱的鳥兒。」

　　說完，她們一道唱起歌來，最靠近搖籃的老婦用滿佈
皺紋的細長手指，輕推著搖籃。她們的歌聲溫柔、充滿憐
愛，像是廣袤森林裡吹拂的微風。她們唱了這樣的歌：

　　　久不見，情轉淡，
　　　紅男綠女，自古如此，
　　　意志堅定，興高采烈，
　　　取走我們的小麥食物，
　　　拿走我們的祭壇基石，

僅憑藉著冰雹、雨水、雷鳴，
我們將鮮紅的心臟轉為灰白，
直至時間的盡頭，我們依然真誠。

歌聲停歇，方才第一位開口的老婦說道：「我們只是想在他的血液中混入一滴我們的血。」

她要奶媽拿紡錘過來，然後用紡錘的鋒利處，在手臂上劃出一道傷口。她將一滴濃霧般灰白的血液，滴入小孩的雙唇間，然後離開屋子，沒入黑暗之中，其他人也一個接著一個靜靜地離開了。在這一切發生之際，小孩一直沒有睜開粉嫩的眼皮，爐火也沒停止搖曳。孩子天真單純，爐火興高采烈，他們不知道是什麼巨大的生物在搖籃旁俯下了身。

老婦離開後，奶媽鼓起勇氣，奔向國王的殿堂，在議會廳裡頭大聲喊道：夜裡，精靈在孩子身旁俯下了身，不知道是祝福還是詛咒。於是國王和詩人、執法者、獵人、廚師、將領，都跟隨著她來到小屋，他們湊近搖籃，像喜鵲般嘰嘰喳喳說著話，孩子坐了起來，直盯著他們看。

兩年過去了，國王在與弗博格的戰鬥中身亡，雖然詩人和執法者以孩子的名義來統治國家，但是他們盼望能在不久的將來，見到孩子成為一國之君，因為從沒見過這麼聰明的孩子。他對於眾神和這個世界的形成，有著無止盡的疑問和好奇。和他有關的傳聞，也在柳條編織而成的窮人屋子中不停地流傳。

一切都很平順，但有一件驚人的事，讓人心生不安。實際上，大家不停地談論著這件事：孩子的頭髮開始長出灰鷹的羽毛。奶媽不停地將羽毛剪下，但沒多久，羽毛又長得更加茂盛。

　　這其實不是什麼大不了的事，因為在那個年代，奇蹟是不足為道的。但是，依據古老的葉利法典，身體有缺陷的人不能登基。灰鷹是天空中的動物，沒坐上過餐桌，也不曾在爐火的火光中聆聽詩人歌唱。只要提到頭上長著灰鷹羽毛的人，人們就可能會聯想到污漬和毀滅。雖然人們讚嘆孩子的智慧，但是這樣的讚嘆，和對非人族類的恐懼，無法分開。

　　不過眾人仍決議要讓他統治國家，因為他們受夠了以前那些愚蠢國王所帶來的動亂，期待在他的統治之下，可以看到國家的繁榮景象。大家只是擔心，他偉大的智慧會迫使他要求自己恪遵法律，而讓平庸之士來代替他治理國家。

　　孩子七歲時，首領詩人召集詩人和執法者，來慎重衡量、考慮孩子的這些事情。孩子已經注意到，周遭的人只有頭髮，雖然他們告訴孩子，他們原先也有羽毛，但是因為祖先犯下的罪行，才讓羽毛都掉光了。不過他們知道，終有一天，當孩子開始在國內各處巡視時，就會發現真相。

深思熟慮之後，他們頒布了新法令，規定在死神面前掙扎的人，都要以人為的方式，將灰鷹的羽毛混入頭髮之中。他們還派遣男人帶著網子、彈弓和弓箭，在國內各地蒐集充足的羽毛。他們還規定，跟孩子透露真相的人，就會被從懸崖扔進大海。

　　日子一天天過去，孩子長成男孩，男孩又長成男人。小時候，他對每件事情都感到好奇；現在，他著迷於夢境中那些奇妙而幽微的想法，還有長久以來被視為相同事物之間的差異，以及長久以來被視為相異事物之間的共通之處。

　　大批人潮從各國前來拜訪他，並請教他對事物的看法。然而，邊界設立了守衛，強制所有訪客都要在頭髮上

插著灰鷹的羽毛。這些人聆聽他說話時，黑暗彷彿變成了光明，樂音充滿了他們的內心。但是，唉，等到他們返回自己的國度，他的話又變得虛無縹緲。人們記得的那些話，變得晦澀而難以理解，無法幫助他們應付忙碌匆促的生活。

　　的確，有些人開始過著不一樣的生活，但是新生活卻比不上過往生活精彩：那些一直在追求遠大目標的人，在得到他的讚賞，回到故土之後，發現他們先前追求的目標變得黯然失色，他們的臂膀也在戰鬥中變得軟弱無力，因為他教導這些人，對與錯只有一線之隔。另外，還有一些人從不追求任何理想，只想在平靜安穩中建立幸福美滿的家庭。而當他向他們展現那些願望裡所蘊藏的意義，他們發現自己過於軟弱，意志也不足以面對苦難，因為他讓他們見到了更偉大的目標。還有一些年輕人，聽過他闡述以上這些事情之後，幾個特定的字句，就像火焰一般，在他們的心中燃燒了起來，使得人世間那些親切有趣的事物，還有人際之間的往來交流，都變得無足輕重，他們因此走上了和先前不同的人生道路，但所有的人都帶著些許懊悔。

　　當有人向他請教日常生活事務，像是領土劃分、牛隻走失、殺人的刑罰所產生種種紛爭，他會向身邊最親近的人尋求建議。大家認為，這是出自於他的謙遜，但沒有人知道，各種想法和夢境充滿他的內心，像是軍隊在他的心中來回馳騁，因此他無暇顧及這些瑣事；而更少人知道，

他的心早已迷失在如潮水般湧進的思緒與幻想中，在孤獨中戰慄地發著抖。

在那些來拜訪、聽取意見的人之中，有位來自遠方小國的公主。他第一眼就愛上她了，她十分美麗，和他的國家裡的女子完全不同，她有一種奇特和蒼白的美，但是偉大的神母黛娜給她的是一顆與常人無異的心，她只要一想到神祕的灰鷹羽毛，就會陷入極大的恐懼之中。

集會結束後，他把她叫了過來，稱讚她的美貌。他坦白直率地讚美她，彷彿她是吟遊詩人所傳唱的神話；他也謙卑地請求她的愛，因為他只有在夢中才會變得心思細膩。

他崇高的名望讓公主不知所措，她搖擺不定，因為她渴望嫁的是能夠用臂彎帶她跨越山峰的戰士。國王日復一日地送她禮物，黃金搪瓷杯、商人從印度或中國帶回的衣裳，但是她始終在微笑與皺眉、接受與拒絕之間拿不定主意。

他在她的雙足之前展現智慧，他告訴她，英雄死後，是如何重回人世間，並再次展開任務；他也告訴她許多連精靈或因時間久遠或因無暇回想都已遺忘之事。她對他仍然欲迎還拒，而他仍懷抱著希望，他不相信在她那堪與智慧比擬的美麗外表下，不過是顆平凡心靈。

皇宮裡，有位高大年輕、擅長摔跤和馴馬的金髮男子。這一天，國王在城牆與森林之間的果園漫步時，從掩蓋住護城河的柳樹灌木叢中，傳來這個人的聲音。

他說：「親愛的，我厭惡他們逼迫你把這些骯髒的羽毛織入你的秀髮之中，也憎恨那隻帶著皇冠的猛禽每晚都得以安眠。」一個國王所鍾愛的銀鈴般聲音低聲答道：「我的頭髮不如你的美麗。現在我將你頭髮中的羽毛拔下來了，我就能夠把雙手放在你的髮絲中，像這樣，像這樣，就像這樣，你的頭髮不會在我心中投下恐懼和黑暗的陰影。」

突然，國王想起了許多一度忘卻而不能了解的事情，像是詩人和執法者可疑的話語、那些他已經合理化的疑惑，還有他一直以來的孤獨感受。於是，他用顫抖的聲音，叫來那對情侶。

他們從柳樹叢走出來，跪在他的腳邊請求原諒。國王俯身，拔下女子頭髮中的羽毛，然後不發一語地轉身朝宮殿走去。

他大步跨入集會大廳，召來詩人和執法者，他站上高台，以響亮而清晰的聲音問道：「執法者，你們為什麼讓我觸犯葉利法典？詩人們，你們為什麼讓我和智慧的奧祕作對？法律是為了人們的福祉而制定，但智慧是眾神所創造，凡人不該依循智慧而生存，因為智慧就像冰雹、雨水和閃電，其所依循的法則，對凡人來說是致命的，整件事情難道不是這樣的嗎？執法者和詩人，去過你們這種人該過的生活吧，然後召喚急躁的伊克哈來統治你們，我要去找尋我的同伴了。」

國王走到他們之中，一根根拔下他們頭髮中的灰鷹羽毛，把羽毛扔在地上的燈芯草中，走了出去。沒人敢跟上前去，因為他的雙眼如同猛禽般閃爍。從此以後，再也沒人看過他或是聽過他的聲音。

　　有人相信，他在邪惡的力量之中找到了永遠的棲身之處；也有人認為，他此後和黑暗又儡人的女神們一起生活，她們整晚坐在森林裡的水塘邊，看著星曜在寂寥的水面上起起落落。

5. 春之心[1]

　　一位垂垂老矣、臉龐如鳥爪般乾癟的男人，坐在佈滿岩石的海岸邊沉思，平坦的小島上長滿榛木，座落於吉爾湖面最寬之處。一位黃褐色臉龐的十七歲男孩坐在他身旁，看著燕子在靜止的水面上捕捉小蟲。老人穿著破舊的藍色天鵝絨衣，男孩穿著起絨粗呢外套，戴著一頂藍色的帽子，老人的脖子上還掛著藍色珠子串起的誦經用念珠。

　　在他們的身後，有座半掩於樹叢中的小修道院。很久以前，這座修道院被女王黨[2]中褻瀆神明的人所燒毀，但男孩用燈芯草重新修葺了屋頂，這樣老人在垂暮之年就能有個遮風避雨的地方。

　　不過，男孩還沒開始整理修道院周圍的花園。花園裡，以前的修士種植的百合花與玫瑰花雜亂地繁茂生長，與蕨類的捲旋葉混雜纏繞在一起了。百合花與玫瑰後方的蕨類，也生長得十分高大茂密，要是小孩踮著腳尖走在裡頭也會淹沒，消失在視線中。蕨類再過去的地方，生長著許多榛樹與幾棵小橡樹。

1　這篇故事名稱為「春之心」，故事中也有很多春天的敘述，但是根據百合跟玫瑰的花季、占星學上的計算，以及愛爾蘭仲夏夜的傳統來看，這個故事應該是發生在六月中。

2　女王黨（Queen's Party），在十六世紀，愛爾蘭人和英國人交戰。這篇故事的時代背景為十七世紀。

男孩說：「主人，您長期禁食，在日落之後，用花楸木杖敲地，召喚那些居住在水中、在榛木和橡樹間的生命。對您來說，這負荷太重了，請您稍事歇息吧。您今天搭在我肩上的手掌，比從前更為沉重；您的步履，也比從前更蹣跚。人們都說，您比老鷹還要年長，但是您卻不去追尋那屬於老年的平靜。」

他熱切急促地說著，整顆心都投入到字裡行間。老人緩慢而慎重地回答，彷彿一顆心仍在過去的遙遠往事裡。

「我告訴你，為什麼我一直無法休息，也是時候讓你知道了。這五年來，你這麼忠誠、甚至是真摯地照顧我，緩和了註定會降臨在智者身上的孤獨。而此刻，因為我的操勞即將結束，我的願望眼看也要實現了，更需要讓你明白一切。」他說。

「主人，請不要覺得我在質問您。我的職責就是讓爐火持續燃燒，讓屋頂密實穩固，雨水淋不進來，強風也無法吹至樹林。我得將厚重的書籍從書架上取下，擁有一顆始終對知識不感興趣卻又虔誠的心靈。上帝從祂的豐饒之中，讓每個生命擁有不同的智慧，而我的才智就是為了做這些事務而生。」

「你害怕了。」老人說，瞬間流露出微慍的眼神。

男孩說：「有時夜裡，你手上拿著花楸木杖在讀書，我往門外望去，見了一位壯碩灰衣人在榛樹林裡趕著豬群，還有許多戴著紅帽的小矮人從湖裡出來，趕著前方的白色乳牛。跟灰衣人比起來，我比較不怕小矮人，因為小

矮人會靠近屋子擠牛奶，喝了泡沫牛奶後就跳起舞來。雖然我知道愛跳舞的人心地善良，但我還是害怕他們的一切。我害怕空中浮現、緩緩在四處飄蕩，有著白皙手臂的高大女人，她們為自己戴上玫瑰或百合花皇冠，甩動著充滿生氣的頭髮，那髮絲舞動著，忽而飄散，忽而又聚攏。我聽見她們彼此用思緒的流動來交談。她們有著溫柔美麗的臉龐，但弗比斯之子安格斯啊！我害怕所有精靈，也怕把他們引來我們身邊的那魔法。」

　　老人說：「為什麼？為什麼害怕古老的神祇？他們為你的祖先創造了矛，讓他們得以在戰爭中變得強大。為什麼害怕小矮人？他們在夜裡從湖水深處出現，與蟋蟀一同在他們的住所唱著歌，在我們墮落的那些日子，他們仍守護著世上的美好事物。我要告訴你，為什麼在別人因年老而進入夢鄉時，我仍要禁食、工作。如果沒有你的幫忙，我做這些事都是徒勞的。等你為我做完了最後一件差事，你就可以離開，去建造你的小屋、耕種田地、娶個女孩為妻，然後將那些古老的眾神遺忘。公爵、騎士、鄉紳給我金幣銀幣，因為我讓他們遠離邪惡的目光，還有女巫用愛情編織而成的魔法。我將這些金幣銀幣留了下來，也保存了公爵夫人、騎士夫人、鄉紳夫人給我的金銀幣，她們要我別讓母牛因為精靈而乳汁枯竭，也要我別讓精靈從絞乳器中偷走奶油。我留著這些錢，就是為了使命完成的那一天，而此時，終點就在眼前。所以，你如果要加強屋子樑脊的強度，或是讓你

的酒窖和貯藏室滿溢，你不會缺少金銀幣。我終其一生都在尋找生命的祕密。我年輕時並不快樂，因為我知道青春終將逝去；我壯年時也不快樂，因為我知道年老終將來到。不管是年輕、壯年、老年，我都致力於找尋生命的奧祕。我渴望生命能夠有好幾世紀那麼長，我蔑視只有八十幾個冬日的人生，我希望能夠，喔！不！我必定能夠像這塊土地的古老造物主那樣。我年輕時，在一座西班牙修道院裡發現一份希伯來文手稿，上面說到，在太陽進入白羊座到離開獅子座的這段時間，有那麼一個瞬間世界會顫抖[3]，不死之神的讚歌也會響起，凡是找到這一瞬間並聆聽歌聲的人，就能夠擁有不死之身。我於是回到愛爾蘭，請教仙人和乳牛獸醫[4]，問他們知否這個時刻，儘管大家都聽聞過這件事，卻沒人能夠在沙漏中找到那個時刻。我轉而在魔法中尋找，在禁食與勞役中度過人生，希望能夠讓眾神和精靈來到我身旁。此刻，終於有個戴紅帽、嘴唇上有著鮮奶泡沫的精靈在我耳邊低語，說那個時刻就要到來了。明天，黎明破曉第一個小時的最後一點點時間裡，就能找到那個時刻，然後我將前往南方大陸，在桔樹林中建立起白色的大理石宮殿，召來勇敢與美麗之人，一齊進入永恆的青春國度，但是我得聽完整首歌。嘴上沾著鮮奶的小矮人告訴我，你要砍下大量的綠色樹枝，堆在我的門邊和窗戶四周，還要在地板鋪上新鮮的燈芯草，再用修士的玫瑰和百合覆蓋整張桌子和燈芯草。你今晚就要行動，明天黎

明破曉第一個小時的最後時刻，你一定要來這裡找我。」

「那時候你會變得很年輕嗎？」男孩問。

「到那時候，我會變得跟你一樣年輕，但我現在還是又蒼老又疲憊，所以你得扶我到椅子上，把書拿給我。」

男孩讓弗比斯之子安格斯待在房間，然後點了燈，巫師的戲法讓這盞燈散發著不知名花朵的甜美香味。他走進森林，從榛樹上砍下蒼翠的樹枝，在小島的西岸割下許多束燈芯草[5]，這一帶的小石子都被微微傾斜的泥沙堆所覆蓋。

傍晚時分，他還沒砍下足夠的樹枝和燈芯草，當他將最後一綑搬回住處時，已是深夜。他又返回採摘玫瑰跟百合，那是一個溫暖又美麗的夜晚，世間萬物彷彿都是由寶石雕琢而成。南方的斯魯斯森林，像是由綠寶石上切割而成；映照著森林的水面，如蛋白石般閃耀；他摘下的玫瑰彷彿是燃燒的紅寶石；百合花也有著珍珠般溫潤的光澤。

萬物像是永遠不會消逝，除了一隻螢火蟲，牠那微弱的光芒持續在暗處燃燒，緩慢地四處飛舞，看起來像是唯一有生命的生物，就像人類的願望一樣，轉瞬即逝。

男孩採集了許多玫瑰花和百合花，然後將螢火蟲塞入這堆珍珠和紅寶石中，一起抱進了房間。這時老人坐在房間裡，半睡半醒，男孩把一抱抱的樹枝和燈芯草鋪在地板

---

3 顫抖的時刻，指夏至。

4 乳牛獸醫（cow-doctor）指能和精靈溝通並擁有治癒疾病能力的人。

5 愛爾蘭傳統中，村子裡的年輕人會在仲夏夜去附近的沼澤割採燈芯草，然後撒在屋子內外。

和桌上，然後輕輕關上了門。男孩躺上自己的燈芯草床，夢想在安穩的壯年時身邊有心愛的妻子，孩子們的快樂笑聲不絕於耳。

日出時分，他起床，拿著沙漏來到湖邊。他在船上放了麵包跟一瓶酒，這樣主人在旅途之初，就不會食物匱乏。然後他坐了下來，等待日出之後的第一個小時。

慢慢地，鳥兒唱起了歌，當最後一顆沙粒落下之時，一切事物似乎都湧出了屬於自己的音樂。那是一年當中最美麗而充滿生機的時刻，人們可以聽見春天的心跳。

他起身去找主人，但是綠色的樹枝堆滿門前，他得清出一條路。他進入房間，陽光照耀在地板、牆面和桌上，忽隱忽現地灑落下光圈，將所有東西都染上淺綠色的光亮。

老人坐在椅子上，頭抵著胸脯，手裡抱緊一大把玫瑰和百合。他左手邊桌上放著一個裝滿金銀幣的皮革行囊，像是為旅途準備的盤纏；在他右手邊，有一根長長的拐杖。

男孩拍拍他，他一動也不動。男孩又抬了抬他的雙手，他的雙手很冰冷，然後沉沉地落下。

小伙子說：「對他來說，也許和別人一樣數著念珠禱告會比較好，而非費盡歲月在不死力量之中尋尋覓覓。他要是願意，可以在自己原本的生活中找到所要追求的。啊，是啊，唸著禱詞，親吻念珠，或許那樣會比較好！」

他看著那件襤褸的藍色天鵝絨衣，注意到衣服上面沾滿花粉。一隻畫眉鳥跳上了堆在窗邊的樹枝，唱起了歌。

6. 火焰與幻影的詛咒

　　一個平靜的夏夜，偽善的費德克‧漢米爾頓率領二十幾位清教徒騎兵，撞開矗立於斯萊戈郡加拉湖畔的白衣修士修道院大門。在轟隆巨響聲中，大門倒下，只見裡頭一群修士圍著聖壇，身上白色長袍在聖燭的沉穩微光中不停地閃爍著。所有修士都跪在聖壇前，只有修道院長站在聖壇的階梯上，手中拿著碩大的黃銅十字架苦像。

　　費德克‧漢米爾頓下令：「射殺他們！」但是沒人敢真的聽令行動，因為這些騎兵才改信為清教徒不久，對十字架和聖燭還是有所忌憚。

　　聖壇上的白色燭火，將騎兵的影子投射在教堂穹頂和牆面上，騎兵們一移動，影子也跟著在突拱和紀念石碑上跳著奇幻的舞蹈。那一瞬間，所有的一切都靜默下來，費

德克‧漢米爾頓的五位貼身侍衛舉起火槍，射殺了五位修士。火槍的槍聲與煙硝，削弱了聖壇燭火微光帶來的神祕氛圍，於是其他騎兵也鼓起勇氣進攻。沒多久，修士們都倒落在聖壇階梯旁，白色的長袍上沾滿了鮮血。

「把屋子燒了！」費德克‧漢米爾頓大喊。一位騎兵聽到命令，出去抱了一堆乾稻草進來，擱在西側的牆邊後就退回原地，仍對十字架和聖燭心存恐懼。

費德克‧漢米爾頓的五位貼身侍衛見到此狀，便衝上前去，每人拿起一支聖燭，點燃稻草，讓稻草熊熊燃燒起來。紅色的火舌迅速上竄，在一根根突拱和一座座紀念碑間忽隱忽現，火勢也沿著地面四處蔓延，座位與長凳都陷入火海之中。影子的舞蹈消失了，接續而上的是火焰的舞蹈。騎兵紛紛退到南側的大門，注視眼前的黃衣舞者四處跳著舞蹈。

有那麼一刻，聖壇安穩地矗立在白色燭光之中。騎兵都以為修道院長被燒死了，但是當他們的目光轉向聖壇，修道院長竟然站了起來，雙手拿著十字架高舉頭上。

他突然大聲喊道：「這群人竟然攻擊安住於上帝榮光之中的人，讓我們為他們哀悼吧，他們必定會迷失在無法駕馭的幻影之中，盲目跟從失控的火焰。」

修道院長說完話，便向前倒下身亡，手中的黃銅十字架從聖壇的階梯滾落下來。

煙霧越來越濃密，騎士們被逼到教堂的內院，前方的修道院陷入熊熊大火，後方的彩繪窗戶閃耀著光芒，色彩

斑斕的玻璃上，滿滿繪製了聖徒與殉道者的圖像，祂們彷彿從神聖的沉睡狀態中甦醒，轉為生氣勃勃且怒不可遏的生命。

騎兵們眼花撩亂，一時之間，眼前都是聖徒和殉道者怒髮衝冠的臉孔。但沒多久，一位渾身上下都是塵土的男子向他們跑了過來。

男子大聲喊著：「愛爾蘭人吃了敗仗，就派遣兩位信差，要集結漢米爾頓領地周圍地區的人，群起攻打你們，要是不設法阻止這兩位信差，你們就會在森林裡遇襲，永遠別想回到故土了。兩位信差沿著布本山和卡什那蓋爾山之間的道路，朝東北方騎去了。」

費德克・漢米爾頓召來那五位最先舉起火槍射殺修士的騎兵，對他們說道：「你們立刻上馬，越過森林，朝著那座山騎去，追上信差，殺了他們。」

騎兵們火速出發，一下子就不見蹤影。沒多久，他們在如今稱為巴克利淺灘的地方涉水渡河，然後衝入森林。他們騎著前人踏出的小徑，小徑循著河流的北岸蜿蜒延伸。樺樹和梣樹的樹枝在他們頭頂上方交纏，遮住了朦朧的月光，小徑一片漆黑。

他們策馬奔騰，不時彼此交談，有時也會看見迷途的鼬鼠或是兔子飛奔而過，消失在黑暗之中。森林裡的陰森和死寂，逐漸籠罩他們，於是他們越騎越近，絮絮地談起話來。他們是多年的同袍，對彼此都很熟悉。

一個已婚的騎兵告訴其他人說，在這場攻打白衣修士

的荒誕長征後，他要是能夠平安歸去，妻子會有多麼高興；而當她知曉幸運如何化解他魯莽的性格可能招致的不幸，又會感到多麼雀躍。

　　五人之中最年長的騎兵妻子已經過世了，他告訴大家，家中的櫥櫃上層有一大甕酒在等著他。第三位騎兵最年輕，有個引頸企盼他歸來的情人，他不發一語地騎在其他人的前方。這時，這位年輕人突然停了下來，大家看見他座下的馬正發著抖[1]。

　　他說：「我好像看見了什麼，但不太確定，很可能只是個幻影，像是一隻頭上戴著銀色皇冠的巨大蠕蟲[2]。」

　　其中一位騎兵將手抬至額頭前方，一副準備要劃十字的樣子，但他突然想起，自己已經改宗了，於是他放下手，說道：「那一定只是幻影罷了，各式奇形怪狀的幻影一直圍繞在我們身邊。」

他們沉默地繼續前行。那天稍早下了雨，樹梢滴落的雨水，打溼了他們的頭髮跟肩膀。一會兒，他們又聊起來了，他們曾在許多戰役中併肩抵禦敵人，此時他們談論起自己身上傷疤的由來，以便在心中喚起過去一同出生入死的強烈同袍之情，藉此忘卻森林中懾人的孤寂感。

　　突然間，走在前方的兩匹馬發出嘶吼，直挺挺地站著，怎樣也不肯往前走。騎兵看見閃閃發光的水波，聽見湍急的水流聲，才發現前方有一條河流。他們下了馬，半拉半哄，費了一番力氣才將馬匹帶到河邊。

　　河流中央站著一位高大老婦，她灰白的長髮在灰色的裙襬上飄盪著，在水深及膝的河水中，不時地俯身彎腰，像是在清洗什麼東西。不久，騎兵們察覺到她正在清洗漂浮在水面上的東西，月亮灑下朦朧的月光，他們驚覺那是一具男人的屍體。正當他們聚精會神地看著，屍體的臉龐順著水流的漩渦，轉至他們面前，五位騎兵在那一瞬間，同時認出那是他們自己的臉龐。

　　他們驚嚇過度，呆站在原地。婦人緩慢而高聲地說：「你們看見我兒子了嗎？他戴著銀色皇冠，皇冠上面鑲著紅寶石。」

1　愛爾蘭許多地區的人們相信，馬能夠和另一個世界的幽靈、
　　精靈溝通。
2　巨大水蛇常出現在愛爾蘭的傳說故事中。

最年長也是最常負傷的騎兵拔出寶劍，說道：「我為上帝的真理而戰，才不會害怕撒旦的幻影。」說完，就衝進河裡，但沒多久就返回。婦人已經消失無蹤，他用寶劍猛刺空氣和河水，但什麼也沒找著。

　　五位騎兵再度上馬，想在淺灘上逼迫馬匹前進，卻一點辦法也沒有。他們騎著馬，從各個方向衝刺，但馬匹總是口吐唾沫，高高地抬起前腳，用後腳站立著掙扎。

　　年長的騎兵說：「我們回頭往森林裡騎，去河的上游。」

　　他們在樹下行進，地上的藤蔓在馬蹄的踩踏下劈啪作響，樹枝也不停敲打著他們的鐵製頭盔。約莫過了二十分鐘，他們騎出了森林，再度出現在河畔。又過了十分鐘，他們在一處水深不及馬鐙的地方，橫越河流。

　　在河流的另一側，林木稀疏，月光被切割成一道道細長的光束，起風之時，雲朵快速輕拂過月亮，細長的光束在稀疏的樹叢和瘦小的冷杉間，彷彿跳起了古怪詭異的舞蹈。樹頂傳出了蕭颯的嗚咽聲，像是逝者在風中呻吟，騎兵們不禁想起，傳說煉獄中的死者會被置於樹木頂端和利石的尖處，接受被吐唾沫的懲罰。騎兵們又稍稍轉向南方騎去，希望能夠重返那條前人踏出的小徑，但尋遍不著。

　　就在這時候，詭異的嗚咽越來越大聲，火焰般的月光也舞動得越來越快了。漸漸地，他們隱約聽見遠方傳來了風笛的樂音，於是滿懷希望地朝聲音奔去。

　　聲音是從一個杯狀洞穴的底部傳出來的，洞穴裡有個

形容枯槁的老人，他戴著一頂紅色帽子，坐在火堆旁，腳邊的泥地上插著一支正在燃燒的火把。老人奮力地吹著老風笛，紅髮垂懸在臉上，就像是生在石塊上的鐵鏽。

洞穴裡的老人抬起頭，問道：「你們有看見我的妻子嗎？她在清洗東西！她在清洗東西！」

「他令我畏懼，我怕他也是精靈的一分子。」年輕的騎兵說。

年長的騎兵說：「他不是精靈，他是人類，我看到他臉上的曬斑，我們得逼迫他當我們的嚮導。」他抽出利劍，其他人也一起抽出利劍。

他們團團圍住吹笛人，用劍指著他。年長的騎兵告訴老人，他們要殺了那兩位愛爾蘭叛徒，他們正騎在布本山和主要支脈卡什那蓋爾山間的道路上，所以老人要上馬，坐在當中一名騎兵的前方，擔任嚮導，因為他們迷路了。

吹笛人轉頭指著一旁的樹木，那裡有一匹年邁的白馬，已經安上馬彎，繫了韁繩，也配了馬鞍。他將風笛掛在背上，拿起火炬，跳上白馬，快馬加鞭地衝到騎兵前出發了。

森林裡的樹木越來越稀疏，地面也開始朝向山頂傾斜。月亮已經下山，星星在遼闊的穹蒼中閃著銀白色的光芒。地面越來越陡峭，最後他們遠遠地離開了森林，來到了平坦寬闊的山頂。森林在他們腳下連綿不絕，南側炙烈燃燒的城鎮，噴發出紅色的火光，但是前方和頭頂滿是銀白色的光芒。

嚮導突然拉緊韁繩，用空出的手，指向前方，淒厲地大叫：「快看，看那支聖燭！」他騎馬快速俯衝而下，拿著火炬四處揮舞。

　　「你們聽見愛爾蘭信差的馬蹄聲嗎？」嚮導大喊：「快點！快點！要不然他們就要逃出你們的手掌心了！」嚮導像是因追逐所帶來的快感，大笑了起來。

　　騎兵們遠遠聽見下方彷彿傳來喀喀的馬蹄聲，但是山勢越來越陡峭，他們向前俯衝的速度也越來越快，他們拉緊韁繩，但是無濟於事，馬匹似乎已經失去控制。

　　嚮導把手中的韁繩扔在年邁白馬的脖子上，一邊揮舞著雙臂，一邊唱著蓋爾語的歌謠。突然，騎兵們在極深的山底看見河水閃耀著微弱的光芒，才意識到自己正處於懸崖的邊緣。這座懸崖在今日稱作魯格那蓋爾，翻譯成英文的意思是「一躍而下的外來者」。

　　六匹馬向前躍下，其中五個人的尖叫響徹雲霄，不一會兒，五位騎兵連同馬匹摔落在山腳的綠色斜坡上，發出又悶又鈍的撞擊聲響。

7. 曙光中的老人

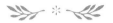

在羅席斯接近「死者之岬」的地方，有一間廢棄的水手屋，兩個像是眼睛的圓形窗戶眺望著大海。那兒有間小泥屋，建於上個世紀，也是一座瞭望台，裡面住著年邁的麥可‧布魯恩，他以前是走私商，子孫也是。傍晚時分，每當巨大的雙軌縱帆船從洛夫萊海港悄悄地駛進海灣，他的職責就是在南面窗戶掛上提燈，把信號打到多倫島上，那裡有另一個提燈會再打信號到羅席斯城。

除了發出這閃著微光的信息，他不太跟人打交道。他年紀很大了，只會站在煙囪旁吊掛的西班牙橡木十字架下，探索自己的靈魂，或是對著石製念珠鞠躬，祈禱能為他帶來一艘滿載法國絲綢與織品的船隻。除此之外，他對什麼事都漠不關心。

一天晚上，輕柔溫順的微風吹拂著，「憐憫之母號」比預計的行程慢了許多，所以他照看著海面好幾個小時。他看見東邊的天色正在轉白，推測這艘船不敢冒著風險駛進洛夫萊港灣，在黎明之後下錨，所以他準備躺在稻草堆上休息。他看見一行蒼鷺，從多倫島慢慢飛向被蘆葦半覆蓋住的水塘，水塘就坐落於小羅席斯的後方。他從未見過蒼鷺飛越海洋，蒼鷺是生存於海岸邊的鳥類。這時，可能

是飛越海洋的蒼鷺讓他從昏昏欲睡中驚醒，但更可能是因為遲遲未到的雙軌縱帆船，讓他的食物櫃空空如也。於是，他拿出生鏽的獵槍，上頭用細繩繫著槍管，然後跟上朝著水塘飛行的蒼鷺。

不一會工夫，他就走到蒼鷺旁，一大群蒼鷺抬著腳踏在淺水裡。他的身體蜷伏在一叢燈芯草的後方，看著獵槍的雷管，低下腰對著念珠輕聲說道：「守護神派翠克，讓我打下蒼鷺，把牠做成餡餅，這就夠我吃個四天，我的食量已經不如年輕的時候了。只要你不讓我失誤，我就在吃完餡餅之前，每晚為你誦念一次玫瑰經。」

要射中站在水中的蒼鷺，就得涉水，他擔心這會讓他得風濕病。於是他臥倒下來，將獵槍放在一顆大石頭上，瞄準一隻站立在橫跨小溪的平坦青草堤岸上的蒼鷺，小溪向水塘緩緩流去。

然而，當他沿著槍管瞄準時，蒼鷺消失了，反見一個年邁的孱弱老人站在那裡，讓他驚懼不已。他放下槍，蒼鷺又出現在那裡，牠低著頭，羽毛一動也不動，彷彿從宇宙初始就一直在那裡沉睡著。

於是他又舉起槍，但他才循著鐵管瞄準，老人又立刻出現在眼前。他再度放下槍管，老人就又消失。

他放下槍，在胸前劃了三次十字，唸了一段主禱文和

聖母頌，咕噥說道：「上帝和守護者的敵人，正站立於平坦之處，垂釣於聖潔的水中。」他仔細而緩慢地再一次瞄準目標。

他射擊了。煙霧散去後，他看見有個老人蜷縮在草地上，一行蒼鷺喧鬧著朝著大海飛去。他繞過水塘的轉彎處，走到小溪，低頭看著老人，黑色和綠色的褪色衣物包覆著，那是古老的樣式，上面還沾著血跡。目睹這樣的邪惡之事，他搖頭嘆氣。

突然，衣服動了，一隻手臂朝向他脖子上掛著的念珠伸出來，細長瘦削的手指差點碰到十字架。他跳起來大叫：「你這個巫師，我是不會讓任何邪惡的東西碰我神聖的念珠。」一想到方才差點讓他碰到念珠，便不住地顫抖。

一個微弱的聲音回答他，像是一陣嘆息，「你只要聽我說，就會知道我不是巫師，而且願意讓我在死前親吻你的十字架。」

他答道：「我聽你說，但是我不會讓你碰我神聖的念珠。」他坐在草地上，離瀕死男人有一些距離。他為槍充填子彈，然後把槍放在膝蓋上，讓自己鎮定下來，準備聽他說話。

「不知道在多少世代之前，我們這些現在是蒼鷺的人，是國王里亥爾跟前的博學之士，我們不打獵，也不上戰場，更不需聆聽德魯依人的講道，甚至連愛情——如果愛情真的降臨——對我們而言，也不過是轉瞬即逝的火焰。德魯依人和詩人多次向我們提起德魯依聖人派翠克的事蹟，大部分德魯依人和詩人都對他很不滿，

有些人認為，他所傳授的教義只不過是以新的象徵意象來闡明眾神的教義罷了，目的只是要讓自己受到擁戴。當他們講述派翠克的事蹟時，我們都聽得打哈欠。最後他們跑過來大喊，說是聖派翠克來到國王的宮殿，和他們爭論了起來。但是我們不願意傾聽任何一邊的立場，因為我們正忙著爭論大小音韻的問題。當他們帶著施了魔法的棍棒經過我們的門前，進入森林要把聖派翠克趕走，我們不受干擾。當他們在黃昏後從森林回來，身上的衣服被扯爛，絕望地哭泣，我們仍然不受打擾。因為我們正在用歐甘文字[1]寫下我們的想法，而小刀刻字時發出的喀搭聲，讓我們內心充滿平靜，就連我們之間的爭論也是充滿歡樂。甚至在早晨，當群眾經過我們，去聆聽那位新來的德魯依人佈道時，我們也不受影響。等那群人離開後，我們有人放下刀子，打著呵欠，伸了個懶腰，突然聽見遠方有個聲音在講話，他知道，那是德魯依人派翠克正在國王的宮殿裡佈道。但我們內心聽不到聲音，我們只是雕刻著、爭論著、閱讀著、一起輕聲笑著。不久，一陣腳步聲朝著屋子傳來，接著兩個高大的人影站在門口，其中一位穿著白衣，另一位穿著深紅色長袍，像是一朵巨大的百合和一株巨大的罌粟。我們知道，那是德魯依人派翠克跟我們的國王里亥爾。我們放下小刀，向國王彎腰鞠躬，當我們黑色和綠色的長袍停止沙沙作響，此時跟我們說話的不是國王里亥爾粗糙的聲音，而是一個令人著迷的陌生聲音，那聲音似乎來

自德魯依的城牆垛火焰後方。那聲音說：『在國王的宮殿裡，我宣揚造物者的戒律，從世界的中央到天堂的窗口，一片寂靜。老鷹展翅，在潔白的空中滑翔；魚靜止的魚鰭，漂浮在微暗的水中。大樹枝上的朱雀、鶺鴒和麻雀，都停下了唧啾不停的舌頭，雲朵像是白色的大理石，河流成了靜止的明鏡，遠處池塘中的蝦子也耐著性子忍受永恆，雖然這的確不容易。』當他列舉這些小動物時，就像是國王在統計子民。『但是當所有其他的事物都陷入沉寂，你們的小刀卻在那根木棍上持續地發出喀搭、喀搭聲，惹怒了天使。噢，可憐的樹根啊，你在冬天被凍傷，雖然夏天在你的身上留下了無數腳印，你也未曾甦醒。噢，你們這些人不曾嚐過愛情的滋味，也未曾聆聽歌聲，你們缺乏智慧，生活在記憶的陰影中。在那裡，當天使飛過你們的頭頂時，他們的雙足無法碰觸你們；在那裡，當惡魔經過你們的腳下時，他們的頭髮無法掃過你們，我將對你們施予咒語，讓你們變成後世的警惕。你們將變成灰色的蒼鷺，站在灰色的水池中沉思。當這個世界充滿嘆息時，你們將輕輕飛過。你們將遺忘星光，也不會看見太陽的光芒，你們將對其他蒼鷺講道，直到牠們都變得像你們一樣，成為後世的警惕。死亡將會出奇不意地降臨在你們身上，因為你們永遠無法確定任何事情。』」

---

1 歐甘文（Ogham）為古愛爾蘭文。

博學老人的聲音停止了，獵人的腰彎到了膝蓋的槍上，眼睛注視著地面。他太笨了，聽不懂。他就這樣彎著腰，要不是有人扯動他脖子上的念珠，將他從夢中驚醒，他大概會一直持續這樣的狀態。博學的老人爬過草地，想把十字架拉到唇邊。

　　「你絕對不能碰我神聖的念珠！」虔誠的信奉者大叫，用槍管敲打老人細長乾枯的手指。

　　他再也不會發抖了，因為老人向後倒在草地上，喘了一聲，然後一片寂靜。

　　他彎下腰，仔細端詳那黑色和綠色的衣服，當他清楚了解他擁有那博學老人所渴望的東西時，他的恐懼減少了，況且神聖的念珠安然無恙，他的恐懼都消失了。他想，眼前這件大斗篷和下面的小件貼身斗篷，如果都是暖和的，而且沒有破洞，那麼聖派翠克就會取走裡頭的魔力，然後留下衣服給人類使用。

　　然而，當他碰觸那件黑色和綠色的衣服時，手指所及之處，布料隨即消失。另一件奇蹟的事情發生了，一陣風吹過水池，博學老人和古老的服飾化成一堆塵土，微風捲走小堆塵土，最後只剩下一塊平坦的青草地。

8. 空無一物之處，是上帝所在之處

　　修道院長馬拉吉涅、德弗修士、禿琺修士、彼得修士、派翠克修士、彼特修士、菲爾布勞斯修士，他們圍坐在火爐邊。一位在修補釣魚線，打算放進河裡抓鰻魚；一位在製作捕鳥的陷阱；一位在修補鏟子壞掉的手把；一位在厚重的書上寫字；一位在敲打收藏書本的黃金盒子邊角。學生們坐在修士腳邊的燈芯草上，將來有一天他們也會成為修士。

　　其中有個孩子叫作奧利歐，約莫八、九歲，他仰躺在地上，火爐的煙從屋頂的洞口飄出，星星在煙霧中若隱若現。

　　他轉向正在厚重的書上寫字的修士，這位修士的職責是教導孩童讀書。奧利歐問：「德弗修士，星星是繫在什麼東西上呀？」

　　修士很高興自己那位最愚笨的學生對事物感到這麼好奇，於是把筆放下，回答道：「天上一共有九個晶狀球體，月亮繫在第一個球體、水星繫在第二個、金星繫在

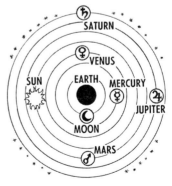

第三個、太陽繫在第四個、火星繫在第五個、木星第六個、土星第七個，這些都是會移動的星星。但第八個球體上繫的是固定不動的星星，而第九顆球體是由宇宙第一因所形成。」[1]

「在那之外呢？」男孩問。

「在那之外，什麼都沒有，只有上帝。」

孩子的目光轉移到黃金盒子上，問道：「為什麼彼得修士放了一顆大紅寶石在他的盒子側邊？」

「因為紅寶石象徵上帝的慈愛。」

「為什麼紅寶石象徵上帝的慈愛？」

「因為紅寶石的紅色光澤就像火焰，火焰能將所有的東西燃燒殆盡，而空無一物之處，就是上帝所在之處。」

孩子陷入沉默。不久他坐了起來，說道：「有人在外面。」

修士回答：「不是的，那是狼群，我聽見牠們在雪地中四處走動好一陣子了。牠們變得很野，因為寒冬把牠們趕下了山。昨天晚上，牠們破壞了柵欄，叼走了許多羊隻。我們一個不小心，牠們就會吃掉所有的東西。」

「不是，那是人的腳步聲，聲音很沉，而且我也聽到了狼群的腳步聲。」

他話才說完，就有人敲了三下門。

---

1 在托勒密的天動學說中，地球固定在世界中心，為九顆行星所環繞，而天堂包覆著全世界。「第一因」的英文為「First Substance」。

「我去開門，一定是凍壞了。」

「不要開門，可能是狼人，搞不好
會把我們全部都吃掉。」

但孩子已經將沉甸甸的木門閂拉
開，而大家的臉孔多數變得蒼白，轉向
那扇緩慢打開的門。

「他戴著念珠和十字架，不可能是
狼人。」孩子說。一個男子走進來，用
溫柔又欣喜的眼神，環視著一張張臉。雪花積在他雜亂的
長鬍鬚上，積在長及腰間、纏結成塊的頭髮上，也從半裹
著憔悴身軀的破爛斗篷上滑落下來。

他站在離爐火一段距離的地方，目光最後落在修道院
長馬拉吉涅的身上。他說：「啊！神聖的院長，請允許我
到火爐邊取暖，烤乾堆積在我的鬍鬚、頭髮、斗篷上的雪
吧，這樣我才不會因山上的嚴寒而凍死，也不會因為存心
要殉道而激怒上帝。」

「來火爐邊暖暖身子吧，吃點奧利歐拿給你的食物。
在耶穌為之而死的人之中，居然有像你這樣可憐的人，令
人不忍。」院長說。

那人在火爐旁坐下。奧利歐取下他正滴著水的披風，
在他面前放了肉、麵包和葡萄酒。他只吃了麵包，把酒放
在一旁，然後要了點水。

他的鬍鬚跟頭髮乾了些，四肢也不再顫抖。他又說話
了：「請安排我做些勞役，給我最粗重的工作，因為我是

上帝管轄的可憐人之中最可憐的。」

　　修士們便討論起有什麼工作可以派給他。一開始，大家毫無頭緒，所有的工作都有人做了。最後，有人想到禿弦修士，他太笨了，什麼都不會做，所以在磨坊裡推笨重的石磨，但是他逐漸上了年紀，所以這個乞丐可以在早上去磨坊工作。

　　寒冬過去了，春去夏來，磨坊從沒閒置著，乞丐也從沒發過牢騷。大家經過磨坊時，都聽見乞丐一邊唱著歌，一邊推著手把轉。

　　而在這個充滿歡樂的團體之中，大家最後一件頭痛的事也消失了，那就是長久以來，愚笨又教不來的奧利歐，突然變聰明了，這只發生在一夕之間，令人更加難以置信。

　　有一天，奧利歐的表現比平時還要笨拙，被揍了一頓，還被告誡翌日的功課要是沒有起色，就會被轉到低年級，跟那些會嘲笑他的小男孩在同一班。

　　聽到這麼一說，他哭著走出教室了。他的愚蠢是與生俱來的，他沉迷於聆聽各種飄盪的聲音、沉思各種飄忽的光線。一直以來，他都是學校裡的笑柄，誰知隔天他來上學的時候，竟然十分嫻熟課程內容，甚至超越了班上功課最好的孩子。從那天起，他成為了學業最優異的學生。

　　起初，德弗修士認為這是他的禱告所致，為此洋洋得意。但是，當他為更重大的事情做虔誠禱告卻都毫無下文時，他認為那個孩子一定是和吟遊詩人、德魯伊教僧侶[2]

或是巫婆打了交道，所以決定要跟蹤監視孩子。

　　他把自己的猜測說給修道院長聽，院長要德弗修士一查出真相，就立即來報告。隔天是星期日，修士站在小路上，當院長和其他弟兄晚禱過後走過來，他一把揪住院長的袖子說：「那位乞丐是聖徒中最偉大的聖徒，也是創造奇蹟之士裡最優秀的一位。就在剛才，我跟蹤奧利歐走進磨坊旁的小樹林，從樹下踏出的小道和泥地腳印來判斷，他去過磨坊旁的小樹林好幾次。我躲在樹叢後方，在小道斜坡處折返回來的地方，我從他眼中的淚水看出來，他的愚昧積習已久，而智慧又來得太遲，所以無法讓他免去對棍棒的恐懼。他進入磨坊後，我走到窗戶邊，往裡面望去。鳥兒飛來停在我的頭頂跟肩膀，因為牠們在這神聖的地方並不膽怯；還有一隻野狼走過，牠的右側蹭過我的長袍，左側擦過灌木的葉子。奧利歐打開書本，翻到我要他讀的那一頁，然後哭了起來，乞丐坐在他身旁安慰他，一直到他進入夢鄉。奧利歐睡得正熟時，乞丐跪下大聲祈禱：『位於在群星後方的祢，請一如初始地顯現祢的力量吧，他的腦中空無一物，讓祢散發出的智慧，在他的內心甦醒吧，九級天使將會讚美祢的名字。』只見一道光劃破長空，環繞著奧利歐，這時我聞到了玫瑰的香味。我因為震驚而稍

2　在古愛爾蘭，德魯伊人是由教士組成的社會階級，被認為擁有魔法般的力量。

微晃動了一下，乞丐轉過頭來，看見了我，便彎下腰說：
『噢！德弗修士，如果我哪裡做錯了，請您原諒我，我願意懺悔。我是出於同情才這麼做的。』但是我卻害怕地逃走了，到這裡一路上沒停下腳步。」

　　所有的修士開始討論起來，有人認為他是某位聖徒，有人認為他是另一位聖徒，又有人認為他不是先前提到的那兩位聖徒，因為他們都還在所屬的同道會裡面，所以認為他是另一位聖徒。整個討論到後來都快成了爭吵，每位修士都聲稱，這位偉大的聖徒來自於自己的家鄉。

　　最後修道院長說話了：「你們剛才提到的人都不是他，因為感恩節的時候，我收到以上每一個聖徒的問候，而他們都還在自己的教會中。他是『安格斯，熱愛上帝者』，是他們之中第一位在荒野中與野獸一同生活的人。十年前，他觀察到派翠克山腳下兄弟會裡的勞動重擔，因此進入了森林，只要人們唱著上帝的讚歌，他便會付出勞力。他的虔誠所帶來的聲望，使得無數人來到他的屋子，他的靈魂吸引著眾人，也產生了些虛榮。九年前，他換上破爛的衣裳，從那天起，就沒人再看過他了。除非他真的是如有些人所看見的，與山中的狼群一起生活，以田野中的青草維生。我們走到他那裡，向他鞠躬吧，因為在長時間的苦苦尋覓之後，他發現，在空無一物之中，就有上帝存在。」

9. 驕傲者寇斯泰勒、麥德蒙之女 和刻薄的話語

　　寇斯泰勒[1]從曠野回來後，躺在自家方塔門前的地上，將頭枕在手上，凝視著日落，猜想接下來的天氣將會如何變化。

　　在英國，伊莉莎白和詹姆斯式的衣服款式已經過時了，但在愛爾蘭的上流社會中，卻逐漸流行起來。不過，他仍然穿著愛爾蘭的傳統厚重披風，多愁善感的臉部輪廓和高大的身軀，仍透著簡樸年代中的驕傲和力量。

　　長長的白色道路，消失在西南方的天邊，他的目光移至落日中一個騎馬人身上，那人正緩慢艱難地行進在小丘上。沒多久，騎馬人靠近了他。在黯淡的薄暮中，可以清晰看見那瘦小不成人形的身軀，穿著愛爾蘭式的長披風，肩上掛著破舊的風笛，騎著一匹毛髮蓬亂的矮馬。

　　很快地，那人就來到他的聽力所及的範圍內，那人大叫：「當高尚的人在純白色的大道上傷心欲絕的時刻，圖茅斯・寇斯泰勒，你這是在睡覺嗎？起來！驕傲的圖茅斯，我帶消息來了，起來吧！從地上起來！你這廢物！」

　　寇斯泰勒站了起來，待吹笛人一來到面前，就抓住他

1　中世紀時，寇斯泰勒（Costello）家族是瑪佑地區勢力龐大的家族。

外套的領子，將他從馬鞍上舉起來摔到地上。

「放過我吧！放過我吧！」那人說，但寇斯泰勒繼續抓著他前後搖晃。

「我有麥德蒙[2]之女鄔娜的消息。」

寇斯泰勒一聽，便鬆開手。吹笛人喘著氣站了起來。

「你剛才怎麼不說你是從她那裡過來的？剛才那樣對你，你一定很嘔吧。」寇斯泰勒問。

「我的確是從她那裡來的。我剛剛被揍，你要補償我，不然我什麼都不會告訴你。」

寇斯泰勒在錢袋裡翻找，費了些工夫才打開袋子，因為他那雙擊敗過無數男人的手，此刻正因為恐懼和期待而顫抖著。

「這是我袋子裡所有的錢。」他說，然後將幾個法國錢幣和西班牙錢幣倒在吹笛人的手中。吹笛人咬了咬錢幣，才開口說話。

「這樣就對了，好價碼，但是要我確實安全了，我才會告訴你。麥德蒙家族的人，要是日落之後在小道上賞我巴掌，或是日正當中時在庫拉芬[3]毆打我，我就會被丟在壕溝裡的蕁麻叢中，靜靜地腐爛，或是被吊死在高大的西克莫無花果樹上，也就是他們四年前在慶祝會上將偷馬賊吊死的地方。」

他一邊說著，一邊將矮馬的韁繩繫在牆上的生鏽長條鐵棒上。

「我會讓你擔任我的吹笛人和貼身侍衛，這樣一來就

沒人敢動你了。沒有人敢欺負圖茅斯·寇斯泰勒的人、山羊、馬匹或是狗。」寇斯泰勒說。

「只有當在我坐在壁爐邊，手裡拿著小酒杯，身旁放一壺私釀的威士忌，我才會跟你透露口信。」那人一邊說，一邊將馬鞍用力摔在地上，「雖然我衣衫襤褸，一無所有，但是我的家族以前是豐衣足食、不愁吃穿的。一直到七個世紀之前，狄龍斯家族燒毀我們的房子，帶走牲畜。我想，我應該能見到狄龍斯家族的人在地獄裡的烤架上尖叫。」

寇斯泰勒領他進入鋪滿燈芯草的大廳，裡頭不見流行於仕紳階級的設備擺飾，卻有著中世紀的淒涼與簡樸。寇斯泰勒指了指大壁爐旁的長凳，吹笛人坐下後，寇斯泰勒斟滿角杯，放在長凳上，再把水罐放在角杯旁。他點燃斜掛在牆上鐵環的火炬時，雙手不住顫抖，然後轉身對吹笛人說：「達利之子杜亞拉，麥德蒙之女會來見我嗎？」

「麥德蒙之女不會來見你，她父親派了幾位婦人監視她，但是她吩咐我告訴你，七天後的聖約翰之夜是她與湖畔麥納馬拉的訂婚之夜，她希望你能在現場，這樣一來，當別人要她向最愛的人敬酒時，她就能夠和你——圖茅斯·寇斯泰勒——對飲，讓所有的人知道誰才是她的內心所屬；也讓大家知道，在這場婚禮中，她感受到的喜悅是

---

2 麥德蒙（MacDermot）家族因其與修道院的關係，曾是洛奇地區最有勢力的家族。

3 庫拉芬（Cool-a-vin）是麥德蒙家族的住處。

多麼微小。我親眼看過偷馬賊，那時他們正在半空中跳著藍鵲舞，所以我奉勸你去的時候，要帶上有本事的人。」

吹笛人的手像鳥爪般緊抓著空酒杯，對著寇斯泰勒大叫：「斟滿我的杯子，願有一天，世上所有的水都縮到海螺殼中，這樣我就可以只喝私釀的威士忌了。」

他看到寇斯泰勒沒有應聲，只是坐著發呆，便大叫：「我命令你斟滿我的酒杯！世上任何一個寇斯泰勒家族的人，都沒有厲害到不用招待達利家族的人，儘管達利家的人只能帶著笛子遊蕩，而寇斯泰勒家族擁有一座光禿禿的小山、一間空空如也的房子、一匹馬、幾隻乳牛。」

「你既然想，我就來讚美達利家族吧」，寇斯泰勒說著斟滿酒杯，「因為你從我的愛人那裡帶來了好消息。」

接下來幾天，杜亞拉四處奔走，招募保鑣，他遇見的每一個人都聽過寇斯泰勒的事蹟，像是他小時候如何擊斃摔跤手，光是拉住他們的腰帶，就摔斷了摔跤手的背；當他長大了些，他為了賭金，拖著兇猛的馬匹穿越淺灘；又當他成人了，他在梅奧地區弄斷了馬蹄鐵；還有其他許許多多關於他的力氣和引以為傲的事蹟，但是他找不到有人願意將自己交給這麼衝動又身無分文的人，何況他還跟冷靜行事又富裕的人作對，像是牧羊人麥德蒙和湖畔麥納馬拉。

於是，寇斯泰勒只好自己去找。在各地聽盡了各種推託藉口之後，他帶回來了一個高大的愚笨傢伙，像狗一樣跟隨著寇斯泰勒，還有一個崇拜寇斯泰勒力氣的農工，另

外還有一個祖先服侍過寇斯泰勒家族的碩胖農夫，寇斯泰勒還找了兩個小伙子來照顧牛羊。然後，寇斯泰勒將他們都帶到空蕩蕩的大廳火爐前。

他們每個人的身上都帶了粗壯的木棍，寇斯泰勒給他們每人一支老舊的手槍，讓他們整晚喝西班牙麥芽啤酒，對著用叉子釘在牆上的蕪菁甘籃菜射擊。

吹笛人杜亞拉坐在壁爐邊的長凳上，用老舊的笛子吹奏了《綠色燈芯草束》、《昂齊翁河》、《布瑞芬尼的王子》[4]。他辱罵射擊手的長相，批評他們拙劣的射擊技術，又罵寇斯泰勒連個像樣的僕人都沒有。

農工、笨傢伙、農夫和小伙子們，都習慣了杜亞拉的辱罵，因為無論是在守靈夜或是婚禮上，都少不了他長而尖銳的辱罵聲，就跟笛子的聲音一樣。他們驚訝的是寇斯泰勒很容忍他，這是由於寇斯泰勒很少參加守靈夜或是婚禮，要不然是無法對不斷咒罵的吹笛人百般容忍的。

隔天晚上，他們朝庫拉芬出發。寇斯泰勒帶著利劍，騎了一匹差強人意的馬，其他人則是騎在鬃毛蓬亂的矮馬上，臂下夾著棍棒。他們越過沼澤，走上山間小路，看見四處插滿了火把，視野所及之處，許多人在泥炭燃燒的紅光中跳舞。

他們來到麥德蒙的屋子，看見門前有一大群赤貧的

---

4 這些都是傳統的愛爾蘭曲調。

人，正圍繞著火堆在跳舞，火堆中央有一個熾烈燃燒的車輪。這轉圈的舞蹈很古老了，甚至當眾神還只是小精靈的時候，就都沒在跳了。門上兩側的窺孔閃著燭光，傳出許多人跳舞的腳步聲，那是伊莉莎白和詹姆斯時代的舞蹈。

他們將馬繫在灌木叢上，繫在樹上的馬匹數量顯示了馬廄已經滿了。他們從站在門前的農夫中擠出一條通道，走進舉行舞會的大廳裡。農工、笨傢伙、農夫和兩位小伙子混入在壁龕圍觀的僕人之中，杜亞拉拿著笛子坐在長凳上，寇斯泰勒越過舞者，來到麥德蒙和麥納馬拉站著的地方，他們正將瓷罐裡的威士忌倒入銀邊角杯裡。

「圖茅斯·寇斯泰勒，你好不容易才忘記過去的仇恨，前來參加我的女兒與湖畔麥納馬拉的訂婚典禮，你做得很好。」老人說。

寇斯泰勒回答：「我來這裡，是因為在寇斯泰勒·德安格羅的時代，我的祖先征服了你的祖先，簽訂了和平契約，規定寇斯泰勒家的人可以帶著保鑣和吹笛人，參加任何麥德蒙家族所舉辦的宴席，而麥德蒙家的人也可以帶著保鑣和吹笛人，參加任何寇斯泰勒家族所舉辦的宴席。」

「如果你帶著邪惡的思想和武裝人員進來，不論你們多麼訓練有素，情勢都是不利於你的。」麥德蒙臉色發紅，「我妻子家族的人馬已經從梅奧郡過來，而我的三個兄弟和他們的僕人也都從斯萊戈山脈下來了。」他說話時，手一直插在外套的口袋裡，像是放在某種武器的手把上。

「不是的，我只是要來跟你的女兒跳支舞道別。」寇

斯泰勒回答。

麥德蒙從口袋裡抽出手，然後走向站在一旁的女孩，她身材高挑，臉色蒼白，溫柔的雙眼直盯著地面。

「寇斯泰勒來跟你跳支舞道別，他知道你們再也見不到彼此了。」

女孩抬起目光，注視著寇斯泰勒，她的眼神中充滿著信任，驕傲中帶著謙卑，狂熱中帶著溫柔，這是女性從最初就注定的悲劇。

寇斯泰勒牽起她，走入跳舞的人群之中。他們很快就被帕凡尼式的節奏吸引，隨著撒拉本舞、嘉莉舞、莫利斯的舞步，翩翩起舞。莊嚴的舞蹈被驅逐出舞池，剩下的只有最具愛爾蘭風格的貴族舞蹈、急速交錯的舞步旋律和早期的古羅馬舞步。他們跳著舞，心中浮現出對人世間的疲乏困頓、對彼此的憐惜，還有對於共同擁有的期望與恐懼所產生的莫名怒氣，那是昇華之後的愛。

一曲終了，吹笛人放下笛子，舉起酒杯。那對戀人彼此離了一小段距離，靜靜地耐心等候舞曲再次響起，也等待著心中的火焰燃燒，再次圍繞他們。他們就這樣整晚跳著帕凡尼舞、撒拉本舞、嘉莉舞、莫利斯舞，很多人靜靜站著看他們翩然起舞。農夫也擠到門邊偷看，彷彿了解到，他們以後會把孫子叫到身邊，說著他們如何看見寇斯泰勒與麥德蒙之女鄔娜跳舞，而在訴說的同時，他們自己也成為古老羅曼史裡的一部分。然而，在舞蹈和笛聲之中，麥納馬拉四處走動，大聲說著話，說著所有人都聽得

出來的愚蠢笑話，老麥德蒙的臉越來越紅，更加頻繁地望向門口，查看門口的蠟燭是否在破曉時分變得昏黃。

最後，他看見結束的時刻到來。在舞蹈的間歇時刻，他大聲宣布，女兒現在要喝下訂婚酒。鄔娜來到他的身邊，賓客在一旁圍成半圓形，寇斯泰勒靠近他右方的牆，吹笛人、農工、農夫、蠢蛋和兩個農場小伙子也站在一旁。

老人從牆上的壁龕取下一只銀杯，那是他的母親和祖母在訂婚時所使用的。他將瓷壺中的酒倒入酒杯，遞給女兒，依照禮俗說：「向你最愛的人敬酒吧。」

她舉杯至唇邊停駐片刻，用清晰溫柔的聲音說：「敬我的真愛，圖茅斯‧寇斯泰勒。」

下一刻，酒杯在地上不停翻滾著，發出像是鈴鐺的聲音，因老人打了她一巴掌，酒杯掉到地上。大廳陷入一片死寂。

僕人之中有許多麥納馬拉的人馬，紛紛從壁龕現身，其中有個在麥納馬拉廚房中是放有盤子椅子的說故事詩人，從腰帶抽出一把法式小刀，意圖襲擊寇斯泰勒，但三兩下就被摔在地上，肩膀撞上杯子，杯子再度轉動鳴響起來。

要不是門旁和擠在後方的農夫開始騷動和叫囂，刀劍的鏗鏘聲早就響起了。眾人皆知他們並非女皇的愛爾蘭後裔[5]，而只是在加拉湖和卡拉湖地區野蠻的愛爾蘭後裔，這些人沒讓自己的孩子的右臂受洗，是為了讓拳頭變得更加有力，據說他們還任命野狼為孩子的教父。

寇斯泰勒的手擱在劍柄上，指節已經發白，但這時他放下手，大步邁向門口，隨從也一起跟上。有些跳舞者讓出路給他走向門口；有些跳舞者憤怒極了，動作慢吞吞，還瞥了一眼那群咕噥不停大吼大叫的農夫才讓了路；不過也有些人因仰慕他的名聲和榮耀，樂意俐落地讓出路。

　　他穿過混雜著敵意和善意的農夫，走到繫著馬匹跟小馬的樹叢。他跳上馬，也命令他的保鑣上馬，然後騎進狹窄的小道上。他們騎了一小段路，騎在最後頭的杜亞拉轉頭望向屋子，麥德蒙和麥納馬拉家族的人就站在一群村民的旁邊，杜亞拉對他們大喊：「麥德蒙，你現在落得這個樣子，是你應得的，誰叫你對吹笛人、提琴手、貧窮的旅人一毛不拔。」

　　他話才說完，三位來自公牛山脈的老麥德蒙家族成員，就衝向馬匹。老麥德蒙一把抓住了麥納馬拉家小馬身上的韁繩，要其他人跟上。馬匹嘶吼著，不停地猛衝暴跳，有幾隻還從人們的手中掙脫，馬匹的眼白也在破曉的曙光中閃耀。要不是村民從爐火的灰燼中拿出幾根還冒著火焰的柴枝，朝馬匹丟過去，雙方早大打出手，死傷慘重了。

　　接下來的幾個星期，寇斯泰勒不斷接到鄔娜的消息，一會兒是賣蛋的婦女，一會兒是前往神聖之泉朝聖的男女。他們告訴寇斯泰勒，他的愛人在過了聖約翰之夜就病

5　女皇的愛爾蘭後裔（children of Queen's Irish），指接受英國統治與文化的人。

倒了，也會跟他說病情此刻是好轉還是又惡化了。村民們仍然記得，夜幕垂降之時，他便會請吹笛人杜亞拉講述《蘋果之子》、《人間之美》、《愛爾蘭國王之子》等等的故事，當傳奇故事中的世界逐漸建構成形，他就會將自己放逐在悲傷的夢境之中。

　　無論故事如何曲折離奇，寇斯泰勒只關心著情傷。鄔娜一人承受了故事人物的痛苦經歷：是鄔娜，而不是國王的女兒，她被囚禁在水底的鐵塔之中，被九眼蟲團團圍住監視。是鄔娜經過了七年的奴役，才有權從地獄帶走她想帶走的東西，但是她只能用疲憊不堪的手指，將一大堆東西掛在裙子的摺邊上帶走。也是鄔娜忍受了整整一年不能說話的日子，因為小妖精將一根施了魔法的荊棘，刺進她的舌頭；也是她的一絡髮絲蜷收在小小雕刻盒裡，發著亮光，人們從日落到日出，不停地議論紛紛，強烈的好奇心被激起。許多國王為了找尋她的藏身之處，流浪多年，或是在不知名的軍隊面前倒下。

　　整個世界與她的美麗相比，都相形黯然失色；所有的苦難跟她所受的折磨相比，也微不足道。因為她是那種帶著熱情在苦行的人，她在愛與恨中始終保持著純潔的心，就像那些信奉上帝、聖母瑪利亞和聖徒的人那般純潔。

　　這一天，一位僕從騎馬來見寇斯泰勒。當時寇斯泰勒正在幫兩個小伙子收割牧草，僕從帶來一封信後就離開。信裡用英文寫道：「圖茅斯·寇斯泰勒，我的女兒病得很重，除非你來見她，不然她會死去。你用機巧之術偷走她

的平靜，我命令你前來見她。」

　　寇斯泰勒扔下手中的大鐮刀，吩咐一個小伙子去叫杜亞拉，因為在他心裡，杜亞拉已經和鄔娜連結在一起了。他自己則去幫兩人的小馬鞍上馬鞍。

　　他們到達麥德蒙的屋子時已近黃昏。加拉湖就在他們的腳下，如此湛藍，卻又那麼寂寥。他們大老遠就看見門邊有黑影晃動，但是走近一看，屋子宛如加拉湖一般荒涼。大門半掩，寇斯泰勒不停地敲門，但沒有回應。

　　「這裡沒人，麥德蒙太高傲了，他不歡迎驕傲的寇斯泰勒。」杜亞拉說。他用力推開門，看見一個衣衫襤褸、渾身髒兮兮的老婦人，正倚著牆壁，坐在地板上。

　　寇斯泰勒一眼認出那是布莉潔‧堤拉尼，一個又聾又啞的乞丐。她看見他們，就站了起來，示意要他們跟她走。她帶寇斯泰勒和夥伴上樓，走過一條長長的走道，來到一扇緊閉的門前。

　　她推開房門進去，走到一旁，然後像之前那樣坐在地板上。杜亞拉也在更靠近門邊的地上坐下來，寇斯泰勒走了進去，望著床上沉睡中的鄔娜。

　　他坐在她身旁的椅子上靜待著，過了良久，她依然沉睡著。門邊的杜亞拉做手勢，要寇斯泰勒喚醒她，但是寇斯泰勒屏住了呼吸，因為她可能需要繼續休息。

　　不久，他轉向杜亞拉說：「我不該留在這裡，她的家人不在，而一般人總是容易指責美麗的人。」

　　他們走下樓，站在屋子的大門口等待。然而入夜了，

還是沒有人出現。

杜亞拉最後開口說道：「那些稱你為驕傲的寇斯泰勒的人們，都是蠢蛋。他們要是看見你在這裡枯等，卻只有乞丐來迎接你，他們應該稱你為謙遜的寇斯泰勒。」

寇斯泰勒和杜亞拉上了馬，騎了一小段路之後，寇斯泰勒拉緊韁繩，讓馬停下來。

過了好幾分鐘，杜亞拉叫道：「難怪你會害怕冒犯綿羊麥德蒙，因為他有許多兄弟朋友，而且老當益壯，隨時可以戰鬥，何況他屬於女皇的愛爾蘭，蓋爾民族的敵人都站在他那邊。」

寇斯泰勒朝屋子的方向看去，漲紅了臉說：「我以聖母之名起誓，在我越過布朗河之前，他們要是不派人來挽留，那我就再也不會回到那個地方。」他繼續騎著馬，但是騎得十分緩慢，太陽都下山了，蝙蝠也飛越了沼澤。

他來到河邊，在河畔徘徊了一陣子，然後突然騎至河流中央，在淺灘上停下馬匹。杜亞拉先越過了河，在水深處旁的河岸等待他。

過了好一陣子，杜亞拉又對他大喊，說著十分刻薄的話：「生下你的人是白癡，養你的人也是白癡，有人說你來自古老的貴族世家，說這些話的人更是白癡，因為你的祖先實際上是面黃肌瘦的乞丐，他們挨家挨戶地乞討，向各戶人家的僕人鞠躬哈腰。」

寇斯泰勒垂頭喪氣越過了河流，站在杜亞拉身旁，正要開口說話之際，前方河堤一陣馬蹄聲傳來，一位馬伕奔

向他們，那是麥德蒙的僕人，他奮力地騎著馬，上氣不接下氣說：「圖茅斯・寇斯泰勒，我來帶你回去麥德蒙的屋子，你離開了之後，他的女兒鄔娜醒了過來，還喚著你的名字，因為你出現在她的夢中。啞巴布莉潔・堤拉尼看見她的雙唇動了，知道她所受的苦痛，於是來到屋子後方，也就是我們躲藏的那片森林。她一把抓住麥德蒙的外套，帶他去看女兒，他見她痛苦的樣子，便吩咐我騎上他的馬匹，盡快將你帶回。」

　　寇斯泰勒轉向吹笛人杜亞拉・達利，從他的腰部將他從馬鞍上提起來，往河中的一顆大石頭上砸去。杜亞拉沉到河水深處死去了，河水流過他刻薄的舌頭，而這或許之後會成為人們口耳相傳的故事吧。

　　寇斯泰勒用馬刺狠狠刺著馬，沿著河岸，使勁地朝著西南方奔去。他一路上不停歇，最後來到另一片更為平坦的淺灘。他看見升起的月亮在水中的倒影，遲疑了一陣，停了下來。他騎上淺灘，越過公牛山脈，再向下朝著大海奔去。一路上，他幾乎一直望著月亮。

　　他不停地策馬前行，這時他的馬匹已經汗流浹背、氣喘吁吁，最終重重地倒下，把他拋到路旁。他想讓馬匹再次站起來，但是徒勞無功，只好孤零零地朝著月光走去。他來到了海邊，看見一艘帆船停泊在港口。

　　前方就是大海，他無法再向前。他發現自己疲倦不堪，而夜晚非常寒冷。於是他走入一間靠近海岸的小酒館，一屁股坐在長椅上。屋子裡滿滿是西班牙和愛爾蘭來

的水手，他們剛走私了一批酒，正在等待另一陣適宜的海風，好再次啟程。一個西班牙人說著蹩腳的蓋爾語，給了他一杯酒，他狼吞虎嚥喝下，開始無所顧忌、滔滔不絕地說起話來。

大約有三個星期，海風要不是吹向陸地，就是過於猛烈，水手們便持續地喝酒談天與玩紙牌。寇斯泰勒跟他們待在一起，睡在酒館裡的長凳上，比誰都還耽溺於飲酒作樂。

很快地，他花光僅有的一點錢，便典當了長披風、馬刺，甚至靴子。最後，一陣溫和的風朝著西班牙吹去，船員將帆船駛出港灣，不久，風帆就消失在地平線那端。

寇斯泰勒轉回家鄉，他的人生在前方張口等著他。他走了一整天，在傍晚時分，來到一條從羅賈拉一帶通往沙洲湖南方的路上。他在這裡遇見一群鄉下人和農夫，他們緩慢地走在兩位神父和盛裝打扮的人群後面，其中幾個人抬著一副棺材。

他攔下一位老人，問他這是誰的喪禮，這些人又是誰。老人回答：「這是麥德蒙之女鄔娜的喪禮，我們這些人是麥納馬拉家族、麥德蒙家族的人和臣僕，而你——圖茅斯・寇斯泰勒——是你殺了鄔娜！」

寇斯泰勒繼續朝隊伍的前方走去，穿越那些對他怒目以視的人群，他對剛才所聽見的字句只有模糊的理解，因為他已經喪失正常人的理解能力。對他而言，像鄔娜那麼溫柔美麗的人，是不可能從這個世上消失的。

不久，他停下腳步，又問了一下要下葬的人是誰。一名男子回答：「我們正抬著麥德蒙之女鄔娜，也就是被你謀殺的人，她將埋葬在三位一體（Holy Trinity）之島。」他撿起石頭往寇斯泰勒丟去，打中臉頰，頓時血流滿面。

寇斯泰勒幾乎感覺不到方才被人打了，還繼續朝著棺材走去。他用肩膀擠入棺木旁的人群，把手放在棺材上，大聲地問道：「棺材裡的人是誰？」

三位從公牛山脈來的麥德蒙家屬撿起石頭，也命令身邊的人撿起石頭。最後寇斯泰勒被趕出馬路，全身上下滿是傷痕，要不是有神父攔阻，他就被打死了。

隊伍繼續行進，寇斯泰勒跟上前去，遠遠地看見棺材被放在一艘大船上。其他人上了另外幾艘船，所有的船隻緩慢地駛向三位一體之島。過了一陣子，他看見船隻都返回，船上的人走入河堤旁的人群中，從大路和小徑散去。

他感覺，鄔娜還在島上的某處溫柔地微笑著。等到眾人都離開了，他循著小船駛過的路徑游去，在傾頹的修道院旁發現了一座新立的墓碑。他整個人臥倒在墓碑面前，哭喊著鄔娜的名字，要她回到他的身邊。

他在墓碑前躺了一整夜，不時地呼喊著鄔娜，要她回到他的身邊；第二天也是如此；但第三個夜晚來臨時，他因為飢餓和悲傷，忘記她的屍體就在正下方的泥土裡，他只知道她在附近的某個地方，而且再也不會回到他的身邊。

在破曉前一個鐘頭，農夫聽見他鬼哭神號地大喊：「鄔娜，你再不出現，我就要離開聖三位一體之島，永遠

不回來了。」在聲音消失之際，小島刮起一陣寒風，一大群身影拂過他的身旁，那些是頭戴銀色皇冠、身穿飄逸長袍的精靈。接著鄔娜也出現了，但她不再溫柔地笑著，而是怒氣沖沖地快步走過他的身旁，賞了他一巴掌，並對他大吼：「那你就走吧，永遠別再回來！」

他大喊她的名字，想跟上前去，但是他們全部升上空中，像朵巨大的銀色玫瑰，衝入灰濛濛的黎明，消失無蹤。

寇斯泰勒從墓地裡爬了出來，腦中一片空白，他只知道他惹情人生氣了，而且她還希望他就此離開。他涉水走進湖中游了起來。

他不停地游著，但是四肢太過虛弱，無法繼續浮在水面上。於是，游了一小段之後沉入了水底，一點掙扎也沒有。

第二天，一位漁夫在湖邊的蘆葦叢看見他躺在白沙上，便將他扛回自己的住處。

這窮人為他哀悼慟哭，等到時候差不多了，便將他葬在三位一體之島上的大教堂。他和麥德蒙之女之間，只隔著一座傾頹的聖壇。窮人也在他們的墓地上種了兩棵梣樹，在往後的日子裡，兩棵樹的樹枝互相纏繞，抖動的樹葉也交疊在一起。

Chapter 3

玫瑰煉金術

噢！他知曉眾神的祕密，蒙主恩寵，喜悅歡騰，
他將自己奉獻給神，也淨化自己的靈魂，
在山中舉行神聖的齋戒儀式，並且縱酒狂歡。

——尤里彼得斯

一

我最後一次見到麥可·羅巴特，已經是十年前的事
了，那一次，也是我第一次和最後一次見到他的朋友以及
他的學生。我親眼目睹了羅巴特和那些人悲慘的下場，也
承受了那些詭異的經歷。這一切改變了我，我的著作變得
冷門、晦澀，也讓我差不多是過著聖道明式[1]的生活。

我剛出版了《羅莎煉金術》，這本薄薄的書講的是煉
金術師，風格有點像托馬斯·布朗爵士[2]的作品。我因此
收到許多神祕學信奉者的來信，他們責罵我，認為我過於
膽怯，他們不認為這麼明顯的感應，只是藝術家對各個時
代觸動人心之事物的感同身受，而且很大部分還是出自憐
憫。

在我初期的研究中，我發現煉金術師所信奉的原理，
不僅僅只是化學方面的奇想，也是能夠應用在物質世界和

St. Dominic

---

1 聖道明（St. Dominic, 1170–1221），西班牙
　教士與聖道明會的建立者，堅守刻苦的生
　活，遊歷講道時，跣足步行。
2 托馬斯·布朗爵士（Sir Thomas Browne,
　1605–1682），英格蘭散文家和醫師。

世人身上的哲理。我也發現，煉金術師想將一般的金屬變為黃金，其實也是想將世間的事物轉變為神聖不滅的物質。於是這讓我的小冊子成了一本奇幻的書，除了企盼將生命轉變為藝術，也傳達出對全然由本質所組成的世界的無盡渴望。

我坐在都柏林舊城區的住宅裡，由於我的先人在城裡的政治勢力，以及他們與當時名流之士的交情，這間住宅頗負盛名。我思索著我在書中所寫下的內容，感受到前所未有的雀躍，因為我終於完成醞釀已久的構思，讓我的房間展現出我所珍視的理念。

那些歷史價值高於藝術價值的肖像畫，都消失了；從門上垂下的掛毯上織滿了寶藍色和青銅色的孔雀，那些和美感與寧靜無關的歷史事件，都被阻擋在門外了。我看著克里韋利[3]的畫作，靜靜端詳聖母手中的玫瑰，玫瑰的樣子描繪細膩精確，與其說是花朵，更像是一種思索。我也細細品嘗著弗朗切斯卡[4]畫中所呈現的灰白色黎明和雀躍的表情，在這些時刻，我能夠理解基督徒所感受到的一切狂喜，卻不需像他們一樣被陳規與習俗奴役。我仔細欣賞我抵押房子所購入的古董青銅眾神像，感受到異教徒在各種形式的美裡面所得到的喜悅，但我不需像異教徒那樣活在永不停歇的恐懼之中，也不需像他們一樣操勞於各式獻祭犧牲，我只需要走到我的書架前，那書架上的每本書都用皮革裝訂，壓印上精緻的裝飾花紋，書皮的顏色也是精心挑選：橘色用來讚頌莎士比亞的偉大，深紅色表達但丁

的憤怒，灰藍色呈現出米爾頓拘謹的沉靜。我能夠體驗人世間的熱烈情感，卻不覺苦痛和厭膩。

我召喚來眾神，因為我並不是只信奉其中一位，我感受各種喜悅，因為我不耽溺於任何一種形式，我讓自己與之保持距離，維持自己的完整和獨立性，像一扇磨亮的鋼鏡[5]。我在這種想像帶來的滿足喜悅之中，看著希拉的孔雀[6]在火光中閃耀，彷若精心製作的寶石。對我的心靈而言，象徵的意象是不可或缺的，這些孔雀就像是我的世界的守門人，將那些不如牠們美麗豐富的東西阻擋在門外。一如往常的許多時刻，某個瞬間，我感覺到自己可以去除生命中所有的苦痛，除了死亡。諸如此類的想法不斷地湧現，在在使我心中充滿激昂的痛處。

因為所有這些美的形式，無論是聖母瑪莉亞沉思時展現的純真、在晨光中歌唱而如癡如醉的臉龐、沉著而莊嚴的青銅眾神，還是那些在各式絕望中湧現的狂暴形體，都屬於一個我無法進入的神聖境界。儘管每個感受皆饒富深意，每種覺察皆細微透徹，卻還是使我渴望那未知的無盡

3　克里韋利（Carlo Crevelli, 1430–1495），文藝復興時期的義大利藝術家。
4　弗朗切斯卡（Piero della Francesca, ?–1492），文藝復興時期的早期義大利畫家。
5　有聚焦能力的金屬鏡，例如望遠鏡中使用的凹面鏡。
6　在希臘神話中，孔雀拉著宙斯的妻子希拉（Hera）所乘坐的戰車，孔雀也是希拉的聖鳥。

力量，並為此感到痛苦。當我處於完滿之時，我甚至會一分為二，其中一個我，以疲倦的眼神，觀看另一個心滿意足的自己。

我的身旁堆滿了從別人的坩堝中所提煉出來的黃金，然而，煉金術師的終極目標是將消沉的心靈轉變為活躍的心靈，而我深信，這樣的目標，之於我自己或之於他人，都是一樣遙遠的。

我走向最近購入的一套煉金器材，佩勒提耶路上的商人向我保證，這些儀器以前是屬於拉蒙・柳利[7]的。我將蒸餾器接上熔爐，並在一旁裝上洗滌池，這一刻我突然領悟了煉金術的精義。所有的存在都是疲乏而困頓的，它們來自靈魂遊蕩的幽谷之中，是一個整體，也是無數個體。而身為一個煉金術師，我能夠理解其他煉金術師對於摧毀事物的強烈渴望，他們渴望瓦解所有終將一死的事物，並將這種追求，藏匿於獅子與蟠龍、老鷹與渡鴉、露水與硝酸鈉種種的象徵符號之中[8]。

我重複唸著貝西・瓦倫泰[9]的第九個重點，他將末日之火比做煉金術師的火焰，將世界比喻為煉金術師的熔

爐，為的是要使我們了解，在至高無上的本質面前，一切事物都會瓦解，無論是有形的黃金或是無形的狂喜狀態，醒轉吧！

雖然我已經摧毀了凡人的世界，住於不滅的本質之中，但我並未獲得奇蹟般的狂喜。

每當我思索這些種種，我就會拉開窗簾，注視外頭的一片漆黑。這些折磨人的思緒，使得佈滿整個天空的微小光點，就像是無數卓越煉金術師的熔爐，煉金術師們不停地工作，將鉛塊變為黃金，將沉悶轉為喜悅，讓肉體化為靈魂，讓邪惡成為上帝。看著他們完美無缺的作品，我將至的死亡，顯得更加難以承受。如同許多在我這個時代的夢想家和知識分子，我大聲喊叫，渴求靈性之美的誕生，企盼能鼓舞心懷夢想而因此肩負重擔的靈魂。

---

7 拉蒙·柳利（Raymond Lulle, 1235–1315），加泰羅尼亞作家、邏輯學家、神祕主義神學家。

8 這是煉金術各個步驟與各個階段的象徵。綠獅代表綠色、硫酸、硝石，也有侵蝕的意象；蟠龍代表煉金步驟開始與結束的兩個階段；老鷹代表物質轉為白色；渡鴉代表物質轉為黑色；露水據說能夠溶解黃金。

9 貝西·瓦倫泰（Basilius Valentinus），十五世紀初期的煉金術師，曾出版煉金術的神學圖案書，並發表鹽酸的製作方法。

二

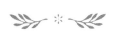

　　一陣響亮的敲門聲打斷我的思緒，我感到格外的納悶，因為我沒有訪客，也吩咐僕人做任何事情都要安靜無聲，以免打擾我內在的幻想世界。我有些好奇，決定親自走去大門。我拿起壁爐架上其中一座銀製燭台，走下樓梯。

　　僕人們似乎都出門了，因為儘管敲門聲從屋子各個角落和隙縫傳出來，樓下的房間卻沒有任何動靜。我記得是因為我生活上的需求很少，也不常處在現實生活的狀態，所以僕人們隨意進出，往往留我一人好一陣子。我逐出世上所有的東西，只留下夢境，但夢裡的空無一物與寂靜，此刻卻突然將我淹沒。我發著抖，拔出門閂。

　　多年不見的麥可・羅巴特現身在我眼前，他亂糟糟的紅髮、銳利的眼神、易怒而微微顫抖著的嘴唇、一身簡陋的衣服，讓他看起來就和十五年前一樣，像個浪人、聖徒或是農夫。

　　他說，他近日來到愛爾蘭，是為了一件重要的事，希望能見上我一面。事實上，那是我們兩人之間唯一一件重要的事。

　　他的嗓音，讓我回想起我們在巴黎求學的那段時光，還有他那能支配我的神奇魔力。我帶領他走上寬大的樓梯，史威夫特[1]曾經一邊說笑、一邊咕噥地走過這裡，而

庫蘭[2] 在從前簡樸的日子裡，也曾經在這裡援引希臘人的話語，說著故事。那時的人心尚未因浪漫運動的藝術與文學，而變得複雜難解。我開始因為他突如其來的造訪，感到些微恐懼，還混雜著更多惱人的情緒，並且為某件即將揭露的事情而焦慮起來。

我感覺我的手在發抖，燭光在法式鑲版上的女祭司身上，搖曳得厲害，使得她們看起來就像是在混沌與空洞的黑暗中，逐漸成形的最初的生命。

闔上了門後，孔雀門簾垂墜在我們兩人和這個世界之間，像是各色的火焰在閃耀，沒來由地，我感覺某些怪異而且無法預期的事情即將到來。

我走到壁爐架前，發現放在歐羅舟・馮塔納[3] 的瓷器作品旁邊的小型無鍊香爐倒下了，裡頭的古董護身符都掉了出來。我一邊整理著思緒，一邊帶著慣常的敬畏，把護身符收進香爐。我一向認為，我們應該敬畏那些長久以來與神祕的渴望和恐懼相關的事物。

麥可・羅巴特說：「我看得出來，你仍然對焚香十分著迷，我給你看這款焚香，這比你見過的都還要珍貴。」他說著，拿起我手中的香爐，把裡頭的護身符倒出來，堆

---

1 史威夫特（Dr Jonathan Swift, 1667-1745），英國和愛爾蘭作家，《格列佛遊記》（*Gulliver's Travels*）的作者。

2 庫蘭（John Philpot Curran, 1750-1817），愛爾蘭律師、演說家、愛爾蘭國會成員。

3 歐羅舟・馮塔納（Orazio Fontana, 1510–1571），義大利的陶藝工匠。

在熔爐和蒸餾器之間。

我坐下來，他也在火爐邊坐下，手中拿著香爐，看著火光，坐了好一陣子。

他說：「我來是要問你一些事情，在我們談話之際，焚香的香氣會充滿整個房間和我們的思緒。這是我從一位敘利亞的老人那裡拿到的，他說這是用花朵做成的，那是有著肥厚紫色花瓣的花朵，生長在客西馬尼花園[4]中耶穌塑像的雙手、頭髮、雙足之上，將祂包覆在花朵的香氣中，直到祂被釘在十字架上，大聲呼喊，抗議自己的宿命。」

他將小絲袋裡的一些粉末抖落至香爐，將香爐放在地板上點燃，粉末中飄出藍色煙霧，上升至天花板又降下來，像是彌爾頓[5]的班楊樹。

這種焚香也如一般焚香，讓我昏昏欲睡。他一說話，我就陷入恍惚狀態。他說：「我來這裡，是要問你我在巴黎問過你的問題，你那時候離開了巴黎，沒有給我答案。」

他的目光轉向我，透過焚香的迷霧，我看見他的雙眼在火光中閃耀。我答道：「你是指，我是否願意加入你的玫瑰煉金術教團[6]嗎？我在巴黎的時候，充滿了未能滿足的渴望，那時候的我不願意加入，而現在的我終於能夠依自己的渴望，過自己想要的生活，你覺得我此時有可能答應你嗎？」

他說道：「在那之後，你改變了很多。我讀了你寫的書，又看到你現在活在這些意象中，我比你還要了解你自己，因為我見過無數個在十字路口迷失的人。你將世界關

在門外，並招引各方神祇，你要是不向祂們臣服，就將永遠感到困乏，漫無目的地遊蕩。人們應該忘記身處這個喧囂塵世，還有時間洪流裡的悲慘狀態，不然就得向那管轄這個世界和時間的大眾，尋求一種神祕的結合。」

他像是對著我看不見的人咕噥了幾句，一瞬間整個空間突然暗了下來，就像是他從前要進行特殊的實驗一樣，黑暗中，門上的孔雀似乎以更濃烈的色彩閃耀著。

我拋開這些幻覺，相信那只是從前的記憶和焚香的微光所導致，我不認為他能夠戰勝我已臻成熟的理智。我問道：「就算我承認我需要精神寄託，還有某種崇拜的形式，我為何非得去到埃萊夫西納[7]，而不是加爾瓦略山[8]？」

他倚身向我，以略帶韻律的語調說話，說著的當下，我又得再度與那幻影搏鬥，那像是比太陽的夜晚更加古老的暗夜幻影，讓燭光變得微弱，遮蓋了畫框框角和青銅神像上的微光，使得香爐的藍色煙霧轉為深紫色，但幻影也

---

4 客西馬尼花園（Garden of Gethsemane）位於耶路撒冷。耶穌在最後的晚餐之後，來到這個花園裡，被猶大出賣。隔日，耶穌被釘在十字架上。

5 彌爾頓（John Milton, 1608-1674）：英國詩人、思想家。

6 「玫瑰煉金術教團」承襲許多玫瑰十字會（Rosicrucian）的傳統。在葉慈所加入的黃金黎明教團（Hermetic Order of Golden Dawn）中，玫瑰也是重要的象徵意象。

7 埃萊夫西納（Eleusis），希臘神話中膜拜豐收女神狄蜜特（Demeter）的地點。

8 加爾瓦略山（Calvary），耶穌被釘上十字架的地方。

讓孔雀閃耀著光芒，彷彿每種單一顏色都有著生命的靈魂。我陷入如夢般的深度冥想，彷彿聽見他在遠處說著話。

　　他說著：「每個人不只跟一位神交流，人越是能進入想像的國度，越是有著過人的理解能力，就能接觸更多的神，與之對話，並且更能接觸以下這些人與眾神的力量：像是在朗謝斯馮山谷中，吹響人們的意志和喜悅的羅蘭[9]；嘆息看著眾神消失的哈姆雷特[10]；在世界各處找尋眾神，但一無所獲的浮士德[11]；無數當代詩人和騎士文學作家的心靈中所浮現出的眾神，還有從古老崇拜中承襲一切，但在文藝復興之後，卻喪失了鳥與魚的牲禮、花冠的香氣、焚香煙霧的古老眾神。許多人認為，是人類創造出這些神祇，因此也可以使祂們消失。但我們見過眾神穿著柔軟的長袍，乘著咯咯作響的馬車駛過；當我們倒臥在死亡般的地溝中，也能聽見祂們清晰的談話。因此我們知道，是祂們持續地創造並毀滅人類，而這只不過發生在他們雙唇間顫動的瞬間。」

　　他起身來回踱步，在我清醒的夢境中變成一只梭子，編織著巨大的紫色蜘蛛網，層層疊疊的蜘蛛網逐漸填滿整個房間，裡頭盡是無法解釋的寂靜，而整個世界彷彿只剩下這張蜘蛛網，還有永不停歇的來回編織。

　　那聲音繼續說道：「所有出現在你的夢境的，所有你在書本裡見過的，都來到了我們的身旁，都來到了我們的身旁！李爾王[12]的頭顱在暴風雨中仍是濕透的，他放聲大

笑，因為你認為自己是個存在的實體，但其實只不過是一抹影子，而他看起來雖然只是一抹影子，但其實是不朽的神；蓓德麗絲[13]也來了，她的嘴唇因微笑而微微張開，彷彿所有的星辰都將在愛的嘆息中消逝；謙遜之神的母親[14]也出現了，謙遜之神苛刻地詛咒世人，因為人們想將他所管轄之地——也就是人類的內心——變成一片荒蕪，但謙遜之母手中握著玫瑰，每片花瓣都是一位神；就在那裡，噢！阿芙蘿黛蒂[15]也匆匆到來，無數隻麻雀的翅膀撒落下了薄暮，她站在薄暮之中，腳邊是灰白色相間的鴿子。」

在我的夢中，我看見羅巴特伸出左臂，右手揮過左臂上方，彷彿在拍打鴿子的翅膀。我有些僵硬地以堅定的口吻，努力說出以下的字句，用力到簡直要把自己一分為二：「你會讓我捲入可怕的未知世界。人的偉大程度，要視他在多少程度上能以心智映照一切事物，就像一面鏡子那樣，精確而分毫不差。」

此時的我，彷彿能夠完全掌握自己了，於是以更快的速度繼續說下去：「我要你立刻離開，因為你的觀念和思

9　出自《羅蘭之歌》（*The Song of Roland*）的人物，法國史詩。

10　莎士比亞悲劇《哈姆雷特》（*Hamlet*）的主角。

11　歌德作品《浮士德》（*Faust*）的主角。

12　莎士比亞悲劇《李爾王》（*King Lear*）的主角。

13　蓓德麗絲（Beatrice Portinari），但丁《神曲》（*Divine Comedy*）中的人物。

14　「謙遜之神的母親」指聖母瑪利亞。

15　阿芙蘿黛蒂（Aphrodite）為希臘神話中的愛神。

想都只是幻覺，在文明敗壞和人心墮落的初始，像是蛆蟲般爬入。」

我突然惱怒了，就在我抓起桌上的蒸餾器，正要站起來丟向他之際，他後方門上的孔雀變得無比巨大，蒸餾器從我的指尖滑落，我被淹沒在綠色、藍色、青銅色的孔雀羽毛海浪之中。在我絕望地掙扎之時，聽到遠方傳來的一個聲音：「我們的大師伊本・西納 16 曾寫道，所有的生命進程都來自墮落。」

光彩奪目的羽毛此刻完全將我覆蓋了，我知道我已經掙扎了好幾百年，最終被征服了。

我墜入深淵之中，綠色、藍色、青銅色的火海，充斥整個世界，向我襲捲而來。當我打旋下墜時，聽見上方一個聲音大喊：「鏡子碎成兩片了！」另一個聲音回答：「鏡子碎成四片了！」更遠的另一個聲音，歡欣鼓舞地大叫：「鏡子碎成無數片了！」一大群蒼白的手伸向我，一張張陌生的臉龐，溫柔地俯身望著我，而那像是慟哭卻又撫慰人心的聲音所吐出的字句，在說出的那一刻即被遺忘。

我從火焰的浪潮中升起，感到我的記憶、冀望、思想、意志，所有屬於我的東西，都融化了。我以某種方式，不單單只是猜想，而是更加確切地明白到，在抬起的臂膀、在細細旋繞的文字音韻裡、在眼神朦朧與半垂著眼皮做著夢之時，我像是從無數包覆於永恆瞬間的同伴們之中，向上升去。

我肩負著世界的重擔，也忍受著奇異難解的心境——

或許是憂愁罷——我穿越那些美麗得幾乎就要消逝的形體，然後走進那本質是美的死亡之中，也進入了所有人未曾停止渴望的孤寂[17]。

所有曾經存在這世上的一切事物，似乎都進入到我的心中，而我也在它們之中。我原先是相信眼見為憑，但現在我進入夢境中，體驗到裡頭的不確定性，並且變成一滴融化了的金子，極其快速地下墜，穿越了繁星點綴的夜空。我的四周充斥著憂傷和狂喜的哭喊，若我不曾經歷這些體驗，我是不會了解到人類終將消逝，也不能了解淚水的涵義。

我不停地下墜，突然那慟哭聲變得只是煙囪裡的風在嗚咽，我醒了過來，發現我用雙手撐著頭靠在桌上，也看見蒸餾器滾至遠處角落左右搖晃，而麥可‧羅巴特看著我，等待著我。

我說：「你去哪裡，我就去哪裡，也會聽從你的任何吩咐，因為此刻我與不朽同在。」

他回答道：「我早就知道了。當我聽見暴風雨的呼嘯，就知道你需要一個答案，就像你先前答覆我的那樣。你要去到遠方，因為我們被命令得在海浪邊、在純潔的人群和汙穢的人群之中，建造起我們的神殿。」

---

16 伊本‧西納（Avicenna, Ibn Sina, 980–1037）：中世紀的波斯哲學家、醫學家、自然科學家、文學家。

17 對葉慈而言，心境代表主觀的經驗。

三

我們駛過荒涼的街道，一路上我不發一語，內心也竟然沒有任何平常會出現的想法和感受。我像是從某個清晰明確的世界中被拔除了，然後全身赤裸地被丟進無邊無際的海洋。

有幾個瞬間，我的幻覺又要出現了，我恍惚憶起了人們的罪衍與光榮事蹟、幸與不幸，並為此感到欣喜若狂或是哀戚悲傷。又有幾個瞬間，我的思考會突然變得活躍起來，然後深刻地體會各式企盼、恐懼、欲望和野心，這些在我先前規律嚴謹的生活裡，一向鮮少出現的感受。想到這些無法理解又無法描述的東西竟然在我的內心裡肆虐，我不禁突然驚醒過來。

在這些感受完全消失的幾天前，甚至是到了現在，儘管我在絕對而唯一的信念中找到了庇護，我竟然也十分能夠包容那些性格變化無常的人，也就是時常聚集在小教堂或是各式無名教派的聚會處裡的那些人。因為我也感受到僵化的常規和教條，在某種力量的面前瓦解了，這股力量是一種異常強烈的激情，雖然也可以說那不過是神經錯亂而已，但是包含在這股力量裡的憂傷的狂喜，使我害怕它將再度甦醒，然後再次將我逐出甫重獲的平靜狀態。

我和麥可・羅巴特在昏暗的天光中，來到了杳無人跡

的終點站，我身上彷彿發生了巨大的改變，我再也不像一般人那樣，只存在於某個瞬間，並且懼怕著永恆。此刻的我就是永恆本身，我為短暫的瞬間悲嘆哀悼，也對短暫的瞬間一笑置之。我們搭上火車後，麥可‧羅巴特很快進入夢鄉，他睡夢中的臉龐，沒有任何先前使我驚恐的表情，反倒讓我清醒，對我此刻亢奮的狀態來說，他的臉就像是一張面具。

這個幻覺在我的思緒中盤旋不去。面具後面的男人，像水中的鹽巴那樣消散了。這張面具聽令於那不屬於人世間的指示，它狂笑又哀嘆，搖尾乞憐又破口大罵。

我不停地告訴自己：「這才不是麥可‧羅巴特：他已經死了，死了十年，甚至二十年了。」

之後，我進入發燒昏迷的狀態。我們快速駛過幾座小城鎮，一路上我不時醒來，城裡的石板屋頂因濕氣而閃閃發亮，寂靜的湖面也在冷冽的晨光中閃耀。我想這些事想得出神，就沒有問麥可‧羅巴特我們要去哪裡，也沒注意他手中拿著的是前往何處的車票。但是從太陽的方位來看，我判斷我們正朝著西方行駛，路旁的樹木朝著東方飛馳而去，看起來就像是衣衫襤褸的乞丐。我們離西海岸越來越近。很快地，我在左手邊低矮的山丘間看到大海，灰色的海面碎裂成無數的白色波浪與水花。

下了火車後，我才知道我們還得再走一段路。我們開始行走，因為風勢強勁，我們扣上了外套的釦子。麥可‧羅巴特沉默不語，想讓我沉浸在自己的想法裡。當我們行

走在大海與巨大海岬的岩石側之間，我深刻了解到，我內心的本質經歷了一些難以理解的轉變，我慣常的思考方式和感受，受到很大的衝擊，因為灰白的海浪、疾馳的泡沫所形成的羽狀煙霧，成為我內心的一部分，如雨水傾注般滿溢，奇妙難解。麥可‧羅巴特指著一幢古老樣式的方形屋子，他說那就是玫瑰煉金術神殿。屋子的背風處，有一間樣式新穎的矮小建築物，從即將倒塌和荒廢的碼頭末端延伸出去。我心中縈繞著一個奇特的想法，那就是海洋以白色泡沫沖刷覆蓋神殿，其實是在宣告神殿也屬於某種無限而熱烈的生命，這股生命力正在向我們規律嚴謹的生活方式宣戰，幾乎就要將整個世界投入黑夜中了，那裡頭就像是古典世界崩解之後的混沌狀態。

　　一部分的我，對這種駭人的奇想抱持著嘲弄的態度，但另一部分沉浸於幻象中的心思，仍然持續聆聽著不知名軍隊間的鏗鏘碰撞，顫慄於懸在灰白跳躍的浪濤上那些難解的奇想。才沿著碼頭走了幾步，我們就遇到一位老人。老人坐在倒置的木桶上，就在泥水匠最近才修補好的碼頭裂縫旁，他前方有個火盆，像是用來掛在焊鍋匠的手推車下方的那種火盆，顯然他是在夜間負責看管這裡的人。我看得出來他也是虔誠的教徒，因為木桶邊緣的鐵釘上掛著一串念珠，我看到時，莫名地打了個冷顫。我們離開他好幾碼後，他用蓋爾語大聲喊道：「遊蕩的人！遊蕩的人！跟你們的巫婆和魔鬼一起下地獄吧！下地獄去吧！這樣鮪魚才會再度回到海灣！」之後，我又聽見好幾次他在後方

大吼大叫、喃喃自語。

「你難道不怕這些粗野的漁夫對你做出什麼瘋狂的事情？」我問道。羅巴特回答：「我跟我的同伴再也不會遭受到任何人的傷害，或是接受任何人的幫助，因為我們已經與不朽的靈魂融為一體，我們死去的時刻，就是我們完成終極任務之時。事實上，除非這些人的神祇再度蓋起屬於祂們的灰石神殿，不然那個時刻遲早也會來到這些人的面前，等到那時候，他們會把鯡魚獻祭給阿蒂蜜斯[1]，或是把其他種的魚類獻給新的神祇。他們身上的枷鎖從未消失，只是在程度上稍稍減弱了一些，因為精靈仍然存在於每一陣風中，也在愛爾蘭球戲裡歡樂地跳舞玩耍，但是他們無法再次蓋起他們的神殿，除非等到殉道者出現並得到勝利，或是久遠前便預言的黑豬谷戰役[2]發生。」

狂吹猛打的浪花與強風，每刻都像是要把我們掠倒。我們緊緊挨著面向大海的海堤牆面，靜靜地走向那座方型建築的大門。

麥可・羅巴特用鑰匙打開門，我看見鑰匙因鹹鹹的海風而生鏽了，他帶我沿著毫無陳設的通道，走上一條沒鋪上地毯的樓梯，再進到一間書架環繞的小房間。他向我解釋，晚一點有人會送餐點過來，但是因為儀式開始之前，

1　阿蒂蜜斯（Artemis），希臘神話中的月亮女神與狩獵的象徵。
2　葉慈在《蘆葦間的風》（ *The Wind Among the Reeds*, 1899）提到：「黑豬谷之役，是明白清楚的世界與古代黑暗事物之間的戰爭。」

我要進行簡單的禁食，所以餐點只有水果而已，待會兒也會有人拿來一本教團規則和實施方法的書籍，我得在這個冬日剩下的短暫陽光中閱讀完畢。接著他離開了，向我承諾他會在儀式開始前的一個小時回來。

我開始在書架上瀏覽，看到了我所見過最詳盡的煉金術藏書。裡面有許多大師的著作：隱士莫瑞諾斯[3]將他那不死的身軀，藏在毛茸茸的襯衫之下；伊本‧西納[4]雖然是個醉漢，但是掌控了無數個靈魂；法拉比[5]將許多靈魂寫進魯特琴演奏的音樂，讓人們聆聽後，或是開懷大笑，或是潸然淚下，或是陷入死亡般的催眠狀態；盧爾[6]將自己變成紅色公雞的模樣；弗拉梅爾[7]和妻子帕尼拉在數百年前就提煉出了長生不老之藥，據說現在仍然和托缽僧[8]居住在阿拉伯；書中也提及許多比較沒沒無聞的人。

書中提到的神祕主義者，幾乎沒有不信奉煉金術的，我相信這是因為多數的人只將自己獻給單一神祇，並且美感受到限制所致，我想羅巴特也認為這是必然的結果。我也注意到一套威廉‧布萊克[9]寫的預言式著作的完整摹本，大概是因為他精闢的闡釋，人們慕名而來，就像「月亮吸著露水之時，海浪中的灰魚」[10]。

我還看到各個時代的詩人和散文家的書，不過他們大多對人生感到些許厭倦。事實上，偉大的詩人與散文家無所不在，但他們澆鑄在凡人身上的想像力，是他們不再需要的東西，因為他們正搭乘熾烈燃燒的戰車，向上飛去。

不久，我聽見了敲門聲，一位女士走進來，放了些水果在桌子上。我看得出來，她一度身材健美，但此刻雙頰深陷。如果我是在別的地方遇見她，我大概會認為那是肉體的快感和對享樂的渴求，讓她的雙頰深陷，但此刻的我認為，那無疑是奔馳的想像力和對美的渴望所造成。

我向她詢問儀式的細節，但她搖搖頭，沒回答我。我想我得安靜等候入會儀式。我吃完水果後，她又出現了。她將一個奇怪的黃銅盒子放在桌上，點上蠟燭，然後把盤子與剩下的食物帶走。很快地，房裡只剩我一人，我的注意力轉到盒子上頭，看到希拉的孔雀尾巴延伸到蓋子的兩側，背景以輝煌的星辰襯托，彷彿宣示著天堂也是孔雀榮光的一部分。

---

3 莫瑞諾斯（Morienus），七世紀的一位基督教隱士。

4 伊本・西納（Avicenna, 980–1037）為波斯醫師、哲學家，對中世紀的伊斯蘭哲學影響深遠。葉慈從《煉金術哲學家》（*Lives of Alchemistical Philosophers*）一書中，得到他的思想。

5 法拉比（Alfarabi, 870–950 年代）為喀喇汗王朝初期著名的醫學家、哲學家、心理學家、音樂學家。

6 盧爾（Ramon Lully, 1235–1316），加泰羅尼亞作家與神祕主義神學家。

7 弗拉梅爾（Nicolas Flamel, 約 1330–1418）為法國瓦盧瓦王朝的煉金術士，研究煉金術界的傳奇物質「賢者之石」，以此聞名。

8 指伊斯蘭教蘇非派的托缽僧。

9 威廉・布萊克（William Blake, 1757-1827）為英國詩人、畫家，浪漫主義文學代表人物，對葉慈的美學有深刻影響。

10 出自威廉・布萊克的作品〈歐洲：預言〉（*Europe: A Prophecy*）中的蝕刻版畫。

盒子裡頭放著一本羊皮紙包覆的書，羊皮紙上的煉金術玫瑰有著淡雅的顏色，並以黃金點綴，許多長矛刺向玫瑰，但長矛的利刺在玫瑰花瓣旁粉碎了。這本書以雅緻清晰的字體，寫在羊皮紙上，依照《太陽的光輝》[11] 的藝術風格，以象徵圖案和插圖點綴。

第一章述說六位凱爾特後代是如何自學煉金術的，各自解開了倍利坎煉金術器具之謎、綠龍之謎、老鷹之謎、鹽巴與水銀之謎[12]。

雖然似乎是一連串的偶發事件，將他們帶到一間南法的小旅館花園裡，但是書中強調這其實是超自然力量的巧妙設計。他們在談話時，冒出了個想法，也就是煉金術是淨化靈魂的過程，為的是讓靈魂準備好超越死亡，進入永生狀態。

一隻貓頭鷹飛過，在他們頭頂上方的藤葉沙沙作響，一位老婦拄著拐杖走進來，在他們身旁坐下，接續他們方才討論的議題。她向他們解釋靈性煉金術的整套原理，囑咐他們創立煉金術玫瑰教團，然後離他們而去，等到他們要追上前去，她早已不見蹤影。

後來，這幾個人成立了教團，發揮他們各自的長處，並分享研究成果。在他們精通煉金術原理後，幽靈在他們之中來來去去，傳授他們更加奧妙的謎團。

這本書繼續詳述下去，因為教團允許新加入的信徒，從一開始就充分了解人類思想中獨立自主的那一部分。根據這本書所說的，這就是所有真正的宗教教義的源頭。

書上寫道，若你能想像出某個生物的外貌，那它就會立刻為一個飄盪的靈魂所據，並且在死去之前，四處行善或行惡。書上舉了許多從眾神身上得到的例子，例如：愛神曾指示他們如何形塑出一個神性可寄居的形體，如何對沉睡的心低語；而阿特[13]曾教導他們如何形塑出容納惡魔的形體，如何將瘋狂或是惡夢，灌入沉睡的生命中；赫密士[14]說，如果你認真想像有一隻獵犬在你身邊，牠就會一直照看著你，直到你醒來，牠還能驅趕走所有的東西，除了最邪惡的惡魔。但是，如果你的想像力貧乏，獵犬就會十分虛弱，這樣一來惡魔就會肆虐，而獵犬迅速死亡；阿芙蘿黛蒂說，如果你用奔放的想像力，創造出一隻帶著銀製皇冠的鴿子，命令牠振翅飛過你的頭頂，那麼牠溫柔的咕咕叫聲，就會讓永不消逝的愛情美夢，從人們的沉睡之中孕育出來。眾神一致警告並悲嘆道，所有的心靈正不停地在創造這樣的東西，再讓它們生出喜悅或是憤怒、強健體魄或是疾病災厄。

---

11 《太陽的光輝》（*Splendor Solis*），著名的彩色插圖煉金術手稿，於1532–1535 間寫成。

12 倍利坎（Pelican）是一種煉金術的容器，圓形的壺身加上細長的壺口，像是鵜鶘彎著脖子餵食幼鳥的樣子。綠龍，沒有精確指向任何煉金術的隱喻或是階段步驟，較常見的是使用綠獅，象徵第三個步驟時物質轉為綠色。綠龍一詞可能是葉慈閱讀《太陽的光輝》時，對雙龍插圖印象深刻。老鷹，是第二個步驟時物質轉為白色。鹽巴和水銀，指的是煉金術中的第一元素（prima materia）。

13 阿特（Ate）為詛咒女神，宙斯的長女。

14 赫密士（Hermes）在希臘神話是眾神的使者、商業之神、旅者之神。

這本書又說道，如果你賦予邪惡力量形體，你就會製造出醜陋的形體，它會因渴望生命而突出雙唇，或者生命的重擔會破壞其身形的比例，而神聖的力量只會出現在美麗的形體中，因為那不過是從存在本身之中，顫抖地出現的形體，包覆了永恆的狂喜，漂浮於半闔上的雙眼，然後進入睡眠的寂靜之中。

　　那些進入到這些形體中的無形體的靈魂，就是人們所說的主觀意識，能使世上發生重大的變革。就好比魔術師或藝術家能夠召喚主觀意識，主觀意識也能夠召喚魔術師或藝術家的心靈。如果主觀意識是魔鬼，他們就會以各種方式，召喚卑鄙之士或瘋子的心靈，然後以人們的聲音和姿態進入這個世界。

　　世上所有重大的事件就是以這種方式發生，主觀意識、神性、惡魔，一開始像是一陣微弱的嘆息，進入人們的心中，不斷持續地改變人的想法和行為，直到黃髮變為黑髮、黑髮成了黃髮，直到各個帝國移動了邊界，像是一堆堆樹葉那般。

　　書本其餘的內容涵蓋了形體、聲音、顏色的種種象徵，還有其分別歸屬於哪位神和惡魔。因此初學者可以替任何神性或魔鬼形塑出形體，並且能夠和伊本·西納一樣，擁有神奇的力量，能夠影響那些生活於眼淚和笑聲之中的人們。

四

　　日落過後幾個小時，麥可・羅巴特回來找我，他要我學習一種古老的舞步，以完成我的入會儀式。我得加入一支神祕之舞三次，因為舞蹈中的韻律像是不停轉動的永恆之輪，無常與偶然都瓦解其中，藉此靈魂就能得到自由。

　　我發現，他要我學習的舞步極其簡單，與某種舊式的希臘舞步相似。我年輕時是優秀的舞者，精通多種少見的蓋爾舞步，因此我很快就上手了。

　　他要我跟他一起穿上像是希臘和埃及混搭的服飾[1]，但是其緋紅的顏色又具有更為狂熱的生命力。他將一個無鍊的黃銅香爐放在我的手中，香爐的玫瑰外型是由當代的工匠精心製作而成。他要我打開一道小門，就位於我方才進來的那扇門對面。

　　大概是因為焚香的煙霧中那股神祕難解的魔力，當我握住門把之時，我又進入了夢境。在夢裡，我似乎變成一張面具[2]，平放在一間小型東方店舖的櫃檯上。許多人進

---

1 所有黃金黎明教團裡的成員，在儀式中依照他們的位階，穿上不同顏色的長袍和腰帶。
2 葉慈曾寫道：「在拜倫的詩作中，人物角色像是個面具，是用來傳達主觀意識的媒介。」

到店裡，他們有著明亮沉靜的雙眼，我知道他們並非一般人。他們將我拿起來試戴，輕笑了幾聲，最後將我扔到角落。但是這整個過程只是一瞬間的事，當我回神之時，我的手仍握在門把上。

我將門打開，發現自己站在一條讓人讚嘆不已的廊道上，廊道的兩側貼著馬賽克拼貼成的一尊尊神像，可與拉溫納[3]洗禮堂中美麗的馬賽克裝飾相比擬，但是又沒那麼樸素。每尊神像前方都有著一個從天花板垂掛下來的吊燈，散發出奇特的香味和顏色，神像的顏色與燈光的色澤有著相似的色調，必定是具有著象徵意味。

我繼續往前走，極度訝異這群狂熱的信徒，如何能夠在如此偏遠之地，打造出這一切美麗的事物。蘊藏在眼前景象的瑰麗寶藏，以及走過廊道時，瀰漫於空中不停變換色彩的焚香，不禁讓我有些相信物質煉金術了。

我在一扇門前停下腳步，門上黃銅色的鑲板有手工打製的波紋，陰影的部分像是駭人的臉孔。門後的人們似乎聽見我們的腳步聲，有個人大聲問道：「不朽之火的成品完成了嗎？」麥可・羅巴特立刻回答：「已經從熔爐中提煉出純金了。」

門打開，我們進入一間寬敞的圓形房間，站在穿著緋紅色長袍緩緩起舞的男男女女之中。天花板上有一朵用馬賽克拼貼成的巨大玫瑰，四周牆面上是眾神與天使間的戰役，同樣是用馬賽克拼而貼成，眾神閃耀著紅色和藍色寶石般的微光，天使則是一片灰濛濛的。麥可・羅巴特對我

低語，他說這是因為天使們仰慕著謙遜而憂傷的神，而捨棄了自己的神性，也拒絕敞開他們各自的內心。

柱子頂著屋頂，撐出圓弧狀的迴廊，每根柱子都有著令人炫目的造型，風之神穿梭在風笛和鐃鈸的樂音之中，熱烈地跳著迴旋舞，長柱間伸出許多捧著香爐的手。

有人要我手捧香爐，然後站上我的位置開始跳舞。當我的目光從柱子移至舞者身上，我看見地板中央鋪著綠色的石子，蒼白的耶穌被架在灰白的十字架上。我問羅巴特那些地上圖案的涵義，他說他們想要「用數不清的雙腳，來干擾祂的整體性」。

地面與天花板上的玫瑰花瓣相互輝映，舞者沿著地面上的花瓣輪廓前進後退，也隨著不知隱身何處的樂器所發出的樂音起舞，那樂器大概是古老的樣式，因為我沒聽過這樣的音樂。舞步越跳越激昂，直到最後世上的風似乎都在我們腳下甦醒。

過了一陣子，我開始感到疲倦，站在柱子旁注視著那些像是火焰的形體來來去去，漸漸地進入半夢半醒的狀態。夢中，我看見那朵巨大玫瑰的花瓣，然後就醒過來了。這時，玫瑰不再是由馬賽克拼貼而成的樣子，反而自充滿濃郁焚香的空中緩慢降落，漸轉變為絕美的生命形體 [4]。

---

3 拉溫納（Ravenna）位於義大利艾米利亞─羅馬涅區的城市。
4 在《神秘玫瑰》裡，也有玫瑰花瓣轉化為永恆生命的意象。

這些模糊如雲霧般的形體開始跳起舞來，越跳形體就越加清晰，我得以分辨出美麗的希臘人臉孔和嚴肅的埃及人臉孔，並且不時能夠依據他們手中的權杖，或是飛越他們頭頂的小鳥，說出某個神的名字。很快地，凡人的雙腳都和不死的白皙雙腳一同跳起舞來。一雙雙憂悒的眼睛，望著無憂無慮的朦朧雙眼，在那些憂悒的眼睛裡，我看見因為極度的渴望而閃現的光芒，就像是在無盡的徘徊流浪之後，終於找到年輕時候逝去的愛。

某些時刻，只是短暫一瞬，我看見一個孤單的模糊身影，蒙著臉，舉著黯淡的火炬，在跳舞的人群之中緩緩飄過，像是夢境中的夢境，幻影中的幻影。這時，比思想更為深刻的知識泉源湧出的頓悟，讓我了解到他就是愛神本人了。他將臉蒙上，因為從世界初始以來，沒有男人女人知道什麼是愛情，也沒有人看過他的雙眼，因為愛神本身就是個幽靈。愛神如果與凡人的內心交融，他將會躲藏在熱情之中，儘管熱情並不是他的本質。因此人們如果以真誠的方式愛人，他們就能在無盡的憐憫、無法言喻的信任、廣博的同理之中，體驗到愛；但是如果人們以卑劣的方式愛人，他們就會在強烈的忌妒、突如其來的恨意、無法平息的欲望之中，體驗到愛。也因此，人們永遠不會知道揭開面紗後的愛情是什麼樣子。

正當我在思索這些事情，一個緋紅的身影對我大叫：「加入跳舞的人群吧！沒有任何事物能夠阻止我們跳舞！進去跳吧！進去跳吧！這樣一來，神就會從我們的內心深

處浮現！」我才正要回答，一陣莫名的衝動就攫住了我，那是竄動於我們的靈魂之中的舞蹈之魂，將我淹沒，我在裡頭不順從，卻也不加抵抗。

我與一位不死的、令人畏懼的女神跳起舞，她的頭髮插上了黑色的百合花，如夢般的舉手投足之間，散發出比星辰間的黑夜還要神祕莫測的智慧，也充滿著像是在水面上低語的愛。我們不斷跳著舞，四溢的焚香環繞著我們，將我們包覆於世界的中心，我們似乎經歷了好幾個世紀，暴風雨在我們長袍的皺褶間與她的秀髮間，時而肆虐，時而平息。

突然間，我發現她未曾眨動眼皮，頭髮上的黑色百合花瓣一片也沒掉落，甚至連晃動也沒有。一陣強烈的恐懼襲上心頭，我突然了解到，和我跳舞的不是凡人，此刻，她正在吸取我的靈魂，就像是公牛在路旁的水窪暢飲。接著，我昏厥過去了，黑暗籠罩上我。

五

　　彷彿是被什麼給喚醒，我突然醒了過來，發現自己躺在簡單油漆過的地板上，不遠處的天花板粗略漆上了一朵玫瑰，四周的牆面上是畫到一半的畫像。長柱和香爐都已消失不見蹤影，我身旁有二十幾位沉睡的人，身上裹著凌亂的長袍，臉龐望著上方，在我的想像中，就像是一張張空洞的面具。黎明的冷冽曙光，從一扇我先前沒注意到的長條形窗戶透進來，照耀著這些面具，外頭的大海咆哮著。

　　麥可‧羅巴特躺在不遠處，身旁有一個翻覆的精緻銅碗，看起來先前裝著焚香。就在我這樣坐著的當下，突然聽見了一陣騷動，幾位男女怒氣沖沖喧鬧著，混雜著海浪的怒吼，我跳起來，快步走向麥可‧羅巴特，想將他從睡夢中喚醒。

　　我抓住他的肩膀，拉他起來，但他卻向後方滑落，發出微弱的嘆息。這時周遭的喧騰越來越大聲，也越來越憤怒激動，還聽見有人使勁撞著通往防波堤的大門。

　　突然，一陣木頭斷裂聲傳來，木門就要被撞開了。我跑到房門口，推開門，進到走道，腳下未上漆的木板嘎滋作響。在走道上，我找到另一扇門，通向空蕩蕩的廚房，我才跨過那扇門，就聽見兩個連續的撞擊聲，接著傳來一

陣匆促的腳步聲和叫罵聲，我想那扇通往防坡堤的門已經朝屋內倒下了。

我跑出廚房，進到一座小庭院，朝著大海和堤防斜坡的方向跑下階梯，再從階梯沿著海濱向上攀爬，一路上憤怒的叫罵聲不絕於耳。防波堤這側的外部，最近才剛以花崗岩塊重新整修，所以幾乎不見海藻的蹤影，但走到較老舊的那側時，發現防波堤長滿了綠藻，又溼又滑，所以我得爬上路面。

我回頭望著煉金術玫瑰神殿，漁夫與婦女仍然在那裡吼叫，但聲音減弱了，大門旁和防波堤上都不見人影。就在此時，一小群人匆忙奔出大門，在一旁堆起的石塊堆裡撿了些石塊。石塊堆是為了防止接下來的暴風雨破壞防坡堤，要用來放在花崗岩塊下方的。

我站在那兒看著他們，一位貌似狂熱信徒的老人指著我，吼叫了些什麼，那整群人變成一片慘白，因為他們全部的人將臉轉向了我。我奮力快跑，幸好那些槳手的雙腳，比他們的雙手和身體還要孱弱許多。我奔跑的時候，幾乎聽不見後頭那些緊追而來的腳步聲或是憤怒的喊叫，因為我的頭頂上空不停盤旋著歡呼和哀嘆的聲音，彷彿像是夢境般，在被聽見的當下就隨即被遺忘了。

時至今日，某些時刻裡，我彷彿還是會聽見那些歡呼與哀嘆，而儘管那晦澀不明的世界對我的內心和理智的控制，已經失去大半，卻又似乎即將要主宰我的命運。但我頸上掛著念珠，當我又聽見那些聲音，或是彷彿又聽見那

些聲音之際，我會將念珠貼在胸口上，並且唸道：「那稱為『群』[1]的東西，就在我們的門前，用模稜兩可的方式來欺瞞我們的理智，用美麗的事物來迷惑我們的心靈。除了祢之外，我們誰都不能相信。」沒多久，我內心的天人交戰就會平息下來，我也再度重獲平靜。

---

1 出自《聖經》的〈馬可福音〉，故事如下：

耶穌在格拉森人（Gerasenes）土地上遇見一位被污靈附身的人，那人遠遠地看見耶穌，連忙跑過來，跪在耶穌面前，大聲喊道：「至高上帝的兒子耶穌，你為甚麼來打擾我呢？我指著上帝求求你，不要折磨我！」（他會這樣講，是因為耶穌已經吩咐說：「污靈，從那人身上出來！」）

耶穌問他：「你叫什麼名字？」

他回答：「我名叫『群』（Legion），因為我們數目眾多！」他再三哀求耶穌不要趕他們離開。

在附近山坡上，剛好有一大群豬在吃東西，污靈就央求耶穌，說：「把我們趕進豬群，讓我們附身在豬群裡面吧。」

耶穌准了他們，污靈就從那人身上出來，進了豬群。整群的豬（約兩千隻），衝下山崖，跌入湖裡，淹死了。

國家圖書館出版品預行編目資料

尋味葉慈故事選：紅髮翰拉漢、神祕玫瑰、玫瑰煉金術 / 威廉‧巴特勒‧葉慈（William Butler Yeats）著；陳珮瑄 譯. 一初版. 一[臺北市]：寂天文化，2017.12 面；公分. 中英對照; 譯自：Stories of Red Hanrahan, the Secret Rose, and Rosa Alchemica

ISBN　　978-986-318-626-7 (25K平裝)

884.157　　　　　　　　　　106018612

作者 _ 威廉‧巴特勒‧葉慈（William Butler Yeats）
譯者 _ 陳珮瑄
編輯 _ 安卡斯
製程管理 _ 洪巧玲
發行人 _ 周均亮
出版者 _ 寂天文化事業股份有限公司
電話 _ +886-2-2365-9739
傳真 _ +886-2-2365-9835
網址 _ www.icosmos.com.tw
讀者服務 _ onlineservice@icosmos.com.tw
出版日期 _ 2017年12月 初版一刷（250101）
郵撥帳號 _ 1998620-0 寂天文化事業股份有限公司